Alas, Hestia

Charlotte G. Morgan

Legacy Book Press LLC
Camanche, Iowa

*To Lynn Pendleton Smith, my grandmother
and first story-teller;
Laura Loe, who made a place for me to write;
and the fascinating women who told me their stories.*

Contents

Epigraph

"You don't love because: you love despite: not for the virtues, but despite the faults."
WILLIAM FAULKNER

"Nothing makes us so lonely as our secrets."
PAUL TOURNIER

Hestia (Vesta)

- Virgin goddess, along with Artemis & Athena
- Goddess of the Hearth & Home
- Every city had a hearth sacred to Hestia, where the fire was never allowed to go out
- Meals began & ended with an offering to her

EDITH HAMILTON

I. THE HOUSE

September 15, 2000

"You're kidding, right? This is IT?" My daughter groans as we turn up the hill toward the fraternity house—her auburn hair so like mine, her strong chin so like her dad's. "Holy shnikies—this looks more like some . . . some damn dump."

"Please don't use that word."

"Shnikies? You don't want me to say shnikies?" She grins a daddy-like grin.

"Smart Alec."

Emma tells me I'm the only mother in Virginia who says Smart Alec and corrects her when she says damn. She's been weaned on crude tales her daddy tells of his college days with his so-called brothers, the Phi Kaps. She's heard his stories of the drunken parties and townie barfights and love-gone-wrong screaming matches for sixteen years, well before she had any idea what he was saying. He'd sing the WVU fight song to her when he rocked her to sleep as a baby.

Up close, the neighborhood of tiny run-down houses perched on uneven sidewalks doesn't look anything like a dump—that's pure mom baiting—but it doesn't have the slightest gloss of a backdrop for Jack's vivid, exaggerated memories either. The rumor of sofas on front porches is clearly no rumor, though. Emma sighs, as if she's expected as much from her dad's grandiose legends.

Now that we're almost here, that flicker I felt a couple of weeks ago, that I needed to come, is just that—a flicker. Old anxieties flutter in my stomach. My hands sweat. What if these women ignore me? What if they're frosty and civil, but standoffish? Treat me with "you sweet thing" faux courtesy. I tell myself I'm not a girl—so why do I feel like a sixteen-year-old about to go to her first school dance? But no matter what happens, I will have faced them, finally, paid my respects to these women who were once my friends, and that will be that. Jack's already here; he'll have my back. Or maybe he'll fall into frat guy behavior himself. I don't want to think about this. Here we are.

Emma's never met a single one of these heroes, antiheroes, goofballs, and rogues her daddy's described with such detail. Most of them have children twice her age—Jack has a son twice her age with his first wife, Simone—but we haven't been to Morgantown together since Jack and I got married. Emma's never been. She's one small reason for this trip. When the guidance counselor started talking about schools for Emma and Jack suggested West Virginia as if it were Harvard or Princeton, I'd almost choked. She acted enthusiastic, though it's the opposite of all the things she claims she wants: small, liberal arts, no sororities. Insisted it was only fair she visit her dad's alma mater. At least once.

Emma takes out her earphones, looks over at me with her serious, sincere face. "I still don't get why I've never met any of these people. To hear Dad tell . . ."

"I know, Emma. Like I've said before—it's complicated. Your dad married Simone D'Espere. End of subject. This weekend you're going to meet everyone . . ." Lately she's been on a "Dad can do no wrong" kick, meaning I'm her challenge parent.

"Even Simone?"

What a horrid thought. "She'd have no reason to be here. She was a townie. I have no idea why she'd come."

She puts her earphones back in. I'm not usually short with Emma, and she isn't a pouter—she knows I'll get myself together. I'm a champ at composure.

After all these years, I can't banish Jack's stories even if I'd tried. They're part of him, much as his devilish eyes are. When he tells them at cocktail parties or drinks on the beach, they're always about him and the guys in the house—he never includes me or the women, thank goodness. Do guys ever tell their wives' stories? Not in my world. There was winning the intramural handball tournament after drinking himself into a stupor the night before. Barfing in the trashcan between matches. Rolling the fire-tire down fraternity hill with the pledges. Crawling through the transom to unlock the kitchen and cook late night steaks for all his brothers. Raffling off a TV set for the fraternity when they didn't own a TV. His connections to that boy he'd been. I'd deliberately buried my connection to that girl. No back story for me.

There it is at the top of the hill: The House. Three stories of plain brick and simple double-paned windows and no recognizable architectural feature to recommend it, just the oversized Greek letters on the door. Nowhere to park, of course. Some things never change. But a young fraternity guy is waving me on—I guess he's going to valet park for us. This rededication thing is a big deal, just like Marc Bonheur said. Emma turns to smile at me. She can't believe we're doing this. I've never told Emma a thing about the women, and she's never heard me add a single detail to a Phi Kap story, though I did have plenty of moments myself. I wonder how everyone will come across in her eyes. Or mine.

"This is it, honey. No kidding."

Out of the blue a few weeks ago, Marc Bonheur calls and says the house is being rededicated and Jack and I have to come—they're trying to get everyone from their class on the '66 composite who's alive to show up. He's calling all the guys he can track down, begging. Marc's still married to Joanne, they still live in Morgantown. Manny and Regina will fly in from Raleigh, Marya and Paulo are driving from Pittsburgh—none of these old friends have divorced, believe it or not. Jack and Frankie are the only two of the guys who've remarried. What are the odds? No b.s., we have to come, to make their class appearance 100%. Frankie Galluci gave something like a million dollars for the renovation, and he's flying in on his private plane with his silicon-valley trophy wife to dedicate the new wing. They're calling it The Galluci Wing. Jack's laughing so hard while he's talking to Marc.

He yells in to me, "Marc says nobody wants to see me. They could give a shit. They all want to see you, Linda, so we've got to go."

It struck me at that moment, crazy as it seemed: I wanted to see them, too. Maybe even needed to in some inexplicable way, to tie up those ragged strands I'd left dangling so long ago. Marya, my very first college friend; Regina, a wild child if ever there was one; and JoAnne; logical, sensible, honest JoAnne. We were grown people now. It hit me: I needed to see the women one more time.

They were the first gals I'd ever met who had their own stories to tell, their own grit, their own way of being in the world that wasn't created to impress some guy. Those three were savvy back when I was green as a gourd. My boyfriend dumps me for his pregnant townie girlfriend, Simone D'Espere, and I'm the one who's too ashamed to face anybody. I'd shut them out, let them down when Jack Vanderbilt nearly destroyed me.

So I'd tried to erase those two years of my life at WVU, like that big long blank on those Nixon tapes. After I didn't answer their phone calls or letters or Christmas cards those first six months, it got harder and harder to get in touch. After a while I felt so embarrassed that I hadn't, I couldn't. Even if I had, what would I have said? Had they let Simone D'Espere take my place at all the parties and get-togethers, just like Jack had? I didn't want to know. They finally stopped contacting me. I hadn't just closed the door; I'd slammed it in their faces.

While Jack was talking to Marc on the phone, I felt a strange flutter, like finding an old black and white photo I hadn't seen in years. We both had a reason to go back. And it might be satisfying to see everyone, to finally cauterize that old, deep wound.

Plus, I wanted them to meet Emma, to see the capable young woman I'd raised, a gal with confidence and competence, like them. Not like freshman me, a blank slate needing to grab a personality and depending on Helen Gurley Brown to keep her from becoming a mouseburger. Sad to say, too, but in all that time since those two years at WVU, I'd never had close female friends. Maybe those friendships weren't real either, maybe I'd idealized them, too, much like Jack polished and elaborated his outlandish fraternity stories.

Though their letters had begged me to come back and swore that Simone was making Jack crazy with her flirting and lying and constant demands, I couldn't trust anybody at that point—not them, certainly not myself. But that other piece, the secret nobody knew—I wasn't going to ever talk to Emma about that. I'd never talked to anybody about that.

When lo and behold, voila, who'd a thunk it, all those years later I decided to marry Jack Vanderbilt after all. I figured I'd put that vulnerable twenty-year-old in her place, had grown well beyond that old heartbreak. Doesn't everyone have one? I'd gotten what I'd wanted in the end, Jack and I got married. On my terms. As an independent woman. But there were flashes when I couldn't ignore how much he'd become part of me: That first ultrasound, the instant I saw Emma's heart beating, and he was holding my hand with tears in his eyes; his heart attack two years ago, me driving to the hospital in a panic behind the ambulance when I thought he might die. My feelings are all tangled around Jack Vanderbilt like Kudzu, and his feelings are still connected to this college part of him, this past, that I've never resolved.

The front hall is crammed with people—it was always narrow, anyway, for a front hall. The composites line the walls—all those oval faces of young men, boys, really, frozen in time, wearing ties and white shirts and sport coats—but I'm too short to get a fix on how the pictures are arranged. Probably by year, and the sixties are pretty far down the hall. Jack is going to meet us here—he'd flown in from a business trip in Boston. Supposedly he got in last night, got our suite, and went to have dinner at Marc and JoAnne's. I haven't heard from him, but the plan's to meet at the house at eleven. Emma and I drove in this morning from Lynchburg; mostly she slept and I listened to an oldies station and conjured up images of my first two years of college.

Thinking about Marya and JoAnne and Regina and the things we did together, all those intense proddings and probings of who we were, who we wanted to be, what we'd do with our lives. For me this weekend isn't about the guys, not even Jack. Or Emma. It's the women I want to see.

I have to admit I'm excited to be here, even a bit nervous, like you are when you think someone's giving you a surprise party. Approach/avoidance big time. I pull Emma into the front room by the hand. She lets me, since it's clear if we get separated in this crowd it'll be hard to find one another. Even dressed up for a celebration, this is such a guy place—always was.

There's a blend of young guys in jeans, older guys in suits and ties, and guys in sports coats and khakis. The sixties men I'm guessing. It doesn't smell like stale whiskey and last night's beer—more like the Clinique counter at Nordstrom's. That's the first surprise. I don't recognize the music, either—in my mind I was expecting Motown, maybe because Frankie is the big donor, but Phi Kaps from every decade are here. Why should our guys prevail with the tunes? The women are an odd mix of polished professionals of all ages, worn housefraus, and tattooed coeds.

I'm pushing toward the bar, thinking a Mimosa would be good right about now, when I see a profile of a face I can't possibly forget: Regina Bello—she's Regina Tambellini now. She's talking to some man I don't recognize, looking engrossed, and she's tinier even than I remember her. Those long dark eyelashes are fluttering, her hair's as brown and blond-streaked as it was our freshman year, and she doesn't look a day older, though I know she's 53, too.

"Mom," Emma tugs, like get a move on, and I turn to her and smile.

"That's Regina Bello, right in front of us, sweetie," I say, and at that instant Regina glances our way and screams "Linda—Linda Lee Barbour! Come here and give me a hug!"

We're hugging and screaming and my inner eighteen wakes up and takes over. I don't think I've hugged a woman and screamed in more than thirty years. My family was not the hugging/screaming type. Regina smells subtle and expensive.

"Look at you, Linda Lee. My god you still have the most gorgeous skin . . . And who is this with you? One of your sisters?" Regina is holding me by the shoulders, standing back and staring like she's discovered the secret to life on earth, and it's clear in that second that she's still the perky package she was when we roomed together sophomore year. Her focus on the person in front of her is like a laser.

"This is Emma"—Emma, eyes wide, sticks out her right hand to shake.

Regina says, "Oh come here and give me a hug, honey, I don't bite."

"Pleased to meet you, too," Emma smiles as she pulls away, pushes a wave of her thick auburn hair behind her ear. Regina is an energetic hugger, even if she's the size of a twelve-year-old.

"Don't tell me your mama's told you so much about me 'cause I know she hasn't," Regina says. "But I'm sure old Jack Vanderbilt's had a thing or two to say. I saw your daddy here just a minute or two ago—." She twists her head around, shrugs her shoulders. "He's still the handsome rogue he always was, isn't he? You don't look a thing like him, though. Your mama always was the prettier of the two." Regina talks like an ADHD poster child, scanning the crowd the whole time she's talking. Her collar turned up, diamond earrings the size of fat blueberries in both ears, she's as stylish as ever, only more polished. "I'm sorry you couldn't get here for JoAnne's last night, Linda Lee. You could at least hear yourself think at her house. Have you seen her and Marc yet?"

"We haven't seen anybody. We just got here."

"Come on, then." She grabs me by the hand and pushes forward. I'm glad to hold onto her. Everyone lets Regina through. A convention of Mac truck drivers would let Regina through: She's a force. In no time, we pull up to a group and I can hear Jack before I see him, his voice riding over at least four or five other men all talking at the same time. "Manny, Jack, look who I found!" Regina calls out.

Everyone turns our way. Jack winks—it's like he's won an Academy Award, he looks so happy to see me and Emma.

"Hey, look who's here."

Manny Tambellini, Regina's adoringly tall husband sporting an Errol Flynn 'stache (not a fan!), and Marc Bonheur, JoAnne's handsome dude of a hubby, have their arms around one another's shoulders. Brothers. Bloody Marys in their free hands. Paulo Santos reaches out to us right away, and Jack keeps on talking.

"Welcome to the party," Paulo smiles, such a cutie, the only one of the guys who's got a big bald spot—and all his curly hair is white. He pulls me so close I can feel his heart beating. He's not much taller than I am, our eyes almost the same level. He waltzes me around a few steps.

"Somebody get Marya. She's dying to see Linda Lee." He'd say that, whether it was true or not. I'd forgotten that Paulo was the gentleman, always the one to pay attention to us gals when the others were busy with their sports or their drinking games.

I pull back and smile. I'm pleased to see Paulo, want to see Marya and JoAnne, too. Whether staying away all those years was necessary or not, being here today feels okay so far. Jack catches my eye again, hurries over and pulls Emma forward, introduces her around, and it's obvious he's pleased we've come. This is when I should begin to relax, rise above the petty past. Odd, though: I feel more awkward standing here with Jack's arm draped around my waist than I felt when Emma and I first walked in the door alone. That's just silly, I know. I'm not Jack's reject any longer. He's the one who found me again, begged me to go out with him, promised he'd always loved me more anyway. We're here together now, with our beautiful, smart daughter. A family. Simone D'Espere was never close with these people. I was. I'm no simpering twenty-year-old running away because a man's thrown me over for another woman. I'm his wife, an experienced nurse practitioner, a well-respected artist in our community. I was successful on my own way before Jack came looking for me. So why am I nervous?

"Linda Lee! Linda Lee Vanderbilt!"

I turn, pull away, as I hear someone calling my name. Jack grabs onto my hand, leans down and whispers,

"Thanks for coming, babe. It's great to have you here," just as the voice gets closer.

"I've been looking all over for you, Linda Lee! Come on, let's jump up on the mantel and dance before they start the boring old speeches! We always could upstage Frankie Galluci!" JoAnne Miller: I'd remembered everything about her—how much smarter she was than the rest of us, how her curly hair never looked contained, how she could run and dance and play guitar just about better than anybody I'd ever met, but I'd forgotten that sassy look in her blue eyes. How could I have forgotten that? It defined her.

"You first, JoAnne. I'll be right behind you," I answered. Like always, I thought.

"I'm mad you didn't come to my house last night. Just like old times—I had to feed Jack. You'd think he was still broke and couldn't afford to take his dates out for supper."

I have to laugh. "Emma had a concert. Emma, this is JoAnne Miller. JoAnne Bonheur, I should say. You just met her husband Marc—the one wearing the tortoise-shell glasses." When did Marc start wearing glasses?

JoAnne studies the three of us. "Your daddy told us you play violin, Miss Emma. Around here we call that the fiddle, you know."

"I know. I'd love to hear some old-time tunes, maybe learn a few." Emma is poised and at ease with all this. I can't help but be proud of her.

"Well one of my boys can teach you. Charles. He plays with a group of old fiddlers and pickers."

Marc Bonheur smiles, a big full-faced smile that starts at his eyes. "Charles is either at the bar or with the band. You'll have to find him, talk to him. He rarely talks to me."

Manny Tambellini chimes in. "Yeah, he's not a bullshittin' glad-hander like his daddy, is he, JoAnne?" Looking at Manny's perfect hair and pale blue cashmere sweater tied over his shoulder, it's hard to figure who's better groomed, him or Regina. I still can't get over the trim mustache; it's so Hollywood.

"Nobody outdoes Marc," JoAnne doesn't crack a smile.

"When the guys told me Marc's been appointed district judge I knew they were pulling my leg," Manny said. "I never thought he'd make it out of law school, much less pass the bar. We all thought you'd be the judge, JoAnne." I remember: Manny is oh-so-polite, but he gets his digs in.

"Guess he's made more friends along the way than I have, given I've defended mostly the downtrodden and the helpless in the great state of West Virginia." Eyebrow arched, mouth upturned.

"Where's Marya? She's got to see Linda Lee." Paulo is still scanning the room for his wife.

"I think I saw her out on the patio with some of the other wives. Let me go get her." Regina hustles toward the new wing. From the back she looks like a child dressed up in designer clothes; those tiny legs are sticks. Could she be ill, like Jack said the guys had hinted? I knew she'd never had children, wondered why. From Jack's recitation of the alumni notes, I knew that JoAnne had the two boys, young Marc and Charles. Marya had a boy and a girl. The perfect family. Maybe Jack had the perfect family, too, if you counted his thirty-one-year-old son Jay with Simone.

Emma nudges me. "Why's everybody calling you Linda Lee?" She's obviously heard that name one time too many in the last fifteen minutes.

I have to laugh. "You've never heard that, have you? I was called that growing up, honey. I changed it when I went to UVA."

"Can't say as I blame you." She smiles, relaxed. That's my clever girl.

My West Virginia parents had actually named me Linda Lou when I was born, but by the time I was old enough to go to school they'd changed it to Linda Lee for some reason I've never been told. Probably some falling out with some distant cousin named Lou. Linda Lee Barbour. It was only when I got to UVA that I realized I didn't want the hicky-sounding double name anymore. I guess it was part of my attempt to break with my past, but I thought of it as more of a kind of maturing, a means of claiming my own identity in my own way. My brothers and sisters didn't much like it, saw it as a bit of "fancifying," but they went along, eventually. My parents never did, but they were both gone before Emma was born. I was the middle of seven. Jack got used to calling me Linda, too, when we got back together. I insisted. So Emma had never heard anybody call me Linda Lee. I'd been straight-up Linda Barbour-Vanderbilt for so long that I didn't think to prepare her for that historical tidbit.

I see Regina hurrying back, and I break away from the group when I recognize Marya. Marya was the first person I'd ever known who'd changed her name. She told us that in Catholic girls' school, she'd gotten sick and tired of being one of many Mary somebodies—she was Mary Margaret Mooney. So, one day when a nun called on her, she said "Make that Marya, Sister Bettina. M-A-R-Y-A. They call the wind Muh-RI-ya." She said she'd gotten five swipes of the ruler on her hand, but the name stuck.

"Look at you, Linda Lee. It's like we were just going over our notes together for psych with Dr. Simpson. Remember?" Marya is thinner than I remembered, her dirty-blond hair cropped closer to her face. She's got way more worry lines than Regina or JoAnne. I wonder why. She's the tallest of the four of us, maybe an inch or two taller than Paulo, but she slumps her shoulders. Her smoky voice is the same—funny, 'cause she was the only one of us who never smoked.

"Paulo's been looking for you—some things never change!" I lean close, but neither of us reaches out to hug. We're both practically yelling, the crowd has gotten so loud. I think the number of people here has doubled since I walked in.

"God I'm glad to see you! It's been *way* too long." She's smiling, but her eyes are wary.

"What are you up to these days? You and Paulo are in Pittsburgh, right? He's a pharmacist?"

"He's got so many businesses I never see the man. Three pharmacies, and now he's into beer. A microbrewery. I told him who needs beer when he's got drugs, but when did he ever listen to me?" Paulo an über-successful entrepreneur. It's hard to imagine. He was the gentlest of the guys, but I guess he had been a pretty serious pre-med student.

"Tell me about you! What are you doing? And I want you to meet Emma . . ."

"I've helped Paulo . . ."

A cymbal sounds and everyone looks around, then looks up at someone yelling into a microphone from the new balcony.

"Let me have your attention, please. Quiet, please. Everybody." Frankie Galluci. I look for Jack, but he's huddled with the guys, whispering and pointing up at Frankie.

Frankie has the trim California haircut, the Armani suit worn with a black tee—he looks like someone has scrubbed and waxed him. Possibly the young woman standing beside him—must be his new wife, Jennifer. I'd liked Donna, though I hadn't known her well. I think she and Frankie were high school sweethearts from the same Pennsylvania mill town. Frankie and Donna had been a solid team, more like our parents, him with his ambitions, her with her work ethic. She adored him, too. Funny they're the ones who divorced. It occurs to me that maybe we're supposed to call him Frank now. I smile.

These guys were the strivers when they were boys. Except for Jack, most were the first generation in their families to go to college. Most had grandparents living with them who spoke next to no English. All the fraternities at WVU had personalities in the sixties. The Dekes were the do-gooders, the SPEs the politicians, the Kappa Sigs the jocks. The Phi Kaps were a newer fraternity, so they were the melting pot, young guys from ethnic families wearing their first Gant shirts, determined to do better than their parents, smart and gritty and grabbing for everything college had to offer. They were the bad boys, and the good girls like me tended to fall for them.

A young man who looks around Emma's age steps up and begins to talk about the fundraising for the renovation. I think how immature he appears—hadn't I pictured us as sophisticated in my mind's eye when we were at the house? The new improved Frankie thanks everyone for donating and coming, and I get a clear image of him our freshman year: The skinny kid always in need of a haircut, clothes just a fraction too small, the guy who'd never dated anybody but his high school sweetheart. He knew even then that he was going to be president of the fraternity one day, get his MBA, own his own company, buy Donna a Cadillac convertible. He was always that intense, but those first few years he was fun, too, and even a bit vulnerable. And me: What had I known then? What had I wanted? Just Jack—had I been that shallow?

JoAnne walks up and nods her head toward our husbands. "Are they arrested at eighteen or what?" Emma cocks an eyebrow, smiles. "Listen, we have tickets for the game this afternoon—Maryland, I think—and Marc would turn us out on the street if a single member of our family missed a single home game. Want to meet up at the Fishbowl later? I think the guys are planning on it."

I look at Emma. She turns to me, raises her eyebrows.

I pat her shoulder, smile. "JoAnne represents the downtrodden." I've promised Emma she can have some time to herself in our suite to do schoolwork or just hang out with the computer, but I don't want to go to the game, either.

"Go ahead, Mom. Dad already knows I have no intention of going."

"Tell you what, Jo: Emma and I will go back to our rooms. Can Jack ride with y'all? Could you drop him by after the game and we'll meet you at the Fishbowl?"

"Sure thing. And let's carve out some time for us to talk. Without the guys."

"I'd like that." There. JoAnne would be the one to bring it all up.

"Come on then, Emma. Let's tell your dad we're leaving and find our way to the hotel." I wave in JoAnne's and Regina's direction. I needed that Mimosa.

I'm starving; Emma and I didn't stop for breakfast, in the rush to get to the House by eleven as promised, and I hadn't even seen the food at the reception. I didn't want to eat standing up elbow to elbow in a crowd, anyway. So we stop for a take-out sub at the Greek's on the way to the motel. Embassy Suites didn't exist when I was at WVU—all the parents who came to town stayed at the Hotel Morgan downtown. Of course, my parents never did—they would've considered it a frivolous expense to stay in a hotel three hours from home, if they'd even seen a reason to come to visit me at WVU in the first place. My older brother, Carl, drove me and my stuff to Boreman Hall North freshman year in Daddy's old farm truck. I hung out with Marya that first parents' weekend. Her folks weren't the visiting type, either.

We throw our bags down on the floor, and Emma can't wait any longer to eat. She clears the table under the window while I look in the kitchenette for a couple of plates. Jack has left bottles of my favorite Pinot Noir on the counter. I search around for the wine opener and a glass. I notice a bouquet of flowers on the coffee table in front of the sofa, too—yellow roses, naturally. His courting flowers.

"Oh my god, this is good, Mama. You better come on or I'm going to eat it all." She's chewing and talking, a major no-no in our family, but my mouth is watering, too. "This is one thing Daddy didn't exaggerate."

I sit down and take my first bite of The Greek's #4, meatball with double provolone. It's as good as I remember, maybe even better. The sauce has that perfect combination of bite and sweet, the meatballs are firm but still juicy, the sub roll is toasted just crunchy enough, not too crunchy.

"I think we should've gotten two whole subs instead of splitting one." I'm smiling, talking while I'm chewing, too. And thinking some things don't change, thank goodness.

"How come you've never said anything about JoAnne and Regina and those other women, Mama? They were sure happy to see you." She grins as she takes another huge bite. "And they aren't too bad for old ladies."

"Watch your mouth with that O word, Missy." We sorta giggle. "Who can get a word in when your dad's talking?"

"True that." Emma wipes her mouth, stands up and yawns. "I'm gonna get some sleep, then work on my storyboard."

"Sounds like a plan. I'll dig out my sketchbook, but I doubt I'll draw for more than five minutes . . ."

She gives me a quick hug, steps back. "How come Dad's the only one with stories, Mama?"

I roll my eyes, get up to pour myself another glass of wine. "Your dad's your dad," I answer, a tad edgier than I intended. This coming back has required all my grown-up grit and adult poise, but I'd made up my mind to do it, at least this one time, to put my childish insecurities—jealousies?—to rest and let that scabbed over part of the past heal. That thing at the House had gone well, but I have to admit I'm still a bit nervous. Emma doesn't miss much. "You know I'm not one for telling tales. Who could get a word in anyway with him around?" I shake my head and she laughs. "Just keep in mind that these guys you met aren't the characters your dad's made them out to be, okay? They're just people, good people. They started from mill towns and mines—some of these guys' parents didn't even speak English all that well."

"They *all* look pretty upscale now." She leans down to hug me. "I remember you telling me once about your mother working in the ribbon factory."

No surprise Emma's probing—I've never been one to linger over my family history. Or anything much about the years before Jack and I married. Like my life started junior year at UVA.

"Hard to picture, I know. This trip to West Virginia has to be a bit eye-opening for you, m'dear."

"Right. Like you slogged to school barefoot in the snow and all."

"Come on, Emma. I never said a thing like that, and you know it. But we weren't dirt poor like some of these guys back then." She keeps staring, like there's bound to be more. "But we were nowhere near rich, either. None of our parents went to college. Most of them didn't even graduate high school. We thought going to college was like winning the lottery." All four of Emma's grandparents were dead before she was born; she's our only, though Jack always wanted more. I'd left West Virginia on purpose, hardly talked about my growing up. Whenever Emma had those genealogy projects at school, she interviewed her dad, who was happy to be the center of attention. My mama worked as a stitcher in a ribbon factory, and my dad was a master machinist there. I didn't have much color to add to his tales.

"Dad told me that Papa Vanderbilt went to college for a couple of years." She puts her napkin in the trash, her plate in the sink, sips the last of her soda. Emma loves saying Papa Vanderbilt, even though she never met him, as if he were one of the richie-rich Vanderbilts.

We get asked about our name a lot. And we always say, "No connection that we've ever uncovered, sad to say."

I sip my wine, grateful for a moment to breathe. "Your Dad was like a rock star. He was the one who talked the guys into joining a fraternity in the first place. I'm sure they'd never even heard the word fraternity before they got to WVU."

Emma shakes her head; she knows her dad well.

"But to tell the truth, we gals did have a few tales of our own." I'm not sure I want to think about them, much less tell Emma. "Not wild and crazy, mind you, like your dad's, but *our* stories, *our* memories."

Emma shrugs. "As if," she says, goes into the smaller bedroom.

I take my glass onto our king-sized bed, kick off my shoes, and crawl in with my clothes on. My sketchpad and pencils are in my briefcase, but all of a sudden, I feel too tired to do one more thing. Seeing everyone at the House has been like drinking some truth serum, making all the memories come back as vivid as the rings on my finger. I close my eyes, and the memories push in.

Even now, I have a hard time unraveling the knots, looking at the tangled strands of what has kept us away all these years and finally brought us back today. I'm nagged by the fact that maybe I should've left all this frozen in time, like one of those embryos that's never claimed.

It's no accident we'd lost contact with the brothers, my girlfriends, the place, and its early role in our lives—once we got engaged, all those years later. I made Jack promise we'd stay away. I'd cut off all contact with Jack and the whole group after he broke my heart at the end of my sophomore year at WVU. That's the part Emma doesn't know. I'm not proud of it, but crazy as it sounds, I couldn't face my friends after he dumped me.

I'd stayed home a semester feeling sorry for myself, nursing my wounds like they were some rare treasure, ignoring my girlfriends' attempts to contact me. I'd get out of bed when my parents made me, sit in the kitchen with the grannies, drawing pad on my lap, but I couldn't even pick up the pencil.

That spring, Mama made me get a job at the Greenbrier in the chocolate shop. I almost lost my mind in that phony world of people from the holler waiting on people with more money than sense. I was bound to lose my faculties if I didn't start over, get away from anything to do with West Virginia.

That next fall I transferred to UVA and told myself I was getting my life together again; that this time I wouldn't be sidetracked by sophomoric parties and fraternity boys and girls no smarter than I am telling their growing-up stories—to what end? To what conclusion? To what satisfaction? All that opening up and getting close only hurt, hurt like hell, in the end. I would study and stay to myself and focus on my nursing program. No more studio art. Daddy was right. I would put some distance between me and my childhood and my first two frivolous years of college, wasted years, when I thought about it, but mostly I'd make Jack Vanderbilt an insignificant part of my past. An unfortunate footnote.

Every morning I told myself my Granny Barbour's saying, "What don't kill you makes you tougher than a bobcat's toenails." I'd always been a private person; Jack's betrayal made me even more so. No man was ever going to matter that much to me again. That eventually he became that man who mattered . . . well, I'll never say life isn't full of irony.

I'd sharpened my bobcat's nails, but Jack hadn't stayed in the past where I'd put him. I did exactly what I set out to do, left West Virginia for good. Some years I went home for Christmas, sometimes it was Thanksgiving, sometimes I didn't go at all. I became a long-distance daughter and sister, the one who showed up for weddings and funerals. I built a career as a nurse practitioner, took adult painting classes, had a community of female artists I traveled with, dated plenty of smart men, was asked to marry a couple of them, but I didn't. Scornful of being thrown over again, I did the throwing. Once burned, twice cautious.

So when Jack found me fifteen years later, I tried to be nonchalant, grown up, to assure myself I wouldn't care. Many of the people I knew were into second marriages, looking up high school and college sweethearts. Foolishness. I told myself I no doubt wouldn't even like thirty-something Jack, much less swoon over him. He wouldn't be that good-looking—half-bald with a paunch, probably. I'd have no problem resisting his play.

When he called, I decided I'd meet him for drinks. I was going to give him a piece of my mind, finally let him know how much he messed up that night at Cooper's Rock, but mostly I wanted to show him what he'd missed. And satisfy myself that I'd outgrown him—in person he had to be a letdown, could in no way measure up to his first love status. This would be a blow for his oversized ego, to let him know he might have wounded me way back when, when we were kids, but it hadn't been mortal, not even close.

Dressing in my simplest black sheath, my plainest gold chain, my best pumps, I wanted him to see the independent woman I'd become, the woman in charge of herself and her own happiness. I didn't need him; never had, really.

In spite of myself, I got that inimitable catch in my throat as soon as I saw him sitting at the bar at Sam Miller's, and drinks turned into dinner, and he spilled the whole sordid business with Simone D'Espere. I couldn't hate him. Uh-uh. Not even close. Why had I remembered him as egotistical—hadn't he always been this open, this easy to talk to? And my god, the eye contact! He somehow got me to talk about my work, my paintings, my travels first, like he needed to know what I'd been doing every minute. I laughed when he told me his crazy awkward early sales stories, thought I'd cry when he described his father's death, leaned in and listened when he talked about being a father himself. It didn't take me an hour to know I wanted him again.

I told myself that I'd satisfy myself, let that long-ago flame have its chance to burn out, and put a stop to it on my terms this time. I didn't need him or anyone. Somehow, though, it was so easy for him to fit back into my life. Did I want him back, or did I want to figure *me* out again and come to new conclusions, conclusions I created? I sure as hell didn't want to be led around by my feelings, like that silly girl all those years ago.

Problem was all those years I was never indifferent to him—I guess that was the key. Jack turned me on like nobody before or since, and when we left the bar that night, I couldn't pretend I was only there to give him a taste of his own medicine.

But I promised myself I wouldn't lose myself in Jack Vanderbilt. I'd lead my life, not just be some female extension of him. I made him swear: No pressuring me to attend WVU football games, no alum gatherings, nada. He couldn't ask me to go back with him. That belonged to him and his years with Simone. If he talked to his WVU buds on the phone, stopped and saw one on a business trip, went to a game himself, I didn't want to hear all about it. I wanted to start fresh with our relationship, make our own new history, bury those two mixed-up, wounded college kids back there in the crazy sixties. People who lived in the past were a cliché.

Jack kept that promise for eighteen years, never once asking if I would go back to WVU with him. That didn't stop him from telling his Phi Kap college stories at cookouts and dinner parties, though, or filling me in on the weddings and babies, and lately, heart attacks and cancer.

Regina, JoAnne, Marya, and I: We were tight. Those memories and stories I'd shut away came spooling back like home movies.

October 12, 1965

I could practically hear my mother saying, "Get on outside, Linda Lee. It's way too pretty to be cooped up in the house." I was sitting on my bed in my dorm room with my essay collection propped open on my knees, supposedly reading "Notes of a Native Son" for comp class on Monday, instead doodling in the margins. After I'd read those lines on the first page, "I had inclined to be contemptuous of my father for the conditions of his life, for the conditions of our lives," I'd stopped reading. Was I slightly contemptuous of my father, of his uneducated ways, his lack of ambition? I was feeling a bit ashamed and sorry for myself when Marya knocked on the door.

"You doing anything?" she'd asked.

"Not really." I didn't know her much at all, certainly not well enough to tell her what was on my mind—an odd mix of homesickness and embarrassment for even considering I could compare a speck of my sheltered life to James Baldwin's growing up in Harlem.

"Great. I need to get out of here or I'm gonna go crackerjacks. Want to go get a sandwich at the Greek's? Or go for a walk or something? I could use some company."

"Sure. Let me grab a sweater." It was Saturday morning of Parents' Weekend, and the dorm was practically empty. I realized as I put on my loafers that in the six weeks I'd been there, the place had never been that quiet. My roommate, a junior from Louisville, was rarely in the room. Her Phi Kap boyfriend had an apartment, and she spent more time there. But the four-story building was a constant racket of music and girls talking, phones ringing, footsteps, doors slamming. The best friend I'd made so far, JoAnne Miller from Clarksburg, had gone to the Air Force Academy for the weekend to break up with her high school boyfriend. She'd already had so many invitations for dates that she had no intention of being tied down a minute longer. My only other new girlfriend, my suitemate Regina Bello, was staying at the Hotel Morgan with her mother and sister. I had met Marya Mooney in my freshman comp class and found out she lived in the same dorm, but I didn't know much more about her than that she was from some small mill town outside Pittsburgh. I was thrilled she'd come to rescue me from myself.

"You hungry?" she asked as I scrambled in the dresser drawer for my change purse back behind my underwear. I kept all my spending money there. My parents had opened a checking account so they could put my twenty dollars a month allowance in it, but I tried to ration that on laundry, school supplies, and stamps. For extras, I'd saved almost every penny I made working at the Hudson Brothers Market on weekends during senior year and all summer long—that day would be the first time I hadn't eaten in the dining hall. Actually, it was my first "extra" since I'd arrived at WVU.

I snapped a five-dollar bill into my wallet. "I could eat a cow. I didn't go to the dining hall for breakfast this morning—I slept in."

"Me too. This place is creepy quiet. How about the Greek's? It shouldn't be too crowded right now."

"Let's find out." I practically ran out the door behind her.

Marya and I walked at a fast clip. The late morning air was crisp but not too cold—one of the days perfect for a football game, with enough bite in the temperature but not too much for the outfits girls had planned to wear all week. I wasn't sad about not having a date for the game—I wasn't interested in football anyway, and I hadn't gotten to know any guys who might ask me out—but I was relieved I wasn't stuck in my room alone.

Marya was a good six inches taller than me, one of those slender slouched girls who would always be a slim woman, even if she ate potato cakes all her life. She wore her dirty blond hair long, with bangs, and gold hooped earrings in her pierced ears. I'd never known anyone with pierced ears. Her dark blue velour pants looked new. The wheat jeans I was wearing I'd had for two years, bought with my own money because my mother thought anything made out of denim was too low class for a girl to wear, except for doing yardwork. The women in my family all wore housedresses and aprons at home, uniforms at work, and clingy dresses and rhinestones to go out dancing at the holiday gatherings at the VFW. Mama couldn't imagine why any teenaged girl would want a pair of jeans.

Walking down the hill, we ran into college students everywhere—they all seemed to be headed up the hill, though, to the fraternity houses. In boy/girl twosomes, too, guys in jackets and ties, gals dressed in suits or Sunday outfits. But I didn't care. I was glad to be going somewhere with somebody.

"Have you finished reading the essay yet?" Marya asked.

"Lord no." I was pleased Marya brought up class. I'd been trying to figure out something to say—maybe that Professor Nicholas is kinda cute, even if he never cracks a smile. His stutter was endearing. "I was just starting it when you came to the door. Funny thing—it made me think about my own daddy right off the bat."

"I read it twice last night. I've never read anything like it. Not in my high school, that's for sure."

"Me either." I don't think we'd ever even read an essay—just lots of sappy British poetry and boring American novels like *The House of the Seven Gables*.

Marya made a scrunchy face. "It sounds kinda pathetic, studying on Friday night, doesn't it?"

"Not really." I didn't know what to say. I'd never studied on a Friday night.

"Reading that got me agitated, it's hard to explain." She looked serious. "All about another world, up there in New York." She shook her head. "I remember the first time I ever saw a colored person."

"You're kidding, right?" I had to smile. That would be like remembering the day I was born. I'd known colored people my whole life, even if we didn't go to church or school together. Half my relatives worked at The Greenbrier, and there were as many colored people in service there as white, maybe more. That's what my family said was the polite thing to say, colored people. The first time I heard anyone call them Black people was the previous week in seminar when the professor was introducing us to James Baldwin.

"Huh-uh. Not a bit. I remember clear as a bell." She nodded her head. "We always took these long vacations. Daddy works turns at the mill—he has seniority—so he gets two or three weeks off at a time. This one summer when I was about ten we drove to Texas to visit family. Me and my sister, Dolly, and my mama. Her name's Dolly, too. Anyway, we were going to my Aunt Martha's, I think." Marya and I were walking in step, almost marching. She touched my elbow. "We stopped somewhere in Arkansas, I think it was, to pick up a Black man hitchhiking. Mama got in the back seat with me and Dolly, and we just rode along for the longest time with the Black man up front with Daddy, nobody saying a word. A couple of towns over he got out, said 'Thank you, suh,' to Daddy, and that was it. I said, 'Mama, that man was brown!' My sister Dolly said, 'Don't be such a little dummy.' I'll never forget it. But I don't think I'm gonna bring that up in class." She grinned.

"Smart choice." I grinned back. "But I don't think my daddy would ever pick up a colored person hitchhiking, much less let him ride up front. Especially if my mama was in the car." I wasn't trying to be critical, but I knew that to be true.

She paused. "When I think about it now—maybe I shouldn't say this—I'm guessing Daddy did it on purpose. He thought the South was so backward—his own hang-up, I guess—I never thought to ask him about it." She shook her head. "I wish I had. He supervised a lot of colored men, but us gals never went to the factory."

"I get it. Everybody thinks people in West Virginia are backward. That's not even considered a prejudice. It's like a fact." We both laughed. "But the Black people in our little town are pretty much a part of the community, no kidding, or that's the way it's always seemed to me. I guess I've never thought much about it, which of course sounds ignorant now. I don't think I'll say that in class, either." I cocked an eyebrow; she nodded her head. "I'm not saying we're all big buddies or anything, but we, everybody, shops at the same store. The only store. The one where I used to work on weekends and summers." I didn't mean to be rambling, but I wanted Marya to understand that I wasn't like that, that I didn't have all that hatred inside. "Nobody thinks about it. At least that's what it feels like to me. They had their own schools until this integration thing got going. But even then nobody back home got all riled up."

"At home it was nothing like what James Baldwin was talking about." Marya shook her head. "All that anger. I went to Catholic Girls School, Holy Mother of Saints, and by high school, we had a few colored girls. My sister went to public and there weren't any coloreds there at all. But she's ten years older than I am."

"At home nobody says Black or Negroes like Professor Nicholas. That other word"— I stared and she nodded—"nobody I hang out with would say that. The colored people who work at The Greenbrier aren't agitated like the riots Dr. Nicolas was telling us about in class, I can tell you that for a fact. The only revolution we talked about in school was the American Revolution."

She smirked, nodded agreement.

"It's hard to believe what he's describing was going on in the nineteen forties right in New York City, and I haven't heard a thing about it."

"My parents never talked about anything like race riots to us. Just think: They happened more than twenty years ago, when our folks weren't much older than we are now, and here we are clueless. Maybe the Catholic church had a thing or two to say, and my parents swallowed whatever the church said, I know that for a fact. But you know I don't see all that many colored people here, either." She looked at me and we both shrugged.

"Just jocks." I laughed. "The jocks lead the way."

"No small irony there." She arched an eyebrow.

"So, like I said, I only got started on that first page, but that little bit got me to thinking about my daddy more than the race stuff. He wanted me to come to college if I was absolutely sure I needed to, but he doesn't think it's all that important. He didn't get past ninth grade himself, and he's a shift supervisor."

"Not mine. He thinks me studying to be a physical therapist is right next door to sainthood."

Teenagers who had a clue what they wanted to do as grown-ups amazed me. People I grew up with fell into what their parents did, like working the farm or the factory or the hotel. "I have no idea what

I'm going to do. Be an English teacher I guess. Or a nurse. Go back home and teach or work in a doctor's office. Airline stewardess is out—I'm scared to death of flying."

"English was always my favorite subject, but no way am I ever going to teach or go back home to live. I've got this thing about being different, doing something important, maybe working with needy people. Remember all those posters for the March of Dimes when we were little? Those poor little children on crutches?"

"How could I forget?" Hudson Brothers Market always hung those posters on the big glass window right up front. "They made me so sad—like how in the world could my few dimes make the slightest difference to something as big as polio? And they sure weren't going to help that little girl."

"And now all these pictures on the news of all these broken guys from Vietnam . . . I just feel like I need to *do* something," she said, raising her voice.

"Those pictures in *Time* magazine and on the news only make me sad. That's such a mess. I don't understand it at all." I was shaking my head now. "Some of the guys from high school joined up—none of my close friends. But still, we've been scared to death my brothers might have to go, but so far so good."

"It's lucky I found you this morning, isn't it? Sounds like left alone you could work yourself into a major case of the blahs." A hint of a smile. "I wasn't about to stay in my room ten more minutes. Pretty pathetic, watching my roomie get all dressed up for her date last night. At least at home I would've been out on a Friday night."

"Me too." We hurry along. "Do you have a steady boyfriend?"

"Nobody special. This time of year I would've been cheering at a football game, though, and going out afterwards with my friends."

"Me too!" We both laughed. "I wasn't going to tell anybody about being a cheerleader, though—not exactly a brainy-girl activity."

"I know what you mean. The guys can talk all night about being jocks, but if a girl says a thing about being a cheerleader, we get all the dumb jokes, like how many cheerleaders does it take to screw in a lightbulb, right?"

"I'll never tell!" We pushed into the Greek's—it was the first time I'd been inside. Nobody was at the counter, the two tiny booths up near the window were empty, but the thick smell of marinara sauce and yeasty baking bread filled the dim space. "I can't believe nobody's here," I said as I looked up at the crowded handwritten sandwich board.

"Everybody's at the fraternity houses or out to brunch somewhere nice with their parents. We're the orphans today. But at least we get the Greek's to ourselves."

"What are you gonna get?"

"A meatball sub, for sure. That's all I've been hearing about."

"I was thinking about a Philly cheesesteak, but I'll get a meatball, too. That sauce smells too good to pass up."

"Yeah. Wait for the cheesesteak till you come home with me some weekend." She smiled. I don't think I'd noticed how pretty she was, before. "Order double cheese. That's what my roomie says."

"Sure." My mouth was watering. A bald man with a brushy mustache, wiping his meaty hands on a stained apron, came from the back room, wrote down our sandwich orders.

"Want to share an order of fries?" Marya asked.

"Sure."

"Wet?"

I looked up at the chalkboard to grab a clue. "Why not?" That was a new option for me—french fries with gravy. We used ketchup at home.

He gave us our Cokes and we settled into the back booth.

"So you said the James Baldwin essay made you think about your daddy? Remember, that's what Dr. Nicholas said, we're supposed to consider Baldwin's experiences of family and community and compare them to our own."

"Right. I think I wrote that down. Like there's anything to compare." I was getting the impression that Marya was a serious student. I'd never had to work for grades—graduated near the top of my class without even trying—so all this talk about an essay outside English class was unusual, but I liked it. "Thinking that was going to be a pretty big leap for me. I mean, he's from Harlem and I'm from a holler in the back of beyond in West Virginia." I couldn't help but laugh. "Not to mention the colored/white thing. And when I started reading right off the bat I was hit with all this rage. And how he never talked to his daddy. My family talks all the time. Nonstop."

"He's mad, all right. His father was crazy as a bedbug. That's a pretty big part of what he's talking about—his daddy being a religious nutcase. What were you thinking about your dad, though? He's not a preacher is he?"

"Ha! No way! Baldwin saying that thing about condescending, though . . ." I took a sip of my soda. I wasn't sure how to say this without coming off sounding snooty. "I love my daddy and all, but he's so satisfied with things the way they are. Working at the ribbon factory. Mama working shifts. All us kids and the aunts and uncles living on the same road—sort of like the Kennedy compound without the fortune, you know? When my counselor encouraged me to go to college, Daddy and Mama were both skeptical—like I was 'going above my raising.'"

Our fries came. I'd never tasted potatoes so good—crispy, salty, the skin still on, with thick peppery gravy on top. I could've eaten the whole order by myself. We ate for a few minutes without saying a word.

Marya sat back against the red booth. "My daddy's the one who suggested WVU to me. He said, 'You're way too smart to sit here with your mama and your sister and look at the stories day in, day out. Why don't you study dental hygiene or something like that? Make yourself some good money.'"

"I didn't even tell Mama and Daddy that the counselor said I ought to study art in college. That would've ended the conversation right there. I can hear Daddy now—'Why pay all that money to learn something you can already do better than anybody you know?'"

Marya ate the last fry. "My daddy will let me pick whatever I want to study, though he's been talking the most about some kind of medical field. He's the one who's told me I've got something special, from as long as I can remember. Mama, she'd want to take the belt to me for the slightest thing, but he'd say, 'Leave her be, Dolly. She's got a spark.'" Marya wiped her mouth with her paper napkin, took a breath. "When I was little that made me feel good, you know? When I got older I'd think, *He wants me to know I need to get out of here. I love my daddy,*" she sighed. "You have a lot of sisters and brothers back home?"

"Two sisters, four brothers. I'm in the middle."

"Like I said, I only have the one sister, and she's ten years older than I am, so I was the baby and then the only growing up. Dolly and I aren't a bit alike. We're not close at all. She's into sewing and cooking—she and Mama hang out in the kitchen practically all the time when she comes to visit. She's already got three kids and another on the way."

"Most everybody I know has a big family. There are still a lot of farms around us, but my people work the ribbon factory or The Greenbrier."

"We're Catholic, and if you don't have a lot of kids, the priest looks at you like there's something wrong. My parents always wanted more children, but I guess something *was* wrong." She shrugs. "I wasn't the slightest bit upset about not having a house full of sisters. I probably shouldn't say so, but it's the truth. I've never had to share a room until I came to WVU."

"Not me—I've never had six inches of space I could call my own. I don't think my parents have favorites, though. My sisters were close, even though I'm closer in age to both of them. And my brothers run around together, play sports, hunt. I've always been kind of the loner, even if we were all crammed into two bedrooms, and I never had a second of privacy in my life. I'd read and draw and pretty much stay to myself whenever I could get away with it."

When the guy put the two sandwiches in front of us we both said we couldn't possibly eat so much, but in no time we were wiping our mouths and our plates were empty.

Marya threw her napkin in the messy sandwich papers. "Want to get a beer? I'm not ready to go back yet, are you?"

I must've looked surprised. I'd never had a beer or an alcohol drink, even though a lot of my friends had experimented, especially the boys.

"Oh come on. Everybody who's going to the game is tanked by now. We could at least get a little in the spirit of the weekend. I don't have anything to do for the rest of the day."

"All right. I can do my reading tomorrow." Maybe today wasn't the time to tell her I'd never had a drink, was still a virgin, was a guilt-ridden, sin-fearing Southern Baptist to boot. I smile. "Here? Want me to order?"

"Nah—let's walk a bit more. Maybe go to Nick's?"

It was a strange and wonderful day—hanging out in town, the sounds of the football game eventually taking over, getting to know Marya as well as I'd known the girls I'd grown up with—maybe even better—all in an afternoon.

Anybody 18 or older could drink 3.2 beer in West Virginia, but I'd never tried it, even though it was legal. The first sip was bitter, but not bad. And it was icy cold. By the second draught I was enjoying it, enjoying the raucous crowd and the earliest inkling of belonging.

That's when Marya told me about changing her name when she was in fifth grade—"I've always wanted to be different, to get away from the Mon valley"—and changing her mind about wanting to be a nun. When she was little, she'd thought that being a nun was holy and beautiful, and she could probably go to Rome and serve the Pope, until she got older and saw how mean and petty and bitter the nuns at her school could be. "At first, I thought being married to Jesus was about the most fulfilling thing a girl could do. Then I found out every big Catholic family in the world dumps at least one daughter on the church. Not me. No way."

By the time we walked back to the dorm, the sidewalks were packed. The game was over, and couples and families were everywhere, spilling into the streets. WVU had won. I felt the slightest bit light-headed: Was it the beer, or the fact that this day had turned out to be so different than any day I'd ever spent back home? These handsome guys wearing bathrobes and carrying canes were actually dancing in the streets, with groups of tipsy students around them cheering them on. This was about as far from my hometown as Mars, and I felt about as much a part of all this as a country girl plopped down in outer space. But there I was, right in the middle of it.

"Come on up to the room," I yelled, not ready to go back to being an orphan, "if you don't have anything else to do."

"Sure!" Marya yelled back, and we headed up the hill to Boreman North.

My room was plain compared to the others on the hall. For one thing, Jeannine and I hadn't tried to "match" like some of the other roomies. She didn't even answer my phone calls when I tried to reach her over the summer. At WVU, they put freshmen in with upper classmen, I guess to cut down on contagious homesickness, but

I didn't like this policy a bit. Jeannine still didn't give me the time of day. Neither of us had posters hanging. She had a bulletin board with some family pictures and leftover programs and favors from games and parties and dances. I didn't even have that. I'd tacked up my first contour drawing, a bike. I liked looking at it, the loose flow of graphite. I was used to painting still lifes and landscapes. That was new for me, drawing all loosey-goosey. My bed was covered with a white chenille spread with a quilt at the foot my Aunt Pearl made for my sixteenth birthday: a double wedding ring pattern. We weren't long on subtlety in my family. My roommate's bed was a plain, ribbed burgundy spread—I couldn't remember the last time she'd slept in it. She was pinned to her Phi Kap. I was pretty sure that meant they were sleeping together—she certainly wasn't sleeping here nine nights out of ten.

"I've got some brownies Mama sent me. She's the number one cook in our town, along with my granny." I opened the tin on the counter under the window, held it out. "These are like gold back home."

"You got a coffee maker?"

"Aren't those against the rules?"

Marya shakes her head and smiles at me. "Do you ever wonder why you smell coffee at all hours of the day and night, Linda Lee? Let me run up and get mine. You do have a mug, right?"

I went over to the desk and dumped the pens and pencils out of my Go Mounties mug. "Let me wash it." I wasn't a coffee drinker. At home us kids had hot tea and toast when we were sick, hot chocolate on cold winter mornings before school. The adults drank coffee, gallons and gallons of coffee—there was always a pot on the stove. I'd never had a yen for any. But I'd been too green all day—I'd definitely drink some coffee.

Marya came back with a coffee kit; she could have sold hers in those expensive catalogs they send around at Christmas. Everything arranged on a flat basket, sugar cubes in a box, cream in a tiny glass bottle with a stopper ("I set it outside the window—never goes bad"), a couple of silver spoons ("Mama collects a spoon everywhere she goes—these two are from Hot Springs and Nashville—she thought I might want to start a collection like hers, but I told her it was a waste of money"), a pottery jar of instant coffee, the little illegal plug-in heater to put in the coffee mug. That's the first time I saw Marya's talent for organizing and making other people feel comfortable.

We ate brownies and drank coffee with lots of sugar and cream and laughed and talked for another couple of hours. Right through the dinner hours in the dining hall.

She's the one who brought up sex. She was telling me about the guys she'd dated—"None of them had any ambition, you know what I mean. Unless it was to get in a Catholic girl's underpants. They'd all heard that the girls at Holy Mother are fast. I made up my mind I wasn't going to be one of those girls who jumped in the back seat of the car with any guy from St. Benedict's who thought he was hot stuff. Not me. I wasn't about to be anybody's dirty joke. Besides, I've never kissed a guy who made me want to do more than kiss him, you know what I mean? Most of the boys in my hometown are such . . . boys!"

"Oh, I could've done a little more than kiss Michael Edwards." I couldn't believe I was saying this! "But I was a Queen in the Girls' Auxiliary. We took a purity pledge. Besides, I was scared to death I'd get pregnant."

"A queen of what?" She laughed, puzzled, like maybe I was a bit more peculiar than she had initially picked up on.

"It's a big deal back home. Us Baptist girls, we pledge to do good works and stay pure. There's this church group, the Girls' Auxiliary . . ."

"So you *are* a goody two shoes!"

Jeannine burst into the room like somebody had pushed her with a broom. "Linda Lee! What are you doing . . ." She stared at Marya.

"This is Marya Mooney, from upstairs. We take freshman comp together." Why was I feeling like Jeannine was some adult who'd found us doing something naughty?

"Great. Two's even better. Look, the house is crawling with freshman guys. They all want to rush Phi Kap, right? Ritchie says to come and get you—we need girls. You can dance, can't you?" She stared at us both like she'd just named us Miss America.

I looked at Marya, she looked at me. Why not? It beat sitting in the dorm on Saturday night eating brownies. "Sure. Should we change?" I hadn't even put on make-up that morning. My hair was in a ponytail.

Jeannine looked us over like she just noticed we were wearing feed sacks. She still had on her tweed suit and black patent heels from the game. "I guess it doesn't matter at this point. They're all pie-eyed anyway. Put on some lipstick and brush your hair, though. Just—come on! The Bonnevilles are playing!"

September 15, 2000
After the Game

"Linda?! Emma?! Where are you?"

From the bedroom with the door shut, I can hear Jack yelling, like he's still at the football game.

"In here," I call back.

"Where are you two? Come on—everybody's waiting!"

I get up from the bed in my stocking feet. I'd fallen asleep thinking about the morning at the house, seeing my former friends again, having them welcome me like nothing had ever gone wrong between us. That had gotten all mixed up with memories of WVU when I was a freshman. I shook it all off; I was adept at making my mind shift gears, a trick I'd learned in nursing school to deal with patients and their families during those life and death moments.

I'd startled awake after about twenty minutes—I never take more than a power nap—and made myself open my blank sketchbook and draw. When I couldn't do more than doodle, I'd tried reading *The Bluest Eye*, but it kept getting me so upset that I started flipping through the July *Art in America* instead, which was almost as disturbing. The Whitney's biennial was becoming more and more disconnected, more "Emperor's New Clothes" to me and my sense of aesthetics. Really, a whole room devoted to painting and sculpture and photographs from pigeon droppings?

"Hey you. I missed you." Jack bursts into the bedroom, grabs me, kisses me hard, and hugs me tight. Jack's exuberance doesn't even fade when he's sleeping; he has shaken leg syndrome. "You been missing me?" He looks down at my loose blouse.

I give him a playful push. "Thanks for the flowers, hon. I had a glass of the wine you brought, too. I'm feeling a bit antsy, to tell you the truth. Probably all the art psychobabble." I nod toward the magazine open on the bed.

"My kinda antsy?" The wiggling eyebrows. Jack is not even slightly understated.

"Remember, Emma's six feet away?"

"What's she up to?" He's rubbing my shoulders.

"She's in there with her computer and music, but still . . ."

"You feeling sexy? We can *whisper-shhhhhh.*" He nuzzles my ear. Jack smells like fall leaves and cigarette smoke and beer—like WVU all those years ago.

"You haven't been smoking have you?"

"Lord no. But you should see the students." He's rubbing his knee against my thigh. "Like I said . . ."

"Didn't you say everyone was waiting?" I kiss his cheek, decide to get changed.

"Awwww, Linda . . . you're killing me here." A disappointed look crosses his face as he walks toward the bathroom. I take off my crumpled shirt and choose my favorite pullover sweater from my bag. Might as well feel cashmere good and look red confident.

"I'll see if she wants to go," he yells back while he brushes his teeth. Jack and I have always been sexually simpatico, so I can't blame him for feeling disappointed. My nerves around this trip have given me a weird libido gut punch. He'd been my first, that night out at Cheat Lake after the fraternity formal. It had meant a lot to me. Old fashioned as that seems now, in the sixties none of the girls I knew jumped into bed with a guy without agonizing over it for weeks or even months. Most of us were "technical virgins"—lots of heavy petting, but no actual intercourse unless you thought he was "the one." Then it was usually only after you were pinned or engaged. And still there was the fear of pregnancy. Everybody knew rubbers weren't reliable. Guys didn't want to use them. My generation may have started the sexual revolution, but it hadn't made much headway from California to WVU when I was there in the mid-sixties. So when I "gave myself" to Jack—God, I really thought in those terms back then—I thought we were already "married" in our own eyes. Of course I knew he wasn't a virgin; male/female double standards were exactly that. But I thought he felt the same commitment to me.

Come to find out, he'd been having sex with Simone D'Espere, too. And gotten her pregnant. She won the sex lottery or lost it—however you looked at that "had to get married" finale. I try not to be cynical, but there it is. Still, him being my first was powerful for me. As we started making plans for this get together, without even thinking about it, I'd lost my desire to have sex with Jack for the first time ever in our relationship. I didn't talk to him about it—couldn't find the words to explain it, since I didn't understand myself. It had helped that he had several business trips right before we got here.

I could hear him in Emma's room. "Come on honey, please? You've gotta see this place! Your mom and I used to go there all the time when we were dating. You'll get a kick out of it." I can't hear what Emma's saying.

Emma hasn't had a steady boyfriend yet, far as I know. And I'm pretty sure I'd know. She and her friends go around in "clumps" of guys and gals, not in couples like when I was in high school and college. She has her orchestra/symphony/music friends—a quirky bunch. Smart and talented. Some of them are already identifying as bisexual or gay, boys and girls, but to hear Emma tell it, none of them are coupling up or *having* sex. Then she has her technology friends (some of them are in both camps, like Emma). They call themselves "geeks" and spend all their time deconstructing science fiction books and movies when they're not doing whatever they do at their computers.

At her private school, there are plenty of preps and jocks and even Goth wannabes, but she's never been attracted to them, so the fact that they don't want to hang out with her doesn't appear to bother her, since she doesn't want to hang out with them, either. Her thing right now is computer animation. Her grades aren't all As; she even gets an occasional C in a subject like religion that doesn't interest her. But put a computer or a cello in her hand and whammo—she's brilliant. I'm floored with what she can create on a Mac. Her group is making animated movies now, not babies. I keep watching for all the warning signs and red flags of alcohol and drugs, but I don't see any. They spend the night at the house, and nobody jumps or looks pie-eyed or stoned if I come into the room. The fact that Emma's gorgeous and certainly well developed for sixteen doesn't seem to fit into her equation of what matters to her friends—or to her, for that matter. They all shop at thrift stores for their wardrobes, and a Goodwill vintage "find" is far more "rad" to them than any brand name on the racks. For Jack, a three-piece business suit guy who's ridden the wave of computer products from its inception, she's his precious, inscrutable ET. To me she's a wise new soul.

He hurries back into the bedroom just as I'm putting on my lipstick. "She won't go. Can you talk her into it?"

"Let her stay here. She's probably working on a story board with Zoe and Witt. Let her be."

"But I want her to see the Fishbowl, at least. Come on, I didn't make a big deal when she didn't want to go to the game. She'd get a kick out of all the notes on the walls."

"She went to the dedication. She'll join us for the dinner. We're lucky she even came."

"Didn't you love seeing everybody? I knew you would." He straightens his tie, looks at himself in the mirror. "Maybe I'll change. Lose the tie. Hey, look out—that sexy red sweater makes me want to jump you."

Mario's Fishbowl isn't really named Mario's Fishbowl at all—it's The Richfood Avenue Confectionary, but I've never heard anybody call it that. Students have referred to it as The Fishbowl since before Jack and I went to WVU. When you walk in the door, all the customers stop what they're doing and cheer; when you leave, everyone boos. Beer is served in iced mugs that look like glass soup bowls with thick stems—the so-called "fishbowls." Today it's as crowded as ever, with students and alums and visiting families. They all cheer when Jack and I walk in around five. The noise is especially loud from the back, where I see the crowded tables of Phi Kaps.

Paulo jumps up and starts looking around for more chairs. He offers me his, beside Marya. She's sipping a glass of red wine, turns her lips into a faint smile when I plop down beside her. She says something I can't understand, so I lean closer, and she yells in my ear. "I can't stand beer!" I have to laugh—didn't she tell me at the house that Paulo owns a microbrewery? "And the wine they serve here is just as bad!" I see Jack hold up two fingers and point to one of the beers on tap. He knows what I like.

I look around at all the worn signs on the walls. The SANITARY ICE CREAM sign is still up—that was old when I was at WVU. And there it is, Mario's Frosty Fish, 50¢. And the sandwiches: Meatballs or Hot Sausage, 25¢. Jack hands over a current menu and I start reading the handwritten notes tacked on the wall closest to me. "flew 30,000 mi to be with my family here." Really? "Martie and Melvin, engaged at the fishbowl, July 4, 1985." Funny time and place to lose your independence. "WVU Socks it to Georgetown, 27-7, September 5, 1987." This place is a regular sociological living organism. I don't remember ever writing a note on the wall. Jack points at the menu and I shake my head no; I'm still full from my half sub back in the room, and we'll be going out to dinner later. There's some kind of tribute banquet we've signed up for. He grins, passes a frosty fishbowl of brown ale through the crowd to me, and I mouth my thanks, lean in toward Marya. "I'm glad I came."

She edges right up next to me, puts her face up to mine, looks like she's preparing to announce that she has an incurable disease. "'Bout time."

I take a long sip of beer. "Ouch. You're right."

"I'm glad you came back, glad Jack came for this." She takes a sip of her wine, stares at me without flinching.

I meet her gaze. "Okay. Let me say what I need to say." She doesn't soften her stare. "Looking back, I know I was selfish, the way I dealt with things. Or didn't deal with them."

"We were all upset with Jack back then, Linda Lee. Him breaking it off with you caught us all by surprise."

On the drive here I'd imagined this conversation, but I'd never envisioned it halfway screaming nose to nose at Mario's. "You didn't know about the late-night sneaking around with Simone?"

"Are you kidding? Paulo swore up and down he didn't know, either." She glared at me. "We were friends. We were *us*. Didn't you think I would've told you if I'd known?"

"I don't know what I was thinking. I don't think I *was* thinking. I went a little nuts, to tell you the truth. When Jack took me out to Cooper's Rock that night, I thought he was going to pin me." I gulp my beer, wipe my mouth with my napkin to hide my trembling. "Or even ask me to marry him." Again I wipe my mouth. "I'll bet anything Marc knew."

"You'd have to ask him. You know what a nebnose he's always been. But JoAnne didn't know. I'm certain."

Nebnose—funny, her saying that. I haven't heard it in years. My family said busybody, but all the guys from around Pittsburgh said nebnose.

"I'm sorry I cut everybody off like that. I really am. But I didn't know what to do. I was wrecked."

"I don't think any of us care about sorry at this point." She points to her glass. "This wine is vile." Marya makes a frowny face, takes a small sip. "What did I think, Mario's would have a wine selection?"

I *was* wrecked, heartbroken and alone and scared to death. President Kennedy's assassination that fall felt personal. I remember seeing Jackie with her funeral veil on, and I wanted to swallow all of her pain, to take it away so she didn't have to feel that way ever again. There's no way I can explain that to Marya, practical as she is, and clearly she doesn't need to dig around in my feelings.

"I mean it. The sorry. I think I went a little crazy when Jack told me that night. Desperate. Ashamed. And I had to get away from anything that had to do with him. It almost killed me. I tried to bury it all, everything to do with us here. Once I got to UVA . . ."

"Why UVA anyway?"

"Oh—the nursing program. Remember I couldn't figure out whether I was going to be an English teacher or a nurse . . ."

"Right. So you picked nurse."

"At the time I didn't want to go to one of the women's colleges, William and Mary felt too claustrophobic after WVU, and UVA only accepted junior women who were in nursing, so voila, decision made."

"I thought you were smarter than that, Linda Lee, to choose something just to get away from home."

"Ouch again, Marya." I take a gulp of my beer. "I guess I deserve that. But I do love it, nurse practitioner. It was the right choice. But you were always the one with the plans to go into the medical field. Physical therapy, right?"

"Yep, me and Paulo both. Pharmacy for him, physical therapy for me. It's been good for us."

"How so?"

"I get to do the pro bono work; he's made the money."

"Right. Helping the suffering, like you planned."

"Doesn't seem to have made much difference, does it?" Up close, Marya's makeup is impeccable, but nothing can hide those worry lines around her eyes and mouth.

"Hey, you two, quit acting like two hound dogs guarding your pups over there, join us. Let's toast our Mountaineer ladies, everybody, what do you say?" Jack gets the whole place lifting their glasses. I smile, but I want to hear what Marya has to say. No way can we continue our conversation in this racket.

"You want to take a walk? It's kinda claustrophobic in here. If I drink any more of this . . ." She points to her glass and makes a face.

Marya has only finished half of her wine, but I've powered through my draught. "Sure. I'd like that."

I push through the crowded tables to let Jack know—his lips sag in a loose smile, his face slightly tipsy—he's talking to Marc and Manny and another of their old brothers, Buck, by the bar. He just gives me a quick kiss and continues his story about some crucial play of some long-ago game.

Marya and I head out the door to the requisite boos, turn right up the hill. The sun is setting, the sky pink through the rooftops and phone lines. Morgantown isn't a postcard-ready town, but it's got character, especially on a day like today, fall in the air, the sun setting in the mountains. Marya is still an energetic walker. I'm in shape, but I have to practically sprint to keep up with her.

"So, Jack tells me you have a boy and a girl?"

"Yep. Samantha's married, has a girl and a boy herself, twins. They're four."

"And your son?"

"He's bounced around here and there. Paulo wanted him to go to WVU, study pharmacy like him, take over the businesses. Samantha's a physical therapist, but she lives in St. Louis and doesn't practice anymore."

"What's your boy's name?"

"Antony. Paulo didn't want a junior, which suited me. Your Emma's a cutie."

"Yeah. Jack talked up WVU, but she's only here as a favor to him."

"It's not like Morgantown's been a second home to you guys."

I decide to ignore the dig. "She's interested in music and computers. More a small liberal arts school than a big university is what she and I are thinking. Jack's on a different page. He's all about business, though he's pretty impressed with her technology talent. She wants to do something creative with computers, but she also wants to please her daddy."

"That's the ticket these days, that's for sure."

"I'd hate to see her move to the West Coast."

"Yeah, Antony's just down in Pittsburgh. He works as a personal trainer. Didn't have the focus or the grades for med school. He'd be great in physical therapy, but he could never sit still long enough to finish college."

"Jack was like that. Remember? But he did okay. Took him five years, but he got the degree."

"I think college was easier then. Plus he had the wife and baby, so he pretty much had to get serious, didn't he?"

I don't know what to say to that, absorb the sting. We walk the hilly neighborhood at a brisk pace. I try to let go of Marya's pointed comments, try to frame what I want to say to her about ignoring her all those years ago, but the words don't come. She'd written a lot—at first short notes telling me she felt terrible, thought Jack was a jerk, wanted to talk, then longer letters describing what everyone was doing—everyone but Jack—letting me know they all wanted me to come back. She'd written the most, the longest.

She breaks the silence. "So are you close to Jack's son? What's his name—John?"

"Jay. We get along fine. When Jack and I got back together, he only came a few days in the summers, and Thanksgivings for a few years. Jack and Simone had been divorced for a while by then. Jay was a teenager, so we didn't even try to push the whole blended family thing. Now that he's grown, it's not even that much."

Marya nods, keeps plowing ahead.

"Jack sees him when he travels for business. Emma's crazy about him. She'd like to see him more often."

"Jack did the right thing, you know. Marrying Simone."

I bristle. "If you put aside the fact that he got her pregnant in the first place while he was cheating on me."

"None of us condoned that, Linda. Hell, we didn't know. Come to find out a lot of the guys sneaked around with town girls. They'd take their WVU girls back to the dorms by curfew, head back to Nick's, dance with the townies. And whatever. I'm sure Marc did, too, though nobody's ever told me so for a fact. Paulo and Manny were the exceptions."

"The good guys, you mean."

"Regina dated around on Manny all the time, right up until they got married. Times were strange, people did strange things."

"What's that got to do with the price of eggs? It's not like any of us girls were into the free love thing. JoAnne was pretty out there, but it was always Marc. I was such a faithful little fool."

"You weren't a fool, Linda. Jack, maybe. Not you." She sighs. "Times *were* different. Everything was so up in the air, Vietnam, Civil Rights. And the so-called sexual revolution."

"Yeah. My parents thought everybody my age was going to hell, me included, the way we questioned everything instead of just doing what we were raised to do."

"You know we didn't think you were a fool. We were all shocked, too. I swear. I had no idea Jack was running around with Simone D'Espere back then."

I shake my head. "Really? Nobody? As close as we all were?"

"Unless it was Marc, and he certainly wasn't about to say anything to JoAnne. Not one of us liked Simone. We talked about it nonstop, thought maybe she was lying about being pregnant. But after the baby was born, he was clearly Jack Vanderbilt's. So what were us gals gonna do? The guys loved Jack, we loved Jack too. In the end *you* were the one who left us."

I didn't know what to say to that. "We talked a lot about situational ethics in psychology, remember?"

"Don't evade the point, Linda Lee. Jack screwed up. For a fact. But I didn't. We didn't."

"You mean you and Regina?"

"Yeah. And JoAnne, too. All of us worried about you for months, from right there at the end of school when we found out that Jack knocked up Simone and you packed up and left without a word. Until pretty much the baby came, and it was obvious you weren't going to get in touch with us. Or come back."

"I didn't know what to do."

"Nobody did. We were your friends, though. It felt like that didn't mean a thing to you."

"It did."

She shakes her head. "You had a funny way of showing it." She half smirks. "And Jack was broken up too, you know. He never loved Simone. Hell, I don't think he even liked her. She was a manipulative little gold-digger."

"You said as much in your letters, but what was I supposed to do? It felt like staying connected to you all would mean staying connected to Jack, and I couldn't deal with that."

"Hiding from everybody who cared about you—how did that work? Did you even tell your parents?"

I jerk my head. "About Jack, you mean? Lord no. They knew I'd been dating somebody, but I never told them that was why I didn't want to go back. They certainly never knew Jack and I had a sexual relationship." I shake my head at the absurdity of me and my mother talking openly about sex. "They made me get a job when I told them I wasn't ready to go to school, that my sophomore year had been so hard I needed a break. They were pretty impressed I made Dean's List, but they weren't about to let me sit around the house. After a few months at the Greenbrier, I told them I wanted to try a different school, had heard UVA had a better nursing program. They were all for nursing."

"You all never were close, were you?"

"Not really." We press on up the hill. "So how's your dad?"

"He died years ago. Heart attack in his early sixties. He went fast."

"I'm so sorry."

"Yeah. Mama didn't live six months after him. They fussed all the time, but she couldn't get by without him."

"I hardly go back home anymore. Unless it's for a funeral."

"What caused you and Jack to settle in Lynchburg anyway?"

"Jack can work anywhere there's an airport. I took a supervisory position a number of years ago coordinating the nurses at the hospital in Lynchburg, so that's home now."

"Sounds important."

"It's demanding. It's a good thing we only had Emma, with Jack on the road all the time and me at the hospital so much."

"I would've had more children, but we didn't. The whole 'be careful what you wish for' thing makes a lot more sense to me in my fifties than it did when we were freshmen, you know? I got to be a physical therapist, work with needy people, and it turns out I'm still no closer to figuring things out. My daughter's more like me than I might've wanted. Her Daddy's girl. Couldn't wait to get out on her own. I don't think I'd get very good grades in the mom department. I'd like to be a better grandma, but the twins are too far away."

"That must sting." Marya nods. "I'm lucky Emma and I are close. Right now. Who knows?"

"I can tell. How about you and Jack? Are you two close?"

"Why . . . sure. He travels right much, but he still insists we have date night every week, surprises me with flowers every now and then, takes me on a trip for our anniversary."

"That doesn't surprise me. He was crazy for you the first time you all met, that night at the house."

"The feeling was mutual."

"Plain as the nose on your face." She turns to smile at me. "That's not what I mean, though. Paulo's always had that sentimental streak— that strong feminine they call it these days—but we've been together all these years and we still want to talk every evening when we get home. We're best friends."

"Best friends? I don't know if I'd say that about me and Jack. I'm more connected to him and Emma than anybody else in this world, but best friends? I don't think so." That old lonely/uncomfortable feeling crept into my mind. Did I even have a best friend? I try to control my quivery lip.

"Why not?"

"Maybe I'm too much of a loner to have a best friend." I can't believe I've said that. But I know it's true. I've been a loner all these years, except maybe where Emma's concerned. "I guess if *he* had to say who his best friends are, he'd still say these guys, even though he's barely spent any time with them in eighteen years."

"Yeah, it's been too long. You know, the guys were so excited to find out Jack was seeing you again. And then boom, he stops coming around, except for maybe a phone call every now and then and a golf game when he's on the road. Paulo's got the biggest heart of anybody I've ever known. He's missed Jack."

I feel slapped. Like I deserve to be slapped. "I wanted us to build a life together, away from his life with her."

"Heavy price you made him pay, I have to say." Her voice is brittle. "But the guys, this whole brother thing is a big deal to them. They'd never hold it against him, not coming around much. They knew how much he wanted you." Porch lights are coming on up and down the block.

Without talking about it, we stop, turn around, head back in the opposite direction. I'm glad for a moment to catch my breath.

"They're great guys. It's pretty impressive what everyone's done," I say.

"We've all had our struggles."

"Who hasn't?"

"And Marc . . . I think he had some days of serious boozing and womanizing. Paulo never told me details, but I think he and JoAnne almost split a few years back."

"You're kidding? They were always so . . . perfect."

"Nope." She lowers her voice, even though nobody's anywhere near. "And Regina. She's probably had the roughest road of any of us."

"Come on. She looks closer to Emma's age than ours."

"Don't be fooled. Lots going on with that one."

We walk a few minutes. Marya's tongue-lashing is well-deserved, but it still burns.

"In other words: What gave me the right to lick my wounds so long, right? Or keep Jack from his fraternity brothers?"

"If the shoe fits . . ."

My throat is scratchy, my eyes watery. "You've always called 'em like you see 'em, haven't you?" We're back at Mario's, can see everybody laughing and talking inside. I take a couple of deep breaths. The positive vibes practically roll out the door.

"So why now, Linda? Why'd you decide to come back now?"

"Honestly, I wish I knew, Marya. But . . ." that telltale lip starts quivering again. "I'm glad we came." I point inside. "Look in there—see? Jack over there by the bar?" We look through the glass storefront. "He's so happy to be here. Everybody loves Jack."

She looks at me, tired, her wrinkles obvious in the glare from inside the bar. "Jack with the big personality. And you always did keep everything deep down inside. You never let any of us get too close."

We stand a while, quiet. I know I need to try to make her understand. "I think those two years here I came closer to opening up than I ever have, before or since, especially with you."

"I tried to be your friend. I really did. I wanted to help."

"I know. I was just too ashamed. And scared. And . . . kicked in the gut."

She doesn't speak and I don't fill in any of the blanks. I know I've done it again—closed up just at the moment when I have the chance to connect. I want to tell her what was going on with me, but the words catch in my throat.

Marya turns and smiles. "What do the kids call it these days? A posse? You had a posse, and you didn't turn to us." We both laugh—at how improbable the word 'posse' is to me and Marya and Regina and JoAnne.

I'm glad she made me laugh—I could cry, right now; I who almost never cry. "Well, Jack and I finally got it together, even if it took us almost twenty years. And here we are today, together again, finally, at Mario's Fishbowl."

"I'll never forget it, you and Jack and the love-at-first-sight thing going on that night at the house. Nobody would argue with that."

Back inside, after the silly loud cheers, Marya heads for the restroom and I find Regina and shove in beside her at the crowded table.

"How does a gal get a beer around here?" I lean down and practically yell. She's sitting with Annette and a woman I don't know.

"Hey, Linda, this is Monica, Buck's friend . . . from Santa Monica!" Buck, the eternal womanizer/best dancer, still with the best elbow candy in the room. We laugh at how silly and improbable her name is. Monica is lovely—at least twenty years younger than the rest of us, and she joins us in the humor of the situation, though she's probably already been introduced that way twenty times today. Her brown eyes are warm, her long brunette hair like one of those Clairol commercials. For some reason I think Spanish. Or maybe Native American. "She's been dating Buck, what is it, ten minutes?" We shake hands. I haven't gotten a chance to talk to Buck yet—the group's perennial bachelor, along with Ekim. Buck owns vineyards in California and apparently changes lady friends like other men change skivvies, or so I've heard. Jack has a million Buck stories.

"May I join you all?" Regina nods and skooches over so I can share the chair with her. "Marya and I took a walk and I've talked myself hoarse. I'm ready for something to drink."

Regina smiles. She has a glass of wine in front of her, but it hasn't been touched. "Good luck, dearie. The service around here hasn't changed a bit. Lousy as ever." The women lean in and continue their conversation about *Cats* closing on Broadway—I've seen it a few times, but right now I'm more interested in a beer. I can't catch Jack's eye—I didn't stop to let him know I was back—so I try to get the waitress myself, which is fruitless. I decide to head up to the bar.

"Excuse me—I'll be back in a sec." Regina pats my shoulder as I stand.

I see JoAnne talking to a group of the guys at the bar, so I wend my way through the crowd of bodies in her direction. She'll know how to get a beer in this chaos; she lives here in Morgantown and probably comes here often after games. She's always been able to get exactly what she wants. When there's a pause, I tap her on the shoulder.

"Oh—," she flinches, then brightens, "Hey, you—hey—y'all coming to the thing tonight?"

"Yep. Emma's coming too. Will your son the musician be there?"

"He will. I'll make sure we get those two together." She raises her wine glass, sips. "I'm glad you came, Linda."

"Me too. You have any clout around here? I'm dying for a beer."

When my Yuengling draft is in front of me, JoAnne leans in. "Even after Jack said yes, y'all would come, Marc was worried *you* wouldn't. That man has more confidence than Bill Clinton, but that had him worried."

I sip my beer, nod.

"And Jack looks good, let me say. After that heart attack, we were all pretty scared. He's always been the jock, the fitter than fit one. For him to have a scare like that . . ."

"His doctors say it was a lucky heart attack, if you can ever call a heart attack lucky—small enough not to do any damage, warning enough to make Jack change some of his old bad habits. Like way too much greasy junk food on the road, not nearly enough exercise."

"He still plays tennis doesn't he?"

"Once a week, when he's in town. But other than that he was pretty sedentary before that happened. Now he's running two or three days a week and working out in hotel spas when he's on the road."

"Like I said, he looks good." She gives me a close stare. "And you look great, too. I wouldn't believe you're what, fifty-three?"

"Same as you. That hasn't changed." We smile. I remember that our birthdays are close together—we're both Gemini. I hadn't thought about that in I don't know when. "So what made you guys settle in Morgantown? You were always the one who was going to move away as soon as you graduated."

"After law school here, it was easy for Marc to practice where he'd interned. He tried the Charleston prosecutor thing, while I got my J.D., but it was cutthroat. We already had one baby by then, you know. Then we both got offers here. And I don't think I could live without these mountains after all."

"I don't know how you did it with children, though—practiced law. With Marc being an attorney, too."

"I've had help. You're a nurse, right?"

"Nurse practitioner. Only I don't really do much clinical anymore. I'm chief nursing supervisor at the hospital."

"Keeping everybody in line. Jack told us about that last night. And about Emma. He's sure crazy about that girl of yours."

"She's pretty great. We can't believe she's gonna be leaving us soon. Where did the time go?"

"Yep, it's been strange without the boys home. But Marc and I stay busy. We still have fun together—season tickets for all the Mounties home football and basketball games."

A few of the guys at the bar must hear her; they raise their mugs and shout "Go Mounties!"

"That's funny—Marya said something similar, about her and Paulo still being best friends."

"Marc's never boring—I'll give him that. But he's been a workaholic. A few years there the boys and I hardly saw him. He was bound and determined that he'd be a better provider than his father."

"Yeah—they all had that hungry ambition, didn't they? Even if they did act like naughty boys half the time." We smile in agreement. "Would anybody have ever imagined Jack owning his own tech company and Marc being a judge? I mean, really?"

"And Frankie Galluci giving a million dollars to renovate the house? Excuse me—Frank!" She clinks her wine glass against my empty mug.

"And us with professional careers, too, when all our mothers expected was for us to get our M.R.S."

"I know. But I remember not having any idea exactly what I was itching for—just something different. Even when Marc and I got married, we didn't have any kind of life plan. I just knew I was *not* going to be like my mother."

"Don't talk to me about life plans." I don't mean for my response to sound so snippy.

"Right. Jack sure didn't. Or if he did . . ." She shakes her head, sips her red wine. "God, to be so smart he certainly was stupid."

"Funny, I've always figured I was the stupid one."

"Oh please, Linda Lee—you, stupid?" She shrugs, tips her empty glass toward the bartender. I hold up my mug, too. "Except maybe when you didn't answer my tenth phone call."

"I can't explain . . ."

"Explain? That was a lifetime ago, Linda. Thirty-some years. We were just kids, trying to figure things out. We lost you. That hurt. End of subject."

I don't know what to say. JoAnne was no doubt a helluva lawyer. She'd always been no-nonsense. I'd been such a worrywart, such a scaredy cat. JoAnne would do what she wanted to do, say exactly what she thought, whether it involved a date or a girl on the hall or one of our professors. How foolish of me to think that my choices had had any lasting impact on her. JoAnne Miller was no softie. Never had been.

"Remember that time I went home with you, for Easter, and you got in this big argument with your sister about marching against the Vietnam war?"

"Yeah, right after you met Jack. At that spring dance at the House—you went with one of Marc's friends—who was it, Sammy Stephenson?—and after he passed out, Jack came up and started hitting on you. So Jack. I do remember."

We laugh. "I thought he was being a gentleman, feeling sorry for the wallflower. Jack's always known how to pinpoint a woman's weakness!"

"Don't sell yourself short, Linda. Jack's been crazy about you since he laid eyes on you. No doubt about it, that night he fell hard."

April–November, 1966

"More peas, Linda Lee?"

"Thank you, no, Mrs. Miller. I don't think I could eat another bite. Everything was delicious." The remains of the hearty meatloaf supper surrounded us in this fancy dining room papered with pink peonies in full bloom.

"Well, it was no trouble. You girls look like you haven't had a decent meal in a while," JoAnne's mother insisted, holding the bowl in my direction. She was an attractive woman; I could see how she must have looked a lot like JoAnne when she was younger. Now she was kind of faded all over. Trying to be polite, I took the dish, set it down beside me.

"I'll just get us some ice cream, then. I haven't made a big dessert for tonight, since we'll be having Easter dinner after church tomorrow. . ."

"Mama, do you mind if Linda Lee and I are excused?"

"Of course not, dear . . ."

"Stay and visit with your mother, JoAnne," Mr. Miller said as she leaned back from the table. "She's been hungry for your company." He was a sturdy looking man, as if all his edges were squared off like his chin. His graying crewcut topped off a strong, tanned face.

"I'll stay if you'll stay, Daddy." She reached over to grab his broad hand and he patted her arm.

"I'm gonna check out the ham station here in a minute." He looked at his watch. "And I've got to be at church early tomorrow. I'm ushering at sunrise service."

"You think the Beatles are more popular than Jesus, Daddy?" JoAnne asked, staring him in the face.

I couldn't believe she brought that up at the supper table. My daddy would've popped his cork if I'd said such a thing.

"Don't be silly, pumpkin. That young man will be ashamed he said something so foolish one day, when he's old enough to have better sense." He patted her arm again, pushed his chair away from the table, and stood. "But he sure has stirred up a lot of people." He grinned. "Thanks for the delicious supper, Sally." He rested his hand on Mrs. Miller's shoulder for a moment and then walked into the kitchen. I could hear him heading down the basement stairs.

"You girls go ahead if you've got something planned." Mrs. Miller stood herself and began gathering dishes.

"Let me help . . ."

"Heavens no! Jeanelle can do this."

JoAnne's sister glared at her mother. Four years younger, she was petite like JoAnne, but not half as pretty. Maybe it was that she was minus the curls. Her hair was straight and limp, and she hadn't smiled the entire meal. The eyes were the same color as JoAnne's, but Jeanelle's didn't sparkle.

"Don't give me that look, Missy. Your sister's got company. Excuse us, Linda Lee. Jeanelle's gotten a little sassy since you've been off at school. You sure you don't want some ice cream?"

Jeanelle got up from her chair and started rattling silverware. JoAnne gave me a quick nod. "Thanks, Mama. I planned to show Linda Lee around town a little bit this evening, if you don't mind."

"Course I don't. I was expecting as much." She pushed the swinging door into the kitchen, her arms laden with serving dishes. Jeanelle sulked behind her with a handful of knives, forks, and spoons.

"You sure?" I stage whispered to JoAnne, who was already halfway to the hallway. My role as houseguest to strangers was new for me. Any time I'd spent the night with girlfriends back home I'd known the families my whole life and I ate at home before I went over, so we didn't have a formal sit-down dinner before we made popcorn and told ghost stories.

"Come on. I've washed those dishes enough times to scrub the flowers off. Let Jeanelle get her spoiled little hands soapy for a change."

JoAnne's house was as different from mine as Christmas is from Good Friday. Her white frame two-story gave the impression that someone was setting a stage for good things to happen, whereas mine was spare and outfitted for sturdy survival in a world that required toughness. The Miller living room had chintz stuffed chairs with a sofa to match, in front of a fireplace with a lacey fire screen. Every surface had framed family photos; the one that caught my eye had a base of bronze baby shoes, topped with a picture of baby JoAnne smiling and reaching for something. It had been tinted so that her dress and cheeks were blush pink. Little pottery pitchers held flowers. Her mother was a homemaker, like we'd read about in home-ec class in school. JoAnne told me her daddy owned a car dealership—only because I was so surprised she drove a teal blue Mustang convertible that was all her own to school this semester. JoAnne looked just right in that perky, new car.

We hurried upstairs to brush our hair and put on lipstick. All the bedrooms were on the second floor. That was different for me, too. JoAnne didn't even share with her sister. She had her own room with matching twin beds. Her very own twin beds! Back home, we had bedrooms wherever we could fit one, upstairs and down, and they all were crowded with big metal double beds that could hold two or three people as need be. My sisters and I shared a room, the boys bunked in one room, my parents had a room, and my grandma had a room. Downstairs, back behind the kitchen, my Great Uncle Bo lived in his small bedroom. I think it had once been a sleeping porch. And behind the living room, my Granddaddy Chick, my mama's daddy, had what could've been a big closet or a storage room. People slept everywhere. The living space didn't have enough chairs for all of us at once, but there was never a time when everybody was home at the same time anyway, so it didn't matter. The grannies tended to sit bundled up in sweaters in the kitchen or outside on the porches all year long.

JoAnne had clicked on the radio, was singing along to "Sounds of Silence" while she primped her hair. "I've got us some dates. They're probably already at Porky J's. We're gonna meet there before we head down to the lake."

"What should I wear?"

"What you've got on, silly." We were both wearing slacks and sweaters. Even though it was Easter weekend, the weather was still cold at night. "Grab a jacket, though."

"Are my shoes okay?" I was wearing flats. I don't know why I asked. The only other shoes I'd brought along were the patent leather pumps for church.

"There's a shelter. It's not like we'll be hiking back in the woods."

"So tell me about these guys." I stood behind her brushing my hair. Maybe I'd put it in a ponytail.

"Old high school buddies. I've dated most of them at one time or another—not dated, dated, you know. Just gone out a few times. Just friends. Nobody special."

I nodded. "How long have you lived in this house anyway? It's really pretty." I pulled my hair into the elastic, checked for lumps on top.

"My parents built it right after I was born. Long as I can remember."

"I love your room."

"Thanks. Mama is Betty Crocker, no doubt about that. But I don't plan to sit home and read recipes myself. I'd be bored out of my gourd."

"Really?" I thought my mother would probably give up a lot to trade places with Mrs. Miller, to stop going to the ribbon factory 300 days a year and stay home and make quilts and put up pears.

"Why bother with WVU if you're only gonna be home changing diapers and cooking pot roast?"

"I don't know. I know I want to do something different from Mama. But I'm not sure what that different might be, especially where art's concerned."

"Use your brain, for starters." She gave me a "duh" look. "I think my mama's days must be brainless. I would go goofy with boredom if all I ever did was go to Safeway and church circle and figure out what my husband wanted for supper."

"We Can Work It Out" came on, and JoAnne started bopping around me, singing, "Try to see it my way . . ." I had to laugh.

"Seriously, Linda Lee. They are testing nuclear bombs out in Nevada. Right here in the U. S. of A. We could all blow up tomorrow. Do you want to be trying a new ground beef recipe when the world goes up in a nuclear cloud?"

"Of course not. But I don't want to miss out on a family, either."

"Who said anything about missing out on a family? I *want* to get married and have a family. I just *don't* want to turn into my parents, even if they are sweet peas." She flipped through hangers in her closet. "I do *not* plan to settle down any time soon, though. Uh-uh."

Funny, I'd been thinking that her parents had it pretty well figured out. "Is that guy from the Air Force Academy home? Will I meet him tonight?"

"No, thank goodness. They don't let them leave for Easter. Some kind of military practice thing." She chose a plaid trench coat. "I don't need to run into him. He's still writing me, begging me to go out with him again."

"You are such a heart breaker." JoAnne had dated about ten guys in the time that we'd been at WVU. I'd never known a girl with a good reputation to be such a flirt. Except of course Regina. I was awed and envious. "So is Marc Bonheur still hounding you?"

She laughed, turned up her collar. "Of course. I'm going with him to a big dance at the House the Saturday after we get back. Didn't I tell you?"

"I thought you swore you weren't ever going to go out with him?"

She leaned close to the mirror and applied hot pink lipstick, puckered her lips two or three times. "He is so stuck on himself. I made him beg. He kept asking me at the last minute, when I'd run into him on a Saturday afternoon at the Olympiad, and I'd tell him no way, he was going to have to ask me the right way, ahead of time, or he could forget it." She stepped back to get the overall impression. "He called me before we left on Friday and invited me for the party at the House next Saturday." She wiggled her eyebrows. "So I had to say yes."

"I think he's real handsome." I looked around for my pocketbook on the chest of drawers. "And kinda naughty looking, too."

"I know." She winked. "He's a junior, an 'older man.' He dated Charlene a couple of times, remember her?. . . then didn't call her again. Charlene ought to be there tonight. She can tell us more. I have to admit, I think he's kind of . . . exciting."

Charlene lived in the dorm, too. She was from JoAnne's hometown. We'd all met in the Boreman meetings early on.

She poked me on the shoulder. "Hey, last time we were at Phi Kap, did I see you getting all up close and personal with Marc's little brother Jack Vanderbilt?"

"We danced a few times."

"I saw that. Looked like the sparks were flying."

"I'd heard he was pretty cocky. But he wasn't like that at all when we talked. He came over after my date got wasted—I was thinking about leaving, actually, but couldn't figure out how to get back by myself without looking pathetic—and he sat down and talked to me, not just staring at my boobs, you know." I blushed. "He got me a beer and we actually talked."

"You don't say? That's a plus. The guys say he's a jock, I do know that. Seems like whenever I'm at the House he's with a different girl, but then I'm never with the same guy, either." She looks my way and shrugs. "And he can dance like American Bandstand. I would never go out with somebody who couldn't dance."

"Me either. You're right—he's a terrific dancer. I loved dancing with him." I bopped around a few steps.

"So there. Marc Bonheur and Jack Vanderbilt are on our radar when we get back. Look out guys—you don't stand a chance!"

About twenty of JoAnne's high school friends were rambling around the parking lot at Porky J's Rib Shack when we got there. All the radios were on the same station, so the music was blasting. "Ballad of the Green Beret." I couldn't stand that song. People were singing as loud as they could. JoAnne introduced me to everybody, but I didn't even try to remember all their names. Eddie Edwards got me a beer from the trunk of his car—he was supposedly my date for the night, which was funny since the guy back home I'd sorta liked was Michael Edwards, but he said they weren't kin. Mostly everybody was just hanging out in a group, anyway, so we didn't spend much time together.

At some point, everybody got some subliminal message and jumped into cars and headed down to the pavilion by the lake. I got in with Eddie and about six other people, including Charlene. We didn't even try to talk, just sang along to the radio. The guys yelled stupid stuff back and forth. "Right on!" and "Bitchin'" and "Hell no we won't go!" I couldn't get the gist of where these remarks were coming from. I was quiet, sipping my beer and wondering if my parents or JoAnne's parents had ever done anything goofy like this. Did my older brothers act so crazy? I couldn't picture it. When Carl was dating Mar-tee Mae, before they got married, had they gone down to the lake at night and caroused?

I didn't even know if I was having fun or not. Part of me felt lonely and phony, like I was observing this from one of the stars outside the car. Did I even belong there? JoAnne was so natural with those people. And I was on that star looking down at the fun. I had been feeling on the fringe at fraternity parties while everybody else was so clearly having a blast, like I was tuned to the wrong station. Except for that little bit of time when Jack Vanderbilt came over and talked to me that one night. That had been different. Dancing with him made me "glad all over," like the silly song. I was being childish to even think like that, though. Jack Vanderbilt hadn't even called me by that point.

He did call, though, on Easter Sunday night after we got back from JoAnne's, around 8:00.

One of the girls screamed, "Linda Lee Barbour, you've got a call," from the phone booth at the end of the hall.

Just luck I had my door open, was bringing things up from the parlor. Right away I figured it was my parents, checking to be sure I'd made it back.

"Hello?"

"Hi. Jack Vanderbilt. Remember me?"

Totally caught off guard. My throat tightened. His voice was deep and confident-sounding. "Oh. Of course. Sure."

"I haven't seen you around. Did you go home for Easter?"

"No. I went home with JoAnne Miller."

"She's a cutey. I've seen her at the House. Just a sec." I could hear him yelling, "Keep it down, I'm trying to talk, here." Then, "So what're you doing?"

"Unpacking." Good grief, could I say more than one or two words at a time? This was more like ping pong than a conversation, but I was so caught off guard I was having a hard time thinking.

"Feel like going for a walk?"

Did a walk count as a date? I'd signed in, but I could sign out again. Curfew was 10 on Sunday nights. "Sure."

"I'll be there in two minutes."

"Okay." I wouldn't have time to change. I ran back to the room to brush my teeth and put on some lipstick. I could hardly breathe.

And like that we started dating. We went for that walk that crisp spring evening and talked nonstop. We leaned in toward one another and strolled along as though we were connected at the hip. We both were crazy about The Shirelles and Bob Dylan and The Beatles. Neither of us were big Elvis fans. We thought Motown was way better than beach music and loved to fast dance. I loved President Kennedy and he did, too. Classes were making us think in ways we'd never thought before, like we'd been half asleep all through high school and now we were wide awake. How had we been so ignorant about civil rights, we agreed. The time went by in a blink as we walked along Woodburn Circle and down by the fieldhouse. When he took my hand and kissed me on the steps behind Woodburn Hall, he didn't have to say a word. I knew we'd fallen in love.

When I got back, I had to tell somebody. JoAnne was sitting cross-legged on one of the twin beds talking to Regina.

"Guess who I was just out with?"

"Ringo Starr," Regina deadpanned.

"Seriously. Guess."

"Well from the looks of you, whoever it was he's wearing most of your lipstick about now." JoAnne smirked and pointed her finger at my face.

I put my hands to my lips. "Jack Vanderbilt!"

JoAnne patted the bed beside her. "Sit! Tell!"

For the first time in my growing up, I had total confidence that a boy was feeling exactly the way I was feeling, that right at that instant Jack was somewhere having the sensation that he wanted to be with me just as much as I wanted to be with him. I wasn't worried in the least that he'd been pretending or flirting or wouldn't ever ask me out again: We'd connected. Love at first sight didn't feel like a Shakespeare tragedy to me. Jack Vanderbilt and I were over the moon starstruck in love.

That spring we were a couple in that new couple way. He told me if he had a handball game after classes. I let him know my music appreciation class required me to go to hear Charlie Byrd play classical guitar. He didn't go to listening parties at the House if only girls from a certain sorority were invited, if it meant I couldn't come. The most mundane details of his life fascinated me: If he liked his bologna sandwiches fried or not; if he used Ivory soap or Lifebuoy; whether he'd ever cheated on a test or not (He had, a sixth-grade spelling test. He still couldn't spell.). His Old Spice was so much better than Brut, so all-male and right. I teased him into talking about old girlfriends, and why he liked me better.

Meanwhile, we couldn't touch each other enough. As soon as we saw one another, he had his hand on the middle of my back or I had my arm wrapped around his elbow or he was pulling me down on the sofa beside him. It was like our bodies were supposed to be touching. In his old Chevy Biscayne, we tangled together like twin babies in the womb, we were that close. Jack was the first boy to touch my naked breasts, and I thought I'd stop breathing at that second it was so wonderful. He was the first man to look at me without my bra on, and I was so proud to see that craving in his eyes. I'd never seen an erection before, much less touched one. I was astonished I could make him feel that way. Little by little, we got to know each other's bodies, but we didn't have full-on sex that spring. Much as I wanted to, I wasn't ready to take that risk, not even with Jack. I learned to satisfy him, but both of us always went back to our dorms wanting more.

JoAnne, meanwhile, had gone to the clinic and gotten the pill. She and Marc were pinned within weeks of Easter, and she couldn't get enough sex. Talking about sex was completely new to me. It had always been a taboo topic at home. My mother depended on the church to set the boundaries, and the church deemed sex outside marriage a sinful no-no. I'm sure she was a virgin on her one-night honeymoon to Lewisburg with my dad. I couldn't even imagine—didn't want to. Her job was to reinforce that "intimate relations" were between a husband and a wife, exclusively. I imagined we'd have "the talk" if I ever got engaged, but we certainly weren't going to sit around with my sisters and aunts on a Saturday afternoon while we were shelling beans and talk about how sex made a woman feel and how often we had orgasms. So the topic of sexual relations was as immediate and urgent to me and my friends as discussing Civil Rights and Vietnam and the fact that cigarettes had been declared dangerous to our health. Maybe moreso.

On Friday and Saturday nights that May and early June, we'd gather in the suite after sign-in and JoAnne would tell all. Marya joined us less and less; she'd made up her mind she wasn't going to have sex until marriage, period.

"I can see why our mamas didn't tell us about this when we were in high school," JoAnne gloated. "There's no way they'd be able to keep us from having sex all the time once we found out how un-be-LIEVE-able it feels." I'd thought JoAnne was pretty the first day I laid eyes on her; now she radiated some kind of extra beauty energy, like she'd been given a secret elixir of the ancient goddesses. She looked more womanly, somehow, while I was still stubbornly girlish and naïve.

"You mean it doesn't hurt? It didn't hurt the first time?" I had to ask, though I blushed when I blurted it out.

"I don't know who wanted it more, me or Marc. It hurt, I guess, but not like any hurt you've ever felt. Like part of you has been hidden your whole life and voila, hello, that part's alive and humming now!"

"Are you and Marc gonna get married?" Regina asked. We were all trying to smoke to appear more sophisticated and worldly, though none of us really liked it, so Regina was lighting a cigarette. The guys didn't like for us to smoke around them, but we tried it in the dorm anyway. I think we'd had one pack of cigarettes for over a month. Regina, usually the most talkative of the three of us, didn't say much that spring during our late-night sessions. I noticed it but credited it to the fact that we wanted to hear what JoAnne had to say, and she did most of the talking anyway. Regina wasn't dating anyone in particular, though she always had a date, and sometimes she was at the Phi Kap parties. But she was my suitemate, and we were tight.

"I don't know. Maybe. But no time soon, I can tell you that. He's planning to go to law school. And I've got a lot of school in front of me."

"He hasn't asked you to marry him? What if he dumps you?" Was I sounding like my mother, all Baptist and worried about sin, being "second-hand goods"? I think not—she would've never listened to such talk. Maybe one of my sisters, though.

"He's nuts about me. He's not about to give me up. Why should he? And who knows, maybe at some point I'll get tired of him and decide to dump him!"

I was horrified. "But, then, if you don't marry him . . ."

JoAnne laughed. "I'll be like a used car, used?"

She was reading my mind. I nodded yes, took a puff on my cigarette. I never inhaled 'cause I couldn't stand that whoozy feeling.

"The times they are a-changing, Linda Lee. Haven't you heard? Men want a woman to be sexually confident. At least the men who have half a brain."

"That's what they're saying, but maybe it's all talk, when you get right down to choosing a wife."

"Believe me, I won't be marrying one of the Clarksburg yokels. I expect my future husband to be smart and educated and savvy enough to know a sophisticated woman will make a far better life partner than some Polly Pure-butt."

Where did she get that phrase, life partner? I'd never heard that. Is that what people were saying instead of wife or husband now? I wasn't convinced she was right, but I was certainly fascinated by the choices she was making.

Regina chimed in. "Suppose Marc has to go to Vietnam?"

"Not as long as he keeps his grades up. And gets into law school. We're not even thinking about getting married anyway. We're having too much fun."

Regina and I took tiny shallow puffs on our Marlboros while JoAnne rubbed lotion on her feet and legs. She'd moved into our suite when her roomie, Charlene, quit school.

"Marc and I are both ambitious. We plan to do something with our lives. I'm finishing WVU, that's not even a question. I might go to law school, too. Marc'll be finishing up by then."

"What?" I just about choked. "You think you could get in? That they'd let you in?"

"I'm at least as smart as Marc Bonheur. My daddy wouldn't think twice about sending me to law school."

"They let in girls?"

"Women, Linda Lee. We're women. And yes, they have to. It's the law." She was pulling off her shirtwaist dress to put on her peejays. She stripped in front of us like there was nobody in the room. She could pose for *Playboy*, she was that stacked.

"Back home in White Sulphur there aren't any women lawyers, I can tell you that for a fact."

"There's a great big world outside West Virginia, Linda Lee. A whole great big world." She dropped her bra and picked up her pajama top. I couldn't help but think that she stripped just that casually for Marc. I wanted to have that ease with my body, but I'd always been self-conscious. Until Jack.

Back home, I'd bought into the common understanding that only the slutty girls had sex, and they didn't talk about it—at least I didn't think they did. I'd never had a private conversation with one of them. None of those girls were in advanced classes with me or my Sunday School class or BTU either, so our paths only crossed in the halls or at Hudson Brothers, and we couldn't exactly strike up a conversation about sex in the store. Not that I would've, or they would've. I'd overheard enough from my brothers to know it was the boys who talked about who was "doing it," and that "doing it" ruined the girls' reputations. The boys got a pass. But here was JoAnne, her family as apple pie and upstanding as they come, telling us she was going all the way and loving it and not feeling the least bit guilty as far as I could tell. Maybe the Methodists were laxer than the Baptists about sex, but I didn't think so.

Marya was dating Paulo, so she and I talked a lot about the "idea" of sex: Whether it was a sin "out of wedlock" (Catholics and Baptists, yes), if we would be able to wait (Marya said she'd have no problem, she was her own boss; I wasn't so sure, since I'd met Jack. I was tempted, no doubt), and if a woman had to marry the first man she "did it" with (absolutely, per Marya; I thought probably so—but it was still an open question). Somehow, without all the soul searching, JoAnne had found a way of being comfortable inside her own skin that I hadn't, no matter how much college students talked about free love. I trusted Jack, but I wasn't ready to break with my growing up so completely, not yet. JoAnne was telling us everything, that was true, but I still didn't quite believe that I could be as sexually free as she described, that there wouldn't be some kind of penalty later on. Sin was sin where I came from.

Jack went home to Pittsburgh that summer to work for his daddy and I went back to Hudson Brothers six days a week. He called long distance at least once a week and we wrote every now and then. He'd send silly postcards with only a sentence or two, like "Promise me you haven't run away to India to join George Harrison" and "When you hear that song 'I Am A Rock' think of me." He'd told me he wasn't much of a writer. I didn't date at all that summer. We weren't pinned, but I didn't want to go out with anybody else. I was sure he'd bring up us going together sooner rather than later.

We only saw one another once that summer, fourth of July weekend, when JoAnne had planned for all of us to gather at Mont Chateau Lodge on Cheat Lake. I had to do some huge convincing to get my parents to let me go. College was one thing, but a weekend away just for the fun of it was quite another, not to mention the expense. They gave permission when I promised we had a chaperone and I'd pay with my own money. I'm sure they thought it would only be girls—they didn't ask, and I saw no reason to bring up the fact that a group of the guys would be there too. We stayed three girls to a room—me and JoAnne and Regina—but JoAnne was never in the room. I guess Marc had a single. Marya couldn't come, or wouldn't. She insisted she had to save her money, but I knew she was a lot more committed to "saving herself for marriage," and Paulo acted okay with that. A weekend at the lake might have felt like too much temptation. They both acted more satisfied with working hard and planning for their future than the rest of us.

Those two days defined my summer. Jack picked me up at the bus station in Morgantown, and we couldn't take our eyes off one another as soon as I stepped off the Greyhound. He was tan, wearing a white tennis shirt, madras long shorts, and Weejun loafers without any socks—the most handsome boy I'd ever seen in my life.

"You look terrific," he said, right off the bat. I was wearing a new sundress Mama had sewed, flowered piqué cotton. "Let me get your bag." Jack was always a gentleman in those ways. "Everybody else is here already, down at The Whip."

Being outside on the water in the heat and humidity of July is an aphrodisiac when you're nineteen. Our touching felt intensified that weekend. We were heat lightning. Sitting on the dock, drinking 25-cent beer in frosty mugs at the bar and grill, we were surrounded by an invisible shield of youthful energy and longing and ignorance. No part of the messy grown-up world could dampen our confidence. We could never be like them. Jack told me about his parents' unhappy marriage, how his daddy had to get electric shock treatments for his nerves. His mother had been a debutante in Buffalo when she met Jack's father, a Naval officer wearing those irresistible whites. Ever after she announced to whoever would listen that she'd married beneath her, even though he was an engineer with US Steel. Jack was an only child; my multi-generational family all living on top of one another struck him as warm and desirable. I don't know what part of my description gave him that romantic impression.

We stretched out in lounge chairs in the dark, under skies crowded with stars, whispering and near naked, touching every part of one another possible to touch, but still I didn't make that final commitment to actual sexual intercourse, though every cell in my body reached toward union with Jack's body like seedlings in a jar stretching for the sun. He never pushed, never tried to make me do more than I was willing. When he took me back to the bus station on Sunday, when we were saying goodbye, he used the words, "I love you, Linda Lee" for the first time. I was certain he meant it.

That fall when we were sophomores, since JoAnne was dating Marc exclusively, the four of us were together a lot. Marc, two years older than the rest of us, was Jack's Big Brother in Phi Kap. That seemed important to them. Plus he could buy beer and booze. While the weather was pleasant, the four of us would head out to Cooper's Rock on Sunday afternoons with a cooler and talk about everything from music to classes to the meaning of life.

JoAnne convinced me to go with her once a week to tutor some of the children in the coal-mining community back in Scotts Run. We were both sobered by the poverty. While JoAnne had a fancier house, neither of us had ever missed a meal or had to go to school without breakfast or in hand-me-down shoes. We'd been to the dentist and the doctor and had all our shots. The little girls we worked with looked at us like we were Miss Americas. With scabs on their bony arms and dirt under their fingernails, they were eager to get as much book learning as we could give. Driving back and forth, JoAnne and I talked about how we might do more, do better. I could be an English teacher in Appalachia. JoAnne would work to change the laws so that the miners got a better shake.

Marc and Jack shook their heads and laughed at us when we told them; they considered us two idealistic college girls off to save the world. I'd get so worked up at their sense of superiority that I wanted to spit.

Marc got tuition exemption as a work study student. He still clerked in the law library a few nights a week, but he'd served food in the dorm his first two years to defray costs. He had goals, personal goals, and he never got tired of saying that he didn't look to anybody for a handout or a hand up.

"Look, my daddy had the smell of grease on him his whole life. He didn't expect anybody to make his life any better except himself. Certainly not some do-gooder college girls."

"But it's not these children's fault that . . ."

"Who said it was? But my parents pulled themselves up. Your parents pulled themselves up. What makes you think these girls can't, too?"

"Women don't get many choices, Marc, in case you haven't noticed."

"Whoa, wait just a minute, Miss High Horse. Didn't I hear you say you were going to study law?"

"My daddy earned every nickel he ever spent. He built that car dealership from dirt."

"My point. You keep making my point, JoAnne."

"It's more complicated than that, Marc Bonheur. You know it is!" JoAnne could get fiery.

We'd go around and around. JoAnne was the idealist, Marc was the pragmatist, and Jack and I typically took up for our pals without much conviction one way or another. I did agree with JoAnne, but I wasn't sure things would change all that much, even if I did my part. I liked the tutoring, though. I was glad I could help those little girls, even if I couldn't help the world.

JoAnne was studying psychology, and we started discussing our motivations and the power of non-verbal communication and hidden agendas—things I'd never even heard about much less thought about in my previous life back home. To see myself and my family through the lens of those new glasses was dizzying. My second-year art studio included life drawing; the first time a nude model came into class and dropped her drape I almost shrieked. It was inconceivable to me that a young woman, another student, could sit up there in front of a group of a dozen other students, girls and guys, without a stitch on, nonchalant as if she were at home in her bathtub. I drew, my hand far more in control than my off-kilter brain. The charcoal gliding on paper felt like human contact, in some strange way, and I loved all the shades of gray and black.

My Brit Lit professor, Dr. Nathanael Hapgood Brown, had us read the unexpurgated (another new word for me) version of *Lady Chatterley's Lover*. As we talked about runaway desire right there in sophomore seminar, him up front in his corduroy sport coat leading a discussion about libidos like he was talking about Huck Finn floating down the Mississippi, I realized that this train I was on, that was hurtling my ideas and awareness through new dark tunnels and across unimaginable overpasses, did not have a reverse.

Along with having my brain scrambled, for the first time in my life I got that sense of belonging at the fraternity house that I'd missed, even in my family. I was "Jack's girl," and that made me somewhat of a Phi Kap sweetheart, since his pledge year was over, and he was a full brother and he lived upstairs. All the guys called me by name and hugged me wherever they saw me, invariably teasing me in some lewd boyish way about dating Jack. Silly as it was, it gave me a connection in that swirling see-saw world that was on the one hand making my brain sore and on the other hand waking my body to unimaginable pleasures.

Their parties were notorious on a campus identified in *Playboy* magazine as a party school. They'd have a band on Friday night, a listening party with records on the jukebox on Saturday afternoon, and another even bigger/better band later that night. I'd never danced so much, drunk so much beer, kissed and petted so often and so passionately.

One Saturday night in October, Dr. William Masters and Virginia Johnson came to speak at "The Festival of Ideas" on campus. Their topic: "Human Sexual Response." JoAnne and I got tickets and were breathless for weeks before the lecture. The guys thought we were crazy to miss The Fabians at the house that night. We told them we'd come by later, but we were dying to hear what these so-called sex therapists had to say.

"If they ask for volunteers you come get me, JoAnne," Marc had teased.

As we waited for the presentation to begin, the air in that dark auditorium was crackling with attention. When those two sat down on stage, it was as if rock stars had arrived, the applause was that powerful. I'd never heard anyone say such words out loud in public: manual stimulation, sexual plateau, clitoral orgasm, vaginal orgasm, ejaculation. Students and professors, women and men, we all sat there listening spellbound as Dr. Masters discussed his slides of graphs and charts about the human body's arousal during sexual intercourse. Every syllable was electric. Virginia Johnson spoke too, answering questions in this well-modulated, confident voice. Yes, women's physiological stimulation during sex could be charted, was measurably cyclical like a man's, all the way through to the orgasm. She spoke about these behaviors as though she were telling us how to make a chicken broccoli casserole. When she said "the vagina is a potential" I may have stopped breathing altogether.

I couldn't envision the research, the two of them side by side in the laboratory watching two strangers having sex. My brain had nowhere to catalog such images. The notion that volunteers would have uninhibited sex while they observed was as unfathomable to me as imagining Martians attending classes at WVU. My sexual reticence appeared provincial by comparison. JoAnne and I talked for hours afterwards; we didn't even go to the Phi Kap House that night.

"They are the strangest, smartest people I've ever heard in my entire life," JoAnne said.

"Did you see Dr. Mitchell and Dr. Mitchell there?" These were two English professors, a married couple, who fascinated us. She was almost six feet tall and slender and always fidgeting. He was no more than five-five, with glasses and a near-bald head and an eerie calm demeanor. "I've never thought about them having sex before, but seeing them there tonight. . ."

"God, I know, it was like you began to think about EVERYBODY having sex!" We giggled like crazy at such a thought.

"There's Dr. Masters up on stage, all proper in his bowtie, but he's been watching naked people right there in front of him doing *everything*." It made me blush to picture the things he must've seen couple after couple doing. Jack and I had still only done our grappling in the dark. We were the couple in my mind, on some hospital bed in some brightly lit room with Masters and Johnson on the opposite side of a glass taking notes.

"And HER. What about her, talking about vaginas and orgasms, for heaven's sake? I tell you, there is no reason on earth that a smart woman shouldn't be in charge of her own body, especially with the pill."

"She is so brilliant. And poised." I couldn't see myself having the required exam and asking for the pill, like asking for an aspirin. The fear of getting pregnant was real to me as I tried to give myself permission to go all the way with Jack, but going to the clinic to get birth control was impossible. If I ever did agree to it, he could use condoms, I figured. Getting the pill felt too definite, like I was scheduling sex instead of getting carried away. Wouldn't that be worse? If I was swept away I could blame my emotions, not my sinful, deliberate, un-Christian decision.

"Which makes this whole thing about sex being sinful pretty silly and UN-scientific, doesn't it?" JoAnne cocked her head.

How did she do it, read my mind like that? "I'd never thought about it being scientific in the first place. But the sin part has certainly been a big deal at my house."

"Where does that guilt come from, that makes it so powerful, do you think? I mean besides the obvious Adam and Eve crap."

"Who knows? The Puritans. To keep children under control, probably, safely paired up two by two." I couldn't believe I was saying such things, questioning my Bible teaching. Thinking such thoughts. I knew my parents believed it would be a sin for me to have sex before marriage, but maybe they were wrong. Maybe we'd all been brainwashed.

"It certainly works." We smiled, sympatico and feeling wise.

And on and on. JoAnne and I had been to the mountain, and each of us knew that our sense of sexual identity forever after would have a changed vantage from that evening on.

Fall Formals were the first weekend in November. Jack asked me the color of my dress, and I was impressed by his thoughtfulness. Silly: We could discuss details about corsages and make superficial plans but couldn't talk about the sex that dominated our thinking. This was the night we'd have "real" sex. He'd be "my first." He'd be a part of my "psyche" (a new awareness) forever. I'd made my choice, we knew this when we agreed we would stay over together after the dance, but we didn't talk about it. Odd: We could talk about everything in the world, we'd both said the L word, but we never put into words the decision to do "it." That would've been too clinical, too my way of thinking. We knew, and that was enough.

The formal dance was in the ballroom at Mont Chateau Lodge, and the Phi Kaps always booked all the rooms, supposedly so they wouldn't have to drive back to town after hours of partying. I knew Jack had booked a room for us. It was a given that I would spend the night with him. I had to lie on the dorm sign-out, something I'd never done before. It was a silly rule, having to sign out overnight to an approved boarding house or another student's home. Men could go to war at 18. I could make up my own mind where I'd spend the night. Or so the situational ethics went, excusing everything in the fall of 1966. I signed out for JoAnne's, she did the same. Regina was dating another Phi Kap, Manny Tambellini, who was giving her the big rush, but she was still going out with a couple of other guys, too, especially a Kappa Sig she told us she liked a lot. But she'd be at the dance that night, too, with Manny. I was glad.

The ballroom was decorated like a magical cave, and the Motown-sound band was the best I'd ever heard. Jack told me I looked beautiful in my pale teal ballerina length strapless gown. I felt beautiful. A photographer took formal posed shots of each couple under an arbor of fake lanterns and rocks. After her turn with Marc, JoAnne called for me and Regina and Marya to get under the bower with her. Arms around one anothers' waists, we four laughed into the camera. No matter what was going on in the crazy world outside the lodge, we were young and desirable, and the night belonged to us and our guys.

Jack and I danced every dance, fast and slow, so that the half dozen "special cocktails of the evening," something called a Fall Fizz I've never had before or since, didn't even go to my head. Instead my brain was buzzing with the wonder of the night. I was no longer up there on a star looking down at myself detached from the fun. I *was* the fun, side by side with Jack Vanderbilt.

Marc and JoAnne were crowned King and Queen of the formal. They danced a spotlight dance to "Unchained Melody." Watching them, I had an intuition that they would get married, despite JoAnne's insistence that she wasn't making a long-term commitment any time soon. JoAnne so lovely and self-assured, Marc cradling her back like he was part of her, looking down into her eyes like he could eat her with a spoon—those two fit together.

After the band played "Stay" and their encore "Shout," we all hung around and laughed and talked in the ballroom foyer. Manny glued himself to Regina; she talked to me and JoAnne and Marya and didn't appear the least bit impressed by his attention.

"I'm staying with Marya and some of the other girls," she whispered to me. "Manny has been after me all night to stay in his room with him, but I don't want to." Jack was holding my hand. She smiled and blew me a kiss. "Have fun, you two!" All the guys looked handsome in their dinner jackets. Manny especially; he had a madras bowtie and cummerbund to match but no boutonniere. He and Jack joked about who had the better moves on the dance floor, each showing off a few steps. Manny was known in the House for being the best. I would've voted for Jack.

As we flowed to the elevators, JoAnne and I hugged goodnight. I felt safe with Jack, but I was anxious, too. I couldn't help it. Not about Jack, but about this thing I was going to do that would be irreversible.

"Hey, you," he smiled as he unlocked the door.

"Hey, you," I smiled back. My overnight bag was already in the room with my toothbrush and shorty pajamas inside. I hadn't gone out and gotten some peignoir or sexy nightie, like a bride. I hadn't known what to bring.

JoAnne had laughed when I'd asked her: "You're going to be naked in five seconds anyway, so what difference does it make? Take some Listerine."

"You go ahead in the bathroom." Jack was taking off his jacket and tie, natural as if we'd done this a dozen times before.

I felt like every motion I was making was intensified, like one of those stop-action, slow-motion movies. I didn't much like him using the word "bathroom," though. That was too crude, not at all romantic. Nobody said "bathroom" in true romance. "You sure?"

"Of course. You want a drink?" He tipped his flask in my direction, picked up a glass.

"No thanks. I'll just be a minute." I grabbed my bag and scooted toward the restroom, as fast as I could. "Oh—" I remembered, and turned back into the room, "would you unzip my dress?" It didn't have a side zipper.

He was stepping out of his trousers, which somehow put me at ease. "Sure. Happy to be of service." He looked cute in his white shirt with the long tail and pale blue boxer shorts. He kissed my shoulder as he undid my dress. "There you go, ma'am."

Back in the bathroom I was calmer, pulling on my pajamas with tiny red strawberries and brushing my hair fifty times instead of a hundred. Should I wash off my make-up or leave it on? Leaning close into the mirror I could see it was smudged from all the dancing, so I scrubbed my face and only put on more lipstick. My cheeks were still flushed, probably from the drinks earlier. I took a swish of mouthwash from the tiny bottle I'd packed, gave myself one final look, and walked back into the room.

Jack had turned the bedspread back and was sitting cross-legged against the pillows, still in his shirt and boxers. Both bedside lamps were on. Did he think we were going to do it with the lights on? I began to feel panicky again, imagining Masters and Johnson watching. He whistled.

"You ask me, you look a whole lot prettier now than you did in that blue dress—and I thought you looked beautiful before."

I did a little curtsy, then felt silly. "Your turn."

"Be right back." He kissed me on the forehead as he passed me going into the bathroom. I jumped under the covers and leaned over to each side, turning the lights out. This felt nothing like being in the car or on a chaise lounge or stretched out on a blanket at Cooper's Rock. I was about to lose my virginity to Jack Vanderbilt and then spend the night with him. I'd never once thought beyond the sex to the fact that I'd be waking up in the same bed with Jack, too. That seemed crazy intimate.

The bathroom door opened, and light slanted into the dark room. "Oh," Jack said. Then, "You mind if I leave this door cracked?"

He came over and crawled in beside me. Now he was naked. "I want to look at you, Linda Lee. I want to be able to see you." He snuggled up against me and pulled me into his arms, his hair damp—had he taken a shower?—smelling of soap and a faint scent of bourbon. His skin was warm like bathwater. "Don't worry—I've got a rubber right here." He patted the pillow beside me.

He didn't hurry. We kissed and petted and he lifted off my pajama top and took his time kissing my breasts—"God, you have the most gorgeous breasts!"—and caressing my back and encouraging me to touch him all over. I did not need to be coaxed. When, finally, he was on top of me, I wanted him inside me so much I think I begged.

"You sure?" he asked, panting. Would he really have stopped? I pulled his hips to me and gasped, that first time he entered me like stone meeting water at the beginning of the world.

The next morning as we all gathered to pack the cars to head back to campus, JoAnne walked over, smiling. "You okay?"

"You were right."

"You sure? No regrets?"

The guys were teasing Manny and trying to mess up his hair. Manny was dressed like he was going to model for some men's fashion calendar, a cashmere V-neck draped over his shoulders, while the rest of us looked like we'd pulled on our clothes for a fire drill. Regina was nowhere in sight.

I leaned toward JoAnne's shoulder, whispered. "I'm so glad Jack Vanderbilt is my first."

September 15, 2000: 9 p.m. The Dinner Dance

Ekim is already drunk. "Linda Lee Barbour. Come on, gorgeous. Dance with me. Y'all know I'm a better dancer than slick ol' Jack Vanderbilt." Hands balled into fists up near his shoulders, he makes a few feeble shoulder and hip contortions to the music, almost stumbling into our table. While he's always been handsome and debonair, the one member of the fraternity with a Middle Eastern background while we were in school, now Ekim Koury is more jaundiced than dark-skinned, more bony than slender. His full head of black hair doesn't have a strand of grey, but at this moment it looks like he just woke up and forgot to comb it. Jack, Emma, and I are seated at a round table with JoAnne and Marc and their son, Charlie, plus Regina and Manny.

"Gimme a dance, Linda Lee. You know I've always had the hots for you, right? Come on. Dance with your ol' buddy Ekim. Pretty please." When he leans down to kiss me, his strong whiskey breath is well ahead of his lips.

I look toward Emma, but she's ignoring us and concentrating on Charlie, thank goodness. This is exactly the kind of old fraternity foolishness I'd hoped she wouldn't bump up against.

Jack stands. "Manny's got us both beat on the dance floor, and you know it, buddy. Where's your table? Let's get you some food before Frankie Gallucci starts pontificating." He guides Ekim by one elbow across the crowded ballroom. At that moment I'm grateful for Jack's people skills. I honestly didn't know what to say.

Emma gives me a *What's going on?* look and I shake my head. "Later, okay?" I mouth. I'm promising more than I'm telling her, it seems. What will I say? None of the girls wanted to date Ekim when we were in school—he was too friendly too fast, too physical. The guys loved him. He was one of the number one athletes on all their intramural teams, from racquetball to golf. After graduation he'd been a helicopter pilot in Vietnam, had served two tours, been shot down twice. The guys swear that's why he drinks too much now. I remember him overdoing it way back when we were at WVU, though. Across the room I see him and Jack talking a few minutes, Ekim gesticulating with his hands, then hugging close before Jack helps him into a chair and starts back towards us alone.

"No wonder he could never get a date," Regina comments, shaking her head. No one at the table so much as smiles. "And he always said it was 'cause he was Lebanese."

"You'll dance a fast dance with him later, hon, okay?" Jack says as he tucks in beside me. "If he eats something and goes slower on the booze. It's too bad he never found the right woman."

"God, you're sounding like a sad slow song, Jack. When'd you get so sentimental?" JoAnne shakes her head but gives Jack an approving, long look. "I don't know why they insisted on this banquet thing tonight. Why didn't they just have a pot of chili back at the House?"

"I doubt Frankie has many pots of chili these days," Manny chimes in. "He's donated so much to the business school that they're giving him an honorary doctorate at graduation this year."

We all stare. "Thank God he didn't give it to the law school," Marc says, shaking his head. "I'll never call him Dr. Galluci. Never."

"Buck, buck buck buck, buck!" Regina is so loud people turn to stare from the tables next to ours. "You guys sound like a cluck of old broody hens!" She hasn't touched a bite of the chicken breast in front of her. The diamond clasp holding her black pearls together pulls toward the "V" of her pale rose silk blouse. Where did she ever find a sophisticated blouse like that in a size small enough to fit her child-like upper body? What's going on with her? She takes a long sip of her white wine. "Yessireebob, green chickens at that!"

Emma leans toward me. "Charlie wants to know if I can go back to his house with him. He's gonna show me his fiddles and mandolins."

Fiddles are they now? I check it out with Jack, and we agree that's not a problem. We decide to swing by and pick her up after the dance is over. "You two can slip out after dessert, sweetie, all right?"

As cheesecake and coffee are served, Jack leans into me. "I've got to go get something. The guys're making a presentation. I'll be right back."

An older alum introduces Frank Galluci and he begins his speech. Jack slips back in beside me as he's starting.

"So Dad calls this big donor guy a white hat, Mama, am I remembering right?" Emma whispers. She's clearly tickled seeing her daddy somewhat off balance.

I can't help but grin, too, nod yes. Jack's black hats and white hats. His boyish version of the cool guys and the nerds in Phi Kap back in the day. Oh please. But Emma's right: Jack has described Frankie—Frank—Galluci as one of the "uncool" guys who turned into the ultimate white hat, a straight-laced rule monger who was destroying the fraternity's out-of-control fun by the time they were all seniors. Jack was married and a father by then. His black hat days should've been behind him, this boyish rowdiness part of his past, but apparently he was still the anointed leader of the guys who avoided growing up by playing pranks and partying. I was long gone.

No doubt Frankie's taste for power and control had cut its teeth in Phi Kap. Perhaps that's one reason he'd donated the major gift for the Galluci Wing. This whole male bonding thing over sports and fraternity foolishness was beyond my grasp. Women didn't have such a vehicle—at least not the women I know. Yet here they were, successful grown men, still clearly feeling the love.

I catch the tail end of what he's saying:

" . . . so without Jennifer I wouldn't have had the vision to give back—she's been the heart of the Galluci family, if I've been the hard-working engine"—Did he know he was making a mess of his metaphors, I wonder—"and I'm thankful that together we've been successful enough to be able to help the Phi Kaps, where it all started . . ."

His second wife, Jennifer, who doesn't appear a day over eighteen, is sitting at the front table, looking like she's enjoying herself about as much as Emma. Marya and Paulo are sitting with her. They must have donated big bucks to the renovation, too. Frankie drones on about his successful company. Looking across the table at Jack, Marc Bonheur makes the gag me sign—never one for subtlety, though he is, after all, a judge now. JoAnne cuts her eyes at him, shakes her head no. In school we'd kidded one another about dating "the bad boys," Marc and Jack, back in the 60s, before it was obvious we'd marry them. Manny folds his hands in front of him and keeps a stone face. He and Regina have refused dessert and coffee. Was Manny possibly jealous of Frank Galluci, like Regina alluded? Why? He was hugely successful himself. I'd always considered these guys "scrutable," if that's the opposite of inscrutable. What you see is what you get.

Had they had more bubbling beneath the surface than I'd considered? Manny had been so crazy for Regina, such a "puppet"—we'd teased him that that was his song, "I'm Your Puppet." She'd dated around on him for two years, apparently, had refused his pin three times before they finally got engaged. He'd always struck me as super confident and determined to get what he wanted. At the front table, Paulo sits there looking happy as can be, a broad smile on his face, his arm around Marya's shoulders. Beside me Jack's about to jump out of his skin. Apparently he's the one who thought up this silly gift for Frankie.

As Frankie stops talking to applause and whistles all over the room, the emcee steps forward. "Brother Frankie: In gratitude for what you've done for the House, your Phi Kap brothers from the sixties wanted to give you something money can't buy. There was only one thing we could even consider." He holds out the box.

Frankie looks at it like it might have a bomb inside. He shakes it. "This is bound to be illegal or immoral. We *are* talking about the sixties." The crowd laughs.

"Are these guys twelve years old or what, Mom?" Emma asks. She's shaking her head.

Regina leans forward, whispers in my ear: "What Frankie wouldn't give for these guys to actually *like* him."

Frankie has wrangled the top off the box and folded back the tissue. He laughs. A big hearty gut laugh. He pulls a black cowboy hat out, puts it on his head. "You are so right, Brother Montana. This is something I could never buy myself. Thanks, brothers." He flashes the fraternity sign as applause breaks out all over the room, even though there are only about ten people in the whole place who get it: The former nerd, Frankie Galluci, has been initiated as an official "black hat," one of the "cool ones." Something all his wealth could never buy. Jack claps, obviously pleased this idea has gone over well. I'm confused, though: Are these guys making fun of their fraternity brother who's made it big, or are they celebrating his success and generosity? Do they even know? And men are supposedly the un-complicated gender.

During the interlude between after dinner drinks and the dance, a photographer calls together each decade for shots for the alumni magazine. The sixties are the biggest group, even bigger than the re-cent nineties. I watch with JoAnne and Regina and Marya as the men crowd together for their picture. Frankie is in the center, of course, sporting his black hat. Ekim, who can barely stand, is supported on the front row between Jack and Marc. While everyone is making final adjustments per the photographer's directions, Ekim fumbles around and puts one hand down the front of his trousers, unzips his pants with the other.

JoAnne interrupts, her voice on edge, "Wait, wait, what's he doing . . ." as Ekim sticks a finger through his zipper. The photographer gets off a couple of shots before JoAnne stops him and goes up to make Ekim rearrange his clothes and pose properly. "Who's going to save him from himself?" she asks, shaking her head when she comes back to stand beside me.

Sure enough, when the band starts—an old-time rock band doing covers from the sixties, seventies, and eighties—Ekim finds us and begs me to dance. I'm glad Emma has left. Ekim is slurring his words badly by now, putting his face so close to mine I can see he didn't shave today, but he insists we get out on the dance floor and "show these bastards a thing or two." I look at Jack—would it be kinder to go ahead and try to dance with him, or kinder to say no so he doesn't make a more public fool of himself?

"You sure you want to dance, buddy? Or would you rather go outside for a snort?" Jack interrupts.

I glare at my husband: Has he lost his mind? Ekim must be close to alcohol poisoning as it is. Jack shakes his head at me, mouths "Let me handle this." He slaps Ekim on the bicep, bracing his hand there.

"I've got some shine stashed in my car. You want to check it out? You can come back and dance with Linda after we've had a few."

Ekim grabs hold of Jack's shoulders, slurs a "Roger that, good buddy," and stumbles out of the room with him, like conjoined twins trying to do the two-step. Marc and Manny follow.

"How long has he been like this?" I ask JoAnne.

"Can we find somewhere to sit down? Where it's a little quieter?" For the first time today, she looks tired to me, a bit of crinkle gone from her eyes.

We leave the party and find a corner of the lobby that's remote from the boisterous scene in the ballroom. I sip my wine and wait for her to tell me what's going on.

In a minute, she leans toward me, her voice quiet. "He's loved these guys, you know, all these years. They're his family."

I shake my head. The desperation of that is beyond sad.

"When he got back from Vietnam, he didn't have anywhere to go. He wore out his welcome everywhere. Since Marc and I were in Charleston, I guess he came to us first. Remember, he grew up there." She leans back in her captain's chair, looks off toward the terrace like she's watching some play being acted out there in the dim light. "I had a baby and was studying for the bar. I didn't take much time with him. But even though he never got home until late from his practice, Marc sat up with him night after night." When she looks back at me, she's visibly tired, rubs both hands up and down her face before she continues. "He didn't say a word about being over there or being shot down or anything. He just relived every single fraternity party and every single night on the town and every single dance out at Cheat Mountain over and over, drinking nonstop. I didn't know what to do. Marc thought Ekim would burn himself out if he just listened long enough. But he never did. He'd just pass out and start in again the next night."

"That's awful, JoAnne. I don't know how you did it," I say, mostly to give her a breath. It's as though telling me this is making her desperate all over again.

"One day, when the baby was taking a nap, I was sitting at the kitchen table studying. It must've been about two o'clock in the afternoon, and Ekim comes stumbling in looking for a glass of water and a cup of coffee."

I nod.

"He reeked, Linda. Like he'd been dumped in beer. I offered to fix him a sandwich." She shakes her head, like she's trying to shake the image out of her head. "He just sat down at the table across from me and took my hand and cried real quiet-like. He talked about growing up first generation American, his daddy's grocery stores, his mother's bossiness, and trying to please them both. And how he loved all these guys, his brothers. Then he said the strangest thing. He said, 'Being a Phi Kap, that's the only smart thing I ever did.' After that he never said another word, just cried for a couple of minutes, then stumbled to the sofa and went back to sleep."

"I had no idea . . ."

"After a few weeks, Marc called around and told the guys what was going on with his non-stop drinking. He had to."

"I don't think Jack knew."

"He knew. Marc always called Jack."

I'm stung. Jack hadn't told me any of this about Ekim when we got back together. Was that because of my line in the sand about going back to WVU, or because he wanted to protect his friend? Or was he just plain embarrassed for Ekim?

"Ekim was smoking pot, too, and Marc was brand new in his practice. It was just too risky. If we even tried to bring up his drinking and smoking, Ekim made a joke, changed the subject. Finally one of the guys, Johnny Montana, I think, gave him a job managing one of his apartment buildings up in Newark, kind of being the on-site supervisor, you know? Handling complaints and doing small repairs. Ekim could barely do that, a guy with a degree in civil engineering, a helicopter pilot, for God's sake. Can you imagine? But he kept him on for a good while. Got him an assistant to cover for the fact that Ekim was either too drunk or too hungover most of the time to do his job."

"How could he have lasted this long drinking the way he does?"

"He's had two or three stints in rehab. At veterans' hospitals. He'd get dry and somebody would give him another chance—Frankie got him a position out in California once, doing something in personnel in his company. Didn't last any time. Buck found him work at one of his vineyards—bad combination. Everybody's tried."

"Jack's never told me a word of this."

"Marc thinks he's living on veteran's disability now, though to hear Ekim tell it he's got an option for his memoirs from some big shot in Hollywood and he's busy writing every day."

Now we both stare out at the terrace. There's nothing there but empty chairs, dark shadows. Even while I'm feeling closer to JoAnne, I'm wondering if I should have come, should have opened these long-closed doors.

"Funny thing, Linda. He's loved us as much as he's loved the guys. Always wondering why he didn't find some Mountie girl to marry like the other Phi Kaps."

"I should've danced with him."

"And what—let him fall down and knock you down with him? He's not going to remember any of this tomorrow anyway. He'll have his own version of tonight."

Regina and Marya walk out of the ballroom double doors into the lounge area. I watch them cross to the ladies' room. They're animated, Regina talking with her hands, Marya leaning toward her. From this distance they look like two beautiful grown-up women without a care in the world.

Jack finds me and JoAnne sitting there. "Marc's driving Ekim back to his motel," he tells us, flopping into one of the chairs in the staged grouping.

"He okay?" JoAnne asks. We all know he's not.

"Hell, I wish he hadn't come."

"You didn't give him more to drink, did you?" I have to ask.

"Damn, Linda, what do you think?"

I lean over and rub Jack's shoulder. It takes a car wreck in front of him to quell Jack's optimism.

"He pissed himself." Jack leans forward, puts his head in his hands.

I don't know what to say, so I keep rubbing his neck. Fortunately, Regina and Marya walk over.

"You all missed Manny doing the funky Broadway," Regina drawls. "I thought those young guys were gonna ask for his autograph."

Marya leans in. "Paulo and Frankie got in the middle of the circle to dance, too, Frankie wearing that ridiculous hat. He looked like somebody gave him an electric shock." She laughs. "He never could dance, could he? Somebody grabbed onto his waist—maybe to stop that pitiful gyrating—and before you know it there's this whole line of people snaking around the dance floor behind him. I don't think I've ever seen Frankie Gallucci so pleased with himself."

"And we've certainly seen him pleased with himself quite a number of times," Jack deadpans. I'm glad to see him perking up.

"Was Jennifer dancing?" I ask. Somehow I can't picture that.

"I think she left right after the speeches."

"You're kidding," JoAnne says. "That's kinda rude, with Frankie the guest of honor."

Marya looks around. "I'm not supposed to tell." She purses her lips. "Jennifer's pregnant."

"What?" Frankie's older than I am—at least 55, maybe a year or two older than that. "He's gonna be a daddy? Again?" I was pretty sure he and his first wife, Donna, had two children. They had to be in their twenties. Or thirties.

"Apparently."

Jack stands. "Lucky guy."

After Emma was born, Jack must have said a hundred times how much he hoped we'd have a houseful. He was so good with her, as doting a daddy as a girl could ever hope for. I'd always been grateful to have one child.

Marc walks through the glass doors about that moment. "Where's the party?" he asks, striding toward us. "Don't even think about hanging it up for the night." He pulls JoAnne up by the hand. "Let's go get a drink, sweetheart. I need to dance with my best girl!" Marc and the leering eyes—I have to smile.

By midnight, the crowd has thinned out considerably, but the band is getting warmed up for one more set and the open bar continues to flow. No table is rowdier than ours. Frankie, Paulo, and Buck have pulled up chairs and crowded around, along with Monica and Marya. Monica must be a really good sport: Regina has been sitting on Buck's lap for the past few hours. Every time we all get up to dance, she manages to find her way onto his knee when we rally back at the table for drinks. We've danced circle dances, cheered Buck and Manny on as they writhed like alligators, clapped for Marc's rendition of "Smooth Operator," but every single time we take a break, Regina finds her way to Buck and plops down on him. Manny appears oblivious.

Gina doesn't appear the least bit tipsy. How can Manny be like that, so unconcerned with her over-the-top flirting in front of everyone?

Jack starts another "Remember when . . ." story so I pull Regina up.

"Let's go powder our noses." We laugh. When was the last time any of us carried a compact?

We're the only two women in the ladies' room. "Mind if we sit down here for a minute," I suggest after we've brushed our hair and put on fresh lipstick, patting the stuffed loveseat in the area with the vanity and mirror. "This is way past a night on the town for me—I'm usually in bed no later than eleven, even when we go out. I need a break."

Regina has brought along her cocktail. "You never were the big party girl anyway, Linda." She sips, her brown eyes daring me, to what?

"I guess you're right. I hadn't thought much about it."

"Jack's the party animal. You know, when you took off you missed all those celebrations with us: JoAnne's wedding, my wedding, Marya's wedding. You missed a lot."

I squirm, wish I'd brought a glass of wine along. "Jack and I didn't have a big to-do ourselves."

"Why am I not surprised?"

"So you and Manny did the whole huge Catholic sacrament of marriage and reception thing?"

"Lord, yes." She flops back against the sofa pillow. "Manny asking Daddy for my hand. Now there was a big to-do."

"Really? By the time Jack and I decided to get married, my parents were both gone. There was nobody to ask except me."

"We'd been pinned for a year. He was already working for GE while I finished my last semester. He drove to the house from Charlerois that June night to ask Daddy. Of course Daddy had already gone to his room—he always went to his room by 8:30. We weren't supposed to disturb him in there. Not that I would've."

I hadn't thought about Regina's tales of her domineering daddy, not in all those years since I'd left. The memory, now, makes me uneasy.

"So Mama tells Manny, 'Knock on the bedroom door, son. It'll be all right.' I thought she'd lost her mind. Mama was the sweetest woman in the universe. She adored Manny, was so thrilled I'd chosen him. But to send him in there after Daddy had shut the door for the night . . . huh-uh."

"When I left that June you were still set on that Phi Psi—what was his name? Dennis somebody."

"Dennis Collins. I never brought *him* home. Daddy would've hated him."

"He's the one—you were on and off with him and Manny both for quite some time, if I'm not mistaken."

"Oh no—you are *not* mistaken." She gives me a look. "More off than on with Dennis Collins. That was never going to work." She takes a gulp of her drink. "But when Manny got to the house, Mama didn't want him to wait even one more day to make sure I didn't change my mind about marrying him, even if it meant catching Daddy at a bad time. When would've been a good time?" She shrugs, clinks her ice. "So Manny knocks on that door—I swear, I wouldn't have been a bit surprised if Daddy pulled a shotgun, told him to get the hell outta there—but he yells for him to come on in. Manny says Daddy was propped up on the pillows smoking a cigar, hardly even looked up at him. He made Manny come into the room, shut the door. He wouldn't come out. Oh no, not my daddy."

"That doesn't surprise me—that Manny would do that for you, I mean."

"And he definitely didn't offer Manny one of his damn cigars. Talk about jumping through hoops." She gives me a wide-eyed can-you-believe-it look, on the angry side for sure. "We had to pay for the wedding ourselves. Daddy told him that night he wasn't about to pay one red cent, and Manny insisted it be the whole nine yards—mass, sit-down dinner, a live band. His sweet Catholic mama wanted only the best for her handsome altar boy."

"And you?"

"Daddy walking me down the aisle. Now that's a phony picture if there ever was one. Good riddance can go two ways." She arches her eyebrows. "Come on, Linda, you know I was no blushing bride."

"No doubt Marya was."

"Take that to the bank." She downs the last of her drink.

I stand, start for the door, but she pulls me back down beside her.

"Sweet as he is, Paulo would've probably killed anybody who looked at Marya sideways. Course she probably would've, too."

We laugh. "I could've killed Simone D'Espere with my bare hands if I'd gotten the chance. And Jack—I would've murdered him, too. Tortured him first, as a matter of fact."

"He was too pathetic to murder."

Why did I even bring that up? That last glass of Pinot Noir must've brought my guard down a notch. "Every single one of you has said some version of that, like you felt sorry for Jack Vanderbilt when he dumped me."

"Hey, don't get all high and mighty." She looks me in the eye. "Jack was here. We didn't make it easy on him or that Frenchy-wench he married. But you wouldn't give us the time of day." She stands. "That was a pitiful little wedding, or so I heard. None of us were invited. Just a thrown-together family thing. No bridesmaids or anything like that—except her twin sister and Jack's dad. He stood up for him."

"Don't ask me to throw a pity party."

"Seems like that's exactly what you did. And silly me: I thought you were my friend." She tilts her head, sets her empty glass on the counter. "God, you and JoAnne could talk for-ev-er about what you wanted out of life. You always wanted so much—more, more, more."

I'm surprised. Hadn't Regina wanted that, too? "What did you want?"

She stared at me like I was nuts. "Are you kidding? I wanted to be safe." She takes one final look in the mirror at her perfect face. "You ready?"

Jack and I slow dance to "If You Don't Know Me By Now." So do Manny and Regina. Buck and Monica have left. Regina beams up at Manny in her flirtatious way, as if he's the only man in the world, and he soaks it all in, adoring her like it's the first time they've ever danced together. They're so close they're practically grinding.

Back at the table after the song ends, I ask her, "Why do you think you two are still so romantic?"

She answers, smiling that powerful smile, "It's just the way we are."

Exams, January 1967

Regina balled up the page of notes in front of her and threw it at me. "It doesn't make any sense. Nothing you can say will make it make a bit of sense to me."

I dodged. I was afraid she was right. I wasn't going to be able to teach her half a semester of Anatomy and Physiology in a single cram session. We were holed up in one of the small library study rooms. The first couple of hours had gone pretty well. Regina had attended the class for about eight weeks, and she had a knack for A & P. In labs she was a crackerjack. Her drawings were precise, exact, if not as lifelike as mine. But she only came to about half the afternoon labs and none of the lectures the second part of the semester.

She'd paced the room and blurted out answers when I'd questioned her, confident she could bluff her way to a C or at the very least a C-. But on the topics that came after she stopped going to class, she'd been a total blank, guessed, had no idea what some of the vocabulary meant, couldn't identify anything on the diagrams. Somewhere around the first of November, she'd stopped coming altogether, hadn't even bothered to skim the book or copy my notes after a while, so she was way too far behind for me to explain it to her now.

"What do you want to do?" I bent down and picked up the paper, tried to flatten it on the table. These were my notes.

"Do? Do? What do you think I want to do? I've got to pass this damn exam. That's all there is to it."

"Okay—calm down. Let's take a break, okay? Let's go get something to eat and figure this out." There was no way I could figure this out; magic was out of my skill set. If she wanted to come up with a way to cheat, she was going to need somebody else to help her. I was no more experienced with that than I was with voodoo. I wasn't about to tell Regina how hopeless this was, though, if she hadn't come to that conclusion herself. I'd never seen her so agitated, not even when Dennis Collins broke up with her the first time. Or the second time.

She stopped pacing. "Maybe I should call Manny. He passed this last year. Maybe he can tell me exactly what to study."

As if she had any chance of covering this in one night. "That's a good idea. You want to go back to the dorm and call him?" I started packing my notebooks and books.

"What are you doing?" She looked at me like I'd pulled a gun.

"Aren't we going to get something to eat? Or call Manny? I'm packing up my things."

"We have this room until closing, don't we? We're coming back! You've got to help me, even if we get an old exam. Especially if we get an old exam."

"Oh, okay." I was guessing it wouldn't do any good to point out that she'd just said that nothing I could say or do would make any sense to her. "We're too late for the dining hall."

"Let's get Manny and Jack to meet us somewhere."

"I think Jack's studying."

"They have to eat. You said so yourself."

In the end, we'd tracked Manny down at the House. Jack wasn't around—Manny said he'd probably decided to play handball to relieve some of the study tension. Nobody would accuse Jack of being a scholar. So the three of us went for a pizza. Manny gave us old exams from the fraternity files, and after the quick supper, Regina and I spent hours going over the answers to the questions on the most recent test. She was smart and determined and we covered those topics as best we could, but by eleven when the library closed, I wasn't too hopeful that she'd be able to pass even if the questions were exactly the same as the ones she'd memorized.

"Come on back to the room with me," she insisted. "Mama sent oatmeal cookies. That's the least I can give you for all your help."

All I wanted was to go to my room and go to bed, but I'd never seen Regina so rattled. I hadn't talked to Jack all day, and I'd been sure he'd call me. But now it was too late. The switchboard would be shut down. I thought I'd talk Regina down for a couple of minutes, I'd try to calm her down then beg off. I needed a few hours sleep if I was going to ace the exam myself, even though I knew it cold. I was exhausted. She was still clearly jumpy, though. She wasn't about to accept no or stay by herself.

"JoAnne doesn't have a morning exam. She's staying over at Marc's. I hate it when she does that. Please don't sleep in her room. I hate being by myself."

"Really? I kind of like it." I'd been staying in JoAnne's empty room as often as possible during exams, for the quiet and independence to keep the light on/off whenever I wanted. We crossed Woodburn Circle. Everything was strangely quiet. A few people were out walking between dorms and academic buildings, but either the cold or the exam tension had subdued all the typical chatter and activity.

"Not me. I hate spending the night by myself. At home I always left my door open and the hall light on. I'd make my sister leave her door open, too, so I could call out to her if I got worried."

Boreman was warm as we pushed through the double front doors, heat wrapping around us like a comforter as we took the stairs up to our suite. I smiled.

"Scared of the Boogie Man? Feisty Regina Bello? I have a hard time picturing that."

She shoved all her books on top of mine while she unlocked the door. As soon as we got in, she lit a candle in the windowsill—"What Mrs. Ordough doesn't know can't hurt her!" she stage whispered—and I traipsed through our connecting bathroom to put my stack of study materials on the desk.

"Hey, I'm going to jump into my nightgown, okay?" I called through to her.

After I had on my long flannel granny gown, I dragged my quilt into Regina's room and crawled up on my twin bed, leaning against my husband pillow.

"Here. My mama makes the best brown sugar oatmeal cookies in the world. She sent these 'cause she knows I'm worried sick about my exams. Let's eat all of them."

I took two—"Yay—no raisins"—and leaned back against the pillow, half asleep. "You must have a mighty thoughtful mama. The rare times mine makes cookies, they never make it from the counter to a tin, there are so many of us. And forget it if you're not around when they come out of the oven—all you get is the smell."

"My sister, Debbie, probably helped her." We both munched a cookie. "We're close, me and Mama and Debbie. And my brother Jimmy, too, but he's much younger, six years."

"Sounds nice." I was nibbling my cookie, having a hard time keeping my eyes open while she babbled. It really was a prize-winning oatmeal cookie—crisp around the edges, soft in the center, full of brown sugar and cinnamon, that fresh-baked smell adding to the taste.

"My daddy will kill me if I fail one of my classes."

When I looked up, Regina was sitting on the edge of the bed, the open tin on her lap, staring at the candle.

"Aw, Regina," I sat up, leaned toward her, "it can't be that bad."

"It's not just A & P. I'm pretty sure I already failed psychology. And I'll be lucky if I get a C in Spanish. I'm going to end up on academic probe."

I sat up. "That's terrible . . ." she looked like she might cry. "I mean, losing all those credits, that's bound to be a blow, but it's not the end of the world. You can take summer classes."

"It will be for me. I'm not kidding. My daddy will kill me." She slumped. "With him it's not even the money, though he'll give me hell about that. It's that no Bello ever fails, at anything. Especially not his daughter."

The way she said "kill me" that second time gave me goosebumps. "Oh, honey," I jumped off the bed and went to sit beside her. "Here, give those to me." I put the top on the tin and shoved it onto the crowded desk. "Come on, try to relax." I pulled my quilt up over both of us and eased her back against the wall. "Tell me what's wrong."

"You don't understand. When I went home at Christmas I tried to talk to Daddy. Tried to tell him I was having trouble concentrating. He just told me to buckle down. He's a hard man, Linda Lee." She shook her head back and forth. "After school, when I was little, me and Debbie and Jimmy, we'd sit in the kitchen with Mama and do our homework. Regular kids. Mama'd be hustling around getting supper ready, singing along to Patsy Cline. Then we'd hear the car coming down the gravel road. She'd turn the radio off. We'd pack up our stuff, run to our rooms till she called us for supper. Nobody wanted to get him riled up. And it didn't take much."

I didn't know what to say. My father was stern when he needed to be, but none of us were afraid of him.

"Debbie didn't want to go to school. She took secretarial in high school. Mama was a secretary, and that's what she wanted, too. And he called Jimmy a pathetic mama's boy. But I made good grades. Daddy called me his little brainiac. When I asked if I could go to WVU, he made the decision I'd go. But he said he wasn't sending me to be a glorified babysitter. He meant teacher by that. So he said I could study science, maybe be a nurse. But once I started something I had to finish it. No ifs, ands, or buts."

"You wouldn't be having any trouble at all if you'd come to classes, Gina. You'd have this knocked."

"I know. School's always been easy. But I've been so damn distracted." She looks at me. "I wasn't allowed to date in high school, not even for my senior prom. So when I got here . . . well, you know how much I've loved guys giving me all this attention. Especially Dennis."

I nod. She had certainly been sidetracked by the boys. I'd only met him once, but as far as I was concerned, Dennis Collins was shallow and no count and not even all that good looking, but I wasn't about to say that to Regina. He was a junior, never had early classes, was always talking Regina into coming over to his place in the morning. And that was that.

"You never had a date before you got here? Come on."

"Nope. Not one. Daddy wouldn't allow it. I was too scared of him to sneak out, even."

"You? Scared?" I had to smile. Regina struck me as so tough.

"Daddy would hate Dennis."

"But he'd like Manny, the perfect gentleman. Any dad would like Manny."

"I can't imagine my daddy liking anybody I dated." Regina was trembling. She kept shaking her head, tears running down her face, but she didn't cry.

I was drop-dead exhausted, but it felt creepy to me, seeing Regina get so upset just talking about her daddy, and I didn't see how I could go to bed at that minute.

"Mama's the one who checks out the guys at our house. She would've been satisfied for me to stay home and date Michael Edwards, my high school sweetie—he's on at the ribbon factory now. I'd probably be there, too, if I hadn't come to WVU."

Regina rubbed her eyes, reached by the bed for a Kleenex. "I can *not* imagine you working in a factory, you're such a book nerd—doing what?"

"I don't know—secretarial, probably. Maybe bookkeeping. Nothing on the machines. I think Michael's a supervisor of some sort—where all good high school football stars go after graduation."

"You're too smart for that."

"He was really cute, and I sure liked kissing him . . . but you're right, I can't imagine us at the high school games on Friday night year after year. Moose Lodge on Saturday. Church Sunday morning. I wanted something more . . . I actually loved school, especially my art classes. My folks liked the fact that I could draw and make honor roll, but they never thought that would make much difference when it got down to being a grown up."

"Daddy never noticed what we were doing one way or the other in school, just checked the grades on the report card—though I'm sure if I'd gotten in any trouble or gotten any bad grades he'd have taken the belt to me. He seemed to hate everybody, teachers included. He even got kicked out of the church."

"You're kidding?"

"Nope. Some argument with the priest. Of course Mama never told us over what, and we would've never asked him . . . but Sundays after Jimmy's confirmation, we all went to mass and he stayed home. It was a relief, really, to get to go to out for a while without him."

"I never heard of the Baptists kicking anybody out. They were always talking about everybody being a sinner, seemed to please the preacher."

"Daddy hated the church along with everything else."

"Not mine. We were at the church doors every time I turned around. Wednesday night prayer group and supper, Tuesday choir practice,

Sunday service, Sunday night Baptist Training Union. Church, school, Hudson Brothers, home . . . that was it for me.”

“Mama raised us to be good Catholics, but she never went on about it, what with Daddy being so mad at the priest and the church. We never said a word about it when he was in the room.”

“Lord, we blessed everything in sight, from the food to the weather, every time you turned around. And if the preacher didn’t come to our house for Sunday dinner he was at one of my aunts’ or uncles’.”

“The priest wasn’t allowed on our property. Except for one time. Did I ever tell you I got shot?”

I sat bolt upright. “Shot? Lord no!” Was I falling asleep? Did Regina say shot?

“Yep. When I was eleven.” She kept on trembling. “By a creek walker.” The way she said that word, all quiet-like, was worse than if she’d yelled. “It was on Good Friday. My girlfriend, Mamie Hendricks, came over—we never stayed in the house when anybody came over, even if Daddy wasn’t home. He said he didn’t want strangers in the house. That’s how he felt about anybody, they were strangers, even if they’d lived nearby my whole life.” She rubbed her hands on her cheeks. “Anyway, Mama packed us a lunch, me and Debbie and Jimmy and Mamie, and we went on a hike. We sat down near an old shack down in the holler. I remember hearing this neighbor’s Doberman, Rex, start barking. Mamie said, ‘Look, there’s people just came out of that shack,’ which was strange, ‘cause nobody lived there. I looked up, and it looked like this scruffy old man had a stick in his hand, and he was pointing it at us. Next thing I knew I was hit—then I heard the gun. No kidding, that’s how it happened—I felt something hit me, then I heard the shot after. Weird. I grabbed my side.” She wrapped her arms around her waist, “And Mamie said to me, ‘Oh my God, blood—that guy shot you!’ I stood up, but it was like I couldn’t breathe. I said to her, ‘Don’t leave me, please,’ and I tried to lift my arm to catch hold of her, but I’d been shot through the arm. Debbie was screaming, Jimmy came running up from the creek thinking we were playing, and I just remember saying ‘I’m gonna pass out, help me, please,’ and the next thing I remember I was in the hospital.”

“You really were shot?” I couldn’t believe that this had actually happened to tiny little Regina.

"I remember this man who was pushing the gurney, he was blacker than night, his name was Rudolph. I don't know why I remember him so clearly, but I do. 'You'll be fine, little Missy,' he said to me."

"Where'd you get hit?"

"It was bad. I'd gotten hit in the arm but turns out it went through my side into my lung. My lung collapsed. That's why I felt like I couldn't breathe."

"What happened?"

"I was in the hospital a good while, then home for about six weeks. I remember Mama called the priest to the house one day to say a special prayer over me, but Daddy wasn't home. I didn't go back to school at all that year."

"And you so . . . petite." I couldn't envision a little girl version of Regina shot. Robbers on *Gunsmoke*, or the Mafia, but not little girls.

"Yep, they told my daddy I could've died. He wanted to kill the guy—I think he would've—but they never could find him."

I didn't know what to say. She was tough, tough enough to survive getting shot. So how could this young woman who'd lived through that be afraid of the dark, scared to spend the night alone? Scared to death to tell her daddy she wasn't going to pass Anatomy & Physiology?

"I wasn't ready for all this, Linda Lee. I got As and Bs in school, but I never studied. Not even in high school. It all came so easy." She snuggled down in the quilt. "I don't see how I'm going to pass this damn exam."

"You've got a chance." What could I say? Maybe she did.

"Thanks for the help." She smiled up at me, patted my hand. "I guess you know Dennis treats me like shit."

I looked away, embarrassed. "I know."

"Why is it a guy like Dennis makes me go all weak in the knees? I mean, why can't I look at Manny and feel that way?"

"Get some sleep, Regina. You're going to need to be sharp in the morning. I'll leave the bathroom light on and the doors between the rooms open, okay? And I promise I'll get you up in time."

"Okay."

She didn't pass the exam, or the class. And she did get put on academic probation. I don't know what went on when her parents got her grades—I never met her parents—but if anything, she was more nervous when she came back from break, and she didn't skip classes at all second semester. And she kept on seeing Dennis and Manny both. Dennis would stand her up or take her out for an hour and bring her back, but she wouldn't stop going out with him. Manny would take her out whenever he could, no questions asked. If he knew she was dating Dennis, he never brought it up, at least not to my knowledge. She came to the House with Manny on weekends a lot that spring.

I was taking eighteen hours and working hard to keep up my Dean's List grades. I had to declare a major in May, and I couldn't make up my mind. I'd kept taking art studio on top of my regular required liberal arts classes, thinking maybe I'd be an art major, though planning to be an art teacher made a lot more sense. I couldn't see myself doing that, though. I loved painting and drawing, but I didn't have any particular desire to teach children how to do it. I'd liked my art teachers all through school—they'd always been my favorites—but all of them encouraged me to make art, to study art, and that's what I loved. I won the painting and drawing prizes in school. The professors there at WVU encouraged me too, especially my painting professor. I loved everything I was studying, but art was still my favorite. I could spend hours working in the studio and never even notice time passing.

Evenings when I had to push on art projects, Jack usually had an athletic event of some sort—he competed for the fraternity on every intramural team except football—but we managed to see one another for a quick meal or beer almost every day. He never studied, was content getting C's just by going to his classes and turning in only what was required. College for him was not so much about the academics.

Marya was definitely physical therapy, JoAnne was thinking psychology with a minor in sociology, and Regina was just trying to get off academic probe—her daddy had some crazy idea she should go into engineering—she was going to have to go to summer school anyway, so she could wait and declare in August. I knew in my heart I wanted art; my painting professor had encouraged me to get my portfolio together in case I wanted to apply to the department, but I knew that my parents would never approve. I could hear my father now: "If you aren't going to teach art, what reason in the world could you have for studying art?"

One night toward the end of the second semester, we decided to take a break. Manny and Jack wanted me and Regina to go see the latest James Bond film with them. Though neither of us cared a whit about spy movies, they convinced us that this was a spoof; it was supposed to be hilarious, and it would give us some relief from studying. I thought it was the stupidest movie I'd ever seen, and so did Regina. Neither one of us laughed once, though the guys carried on like tickled babies. I thought it was fun to see some of the old-time movie stars up on the screen, my parents' favorites like Deborah Kerr, Orson Welles, Charles Boyer, and William Holden, but that didn't make up for the sheer stupidity of the plot. If that was their idea of funny, we figured their emotional age at about fifteen.

"That was a waste of two hours," Regina said as we headed up the hill. This was one of the rare Sunday nights when nothing was going on at the House.

"That Mata Bond and The Detainer were babes," Jack laughed. "But Ursula Andrews—she's like every guy's wet dream."

"I think you mean Andress, Jack—and you don't need to be gross," I shoved him in the side.

"No better looking than Regina and Linda Lee, you have to admit," Manny chimed in, reaching over to grab Regina's hand. She shook him off.

"You guys are so easily amused," she remarked. "I agree with Linda Lee. What a waste of time." She quick-walked a few steps ahead of Manny. "I think I'm going to head back to the dorm. I've still got some work to do on a paper I need to turn in this week. And it's got to be good."

Manny hurried ahead to catch up with her. He leaned down toward her ear. I couldn't hear what he said.

"What's with Regina?" Jack asked, pulling me toward him.

"She's worried about keeping her grades up."

"Guess we should've gone to the movie without you two—I knew you weren't going to like it—but Manny insisted."

"It's okay. I didn't mind."

"You want to come up to the room for a little while? You've still got a couple of hours until sign in."

"Nah. Not tonight."

"Are we okay? I know it was a stupid movie, but . . ."

"Oh, no, we're great—but I think Regina's in a pretty bad place right now, worrying about grades and all. I know JoAnne's not upstairs, and she'll probably want to talk. She hates to be alone." JoAnne was at Marc's apartment as long and as late as she could be every night, never worried about lying on the sign-out sheet. I would've freaked.

"She's gonna be writing that paper. Come on up for a little while, anyway." He tugged at my hand.

Regina stopped walking, turned back toward us, and grabbed Jack's other arm. "You know I have to get all B's. Please tell Linda Lee it's okay for her to come help me tonight." She sounded serious, even desperate.

I felt bad for her. "Do you mind?"

"I do. Mind." He gave me a quick kiss on the forehead. "But what can I say with you two double-teaming me? Promise, tomorrow night."

"Tomorrow night. I promise." We kissed quickly and Regina and I peeled off for Boreman while Jack and Manny headed up the hill for the House.

"What's going on, Regina? Why are you all worked up?"

"I really do have to go over that sociology paper one more time, no kidding."

"I know. Want me to look it over?"

"Would you?" We buzzed into the dorm.

"Sure. But I'm sure it's good. You're a good writer."

"Thanks. It's just that I'm worried sick about making all Bs."

"So far so good, right?"

"Yeah. Right. It's these damn exams." We climbed the stairs. "Look. Manny's really putting the pressure on. He wants us to be pinned."

"I can tell."

"And he can be so vain and childish and *un*-aware."

"Can't they all." We laughed as we unlocked the door.

"And I don't love him, Linda Lee. I wish like hell I did. But I don't."

JoAnne, Regina, and I all had second year sociology together; Marya was taking all these pre-med courses instead, and we didn't see her much except at the house these days. A week earlier, we'd all three been assigned to attend the Foreign Film Festival's showing of *The Umbrellas of Cherbourg*, our offbeat professor's means of opening a discussion regarding feminist issues in our culture and whether rights were accessible only to middle and upper class women. One more way of delineating the haves and the have nots, he'd suggested. Regina's paper was on the topic of a woman's right to her body, whether she was married or not, and I found her writing clear and convincing. She concluded that such self-determination was possible only for those rare women who were financially independent themselves, which softened the danger of the husband discovering her infidelities and demanding divorce, which was always an economic disaster for the dependent woman. She'd pulled in references to Masters' and Johnson's studies on female orgasm and the use of surrogates —how was that in fact different from prostitution, she inquired? In either case, didn't a woman have the right to decide for herself?

While I was copyediting, she asked, "Was the type of high class prostitution portrayed in that ridiculous Bond movie any more or less repressive than what's going on on America's streets right now? They made it seem so glamorous, but it's always the woman who pays if she gets caught. Why does the law criminalize women for selling their bodies, and not men for buying?"

I look up from the page. "What's got you so fired up?"

"So Dennis says he doesn't want to go out with me anymore. Again."

"Come on, Regina. Take your own advice." I held up her paper. "You don't have to go out with Dennis *or* Manny, right?"

"You know I've been sleeping with him all along, don't you? And I haven't slept with Manny?"

None of this surprised me, though this was the first time she'd actually said so. I nodded my head yes. She understood I'd been sleeping with Jack ever since the Fall Formal, too, but I never talked about our intimacy like JoAnne talked about hers. It was private between me and Jack.

"Denny can be *such* a jerk. I *know* that." She bit her lip. "MEN! I wish my daddy would die. I mean that. I wish he would just drop dead. You have no idea . . ."

"You're serious, aren't you?" I set her pages down. I'd never felt like that about anybody in my family, wishing they'd die, and she'd said it with so much force. And venom. I could tell she meant it. Talking about Dennis and Manny and her daddy all at the same time—I'd studied Freud, but this jumble confused me.

"Damn straight." Her eyes looked determined. "He's the meanest man walking the earth."

I didn't say anything. What could I say?

"And Dennis treats me mean, too. Like dirt."

She was saying this. I wouldn't dare.

Regina started pacing. "Why in the world can't I feel about Manny like I feel about Dennis? No man has ever treated me like Manny does—like I'm his goddess. I can do no wrong in his eyes."

That was certainly true. Manny doted on her, put up with her dating other guys, acted like he didn't even notice, or if he did, he didn't care.

"What would you do if you didn't settle for either one of them? If you were independent, in charge of your own body, like in your paper?"

"I'd change my major to recreation. Be a Recreation Director on a cruise line, maybe. Have my own apartment in New York. Travel the world."

"I can see you doing that." Would I? Live in New York alone? Or with a girlfriend?

"And if I couldn't do that, which is certainly possible, I'd be an airline stewardess. If I'm not too short."

"I bet they'd take you."

"Why can't I get that damn Dennis out of my head? He's always standing me up. When we do go out, he makes loud remarks about every other girl in the room—her big boobs or killer ass. It's like being attracted to poison, there's no denying it."

She was right, of course, but I held my tongue.

"Whatever happens, I'm never going home again. I will NEVER live with that domineering S.O.B ever again."

Seems like she'd made her choice already, though I wasn't sure she could live by it. Dennis hypnotized her every time he bothered to call, like some snake charmer. Much as we talked about what we'd do on our own, I couldn't picture Regina out there traveling the world alone, not after the fears she described.

I heard a knock next door, at JoAnne's room. "Let me check and see who that is, okay?" I stepped out in the hall.

"Hey, Linda Lee—have you got any tampons?" It was Marya. She had one of the few singles in the building, no roommate, no suitemate. Some former hall monitor's room.

I was relieved to see her. "Sure, come on over. Regina and I are just talking."

That ended the talk about Dennis and Regina's crazy daddy for the time being. Marya wouldn't be sympathetic to Regina's continued attraction to Dennis. She was no-nonsense. Anyway, I was ready for a change of subject. Regina's man drama wore me out.

After she left, it occurred to me that Marya would never run out of tampons. Me, Regina, JoAnne, either one of us could get caught without, but not Marya. She'd only said about two words then begged off visiting; she was working out some chemistry questions, she had to get back to the books, blah blah. The books I could believe; the feminine products I could not.

"Okay, Gina, retype the pages I've marked, okay. I'm going to take some extras up to Marya. In case she can't get to the store first thing."

"You're coming back, aren't you? You're going to go over these last pages, right?" Her worry face was on.

"Of course. Type!"

I went through the bathroom and got an almost-empty box of tampons—I had another full one under the sink—and headed upstairs. Marya's door was closed, so I tapped lightly, in case she'd decided to turn in.

"It's me, Linda Lee."

"Hey, come on in." Her happy voice.

"Here, take these—" I handed her the box, "if you really need them."

"Of course I need them. Why else would I say that?" She sat in the desk chair—looked like she had been studying chemistry—and I flopped on her bed.

"I thought maybe that was a cover . . ."

Marya started to blush. "I can't believe you."

"What do you mean?"

"I did come down to talk to you. About something else. Something . . . private. But you and Regina looked busy." I could tell it was hard for her to say that, "private."

"Sure, Marya. Whatever you need."

Marya was usually the quiet one during JoAnne's glowing reports of sex with Marc; she didn't provide many "dirty details," but she did like to rave on about how great it was, how alive she felt, how

Marc was definitely worth the wait. Regina tended to prod, I tended to egg her on, but Marya . . . she'd mostly listen.

Now she leaned back against the chair, looked at the ceiling for a minute. "You know I'm not having sex with Paulo, right?"

"Yes."

"And I know you *are* having sex with Jack."

I pulled my head back and stared. I'd never told her this. "And?"

"I need some help . . . some advice . . . and I can't talk to Gina or Jo."

"Okay."

She came over and sat beside me on the bed, turned to look directly at me. "You know I like math and science and things you can solve or fix or figure out."

"Uh-huh."

"And you know I went to Catholic girls' school, I told you, didn't I? Where I was a 'good girl'—said my prayers, followed the catechism. Wasn't really ever tempted that way, to tell you the truth."

"Uh-huh."

"And at school we never talked about sex. I mean, the nuns talked about 'the sanctity of marriage' and 'saving yourself for your husband' and 'the value of a virtuous wife,' all that stuff."

"Right. We saw a movie . . ."

She looked flustered. "And my mother is not the sex-talk kind of mother. She's the let's bake brownies and you ask me anything you want to ask type. So we've never talked about sex either."

"Got it."

"Paulo and I, we've promised ourselves to one another . . ."

"Great, that's great, Marya. He sure looks like he's nuts about you!"

"I know it's only been a few months, but we both know. He swears he's known since the first date." She smiled. I could believe she loved him, that downright contented look on her face something new, becoming.

"That's great. I'm happy for you . . ."

"And he's fine with waiting until the honeymoon to . . . you know . . . go all the way. No problem."

"I have no doubt he'd wait for you, Marya. No problem's probably a stretch . . ."

"But . . . things have heated up. You know what I mean?"

"Of course."

"And we both get so crazy for one another, so . . . I don't know how else to say it . . .so hot!"

Now I laughed, and she smiled, finally. "Hot would be the word."

"So . . ."

"So . . . go on. Tell me."

"So we've been doing some things that aren't, you know, doing it, having sex . . . I couldn't get pregnant . . . we're not anywhere near having actual intercourse . . ."

"Pretty great with somebody you love, don't you think?"

"Oh, yes! But here's the thing . . . he wants me to . . .I guess we both want me to . . . you know, touch him."

I grabbed her hands, looked at her directly in the eye. "I'm gonna help you here, Marya. Sounds to me like you're talking about a hand job."

"Uh-huh . . .I mean, I want to . . ."

"Just a hand job? How about a blow job?"

Marya threw her head back, muttered something that sounded like "I cannot believe this." She took a deep breath, looked back at me. "Yes."

"Hand job? Both?"

"Both." Her face was as rosy as cupid's nipple; I could tell that this was painful for her. "And you and JoAnne know so much, you seem so sure of yourselves, I thought . . ."

"Do you want me to tell you HOW, or do you want me to give you permission?"

She laughed, granted a nervous laugh, but she laughed. "Would you?"

"Come on, Marya . . . would I what?"

"Oh hell, I don't want to do it *wrong*, but I swear, I want to do it! I can't believe I'm even saying that."

I hugged her. "Marya, when you're in love, this is as natural as... as natural as breathing."

We both laughed then, real laughs. I was pleased that Marya had come to me for advice. She'd been my first college friend, rescued me from my lonely dorm room when I didn't know a soul. Now I could help her. Weird, my girlfriends at home were besties one day, mad the next, or ignoring me for some boy of the hour. But Marya—and Regina and JoAnne, too—they felt like real friends. Friends for life.

September 16, 2000

We follow JoAnne and Marc home. I'm exhausted but wired at the same time. All that awful Ekim story, plus the crazy Black Hat/Frankie Galluci thing, not to mention being with the gals again for the first time in forever. The Jack/Simone/running away thing still between us, though they're talking to me. More than that, I have to admit. Now going to JoAnne and Marc's to pick up Emma, I can hardly keep my eyes open. My head is swimming. So much to think about.

When we pull up in their circular driveway, I'm astonished, though I shouldn't be. JoAnne and Marc's house looks like a grander version of the governor's mansion in Williamsburg, and it's right on the point at Cheat Lake.

"Nice digs, huh, Linda?" Jack says as we get out of the car. I remember: He was here the night before, has probably been here on other visits to Morgantown.

Marc beams as he walks over to the car. "It's quite a story how we got this house. JoAnne made it happen."

"Come on in for coffee?" JoAnne asks. She looks as tired as I feel.

Marc is chipper, though. "I'll make my famous Bonheur eggs. We can sit by the fire and catch up."

Inside, the foyer sparkles—polished wood floor, blue porcelain, a grand staircase carpeted in white; elegant, but still warm and inviting.

"This is beautiful, JoAnne," I mumble, and she smiles like she'd heard that a million times. "Emma, time to go, hon," I call, and I hear her laughing deep inside the house. Jack shrugs.

We wander back to a huge, comfy family room, where a fire is blazing, and Charlie is playing mandolin. Emma sits on a footstool looking fresh like Sunday morning.

"Mama," she whispers, pointing to Charlie.

He finishes his song with a flourish and stands, smiles. "Hello again, Mr. and Mrs. Vanderbilt. Thanks for letting Emma come over."

She beams. "Charlie's like some old time genius. He knows everything! He's taught me so much in one night . . . I wish I'd brought my cello!"

Jack and I both smile to see her so happy and engaged. Was I ever that unguarded?

JoAnne bustles off to the kitchen while the guys look at Marc's Doo-Wop collection. I follow. I couldn't bustle if somebody offered me a thousand dollars.

"Please don't make anything for us. We've got to get some sleep."

She turns, coffee pot in hand, "You sure? It's no trouble." I can see she's relieved. "Marc can talk all night."

Polite like I'm company. I guess I am. "JoAnne, you're just as pooped as I am." I look around the fresh, spotless kitchen. "Let's do it another time."

"We'll talk first thing in the morning, then. Maybe we can go out for brunch or something, without the guys." She sets the pot down.

"I'd love that. I'll call you when I wake up."

She hugs me. That woman hug is so comforting. No matter how "big" JoAnne has gotten as a defense attorney, she is still one of the easiest women to be around in the universe.

"It's a date. Now get some sleep." She smiles, sparkle on low, but still sparkle.

"Tomorrow. I promise."

Emma talks all the way to the hotel. I close my eyes and lean my head against the headrest, absorbing her excitement.

"Charlie's as passionate about his music as I am about animation, Mom. And the cello. He's the real deal. You've heard of *Old Crow Medicine Show*, haven't you? One of those guys plays cello."

All I offer is "Um-hum." That's all she needs, if that.

"And we were thinking maybe his music could be background on some of my shorts. Like this out there merging of the old and the new. What do you think? Doesn't that sound wild? And wonderful?"

"Um-hum" again. Jack doesn't answer.

"We plan to get together tomorrow. That's okay, isn't it? I don't need a campus tour this weekend. Dad can bring me any time. Lynchburg's not that far."

"That's fine, honey. If it's okay with JoAnne and Marc." Jack sounds as tired as I feel. I know dealing with Ekim has taken a chunk out of his pleasure this evening. Mine, too.

"They are the *nicest* people, Mom. And that house? I mean, I'm not all that into big houses and all, but it's like them, don't you think? Like they really want you to be there?"

"I'm sure they do, honey. They've both always been that way."

"I can't believe you and JoAnne aren't still close, Mama. That doesn't make a bit of sense to me."

As she babbles on, I can't help thinking, *Not to me, either, Emma.* It never did make any sense. But what does sense have to do with it?

I'm too tired to brush my teeth. It's all I can do to undress. Jack and I fall into bed without talking. He's snoring in thirty seconds.

My eyes are closed, but the phone keeps ringing and ringing. I've had a restless night, going over Marya challenging me, JoAnne telling me all that about Ekim, welcoming me into her home, Regina dancing with Manny like they'd never left WVU. Still uncertain whether coming was the right thing. What had I expected? That was it—I hadn't let myself expect anything. I'd long ago stopped envying Simone D'Espere. She and Jack had been horrible together, that was clear; their son, Jay, the only good thing to come of that unhappy union. When Jack came back to me, I'd relished the idea of being cold to him, uncaring. I needed to see him as the two-timing creep he'd become in my head. But instead he'd been the same sweet Jack.

Jack had always been self-confident without being cocky, self-assured without arrogance. Those were reasons I'd fallen in love with him the first time. And the second time, too—if I'd ever *not* loved him. I certainly hadn't fallen for anyone else in the interim. For some reason, I agreed without too much coaxing to come back to WVU that night Marc called. Why? Did I think it was now or what, never? After all these years, what had made me give in? I had no idea. And now Emma, so oddly at home here—what was that about, my quirky daughter? This mind meld with Charlie Bonheur. I eventually fell into a deep sleep around two thirty.

Jack finally answers the ringing phone. I don't raise my head from my pillow to look at the clock. With the black-out curtains pulled, it could be five in the morning or noon. My scrambled brain feels more like five in the morning.

"I'll be right there," Jack said in that dead serious voice, like that heart attack night when he said, "I need to get to the hospital."

I sit up, frightened. Is Emma okay? "What?"

"Ekim's in the emergency room." He's pulling on a shirt and jeans, jumping around to get his socks and shoes.

"Should I come with you?" I am, after all, a nurse. What could be wrong? Overdose? Heart attack? Stroke? Would my medical knowledge be helpful?

"No. Stay with Emma. I'll call you." He's out the door before I get details.

Now of course I can't go back to sleep. I clamber over the king-sized bed, go through the living room to check on Emma. She's sound asleep, still, in her room that's darker than night.

What should I do? Call the hospital? Order a pot of coffee? I go back to the bedroom for my robe, notice the clock says 7:41. My book and magazine are impossible. Maybe I'll sketch—but my hands are shaking. I call room service for coffee. The morning sun streams in the windows in the living area. I feel so alone—but realize I'm used to this feeling. I do my deep breathing, try to calm myself so I can at least draw until the phone rings.

When it does, it's JoAnne. "You okay?"

"Oh . . . I guess. Just waiting here. Do you know what happened?" I'm on my third cup of coffee, Emma's still sound asleep, no word yet from Jack. "What time is it?"

"Almost nine. I talked to Marc a minute ago. He said Jack wanted me to call and let you know what's going on."

"I've been pretty anxious. Is Ekim okay?"

"Not really. He's in a coma."

"A coma? What happened?"

"People in the next room called and complained to the front desk. Said this man was screaming and wailing so loud they couldn't even think, much less sleep. Nobody answered the phone in his room, so the night manager finally went in and Ekim was passed out, barely breathing, looked like he'd vomited. This is what they told Marc."

"Must've aspirated his vomit. That would be bad."

"What? Yeah . . . that's what happened. So he hasn't come out of the coma. They're calling it alcohol poisoning. Waiting for the blood tests to see if anything else is involved."

"Pot would be dangerous—suppress his system even more, if he used enough of it. Awful combination."

"Are you okay? You sound like you're reading from a book, Linda."

I take a deep breath, start trembling again. "What's the . . ." my voice cracks, "What's the prognosis?"

"It's too soon to tell. Are you okay?"

I lower my voice. "Emma's still sleeping. I hate to wake her like this."

"Let me come and get you. Just have her throw on some clothes . . . or, if you don't think she'll freak, I'll bring a quilt. Get her to put on some socks or slippers. She can go back to bed here. I'll be there in ten minutes." She hangs up.

I need to get dressed, but I can't get up off the sofa.

When JoAnne knocks on the door, I've thrown my running clothes on but I haven't tried to get Emma up. JoAnne goes into her room, shakes her shoulder gently, says to put on her slippers, she's coming to her house, "Come as you are." Groggy, Emma does what she says— she wears those cotton pants and a t-shirt to bed anyway—wraps the quilt around her shoulders, makes her slow way into the living room.

"Mom? Seriously?" Her eyes are confused.

"We're going to JoAnne's. For coffee."

"Coffee, I don't drink coffee. Why now?" She looks at JoAnne for some answer to this implausible situation.

"I'll bring you back to get dressed in a bit, Emma. You and Charlie can listen to his CDs. I'll fix us a big breakfast later."

"Like this?" She shrugs.

I force a smile. "I told you this trip would be full of surprises, didn't I?"

Emma wanders to the door. JoAnne takes her elbow, and we walk out into the dim hotel hallway. I still don't know what I'm going to tell her. Not surprisingly, JoAnne has taken over. I don't know whether to be grateful or insulted, but I follow them, wishing Jack were here.

Emma has gone back to sleep in one of the upstairs bedrooms. Amazing how teenagers can sleep through anything.

Standing in the kitchen, holding my fourth cup of coffee, this one much better than the first three, I watch JoAnne as she moves about her workspace as if she could do this with her eyes closed. She probably could.

"How long have you all lived here?"

"We got this when young Marc was little. And then Charlie came along, our caboose. Or surprise. They both grew up here."

"That must've been great."

"We've all loved it. I can't imagine what we're going to do when Charlie graduates from college. It'll sure be empty when he's gone for good."

"He didn't try WVU?"

"Nope. Neither did young Marc. Guess they thought they couldn't go to school in their father's shadow."

"Or their mother's. Though Marc's is quite a shadow, I have to admit."

We smile. It's comforting to share a smile, a memory, even for a second.

She continues to look in my eyes. "We're all really glad Jack's here, and you, too, Linda. It means a lot."

I look down at my coffee cup. "I'm glad I came, too, . . . or I was glad, until . . ."

"I can't believe Ekim did this!" She starts beating the eggs in a bowl like she's beating off a crazed cat. "You don't think he did this on purpose?"

That thought had occurred to me.

"Oh of course not . . .," she wrings her hands, "he's too loyal to these guys for that . . . these guys would never get over it if . . ." She sets the bowl and whisk down on the counter, braces her arms, squares her shoulders. "I just hope he comes out of this coma. Not that I think he'll ever stop drinking." She picks up the eggs again, continues with less frenzy. I imagine Ekim and JoAnne sitting in this sunny kitchen all those years ago, her with her law books, him crying. It's still that sad.

"Does he have any family we should call?"

She continues the breakfast preparations for a moment or two without answering. "His parents are dead. He's got sisters and brothers, but I wouldn't know how to find them."

"Don't you defense lawyers do that? Find people?" My weak attempt at humor goes unnoticed.

"Maybe I'll try later. Right now I wish Marc would call."

"I hope Jack doesn't try the hotel. He'll worry."

"Marc knows I was going to come get you."

Just as she pushes the toast down, the phone rings. She hurries to answer.

"Hey, hon—what's the word?" She listens, scowling. "Okay. I'm getting breakfast ready now. How many?"

Turns out Marc's bringing everybody back to the house to shower and eat. No change in Ekim. I insist on helping, even though she maintains she can do this alone. What kind of friend would I be if I didn't help?

They've all come: Marya and Regina and Annette Montana, too. I'd only seen her across the room at the dinner/dance. Regina and Manny are the only two who look like they've taken the time to groom—their appearance is impeccable. The rest of us are thrown together. Paulo and Johnny Montana take showers. Jack gives me a quick hug, says he'll wait, though I know he's dying for a shower and clean clothes. I know not to suggest we go back to the hotel. He needs to be here.

"You okay?" I hold onto his waist.

"Sure. Nothing we can do at the moment." He kisses my forehead, goes in by the fire with the other guys.

JoAnne makes enough food for the entire fraternity. She lets me prepare the toast and English muffins and butter them, put them on a silver tray covered with a cup towel, directing me the whole way. She's an efficient wonder in that kitchen. Somehow, when she finishes the food the room is clean. I'm organized, but I've never been that organized.

"Where's Frankie?" I finally squeeze in beside Jack on the sofa when JoAnne calls everyone to eat. Marc has the fire blazing.

"He didn't come. Maybe Marc didn't call him."

Regina leans over to us, says in a low voice, "Frankie and his bride took off in his plane early this morning. Before we got the news. They needed to get their asses home. Guess she's not feeling too great." She wiggles her eyebrows. Regina always has the scoop, somehow.

I look around the room. "What about Buck? He should be here." From me, that's pretty brazen, I realize after I've said it.

"They flew out with Frankie."

"Oh." I know the guys will wish Buck was here, too, even if they don't miss Frankie.

When we get our plates, Jack eats like he's been in prison camp. Nobody says a word about Ekim, the hairy mammoth in the room. They all eat, occasionally mutter something about the Mountie game. They've probably talked enough at the hospital. Just as well to try to enjoy the food, even though Ekim is certainly on everybody's mind.

Charlie and Emma wander in, my daughter wrapped in JoAnne's colorful homemade quilt, making me think, immediately, of my grannies—I'm certain some of her people made it.

Charlie stands in the doorway, jeans and a hunting shirt, bare feet. "What's going on?"

"Come help me get some more firewood, son," Marc insists, putting his plate on the hearth. Charlie complies without a question, and they head out the sliding doors. They have raised that young man right.

Emma looks at me, an eyebrow raised slightly. "Let's get you a plate, honey. Have you got any yogurt, JoAnne?"

"In the fridge, bottom shelf. Help yourself."

I'm grateful she doesn't get up to get it for me. I take my time going into the kitchen. Emma tags along dragging the quilt.

"So when are you going to tell me what's going on, Mom? This breakfast thing definitely wasn't on the list of what we were planning this weekend." She glances down, opens the quilt slightly to reveal her rumpled clothes.

I move things around in the refrigerator. It's organized like an upscale grocery store. No surprise. When I stand up with the vanilla yogurt, Emma doesn't reach for it, though I'm sure she must be starving.

"Want a banana?"

She's not buying. "Mom? Really?"

I put the carton on the counter, meet her look. "Ekim's in the hospital." As much time as I've had to plan, I haven't come up with a better way to tell her. No way to keep it secret anymore, though, with everybody in the other room looking all worried, Charlie out getting the word from his dad.

"Why? What's the matter with him?" She's only just met the man the night before, and he was acting like a drunken idiot, but I can tell she's concerned. My big-hearted girl. She'd be worried about her dad. Many of his stories involved the athletic wonders of Ekim, his drunken pranks when that's what they were, boyish pranks.

"Nobody knows for sure. It's bad, though. He's in a coma."

"What?"

"I know. We're all shocked." I don't tell her the vomit part; what good would the graphic details serve?

She takes the yogurt and searches in the cabinet for a bowl, not speaking. I know she needs to work through this in her own quiet way.

JoAnne walks in. "Want me to find some clothes for you, Emma. I've got some sweatpants I think would work."

When Emma turns around her eyes are solemn but clear. "That would be great, unless Mom wants to take me back to the hotel." She raises her eyebrows at me.

"Come on upstairs with me," JoAnne says, making the decision for us.

Emma sets her bowl down, follows JoAnne. I stand there, hugging myself. I should probably tell JoAnne what I know. Would she really want to know? The first eight hours tell the tale. If Ekim doesn't die, he'll probably have permanent cognitive damage from the loss of oxygen when he choked. Or he'll get pneumonia and die anyway. One or the other. This isn't going to have a happy ending, and all these people who love him will feel terrible. Jack, especially, since he hasn't talked to him hardly at all over the years. Me, remembering I didn't dance with him last night when he asked. I'm uneasy but I need to stay calm. Should I tell the others this medical reality, that we should know the medical outcome by dinner? Or should I keep my mouth shut and let them hope?

While I'm standing there, paralyzed by indecision, Annette Montana bustles in carrying dirty dishes. JoAnne has rinse water in the sink, and Annette starts scraping.

"Let me help, please," I say, opening the dishwasher. Of course it's empty.

"I need to do these before we leave. Johnny wants to head back to the hospital pretty quick."

I remember now: Johnny Montana was Ekim's big brother in the fraternity. Johnny never was much of a talker, but he loves the guys like their grumpy father. Annette and I haven't had much of a conversation beyond hello. This was awkward.

"Is Johnny okay?"

She turns to look at me, those deep hazel eyes unblinking. "What do you think, Linda Lee?"

"Of course."

"Johnny did everything he could when Ekim came back from Vietnam. Gave him a job, gave him money when he blew all his on that Corvette and couldn't pay his rent. His heart's breaking. All these guys are hurting, big time."

As she leaves the kitchen to gather more dishes, I face the fact that she's angry I'm here. She's the first person to send a hint that I don't belong, that I don't have the right. Maybe the others are just better at hiding their resentment. I head for the powder room on the first floor before I have an anxiety attack. This is too much. Maybe I should tell Jack what I know—that Ekim probably isn't going to make it. Maybe deep down he's mad at me, too, for keeping him away all this time. I can't figure out a right answer. I turn on the water and have a good, quiet cry by myself.

They all go back to the emergency room except me and JoAnne and Regina. Marya, of course, goes with Paulo, and Annette leaves with Johnny. Jack and I never got to talk by ourselves. He was preoccupied with Ekim, anyway, and I couldn't bring myself to tell him my medical judgments.

He hugs me hard when he leaves, whispers, "I'm so glad we're here, thank you, Linda," and is gone. Emma and Charlie are upstairs somewhere playing music. I faintly hear the fiddle—it's amazing; it could be a record—and I think Emma's trying her hand at mandolin. Thank goodness she's enjoying herself. Every now and again they sing, laugh.

JoAnne adds some logs to the fire, plops down in what must be her regular chair, puts her feet up on the matching ottoman. "This is nowhere near the day I'd hoped for," she sighs.

"Manny and I were going to head home late today, but he's reserved the room for the next few nights. Who in hell knows what'll happen this afternoon." Regina is standing in front of the fire. Good grief she's bony.

"You staying, Linda?" JoAnne asks.

"That's up to Jack," I answer. When she doesn't meet my eyes I add, "I'm sure we'll stay." I have work on Monday, but I have plenty of days banked. I'll call the hospital when we get back to the hotel. What'll we do if Ekim dies? I'm sure he's bound to die. Or be a non-person in some veteran's hospital somewhere, with all the guys obliged to visit him. Jack will want to be here. What do I want? Oddly, I'm not ready to leave either. Jack belongs here, that's clear, but do I? It comes to me in a flash: I want to belong here. I look up, look around the room, dazed.

JoAnne sits forward, meets my eyes, searching, "So what's your medical thinking, Linda. You ever see anything like this?"

Regina comes to sit beside me. She smells of fire smoke and Chanel #5. I have a bottle I've hoarded for special occasions for years. I love that subtle scent. "Yeah, what do you think we should expect?"

I can't look away, can't avoid their questions any longer. "When I was doing clinical, I'd have emergency room rotations. I've seen this kind of thing . . . more than once."

"So? What's the best-case scenario?"

"In my experience, . . ." I hesitate. I have to be truthful, "There is no best-case scenario."

"What do you mean?" Regina's eyes are about to pop out of her slender face.

I look from one to the other. "There's no happy ending. At least not from the cases I've seen. Course it all depends on how long he was out before the emergency personnel got there . . ."

"Manny says the manager told him he took a while to get to the room . . . maybe ten, fifteen minutes. By then there wasn't any more screaming . . . but the asshole wouldn't touch Ekim, he waited for the God damn ambulance . . . that took, probably, another twenty,

twenty-five minutes, Manny told me, from what he could get out of the EMTs. You know Manny. He could get a stone to talk."

Again they look at me for answers. I shrug. "That's pretty bad. I hope the manager at least turned him over on his right side, cleared his throat . . ."

Regina shakes her head. "Manny says the guy didn't touch him. Stupid-ass motel liability thing."

"Where was he staying?" JoAnne asks, as if it mattered.

"Motel Six, I think he said."

JoAnne leans back, deflated. "Figures." Then, "We should've asked him to stay with us."

I decide not to give them the two worst case scenarios. These are smart women. "I'm sure he's getting great medical care. It's a teaching hospital, and they probably have the best equipment . . ."

"Manny and Johnny, they're praying for a miracle, I'm sure." Regina crosses her arms. The good Catholic boys and their so-called miracles. They still must have that kind of blind faith. "What about Jack, did he tell you anything?"

"Not a word. You know how upbeat he is, but this has knocked all the mischief out of him."

"Marc, too." JoAnne looks more defeated than she has all morning. Closing her eyes, she says quietly, "This'll be the first one."

There's nothing to say to that.

Regina perks. "How 'bout some wine? I think we could all use a glass."

We're finishing a bottle of delicious Pinot Noir about an hour later. We haven't talked much at all, but JoAnne has put on a couple of Marc's Doo-Wop CDs, and we've inserted snippets about old times every now and then, when one of the great songs we loved back in school comes on. Phil Spector's "Be My Baby." The Ronettes. I can't help but smile, remembering Jack's stories of Manny primping in front of the mirror while he sang along to that song. The jukebox at the House. Charlie and Emma have come down and asked to go out for subs. They plan to meet some of his fellow musicians. She looks so . . . pleased. And he's a handsome guy, a strong blend of the best of his mom and dad, though he dresses like a down and out country boy in faded jeans and an obviously worn flannel shirt. I try to perk up for them, but they don't seem to notice. I'm relieved when they leave. Fire, music, and wine have lifted us gals out of our gloomy thoughts, at least momentarily.

All three of us jump up when we hear the back door open. Marc hurries into the room, frantic, kneels down and grabs JoAnne, his head against her stomach.

She mutters, "Oh, no," and I can tell Marc's crying. Regina runs to hug Manny, and they walk outside together, whispering. Jack stares at me, his face as sad as I've ever seen him. I pat the sofa beside me and he walks over, shaking his head.

"I know," I say. And I do. He falls against my shoulder but doesn't say a word.

We've come back to our hotel suite to wash up and figure out what's next. We leave Emma at the Bonheurs again, napping, us promising to bring clean clothes. JoAnne has sworn to call us as soon as Emma wakes up if we're not back by then. She's tracking down Ekim's family, Marc is making arrangements with a funeral home, and Johnny and Annette have gone to the Catholic church to light candles. Jack and I pull back the covers and crawl into bed in our grungy clothes, holding on to one another.

Jack hasn't cried. His stillness is disturbing. I cradle his face in my hands. "How can I help?"

He shakes his head, leans back against the headboard.

I get up, pour him a Scotch straight up from the bottle we brought. Again he shakes his head, so I set the glass on the bedside table and crawl back in beside him.

"Jack, I'm so sorry. If he hadn't . . . died," I swallow, "he wouldn't have really recovered, Jack."

He shakes his head again, says, "Shhhhh."

I lean against his chest, but he doesn't put his arms around me to comfort me. That's not like him at all—he's always looking out for me and Emma before he looks out for himself.

I breathe in sync with his heartbeat.

Finally he speaks quietly. "You know what Marc said?"

I lean back to look at him. His face is stoic. "What, hon?"

"Marc said Ekim wanted to stay with us, didn't want to leave."

"Oh, Jack . . . do you think so?" My mind flashes to Ekim, slurring his words, his big smile hopeful on his blurry face, asking me to dance. "That is the saddest thing I've ever heard."

June–August 1967
Cooper's Rock

It's a beautiful night. The whippoorwill is calling—I love that sound. We've driven out because it's our last night before we have to go to our separate homes for summer. Jack hasn't said much on the drive from campus, but neither have I. I know why he's so solemn: He's going to give me his pin, or maybe even ask me to marry him.

We've been together all year. He's been loving, always thoughtful, treating me like his best friend and his girlfriend. We talk every day, see each other almost every day, and I'm so safe with him. I've made my best paintings ever, gotten all As, I'm sure. I've declared a studio major, worked up the courage to tell my parents when I get home. Jack and I are already totally committed in every way. I plan to ask him home to meet my folks, sooner rather than later during summer break. And when we're there, if he hasn't asked me yet, I'm sure he'll talk to my daddy.

He reaches for my hand. "I brought a flashlight. Let's go to the rock."

"Sure." I squeeze his hand. He comes around and opens my door. Jack never forgets the niceties like some of the other guys at the House. He still treats me like I'm his special gal whenever we go out.

The light is beautiful on the rocky path in front of us. We hold hands and walk, each deep in our own thoughts. We're that kind of couple. We can be together without talking. That pleases me, since Jack's such an outgoing person. We can be quiet. There are so many thoughts bumping together in my brain, but I'm savoring this last lovely time together for a while. This is right. This is our moment.

Jack guides me out onto the rock ledge, where so many couples before us have carved their initials, told their secrets, made plans. I lean against him, staring out at the starry sky. It's as if the natural world is celebrating with us.

"You okay?" he asks, also looking out at the vista.

"Of course I'm okay. Except I'm not ready to say good-bye."

"Me either."

"It won't be for long . . . I want you to come meet my folks soon. I just have to figure out the arrangements—some of the boys are still at home, and they'd have to squeeze you in."

He doesn't answer.

"We'd never be able to sleep together at my house . . ." I can feel tension in his chest, now—I guess I hadn't picked up on that until right this moment. "You're all tense. Is something . . . wrong?" I don't want to ruin this perfect evening, but, "If something's bothering you, Jack . . ."

"We should sit down."

I don't like the sound of his voice one bit, kinda brittle, and I look at him, but his profile is still. His face is shadowy. I haven't brought a blanket, and neither has he. He takes off his windbreaker and spreads it underneath us. He sits, pulls me up against him. This is more like it.

"Did you wish on stars when you were little, or is that just a girl thing?"

"I did, Linda Lee. I didn't tell anybody, but I did."

"What did you wish for?"

"You first."

"It's kind of embarrassing . . . I was such a little loner . . . I'd wish for a special friend, just for me, not one of my sisters or my sisters' friends."

"That's so you." He squeezes my shoulder. "Even if it took a while, your wish has come true."

He's right. "Now you."

"Don't laugh." He's half laughing, kind of embarrassed. "I wanted to be Superman."

I can't help but smile. "Of course you did."

"So you got your wish. You've got Regina and JoAnne and Marya."

"I know. They are the best. Do you still want to be Superman?"

"Not likely."

"You're super enough for me." I laugh, so he knows I'm teasing. We're never corny like that. I lean over to kiss him, but he pulls away.

"Don't say that, Linda Lee."

"What? Why not? I'm just playing."

"I know, but . . . I've got something serious I've got to tell you. Something serious and . . ."

I sit back, try to stare into his face, but it's so dark it's hard to see. His eyes are so dark, anyway—I can't read them out here on the ledge, even with the stars. His voice doesn't sound happy. Not at all. "What? Is something wrong with you?" This can't be one of those things where he's sick, really sick, like some soap opera. My throat gets that choked up feeling, and I'm scared.

He reaches for both my hands. "This is so hard. I love you so much."

"Jack! What?!"

He looks away from me. His hands are sweaty. "There's this other girl . . ."

"What?! What are you talking about?!" I almost stop breathing. He can't be saying what I think he's saying.

"Wait. Let me get this out. I've been seeing this other girl . . ."

Now I stand, scream. I can hear myself screaming.

"Linda Lee, Linda Lee," he jumps up and reaches for me, but I push away his hands, keep on screaming no, no, no.

"She's pregnant, Linda Lee. She's pregnant . . . it's mine."

"That's not true. That can't be true. Why are you saying such a horrible thing to me?" I'm pounding on his chest. He's struggling to hold onto my fists.

"Stop, Linda Lee. I don't love her. I love you."

"You stop! I mean it!" I'm flailing my arms now, trying to avoid Jack touching me at all. "Take me back to school. Take me back right this minute!" I start stumbling over the rock outcropping, but I can't see anything in front of me. Jack grabs my arm.

"Let me get the flashlight. Please stop." It sounds like he's crying, too, but I don't care. I can't be here. I can't be with him.

I cry all the way back to campus. He tries to talk to me, begs me to talk to him, but I lean against my door with my hand on the handle and weep. I can't look at him. I don't turn on my light when I get to the room. JoAnne and Regina are gone; JoAnne's side is stripped bare. She left days ago. I've stayed until the last day before dorms close, to drag out my time with Jack. I fall on my bed, try to smother myself in the pillow, anything to keep from breathing and thinking. I might be screaming, but my face is in the pillow.

Jack has been with some other girl, has gotten her pregnant. My Jack. Not my Jack. Not really. Never. How can that be true? He said so. He said he loved me. I could throw up. I can't throw up. He was going to drive me to the bus station in the morning. How will I get there? I've got to get out of here. I won't see him. I won't look at him ever again. I'm gasping into the pillow. I've got to get up and leave. How to get to the bus station in the morning? My trunk's stored—I'll have to have it sent, shipped home. How will I do that? How will I do anything? Jack. Jack. Jack.

In the morning I do throw up. I throw up until there's nothing but bile. Early, at first light, I get down on my knees and throw up and throw up. I gag and gag. I don't want to even think his name but it's all I can think. Jack. Jack. Jack. I call the operator, can barely talk, but she gets me a taxi. I grab my suitcase and overnight bag and laundry bag, stuff the double wedding ring pattern quilt into the laundry bag—I'd like to burn it—I can't leave it, my mother would kill me—and I go down the hill to wait for the taxi just as the sun is coming up.

I have cash for the taxi and my bus ticket already. My mouth is sour from throwing up, my eyes burn. I might still be crying but I can't tell, I'm so disoriented. I wish for Regina or Marya, can't figure out where they could be, remember they're home already. I'm the last one of us here. I couldn't face them anyway—what would I say? Do they know already? Except Jack's here—he had a morning practicum of some sort—he won't come by until after that, and I'll be gone.

I can't think of seeing Jack. Now I really am crying, sobbing when the taxi drives up. The elderly driver gets out and takes my bags—he must see crying coeds all the time—and I swallow and struggle for a deep breath, get out "Greyhound Station," and tumble into the back seat.

Back home no one meets me at the station—I wonder if I've even told them what bus I'll be coming in on? But I'm not on that bus. I've been so preoccupied with my last days with Jack I can't remember if I told them a time or even a day. I lug my bags to a phone booth. Home is more than five miles from White Sulphur, and even if I could've walked any other time, I couldn't possibly walk now. Nobody answers the phone—the grannies must be on the porch, everybody else must be at work—so I sit on one of the wooden benches for I don't know how long.

Jack is going to be a daddy. Jack is going to have a baby. Jack has someone else. Jack is with another girl. Woman. She'd be a woman now. Pregnant. And what about me, too? I was one of those "poor little fools" in the stupid song. Poor little fool. How could I have believed him so completely, so deeply, without a single question in my mind? This is what it's like to be fooled. Fool. Foolish. A fool in love. Isn't that another song? Me. Jack.

Of course he'll do the right thing and marry her. Jack, right thing, how absurd. He's a cheat. A liar. Who could it be? I have no idea. No idea whatsoever. He's said he loves me for how many months now? A year—it will be a year on the fourth of July. Happy Independence Day, fool. What does that mean, he loves me? He loves me not? Do I love him not? Would I be so sick if I didn't love him?

I call home again. It must be around four. Carl answers—what is he doing at the house, but I ask if he can come get me at the bus station and he says, "Sure." That's all.

When he pulls up in his truck and I put my stuff in back and get up in the cab, he looks at me and says, "What the hell?"

I don't mean to cry, think I am cried out, but I start sobbing and he says it again, "What the hell, Linda Lee?" I shake my head and cry and we sit there in front of the Greyhound in the pick-up only section, and Carl stares at me while I shake my head. When it's clear I can't say a word, he turns on the ignition and heads the truck down the familiar road to home.

I go straight to bed without seeing anybody else but the grannies. They ooh and oh and say, "Is that you, Linda Lee? Are you okay, honey? Want some tea?" I don't try to answer, just go up to the girls' room and flop on the first bed and fall sound asleep.

When I wake up, Mama is by my pillow with tea and toast—I know what it is automatically, just by the smells: hot tea with honey and milk, plain white toast. Our sick food my whole growing up. My eyes feel like they're glued closed, my lips are dry. I feel like I might puke. I think, *I can't talk.* I don't want to talk, but I can't talk, even if I wanted to. What would I say?

"I thought you might need this, Linda Lee. Granddaddy Chick said you looked mighty peaked when you got here last night." She sets the dishes on the wicker table by the bed.

I shake my head, no idea what message I'm conveying, wanting to send the "leave me alone please" thought. It's daylight. My sisters aren't in the room.

Mama puts her palm on my forehead. "You're a tad warm, and you've been in the bed over twelve hours now."

I shake my head again.

"I'll just leave this, then. I need to get to work. Granny Sadie says she'll check on you."

When I hear her feet hit the bottom of the steps, I bolt up, run to the bathroom, and try to throw up. I gag and gag, which makes me cry. Nothing comes up, but I want to vomit, want to throw up everything inside me, my kidneys and my liver and especially my heart. I hate Jack Vanderbilt. He makes me sick. I never want to see him ever again. Or even think his name.

I stumble back to bed, weaker than a newborn calf, sicker than a dog with worms. I don't want to do anything but sleep a dreamless sleep, to begin to forget, to start whatever I'm going to start without Jack Vanderbilt as a part of it.

That evening, it's my daddy by my bed. Granny Sadie has been up a couple of times during the day, felt my forehead, taken away the old dishes, replaced them with new. That must've been hard for her, with her arthritis. I've kept my eyes closed, though, stayed still, so she wouldn't try to talk to me. That won't work with Daddy.

"Your mama says something's wrong, Linda Lee. That's plain to see." Daddy's voice is insistent.

I push to my elbows. "Exams, Daddy. Final projects." My voice sounds croaky, or is that just in my head?

"That it? Schoolwork never made you sick before, girl. Never so much as wore you out that I could tell."

I nod. This is true. "Maybe I took on too much, Daddy." What did Granny Sadie always say? *I can see the lie on your face.* I felt like Daddy was bound to know I wasn't being entirely truthful. The less said.

"You need to eat. Your mother's fixing a pan of chicken and some early peas. Granny Sis made light rolls. I expect to see you at supper." He pats my shoulder and leaves the room.

Sitting up is a start. I'll take a bath. I look around this room—the only room I've ever known, except the two at WVU. I don't even have to have my eyes open to know what's in this room: the one double bed, always Jenna's cause she was oldest, and the two single metal beds, mine and Cassie's. The big bureau for all our clothes—we each had a drawer, growing up, but I guess Cassie has taken over Jenna's. And the dressing table we shared. With the big oval mirror and tiny drawers for make-up. We each had our own jewelry box. Mine had been blue. I would've liked Jenna's red or Cassie's pink better. Had Cassie slept here last night? Jenna lived down the road a bit, with her husband, Penn, and the baby. Cassie was working in an office at The Greenbrier—had she come and gone? I never heard a thing last night. Maybe she slept at Jenna's. They'd always been close. More alike, loving fashion magazines and hairstyles and girl get-togethers. Jenna and I were closer in age—Cassie and I were close in age, too—but those two got along. Always had.

Carl was next after me, then Michael, then Cassie. Stair steps from Jenna to Cassie, a baby a year. How had Mama done that? Five children in five years? And her so, what would I call it, together? No nonsense. It was another five years before John Charles, then wham, Baby Richard. That's what he's always been called. Baby Richard. Those two are still in school. The boys all live at home, even Carl and Michael.

Funny that the upstairs is so quiet. The two younger boys must have had school today—college lets out earlier than high school for some reason. Everybody else must be off to work. The house is never this quiet—never was, that I can remember. I stumble to the bathroom and run a bath. I'll make it as hot as I can stand it.

That supper could be any one of six thousand of my growing up, with a few rearrangements of people in the chairs. Granddaddy Chick at one end of the table, Daddy at the other—never changing. Granny Sadie sits on Granddaddy Chick's left, Mama on Daddy's left. Baby Richard is by Granny Sadie—he's always been her pet. John Charles sits by Baby Richard. Cassie sits on the other side of Daddy. When she'd been home, that had been Jenna's spot. Carl, solid as a tree, is planted next to Mama, Michael hovers next to him, and I sit next to Michael.

Neither one of us talks much anyway, so it's no big deal that we don't say much this evening. Great Uncle Bo, because of his uppers and lowers that never fit quite right, always takes his meals by himself. Granny Sis serves—I'd never known her to sit at the table, not even at Christmas or Easter. Even if someone is off somewhere—which is rare, at supper time—Granny Sis serves. She is no bigger than a minute, can flash around the table refilling platters and glasses without you even knowing you've drunk all your tea or milk. She dotes on Daddy and likes to be busy. She would've been uneasy sitting long enough for a meal. Even when she's on the porch with the other grannies, she is always knitting or crocheting or quilting. I've never seen her sit idle.

I know Mama has made this meal for me, with all my favorites. I serve small portions on my plate, eat a bite or two or everything—force it down is more like it. Mama has always been the choir director at supper, the only meal we all even try to eat together, since people leave the house at different times in the morning, and Granny Sis has always been in charge of lunch since we were small, 'cause Mama works. The peas and potatoes and chicken all taste exactly alike, like an old cold roll, though the rolls are hot and made that afternoon. It's all I can do to swallow. Cassie talks about goings on at her office, Mama worries about Jenna letting her baby get away with too much, Daddy gets in a word or two about what the boys need to do before school in the morning. The normal rhythm of my family. I guess it should comfort me, this predictability, this stability. I can only think, *I want to scream. Breathe. Swallow. Smile. Breathe. Swallow. Don't scream. Smile. This is one meal. That's all. One meal.*

I act like an invalid as long as I can get away with it, which isn't long. Those first days I can understand what it would be like to slip into helplessness. After about a week, one evening when Cassie is out on a date and the rest are downstairs looking at *Bewitched*, Mama comes up and sits down at the dressing table bench and says, "Let's talk, Linda Lee."

"Okay." I'd been drawing a little, reading a little, helping clean up in the kitchen after lunch a little, but mostly I'd stayed in the room by myself.

"What's wrong with you? I've never known you to be moody."

That's my mama—get right down to it.

"I had a rough semester at school, that's all."

"How rough?"

"I took on too much, too many hours." I realize Mama might not get the idea of course hours. "Too many classes, with two studios."

"Why'd you do that? What's the hurry?"

"I don't know—I couldn't make up my mind. I didn't really want to major in art education, but I didn't want to give up art, either. I wanted to finish all my general requirements, too, so I could maybe double major." All this is the truth—just not ALL of the truth.

"Doesn't sound like you at all. Taking on more than you can handle."

"I know. Which is probably why I got so burned out."

"That's what you're calling this, burned out? I would've called it beat down. Or run ragged."

"I know. I don't want you and Daddy to worry."

"Of course we're worried. You're not yourself."

True. So true. "I'm not going to go back to WVU. That's one thing I'm sure about."

"Well that's the smartest thing you've said since you walked in the door. Thank goodness for that."

"I hate to quit. Daddy's not going to like me quitting . . ."

"Well he certainly doesn't want you to go on like this." She pats my knee. "And neither of us understands why you won't talk to these girls who keep calling long distance."

"I don't want to talk about it—not going back." It's like I've failed or something, when really I made Dean's List, but I don't want to try to explain all that yet, and the Jack part never. "They're going to want to talk me into coming back."

"They sound awful friendly. And they really want to talk to you."

"But I don't know what I'm going to say. Or do. I need some time."

"It's clear you need to rest. We can all see that." This coming from my mama who has never taken a nap in her life to my knowledge.

"So maybe if it's okay I'll help out around here until I get my head together . . ."

"Get your head together? I was thinking it was your body that was beat into the ground. What does that mean, 'get your head together'?"

"Figure out what next."

"Okay. Get better. I'll let your daddy know about school. They're hounding him for money already. If you're sure?"

"I'm sure. That's the only thing I'm sure about."

And that's that. She accepts my lame story about too many classes and lets it be. That's my mama. One foot in front of the other. Do what you have to do. Grab pleasure where you can. Work hard. Hold onto your own. Do your part. I know I'll be expected to do my part, eventually. But for the moment I've bought some time. Now maybe I won't feel like I have to throw up all day every day, no matter how little I eat.

But I keep waking up needing to throw up, and when I think about my period I wonder, *When did I have my period last month?* I'd been so crazy busy with final papers and art projects and exams. I'd always been regular, never had cramps, so it was easy to go from month to month without noting the dates. But I'd been home two weeks—I should've had a period. I'm certain of that.

I start walking back in the woods early every day, thinking that I'd been so bedbound and housebound and weepy and inactive that I've messed up my cycle. Jack Vanderbilt has screwed up my brain and my emotions and now he's royally messed up my body, too. I should've known. There are more old hunting trails back behind our property than trees, practically, so I can walk forever without running into a soul or seeing the same scenery twice. Not that I'm paying that much attention. I walk myself exhausted. I still feel nauseous, but I blame that on the gut punch from he whose name I don't want to think any more. He'd literally made me sick. Sicker than a dog. That

I might be pregnant myself isn't even on my radar these first couple of weeks when I try to walk myself back to some semblance of health so I can maybe begin to think about what to do next.

When I am eating better at supper every night and looking better—everybody at home says so, even Cassie, and they all stop giving me funny what's-wrong-with-you looks—I get worried. Not just sad and lonely and mad and unwanted, but worried. I walk down to Jenna's and help her with her son a few times, but I can't bring myself to ask her anything about being pregnant, how she figured it out that first time.

I go to the White Sulphur library, to the medical section, and look up early signs of pregnancy. Swollen breasts—mine don't look or feel any different to me. Nipples changing color. I don't notice any change. Exhaustion. Well, yeah. I am exhausted. But I've been dumped by the man I've entrusted with my whole entire self. I'd cried nonstop for days. Now I'm walking miles every morning. Wouldn't I be exhausted? Morning sickness. I've been sick round the clock for a couple of weeks. I'm not nauseous all that much anymore, not like I was those first days. Wasn't that the shock of what he told me? Besides missing my period, I can't talk myself into actually being pregnant, so I walk home relieved—though still worried. Maybe I'm cracking up, but I certainly am not pregnant. We'd always used condoms, that ex-boyfriend and me.

Had he used condoms with Simone D'Espere? That's her name—Marya told me in her letters. They all told me in their letters. Some townie with immigrant parents, her daddy working in the mill. I let myself think her name—hate her name. Simone D'Espere—never Simone Vanderbilt. I know they're getting married. Jack didn't need to tell me that part. I refused to hear it. Probably hadn't used protection. Probably it was all drunk grappling. Who am I kidding? That's what I want it to be. Why? He'd been unfaithful to me, betrayed my trust all over the place, so what difference does it make if it was a quickie or a one-night-stand or a long-time sneaky behind-my-back second girlfriend? He's a no-count cheater who's tricked me and used me and chopped me up in pieces I'm having an impossible time putting back together in any kind of semblance of a whole me. Not funny, Humpty Dumpty. Not the least bit funny. Did he get out of bed with me and into bed with Simone D'Espere? I don't want to know, not really, but I can't help imagining. Cracking up is what's wrong with me—I'd never had my heart broken, my body used and abused and thrown over like yesterday's beer bottle. Ugh. Self-hatred is another possibility. But not pregnancy. We'd been careful.

Two weeks later when my boobs are ballooning over the tops of my bra cups, and I want ice cream all day long, I can't ignore the reality—I'm pregnant. Too. Simone D'Espere is planning her wedding to Jack Vanderbilt (I can't avoid thinking his name, much as I try) because she's pregnant, and I'm pregnant. Too. I start walking/jogging the five miles to town and sitting in a rocking chair outside The Greenbrier ice cream bar until it opens at 11—sometimes I carry a drawing pad and pencils in my backpack, sometimes I take a book, sometimes I just sit—and wait until I can get a sundae or double dip cone, or once in a blue moon, a banana split. I'm ravenous, have a hole inside me I can't fill with ice cream or buttered rolls or chicken with gravy. Or rather a growth inside me I have to feed. Not a baby. Never a baby.

In those weeks, I don't allow myself to think *What now?* or *What next?* I know I'll have to do that, but for those few weeks I am the ice cream blob. The walking, running, drawing, reading, sleeping ice cream blob. I push aside any serious thought that tries to wedge into my brain and put the spoon or the straw or the bite into my mouth instead.

After I've been home about a month, I wake up one morning and I'm crying. Have I had a bad dream? Nothing registers. But tears are running down my face. *Is this what's called a moment of truth?* I think, giggle at the absurdity. Now you have crossed the line into crazy, Linda Lee Barbour. Get a grip. Grab on. To what? I AM PREGNANT. Face facts. All the walking ice cream eating ignoring in the world cannot change that physical fact. I AM PREGNANT. And the man I love—the man I thought I loved—is marrying Simone D'Espere. Has chosen Simone D'Espere. I need to DO something. To make this right. This will never be right. Jack Vanderbilt made his choice. To do the "right thing." Now I have to make mine. By myself. A CHOICE? Do I really have a CHOICE? As in options? Now I giggle again. And cry. Options? That's a crock. A pile. A joke—a sick joke. Jack Vanderbilt is already having a baby. Is already getting married. Has already made his CHOICE. This is what's called TOO LATE—as in TOO LATE. You are stranded. Up the river without a paddle. On your own. Nobody to save you. No savior. Jesus Christ could give a shit. This is no immaculate conception. No angels involved. Just me and Jack Vanderbilt and he's made his choice. Now I have to make mine.

I'm crying hard now, because I know it's no choice at all. It's a fait accompli, as I learned in French so handily. Done. A done deal. I can't have this. I can't have any of this. All the ice cream in the universe can't make it any better, can't make it change or go away. I am not having a baby. No way. I'm on my own, Simone. That's not funny. Not a tiny bit funny. I weep now, not because I've lost Jack, but because of what I know I have to do if I have even a shred of a chance of getting past this. I can't bring my family into this. I haven't even been able to tell them the truth about my heartbreak. They're too good, too honest and true. It has nothing to do with them. I'll never get over this, but I have to get past it. There's no "right thing" for me to choose. I have to do the only thing left to me.

West Virginia won't do it. Virginia will, if a woman has a letter from a lawyer saying she's been "violated." Damn straight I've been violated. That letter is easy enough to create, with the yellow pages and a typewriter. I who have never cheated on so much as a weekly spelling test write this lying letter, design a plausible looking heading. Such things are always hush-hush, no one saying the word rape out loud, no one, not even lawyers, wanting to be candid.

The closest Women's Clinic is in Richmond, Virginia, I discover. That euphemism—women's clinic. It's the only place anywhere near, if you can call Richmond near, that does legal medical abortions because of rape or "danger to the mother's life." This is dangerous, I tell myself. I have my $385, saved from Hudson Brothers. I know how to get anywhere on a Greyhound. I've learned to tell "bald-faced lies," as Granny Sadie calls them, without flinching. So I tell the family I'm going to stay over a few days with my college friend Annette Zamboni, who lives in Richmond, which they consider a clear sign that I'm so much better. Annette doesn't live in Richmond, not even close—she's from somewhere in Jersey—but she's not one of those who's been calling and calling, so there's no chance Mama will ask her about the visit.

I have to face my fears, go alone and stay in a lousy motel room afterwards for at least a night to be sure there's not unexpected bleeding. That's what they say on the phone, "unexpected bleeding." I make my appointment and reservation and buy my bus ticket and that's that.

I go to Richmond, to the women's clinic. Alone.

September 16, 2000

We're at JoAnne and Marc's within a couple of hours, early enough to be back before Emma has gotten up from her nap. It's dusk, and the others are lingering out on the patio, down by the firepit out on the dock. I've been sitting in the guest room while Emma sleeps, doodling, trying to wrap my head around everything that's happened. That clean Emma smell—her unique combination of Dove soap and lavender oil natural essence, her musty Bert's Bees hair—gives me some small comfort in this house that isn't home to us.

"Mom?" She's wrapped in my college quilt I brought back with me from the hotel, has that blurry *Where am I?* look on her face as she props up on an elbow. "Where's Charlie?"

"Downstairs with his dad, I guess." I walk over, sit on the bed beside her. "I've brought you your toothbrush and some clothes. Want to take a shower now?"

"Here?"

"Everybody's gathered here, Emma. Dad and I have already changed."

She looks at me, at my freshly made-up face. "What's going on? What time are we leaving?"

"We'll probably stay at least tonight." I've been here almost half an hour, trying to draw her while she sleeps, and I still haven't figured out a way to tell her that Ekim is dead. My nurse training does no good when I have to tell my own innocent daughter that someone she just met died today. Does she even remember which one of her dad's fraternity brothers Ekim is? Probably—his behavior was rather memorable last night.

"School?" She looks at me worried, like I must be having some kind of breakdown; if she were a sassier child, she'd have a "Duh, Mama" look in her eyes, but that's not our Emma. We both know I'm a stickler for going to school unless you have a fever or "blood and guts" accident.

"I know. I hate for you to miss." I should just say it, have insisted to Jack that I be the one to tell her, just me and Emma, but I keep stalling. Me, usually so matter of fact at the hospital in the midst of news nobody wants to hear. "But, like I said, we need to stay."

"Is that guy Ekim . . . better?"

"He died this afternoon, while you and Charlie were out."

"How?" She sits up so startled, eyes wide, voice shaky—*How could we come here for a stupid fraternity reunion and have somebody die?* her face says. Like life's supposed to make sense.

I touch her shoulder. "I know. It's insane. Apparently he's had a drinking problem for some time now . . ."

"Charlie told me all about that. But *dead*? How's Daddy?"

"He's wrung out, but these men are handling this pretty well. They're trying to find Ekim's relatives and take care of the legalities while the gals are getting together some kind of gathering for the Phi Kaps who are still in town. Here. Food and wine and all that. Just a place to be together."

"Some kinda wake thing?" Standing up, Emma wraps her hair around one hand, rubs her face with the other. No one in our family has ever died while she's been alive. "This still isn't making any sense. You say you've got my clothes here? And you want me to shower here instead of the hotel?"

"Yeah. I know. Maybe you and Charlie could help out, check and see what JoAnne and Marc need. I have an idea it's going to be wall to wall people for a while."

"All right I guess. Where's my stuff?"

She trails into the bathroom, and I stare down at my tablet. All around a sketch of my sleeping daughter I've doodled circles, so many circles so many sizes that now they look like bubbles, a page full of crowded bubbles pushing the edges, going where?

I want to be useful, so I go down to help JoAnne and the others any way I can. They work together seamlessly. Regina is out on the patio setting up coolers and an outdoor bar; she doesn't look like she needs a hand. Marya, Annette, and JoAnne are in the kitchen, well into dicing potatoes (homemade potato salad? Not just Kroger's deli?) and chopping vegetables for salad and making burger patties. They each look up when I enter.

"Emma okay?" JoAnne asks.

"She's getting a shower. Is Charlie around?"

"He's out with his dad and some of the guys, checking out the motels and hotels, the House, trying to contact as many brothers as they can find. Paulo and Johnny are at the church, talking to the priest."

"Oh." I go to the sink to wash my hands. "Put me to work."

Marya looks up, smiles. "How are you at devilled eggs? Or pie crust?"

"I told you I'll do the pie crusts," Annette chimes in, "as soon as I'm done with the potatoes and dressing. You could chop some onions and pickles. Or make the filling—it's easy."

JoAnne wipes her hands on her WVU Tail-Gatin' Phi Kap apron. "Tell you what I really need, if you don't mind."

"Sure. What?"

"I've been to the store twice today and I still think I need more beer and ice. And maybe more lettuce and tomatoes for the burgers. I'm just not sure how many . . ."

"Of course. Glad to do it. Any particular kind of beer, or just a variety?"

"I've already got Coors and Rolling Rock and Miller Lite. Maybe some imports? I don't drink beer, so I only get what Marc tells me."

"I'll get my keys and Emma, and we'll head out."

"How 'bout some good dill pickles, too?" Annette calls as I head for the back stairs.

Emma and I drive around looking for the grocery store, finally stop and ask at a Sheetz. I don't have the peppy purpose that the other women appear to have generated in the face of this mess. In fact, I'm feeling downright flat—not feeling. Emma doesn't say much, finds Santana on the radio and settles back, singing along or humming. I put myself on cruise control until we get the groceries.

We load the car and settle back into the front. "So, Mama, what do you think of Charlie?"

I edge out of the parking lot. "He seems fine—I haven't spent much time with him, remember, except for dinner last night. And he wasn't exactly the focus of attention then."

"I like him a lot."

"I can tell. How old is he?"

"He's a junior this year. He only came home for this fraternity thing, too. He's known these guys all his life."

"He tell you anything about his brother?"

"Young Marc? Apparently he's on the West Coast doing something legal for actors and musicians and he couldn't get back. You know he's a lot older than Charlie, right?"

"I figured that. So how old did you say Charlie is?"

"Twenty one."

I turn for a quick look in her direction. "That's pretty mature to be hanging out with a sixteen-year-old, don't you think?"

"Mom. You're the one who's always said how 'precocious' I am—your word, not mine."

"College is a world away from high school, Emma. Take my word."

"He doesn't act all college superior, if that's what you're getting at." She puts one hand on my shoulder. "Or lech-like, if that's what's really worrying you." She pats my shoulder. "So is now when you can tell me about you leaving WVU?"

"It's not a big thing, really Emma." I smile at her, look back at the road.

"So tell me then."

"I *wasn't* precocious, like you." I stare at the road. "I was a girl from the sticks in West Virginia who'd never looked beyond her nose. I decided on WVU without giving it two seconds' worth of thought. And it wasn't for me."

"Oh, come on—these women, not one of them seems snobby or prudish—or the slightest bit hillbilly. Like you . . ." She smiles. "I don't get what you're saying, *not for you.*"

"The nursing program, for one thing . . ."

"Oh please. Weren't you and Dad dating while you were here?"

"Yes. We were. But he married Jay's mother, remember?"

"Of course I remember. So you didn't fall for him till you two got together later?"

"I didn't say that." I sneak another quick smile, reassuring I hope. I don't want to lie to Emma—that's never been my mom modus operandi—but I don't see any reason for her to know the whole dingy break-up thing either. "I was pretty crazy about your dad—we were just so young. That's what I'm trying to say. The distance between sixteen and twenty-one is like from Virginia to California. Huge maturity gap. But when you're in your thirties, five years either way is no big deal."

"So you just left dad and your girlfriends because UVA had a better nursing program? Seriously? You are such an academic nerd, Mama, but I'm not buying it."

"I've always had my art, even back then, like you've had your music." My paintings are all over the house and I belong to a regional co-op. I've never stopped drawing and painting. Even when Jack and I broke up. "Career choices were pretty narrow, don't forget. My parents weren't going to approve of me majoring in studio. And I didn't want art education."

"JoAnne became a lawyer. Marya's a physical therapist. You told me so yourself. So much for narrow choices."

"They were always more 'out there' than I was, even when we were freshmen. I wasn't exactly a risk taker."

"But you left WVU and transferred to UVA. I'd call that pretty bold."

"Smart choice on my part. But it cost me, didn't it?"

"How so?"

"Women friends."

"They're happy to see you, Mama. Anybody can see that. Dad's smiling all over himself—I guess I should say he was, until this Ekim thing."

"Those women, they all fit together, like those puzzles you had when you were little—remember? Some of them had farm animals, some had jungle animals, some had pets? A slot for each one in each category, shaped exactly like the piece? They'd be an amazing lifelong female friends puzzle. I'm not a part in that. I gave that up."

Emma nods; she'd loved those puzzles. "You are SO visual, Mama. But I don't remember you being so half empty. You're more a half full person."

I pat her knee. "Thanks, Em. Remember what I always told you whenever you were scared?"

She rolls her eyes, but it's playful, not mean. "Are you kidding. I can hear it like some school cheer: Face your fears, Emma Bear."

I have to smile. "Right you are. Every time something tough came along: 'Face your fears.' I learned that lesson when I left West Virginia and went to UVA."

She nods. That's been a family mantra as far back as she can remember.

"That day you went to 'real' school with bells and twenty students in the class, instead of Miss Sabrina's Toddler Care Center—like day-care heaven, and you were her pet. She even put one of your drawings on her business card, remember?—you were terrified of real school."

Emma nods. "All that weekend you kept saying it: 'Face your fears.'"

"And when you were scared to join the swim team, but all your friends were doing it. Going off the high dive that first time. Trying out for Honors String Band. Every single time—'Face your fears.' And you would. Daddy and I were so proud of you—our daring, brave girl."

"How could I forget?"

We ride along without talking for a while. I have no idea why this is coming up today, but it feels okay. "I tried to let you see me do those things, too. Like when I was scared to death of running the art benefit for your school, but I did it—asking people to donate work, raising money, like the sixth and seventh rings of hell for me—but I did it, so you could see I'd face my fears, too. And when you and your dad wanted to get a pitbull, and I was terrified of pitbulls, but I went with you to the breeder, and we got Frieda and she's a big ol' love bug."

"I miss Freida."

"Me too." We both sigh. "And don't forget I quit my job with Dr. Fitzhugh—everybody loved Dr. Fitzhugh, nobody could believe I'd leave as his senior nurse—because he was a sexist pig behind his women patients' backs."

"That's my mama all right—assertive as all get out. Except you can't find your way from point A to point B, can you? Are we lost?"

"No. I just haven't been in any hurry to get back." My shoulders are relaxed.

"Well the ice is going to melt."

"Yeah, and maybe Charlie's back by now, right?"

Emma wiggles her eyebrows, turns up the radio again, and I'm quiet until I turn in the gate into JoAnne's neighborhood. That went well, I tell myself. Emma's had her questions answered, seems satisfied. But I'm feeling raw about facing my former friends again, ever the outsider, decades apart, shared memories and experiences hazy compared to present reality.

There are so many cars crowding the driveway that I have to park out on the grass on the circle in front of the house. Apparently the guys were successful at finding other brothers before they took off for home. Emma grabs a couple of the bags of ice and runs ahead for help while I follow with some of the grocery bags. A few of the men standing out on the patio offer to get the others.

"There you are," Jack booms across the parking area, smiling and walking toward me as I hand over the bags. "Come meet these fellas, babe."

I wave. "Gotta help in the kitchen, hon. I'll see you in a little while."

Emma is handing over ice to Charlie, the two of them with their heads together. So what if he's in college, I tell myself. She's a smart gal, and this is just one of those momentary circumstances. We'll be in the car on the way home tomorrow.

"Good morning, Ms. Vanderbilt," Charlie says. "Anything else in the car?"

"There are a couple more bags of ice, if you don't mind."

"Not a problem." And he and Emma go out the door to ice down the coolers.

"Did you say you needed help with devilled eggs?" I ask the women in general. There are more now, some I haven't met.

Around eleven that evening, most everyone is gone, and JoAnne and Marc, Paulo and Marya, Emma and Charlie, and Jack and I are sitting out by the firepit in the back yard. I'm too tired to move, but everyone else sounds wired from the crowded, busy Sunday. Charlie has his mandolin; Emma is strumming on one of his guitars—they're on a bench a bit away from the rest of us. The guys have been telling Ekim stories all evening—wouldn't he have loved to have been with us today, to hear how much they remember, how much they've loved him?—and it's all a blur to me. I can't focus on what Marc's saying, only that they're laughing in that breathless way men have when they're five words into a story they all already know and they can hardly get it out, they know it so well. Telling it the eightieth time is still obviously not one time too many.

JoAnne leans over from her Adirondack chair to mine. "Charlie and Emma have hit it off with the music, don't you think?"

"They sure have. She's a music nut."

"So's he. Always has been. I don't know where he gets it. Marc can't carry a tune, and I'm strictly a sing-along guitarist. I hated piano lessons."

"Jack always sang to Emma when she was a baby. I did, too, but I was 'Hush Little Baby' while he was 'Like a Rolling Stone.' She heard music all the time—I had those classical tapes for babies, for white noise."

"Not us. I was so busy when Marc Junior was a baby—both of us were—I never even read to him, much less sang. Law books aren't exactly baby ready. I did read to Charlie—things were different by then, economically, career-wise. But Marc was never around to read to either of them. Work, work, and more work. By then I had a housekeeper so I could pay attention to Charlie when I got back from the office. I guess we always had our music playing on the stereo when he was growing up, but neither of us sang to him."

"Emma says he's like a genius."

"She could be right. He is SO focused—blows my mind. And he knows every old-time musician in Virginia and West Virginia, I think. When he goes to these festivals they all want him to come jam with them. This since he was thirteen or so."

"Emma's smart, but she's pretty naïve, too."

JoAnne laughs. "Charlie's no player, if that's what you're getting at. Girls haven't been on his radar, unless they play and sing. Maybe to worship from afar, like Allison Krauss. And then only *because* they play and sing. Now if Marc Junior were here I'd tell you to watch out . . ."

"He's about Jay Vanderbilt's age, isn't he?"

"A couple of years younger—way out of Emma's league. But in his industry young is a cult."

"Emma's never had a serious boyfriend. Her friends tend to hang out in clumps, not couples."

"Honestly, you don't need to worry about Charlie."

"They're nothing like we were, are they?"

"I don't know if I agree with you. We were all pretty smart. And you painted. I didn't have much of a direction . . ."

"But look what you've done?"

"I'd say the real difference is that these kids didn't grow up anything like we did."

"Certainly nothing like I did. You and Jack had it pretty good, don't you think?"

"I guess the four of us had a push or a cushion or something—not like the up from the mines background of some of the guys, most of them, really."

"Including Ekim."

"Yeah, his growing up was pretty hardscrabble—and maybe the ethnic thing was something we never gave enough credit, you know?"

"He was the one always making the jokes about it, not us. Calling himself Ekim the Egyptian Houseboy, when he wasn't even Egyptian."

"True. But still, maybe it was part of his pain, his sense of not fitting in."

"Phi Kaps. Brothers for life. He knew that."

"Big so what in the end, right?"

"God it's awful." We both polish off the wine in our glasses. "I think Jack and Emma and I had better head back to the motel. If everything's cleaned up . . ."

"Done. Place is cleaner than when we started."

I turn my head toward the young people. "Emma? Time to go."

Jack and Emma both look over at me.

"I didn't get a nap this afternoon, Miss, like somebody I know." I raise my eyebrows. "Jack, you ready?"

"I'm pretty beat, Emma," he agrees.

She looks from one of us to the other.

"She's welcome to stay here, Linda, if you guys don't mind."

"I'd drive her home in a little while, Mr. Vanderbilt, but I've had a few beers . . ." Charlie offers.

"Come on Mama, Daddy, could I please stay? Charlie's showing me some progressions . . ."

"If it's all right with you and Marc, JoAnne," Jack says.

"Not a problem. She's already got her toothbrush, right?"

Emma has stayed with guy friends for years. I don't know why this time it's making me uneasy—well, probably because there were always other girls and guys there, too. But Marc and JoAnne are here, Charlie is clearly no predator type, and Emma's been such a good sport about all of this wacked-out weekend.

"Okay, if you're sure it's no trouble."

Jack holds my hand, and we head down the front driveway for the car. The evening is crisp and clear—all's right with the world, the evening birds suggest—one of those West Virginia moments that other people have no idea about.

"It's weird I know, Linda, but even with Ekim and all, it feels so right to me, being here."

"Um-hum." I don't want to pop his bubble, to tell him that I still have mixed feelings about the women, about everyone, really—wanting to be with them, feeling welcome by them, but still having a sense I'm observing from the wings. And this Emma/Charlie thing: Why should it bother me? But it does.

When we get to the car, he hugs me and we lean up against my door. He smells like the fire and beer and a faint hint of his shaving lotion. I love the softness of his old cashmere V-neck. When he kisses my forehead, my cheek, gently kisses my lips, I lean in.

"Thanks for coming, for bringing Emma. It's good to have you both here."

I hug him for a moment, reach down for the door handle. I want to say *I'm glad I came*, but the words won't come. "It's been a long day, Jack. A really long day for all of us. Let's decide what we're doing in the morning, okay?"

He holds the door for me. "Whatever you want, babe. We'll figure it out tomorrow."

II. The Hearth

September 17, 2000

Waking up in a hotel in Morgantown on a Monday is a strange sensation. In the first place, Jack is always up before me, but he's still snoring lightly when I look at my phone at 7:16. He never sleeps until seven. In the second place, I'm up by 6:30 on a school/workday myself, so I've overslept, too. I realize that the third and weirdest vibe is that the three of us have never been together in a motel on a Monday morning in West Virginia, ever. No wonder I feel like I'm in some parallel universe watching myself in a movie without a title.

Then it strikes me: It's only the two of us. Emma isn't here. She's at JoAnne's. And Charlie's. She spent the night.

"Jack," I say quietly. He's been startled enough the last few days. When he only settles a bit and doesn't wake up, I ease out of the bed, tiptoe to the bathroom, shut the door with caution. My cell phone light is the only light.

I've saved JoAnne's number, so I call her. She answers on the first ring. "JoAnne?"

"Hello. Is that you, Linda Lee?"

"Yes."

"Why are you whispering?"

"Jack's still asleep. I'm in the bathroom so I won't wake him."

"Oh. Is something wrong?"

"No. Not with us. I was thinking about getting together today?"

"Marc's already trying to arrange golf for the guys. Jack will play, won't he? There's not a thing they can do today for Ekim. The mass will be late tomorrow. They've found some of his relatives who want to get here for it."

"Oh. Tuesday afternoon?" I hadn't heard that last night, or if I did I don't remember. I'd just assumed there'd be a funeral in the morning, and we'd head home after. "I don't think I want to stay here by myself . . ."

"I thought a few of us gals might go out to lunch?"

"You did the hostess thing all day yesterday . . ."

"I'm ready to catch my breath, you know?"

"Don't I." I switch ears. "Say, is Emma still asleep?"

"Those two stayed up half the night and crashed in the family room."

"Oh."

"She's fine, Linda. I checked when I came down."

"I know she is, JoAnne. Everything feels so . . . fractured, though . . ."

"Let me talk to Marc and call you back, okay? Y'all want to come for breakfast?"

"Thanks—no. I'm going to let Jack sleep as long as he can. I'll get some coffee at the restaurant. I'll take my phone."

REGINA
AT THE HOTEL MORGAN, 7:23

Regina drew the first jolt of morning nicotine, her body getting that initial tingle of dizzy delight, her head going woozy in that delicious way.

This was a hotel no-no, but she didn't care, she'd never get caught. She'd done this all over the world, from the days when hotels didn't mind if people smoked in the room. This tiny indulgence was an accepted secret between her and Manny: As long as it was no more than two cigarettes a day, both when he wasn't around, and she never, ever smelled of cigarette smoke, it was their little acknowledged-but-never-spoken-of secret.

The second drag was almost as good as the first. She leaned over the edge of the balcony. Even now, after she'd finished her walk, no one was rustling about. In the pale morning light she had her 7:30 cigarette to herself, the way she liked it. First buzz of the day. She unzipped her warm-up suit jacket a tad, letting the cool morning air hit her chest. She'd put in her healthy five miles. This one morning ciggie-poo was her reward. Tempt the cancer goddesses, see if she cared. Her heart had a mind of its own.

She was insulated in one of the most expensive suites in Morgantown, her doting husband sleeping a room away. This unexpected Ekim bend in the road could not upset their well-ordered sense of control. They knew one another so well. They agreed: Routine was a key to a good marriage. That and cheerfulness. Always be pleasant, that was their motto. Never ever raise your voice. And absolutely do not, in any form, complain about your spouse.

This Ekim nightmare had her a tad shaky, she had to admit. Poor Ekim. How did he get to be such a wreck? She smoked and pictured him stumbling around at the dinner. How had he gotten so—out of control? That night, the last time she'd seen him at the dinner thing, she'd tried to cheer him up, even sat on his lap and flirted with him.

"Gina, Gina, ballerina," he'd laughed. "Give ol' Ekim a kiss." His breath reeked of brown booze—scotch or whiskey or bourbon. Regina didn't drink brown booze or red wine. Teeth, breath, clothes. Poor Ekim—he was so far gone she'd kissed him on both cheeks and skedaddled. She shuddered. Within hours he was in a coma. Now he was dead. How was that even possible?

Regina didn't like surprises. Or messes. Not one bit. And messy surprises—ugh. She shuddered again, drew on her cigarette. Calm. She liked calm. And predictability. Not knowing when the funeral would be, not being certain when they'd be able to head back to Raleigh, not having the right clothes—it was hard to find stylish clothes in her size anyway. Would Morgantown have anything?

And her regular Tuesday hair appointment? She'd miss it. Who could she trust here to do her hair? JoAnne wouldn't know—she did her own hair, curly as a sheep's. If you could call that mess "done." Not too stylish these days, Jo-Jo. Don't lady lawyers need to keep up appearances? Maybe in a little bit she'd call JoAnne to go shopping with her for funeral clothes. That would mean they'd invite Linda Lee, another slight bump on the reliable road—erase that, she called herself Linda these days. Linda Vanderbilt. It was hard to find a place to fit Linda Lee Barbour, she was so approach/avoidance.

Heavens, freshman year Linda Lee wore those awful wheat jeans and bulky sweaters her grannies knit. Hill through and through. Gina had talked to her about everything, back then: clothes and Dennis and her daddy. She'd never been such a chatterbox before or since. Lesson learned. How in the world had Linda Lee Barbour managed to get Jack Vanderbilt to marry her, after she'd turned her back on each and every one of them, like they had cooties or the clap? She was way more put together now, no doubt. How had she ever forgiven ol' Jack for being a two-timing cheat with that townie whore, Simone

D'Espere? Manny would never cheat. Jack had always been a flirt, and Linda Lee was Needy Nellie. The two of them deserved one another. She shook her head: No nasty thoughts, Gina-Girl. Manny would not approve.

Manny had never been much of a sex slave. He'd rather have a candlelight dinner than the action that came after. Which was fine with her nowadays. Back at WVU, well . . . she'd certainly been hot to trot . . . Gina smiled. That part of her history was best left in the past. That's what happened when Linda Lee showed up at this reunion—the women started all that back in the day mess that the guys swore by. The Ekim deal would take care of that, though. It would take over front and center, certainly with the guys, probably with the gals, too. He'd never had a steady lady that Regina knew of. Too bad. He could've been kind of . . . what was the word . . . dapper? Exotic? . . . if he hadn't been such a falling down drunk. Poor guy—when she sat on his lap, he didn't even get a woody.

Regina stubbed her cigarette out in a wad of tissues, walked into the bathroom and flushed it away, brushed her teeth, gargled minty mouthwash, brushed again, gargled again. Washed her hands three times. The ritual made her calmer.

Manny wouldn't be up for another hour. Up late with international calls. Had to have his beauty rest. This was her no-man's-time, exercise and grooming time, so she'd have on her face before he saw her first thing. Her skin was still taut, thanks to the care she took, but she'd never hesitate to get a little lift if it came to that. She pinched her cheek. Still had good tone, good natural color. Pretty damn good. She'd taken care of herself.

Before she got in the shower, while she was checking her nails, Regina eased over to Manny's dresser, where he'd put his wallet, money clip, and rings before bed. Every day he was home, she checked his wallet and took a bit of cash from the money clip—all part of her morning ritual. She didn't need the cash, what with the money he socked in her account. He knew she took it—it was part of their routine. A little mischief. And Regina wouldn't want to be caught short. Manny wouldn't want her to be caught short. It would reflect on him.

The shower was as hot as she could stand it. Face first, with her cleanser she could only buy at the Nordstrom's counter. The travel size should last—what if she ran out? Not gonna happen. Under the hot spray, like a robot, she did her underarms, legs—zippety do dah. She used a dib of her facial cleanser on her V-Jay-Jay. *When we're on vacation, she's on vacation*, "she" as in Her Highness. That always made Manny laugh, her fingers in a V in front of her bush. "Manny knows better than to even try when we're out of town," she'd said the other night at JoAnne's, when the girls had their feet up in the den while the guys smoked cigars out on the patio. Marya looked a bit scandalized. Gina liked that. They were all so self-satisfied and *good.*

She finished up, singing "Will You Still Love Me Tomorrow" in her whisper voice. On the final "to-mor-row" she turned off the water and tucked the white fluffy bath towel around her. The hotel robes were always too big and bulky.

Rubbing herself dry, she missed hugging Nugget, their champagne standard poodle. Every morning, they walked five miles together, mostly around the golf course and down by the lake. She liked her morning routine. So did Nugget. That was another thing—he got sad at the kennel. It was more like a doggy spa, but still he missed her and Manny something terrible. She'd call around nine to let them know—what? That she didn't know when they'd get back? Manny said they'd found Ekim's sister out in Seattle—Seattle?—and she gave him the brother's address, still somewhere in Charleston. She hadn't half paid attention to what he was saying. Today she'd get it straight.

Fortunately, her hair still looked perky and shiny, but she didn't want to push it. JoAnne would know somebody who'd know somebody. She finished her face—tadah!—and tugged on her white silk blouse and black slacks. Still half an hour before Manny got up. Quiet as a shadow, Regina tied a cream-colored cardigan around her shoulders, stuck the cash in her small Coach bag, and left the suite.

The Hotel Morgan's coffeeshop was old-people staid and formal— she could've been eighteen again, it had changed so little since she used to come shopping with her mama and sister and stop in for an ice cream. Manny's business accounts took him all over the world, and she'd waited for him all over the world. Not that she only sat and waited. No—she took Portuguese lessons in Rio, Spanish and tango lessons in Buenos Aires, pastry-making and French lessons in Paris, and chocolate-molding and more French lessons in Belgium. She could wait in any number of languages. But she always got the morning paper in English, for American news and the crossword.

"Hey, Baby Doll. Don't you look gorgeous today?" Manny kissed her on the cheek, so he wouldn't muss her hair or lipstick and sat across from her at the table for four. His face smelled so yummy—Bleu de Chanel. He'd been using it now for what, almost ten years, ever since she gave it to him that Christmas? Before he could unfold his napkin, the good-looking waiter had a cup of coffee in front of him. "Thanks. Nothing else for me this morning."

"Yes sir."

What was that lilt? Jamaican? So sensual, like a comfy wave in the Bahamas. Gina smiled: Sex on the Beach. That was a drink. Not one of hers, but she liked the name. Nope, she'd order something simple, gin and tonic, vodka and a twist of lime. Something cool and fresh, without all that sugar and mess. She put her paper aside, tucked the mechanical pencil back in her bag. Manny had given her that pencil, with her initials, for her puzzles. She and Manny never ate breakfast—just tea for her, coffee for him.

"You sleep okay?" He sipped his black coffee. Manny made this little sippy sound when he drank his morning coffee. He didn't make it with any other beverage any other time.

"You know me—I sleep, then I don't sleep, then I sleep some more." Manny slept like he took sleeping pills, eight hours, she could bank on it. Nothing worried Manny or caused him to lose sleep. Nothing.

"You look like a hundred-dollar bill, Gina."

"You too." Manny was always the best-groomed man in any crowd, one of his ways of standing out from others. Had they had a senior superlative at his high school, best groomed?

"More coffee, sir?" That lilt again, so sexy. Manny shook his head no.

"Want to go with me to light a candle for Ekim this morning?" he asked.

"Sure. Maybe we could check with Father What's-His-Name about the service?"

"Father Ambrose? He said day after tomorrow, I guess that's tomorrow now. In the late afternoon."

"So we won't leave here for a couple more nights? I need to call about Nugget."

"Right. We'll have a send-off after the service. We won't want to drive after that."

"At the church?"

"Hell no. Some of us are looking into the Country Club. Or Cheat Mountain Club. Ekim would never want some punch and ham biscuit send-off."

"I see." She wiped the corner of her lips with the cloth napkin, didn't want to muss her lipstick. "JoAnne'll probably want to have it at her house. She is *so* Betty Crocker these days." Gina twinkled a smile so Manny would know she wasn't being catty. "Good to see Linda Lee, though—Jack's sure happy."

"The daughter seems nice."

"Um-hum." Gina knew Manny had no idea what the girl's name was. He probably couldn't pick her out in a line-up of four teenage girls. He wasn't at all interested in the guys' children.

Manny leaned forward, took her hand from the table. "Are you worried? 'Cause Ekim's the first of us to go?"

She put on her serious face. He was spooked, dear ol' Manny—leave it to him to express the obvious. No doubt they were all spooked. "I know. We're all on edge, I guess. Not exactly the reunion Marc planned."

"So let's get to church and then we'll see what the others are doing."

JoAnne had given Regina the numbers she needed, and Regina had her hair and nails done. Manny dropped her off at the salon and afterwards she took a taxi to meet JoAnne and Linda Lee for a late lunch, feeling more like herself than she had all day. The stylist had directed her to a boutique down the street, and they had a perfect black silk dress in petite zero that fit like it was made for her; the sales gal said it was French sizing. She almost didn't even try it on. Plus the snazzy new black heels with the toe cleavage. She'd look trés chic at the service. She'd add that Hermes scarf for color. Voila.

She finger-waved hello to JoAnne and Linda Lee across the restaurant, both brightening when they saw her. "I hope y'all ordered without me. I'm not all that hungry."

"No, we waited," JoAnne said, patting the empty chair beside her, signaling the waiter to bring more wine. Linda nodded hello. "Linda's only been here a few minutes herself."

"And don't you look like the first rose of summer," Linda said, all pleasant. That was Linda: pleasant. All "I'll be your best friend" until one day, "Wham, Bam, no thank you ma'am." For what? A guy? For how long? Over thirty years.

Regina smiled her big smile. "Where's that daughter of yours, Linda Lee? I thought she'd be joining us. Emma, is it?" Regina prided herself on being excellent with names and faces.

"She went with Charlie to track down some musicians he wants her to meet."

"Those two have hit it off," JoAnne added.

Regina noticed that Jo's hair was a bit tamer today. Maybe she had a blow drier after all.

"Yeah, Emma's easygoing. She's fit right in," Linda said.

Now that she was closer, Gina could see that Linda's face looked a tad strained. Maybe she and Jackie-boy weren't as hunky-dory as they acted.

Linda picked up her water glass, smiled again. "She certainly doesn't get that from me. I'm the one who's worried about her missing school."

Regina tipped her glass toward Linda. "You *were* a bit of a worry wart back in the day, when it came to school." She took a sip of her water. "What about Marya? And Annette?"

JoAnne looked around, shrugged. "I invited them, but they said they were going shopping. They might stop by to see if we're still here later. . ." She shrugged again, a "Who knows"? "Marc had to go into court for a few hours."

"I went with Manny to church first thing, not for mass—to light a candle and talk to the priest—"

They all looked at one another, Ekim no doubt running through everyone's minds.

"And then he dropped me off at the salon. He didn't tell me what he was up to. Just that he'd see me later at your house." She tipped her glass toward JoAnne.

Thank goodness we didn't get off on Ekim again, Gina thought. What more was there to say?

"I think he and Jack made plans. They're tracking down some of their old stomping grounds," Linda offered.

"Memory lane. The guys never get enough of that," JoAnne added.

They ordered salads—Regina asked for a gin and tonic—JoAnne and Linda ordered glasses of white wine. This waiter had to be sixty if he was a day, Gina noticed. Life had not dealt him a particularly good hand. She gave him her understanding face. Imagine being his age and waiting tables.

A silence settled as they unfolded their napkins and took sips of water.

JoAnne spoke, "Linda, we know what Jack's been up to. What about you? Besides being a mom and a nursing supervisor? He told us about that the other night. I mean, what about you-you?"

Linda reached for her water glass again, took another sip, shook her head like she was saying no. "It's nursing administrator," she smiled. "That's about it. I paint, still." They didn't speak while the waiter served the drinks.

"You were so good. I thought you'd do something with your art," Regina prodded.

"That was never in the cards. But I still love it. And I belong to the local art group. How about you, Regina?"

"Me?" Regina took the first swallow of her drink. That tingle— almost as good as her cigarette. "I never was a rec director on a cruise ship . . ." She stifled a giggle.

JoAnne interrupted, "Like that's what you really wanted."

"You got married to Manny pretty fast after I left?" Linda asked.

"No. Actually, JoAnne got married before I did," she looked over at JoAnne, who nodded. "I came back and finished my rec degree. Manny was already finished and working for this import/export start-up, making good money. We saved, paid for the wedding . . . my daddy wouldn't pay a nickel . . . and as soon as I finished, I joined him in Brazil."

"Brazil?" Linda's voice went up on "zil," clearly impressed.

"Rio first, yeah. Then Argentina—Buenos Aires. By then he was chief of sales for all North and South America for his company—

heavy-duty responsibility, but they were new, then, and he always was a go-getter—so I tagged along."

"Sounds glamorous."

"Sounds more glamorous than it was. I spent lots of time in hotel suites and executive apartment buildings—they're all pretty much the same from place to place. Seems weird now—I'd only ever stayed in the Hotel Morgan with Mama before Manny."

The salads arrived and they each took a few bites. Regina noticed that Linda didn't use dressing—one way she stayed slim, probably.

"I learned to play tennis, believe it or not. I played a *lot* of tennis." Regina dipped her lettuce in the dressing on the side.

"No golf with Manny?" Linda asked.

"My daddy always said it wasn't a sport if you hit a ball that was just setting there, still, waiting to be hit. Nope, Manny plays golf—almost as much as he works. Sometimes I think he has an office at the golf course—has his secretary follow him around in the cart."

"Marc's always been a workaholic, too," JoAnne agreed. "Ever since law school."

"What about you," Linda turned to JoAnne. "Breaking into law when you did, it must've taken all your waking hours, too?"

"It's not the same for a civil servant"—JoAnne held her wine-glass up and the waiter nodded. "And I was always a better student than Marc. It came easier for me. But true, still, being a woman and a mom, it was hard."

"Tagging all over the world after Manny," said Gina, her voice smirky, "Now there's a tough job."

Linda shrugged, turned back to JoAnne, eyebrows raised.

"Working with the indigent, a legal aid lawyer doesn't have to put in all those billable hours like a young attorney trying to make partner."

"So that's what Marc did?" Linda asked.

"He tried that route. Then he decided to go into practice for himself, which was even worse, from my point of view, in terms of his time with me and young Marc. That boy got the worst of it from both sides, I'm afraid."

"Gina—you probably know all this," Linda turned her way again, apologetic.

"Nope, Manny and I had been out of it, pretty much, too, for a long time, until the last few years. Especially after the company expanded to Europe. We've only been back in the States permanently for four or five years. Just before his mother died. I don't know much more than you know."

"Oh." Linda sipped her fresh glass of wine. "I figured you and JoAnne stayed close."

"We stayed in touch. It wasn't like we didn't keep up . . ."

"Christmas letters and all that," JoAnne added.

"But in terms of actually *being* here . . . Manny's been back to Morgantown to visit a lot more than I have."

Linda looked from one to the other. "You're so natural together, like . . ."

"The last couple of years we've made a point of . . ." JoAnne and Regina looked at one another, JoAnne tailing off. "Were you going to tell her? I'm sorry."

"Well I guess I have to, now," Regina looked down, fingers twisting her napkin, looked back up and smiled at JoAnne. "It's okay, you're right." She patted JoAnne's hand.

"What?" Linda Lee looked from one to the other.

"I had a heart thing a few years ago . . ."

"A heart thing?" Linda stared at Regina.

"Actually, a heart attack. Or a couple of tiny heart attacks, is what the doctor ended up saying."

"You did?" Linda gawked. "Good grief—you know Jack had a heart attack, right? It scared me to death. And I'm a nurse!"

"Uh-huh. Mine was before his." Gina had NOT intended to get all serious, but here it was.

Linda sipped her wine. "Damn. I'm so sorry."

"Manny had been out of town for a couple of weeks. I hadn't been feeling too good, like I'd had some kind of bug, you know, but I was fighting it."

"Women aren't allowed to be sick," JoAnne shook her head.

"So Manny and I were out to dinner with clients . . . like I said, he'd only been back a couple of days, and he had to tie up some lose ends of this major deal . . . these top guys had flown in from Pittsburgh, so it was me and these guys and Manny in a private room...

I'd ordered a salad as an entrée, because I didn't have any appetite . . . still blaming it on some bug . . . and my shoulder started to feel sore. I hadn't played tennis in a week or so, cause of feeling off, you know, so I pretty much sat there like a stump and smiled every other minute like the village idiot wondering why my shoulder hurt."

"Were you nauseous?"

"Not then. It was mostly the shoulder and the lack of appetite." She smiled. "I've never had a big appetite." She nodded toward her barely touched salad. "I made it through dinner, but in the car going home, I told Manny I felt pretty bad. He said he could tell something was wrong, thought maybe I just didn't like the two assholes he'd had for dinner. But he knew I'd never act unpleasant around business associates, even if they were pompous jerks, but it wasn't like me to be so quiet. He wanted to drive to the hospital right then and there, but I told him I needed to get home and get to bed, I felt so tired."

"Oh, Gina, . . ." Linda said.

"I know. Stupid, huh?" Regina shook her head. Linda was looking like maybe she meant it. "Anyway, I woke up sick as snot in the middle of the night, my shoulder throbbing, my back hurting, dry heaves. Manny drove me to the ER, and sure enough, I was having a mini heart attack—the doc said it looked like I'd already had one earlier, too. They prepped me for surgery right then and there, and forty-five minutes later I had a stint. I watched the catherization—85% blockage, they said. And me weighing 93 pounds. Can you believe it?"

"Did your daddy have heart trouble?" JoAnne asked.

"You mean did he have a heart?" She shook her head. "No. No heart problems that I know of. But all of Mama's people did. They were big as bulldozers. And never exercised except to go from the sofa to the fridge." Regina shrugged. "Go figure. Anyway, they kept me in ICU three days. I thought they were gonna have to put Manny in with me, he was such a wreck."

"No doubt." JoAnne smiled. "He's your puppet," she sang.

"I know." Regina shook her head. "He's a mess. Still treats me like I'm made of porcelain. Or Blenko glass."

"He always did." Linda agreed. *Was that a wee bit of the old green monster in her voice?* Gina wondered.

"So lots of tennis. And I walk every day. Not so much tango—I took lessons, but Manny never did. And I volunteer at the hospital's NICU three mornings a week."

"That's pretty great." Linda looked relieved.

"Rocking these poor tiny sick babies. Touching little teensy toes. Every now and then patting scared moms and dads on the back, though I much prefer the babies."

"That's so sad," Linda looked directly at Regina, her own eyes shiny, "when one of them doesn't make it."

"I don't think I could do that," JoAnne said. "But I'll bet you're good at it."

"It's not a big deal. I mean, it's not like they're mine." She took her time with her drink, looked over at JoAnne. "But you, you make the world a better place, one poor destitute person at a time." Regina wasn't being snide—okay . . . maybe just a teensy bit, secretly snide.

"It's the only aspect of law that's ever interested me." JoAnne looked uncomfortable. "Remember when we tutored those poor kids, Linda?"

"How could I forget?"

"Yeah, you two were always gonna save the world." Regina hadn't meant to blurt. She was NOT a blurter. But that had slipped out. Those two had been so damn serious about stuff like "the meaning of life," instead of just living, for crap's sake.

"Making people happy isn't such a bad ambition, Regina." JoAnne the sensible one, ever making things right. "You would've made a great airline stewardess—or rec director on a cruise ship—or the person at the old peoples' home who gets them up and active. I can see you leading the sing-along. And you're still so . . ."

"Perky," Linda filled in.

"Thanks. Perky. I've spent my adult life trying to get over being cute . . . so I guess I can live with perky." So what was she expecting? Dynamic? Irresistible? Classy? She held her glass up to Linda as if to propose a toast. "Keep those goals high, right? My daddy was determined I wasn't going to be some glorified babysitter."

Linda started to interrupt, no doubt insist she'd meant perky as a compliment. Regina charged on. "That's what he thought of teaching. Or a bedpan dumper, better known as a nurse." She raised her eyebrows at Linda. "His words. Nope, he thought if I wasn't going to be an engineer then I'd thrown my education—and his money—down the tubes. So now I sing lullabies to other peoples' babies. For free. How's that for irony?"

JoAnne and Linda shook their heads. *That shut 'em up,* Gina thought. No Daddy Dearest dirty laundry here at this classy restaurant, with these squeaky-clean ladies. Uh-uh.

"You should be proud, Gina. Not many people can do that," Linda reached in her direction, but Regina wasn't about to do that touchy/feelie do-gooder stuff.

Linda dropped her hand on the table. "He didn't know you very well."

"Now that's the truest words spoken today." Regina pushed her salad plate away, pointed toward her empty glass and the waiter nodded. Let's just turn the corner on this thought. "Guess in a way I have been a glorified babysitter," she grinned.

JoAnne and Linda looked puzzled.

"Manny? A big baby?" They laughed, nervous and awkward. Gina wanted to stop being so damn serious.

Linda asked, all quiet-like, "Do you ever wish you'd had children?"

Ooops. Serious alert. That HAD to come up, like death and taxes. "Lord no. Manny's all a woman could handle." She grinned her female conspiratorial grin, took a sip of her fresh gin and tonic. Babies. She'd seen way more than her share of pitiful, helpless, needy babies. Nope, not in the cards for her. Talk about an old, worn-out subject.

"Jack wanted more than one." Linda offered.

Phew. Subject changed. "I guess you were pretty far along in terms of your nursing career by the time he showed up again."

"Showed up is right. Out of the blue."

"Why didn't you tell him to go bite himself?" Regina asked.

"Now that's a term I haven't heard in a while," JoAnne laughed. All three laughed, this time without the edge.

"I don't know." Linda Lee looked puzzled.

"Really? Come on. It would've been easy to tell him hell no after what he did to you." Regina was feeling feisty now after her two gins. Maybe she'd have a third. Why not?

"Well, I have to admit I was curious . . . how did he look? Was he fat and bald, down on his luck?" Gina was pleased Linda had loosened up a tad. Not exactly the old Linda Lee, but still.

"Jack Vanderbilt? Not hardly." JoAnne the realist, Madam Legalistic.

"And was he miserable? Or an asshole?"

"Now you're talking, sister," Gina added.

"Curiosity killed the cat." Linda shrugged, a guilty look on her face. Gina had to admit that she was attractive, even pretty; she couldn't take that away from her. In that pretty but not all-that-glamorous way, sorta feminist casual. Hair, eyes, skin—all fine. Neither Jo or Linda was particularly polished, she noted, though they both dressed well.

"You're right, Gina," she went on. "Being all that curious was probably only part of it, if I'm honest with myself. And you two."

"Tell!" Regina said.

"So," she took a deep breath, "I had this meanie idea, maybe I'd do to him what he'd done to me."

"Oooh la la—human," JoAnne said.

"I'm not exactly proud of that sentiment."

"And honest," Gina tacked on.

"So put all that together: Curiosity, a need for long-overdue revenge, and plain ol' female sixth sensitivity, something about unfinished business. I couldn't say no." Linda looked relieved, like she'd admitted she'd cheated on an exam and was grateful to finally get it off her chest.

Ah, Gina, thought, *Now she's talking*. This might get juicy. "How many times did that get me in trouble, not being able to say no?" Regina laughed.

"Especially with Dennis What's-His-Name?" JoAnne looked pleased.

Startled, Linda said, "Now there's a blast from the past." She shook her head in Gina's direction, looking almost girlish. "Truly. You were so crazy ga-ga over him."

"Let's just say crazy and leave it at that."

"But you chose Manny . . . which has turned out pretty great?"

"Indeed I did. But I have to admit it hasn't *all* been easy. His mama thought her baby boy, Manny, was the Angel Gabriel and the Lord Jesus all rolled into one."

"Spoiled?" JoAnne raised her eyebrows.

"Spoiled? He was incubated in spoiled, more so than those little NICU babies I rock." Regina shook her head. "His mama thought he could do no wrong." She rattled her ice cubes. "But you know what? He adored his mama and she adored him, and somehow for all that preferential treatment, he turned out pretty sweet."

"He spoils you, too, doesn't he?" Linda asked.

"Some women might say that."

"Emma said, after the dinner, that you two look like you're still dating."

"Manny always was the romantic." Truer words. He was not a thing like Denny. Whiz, bam, thank you ma'am. That song, "Smoothe Operator," flashed into her brain. That was so Denny. When it came out in London she had to go out and buy it that very day. Her little private pleasure.

JoAnne laughed, "Except that one night at Cheat Mountain."

Linda laughed, too, but Regina was confused for a moment. What night? Manny never let his guard down. Not in public.

"Come on, Gina—when he was voted Man of the Year and you were named SweetHeart?"

Gina's eyes opened wide. "THAT night!" She could see it now— plain as day. What a disaster—Manny passed out in his own mess. No wonder she'd pushed it out of her head. No wonder they never relived that gross night.

Linda shook her head. "That was the last formal I went to with Jack . . . before . . ."

"Right. The Spring Formal. I've blotted that out of my mind, 'cause it's so not a thing like us!" She'd raised her voice the slightest bit. That wouldn't do.

"Cause Manny was blotto." JoAnne said. "Remember? He passed out on the floor in the bathroom, and nobody could open the door? So the guys left him there?"

"Oh my gosh—I had to spend the night with you and Marc? And he was sick as a dog when he woke up the next morning?"

"The guys tell that story like Manny's some kind of overachieving party animal," JoAnne adds.

JoAnne and Linda laugh like it's the funniest thing since *Laugh-In*.

"I broke up with him after that," Gina reminded them—and herself. She'd gone back to Denny for a while, but he was such a user . . . "And a few weeks later . . ."

"You left. Without a word." JoAnne had turned to Linda, serious now.

"I didn't have a hint that Jack Vanderbilt had deep dark dirty secrets he was going to spring on me." Linda sounded defensive.

"And I thought Manny was out of my life forever." Gina didn't want this get-together to go south, all serious. Who needed that? Manny would be mortified to think the women were talking about him wasted, out of it, passed out on some bathroom floor. Didn't they already have Ekim dead? Wasn't that more than enough serious? "Manny would hate it if he ever heard the guys tell that story. It's so not Manny."

"It's like some guy code—Never Let Another Guy See that Something Hurts," JoAnne said. "After that awful night, Marc told me Manny hung around the fraternity, took his exams, pretty much kept to himself after you broke up with him. He was a pathetic, whipped puppy."

"But then the Jack/Linda Lee/Simone D'Espere mess topped the charts," Regina said with a giggle.

"Good to know my misery did somebody some good!" Linda shut her eyes for a second, opened them and looked at Regina and JoAnne. "Things sure can change in the blink of an eye, can't they?"

"Yep, look at Ekim," JoAnne said, patting Linda's hand.

"Not Manny." Gina smiled, feeling a tad buzzed. These gals needed to lighten up. He was steady Eddy, had never messed up once since that awful night. "Like I said, he still treats me like his baby doll."

"And here we are, back in Morgantown, together—who'd a thunk it?"

"JoAnne!"

They turned toward the sound.

Marya scurried up to the table. Regina looked at her and thought, *She could use some of my facial products. Why in the world would she put up with those wrinkles? She looks ten years older than the rest of us. What's she got to worry about? Maybe I should say something . . .*

"Get me a wine list. Right this second," Marya said to the startled waiter. "Please!"

"Yes ma'am."

Linda looked off balance, confused, "What? What's wrong?"

"You will never believe who I saw on the altar guild at the church just now. NEVER." She grabbed the wine list from the waiter. "This is it?" The list only had a few selections of wine, on one side of the page. "Good grief. I need to talk to your buyer." She pursed her lips and gazed at the page. "Ah! Thank goodness there's one Sancerre—I'd like the Sancerre Sauvignon Blanc, please, and make sure it's chilled."

"Of course. A glass, ma'am?"

"Good grief no—a bottle." Marya pulled a chair up and sat. "Let me get my breath."

"Manny and I were there this morning . . ."

"I know. We talked to Father Ambrose," Marya, her eyes still wide, held up one hand as she calmed herself, the other hand resting on her chest. She nodded yes when the waiter showed her the bottle, then waited for him to open it, pour a bit in her glass. She took her time twirling it, sticking her nose down in the bowl of the wineglass, and tasting. Regina felt like she'd pop.

"Fine," she told him. "You all having any? Bring them fresh glasses." The man hurried off.

Marya sure could boss people around. Regina finished her gin, nodded yes for wine. She couldn't have her second cigarette until after four, that was the rule, but boy was she wishing she could duck into the ladies' room right this second. Or maybe in a minute, after Marya finally told them whatever she was going to tell them. This lunch just got way more interesting.

"There's no easy way to say this." She eyeballed Linda. "Simone D'Espere—I mean, Simone Vanderbilt." She shook her head, like she couldn't stand what she was saying. "You know she's kept the name Vanderbilt, right? Even though she's been married at least twice since Jack?" Marya stopped, caught her breath, sipped her wine.

Linda was pale. *Now this is quite the shuffle of the cards,* Gina thought. No wonder Marya was breathless. The waiter poured wine in everyone's glass.

"We'll need another bottle," Marya said. He nodded and backed away. Marya could take over a situation, that much was clear.

"Where's Annette? Weren't y'all together?" JoAnne interrupted, maybe trying to shift the subject. Probably cause Linda Lee looked like she'd been hit by a rock.

Regina knew she was going to feel a second glass of wine, since she was already a bit tipsy, but she wouldn't say no. That was one advantage of the years in South America and Europe—people drank wine any time, day or night.

"She took off with Johnny after we made all the final arrangements. Johnny insisted on buying a new suit for Ekim to be buried in." Marya took a sip from her glass. "That is such a good wine."

"He would," said JoAnne.

"Anyway, I got here as fast as I could. I was afraid I'd miss you."

Linda still hadn't spoken. Regina sipped her wine and looked at her for clues, but she'd composed a poker face. Maybe the wine would loosen her up. This was what—her third glass?

"You would know her in a second if you saw her." Marya looked at each of them, serious as if she were announcing the lottery winner. "The only thing different is her hair—it's short, kind of in this angled "V" toward her face, very flattering—but otherwise she's the same. Still tiny, blond. That would have to be dyed now, right? She's fighting to look young, you know? I'll bet she's had a boob job."

JoAnne nodded agreement. "She was a few years younger than we were . . ."

"Right, but still she has to be pushing fifty. And she looks . . . like somebody gave her a free pass on aging." Marya shook her head. "How unfair is that?"

"She never had any children except young Jack," JoAnne said. "Having that second . . ."

"He's not called young Jack. At least . . . that's not what Jack calls him. Or me." Linda spoke quietly, slowly, as if each word were costing her.

JoAnne shrugged. "All I knew was he was named for Jack."

"Jack calls him Jay. That's all we've ever called him. Jay."

"Do you and Jack see him often?" Gina asked. Juicy as it was, there was no point in hammering Linda any more with this Simone D'Espere update.

"That woman walked right up to me and hugged me, like we were long lost friends," Marya continued, "and said how sorry she was about Ekim. Guess nobody ever told her about personal space."

"No kidding." JoAnne still looked stunned.

Linda shook her head no.

Regina said, "Oh," and looked back at Marya. "I've never seen her."

Now she really did need to go to the ladies' room, but she wasn't about to miss a word Marya was saying.

"She's one of the women who'll prepare the altar for the service, the Altar Guild, so Father Ambrose wanted them there. Don't ask me why. Maybe cause nobody in the church knew Ekim or any of his relatives, and they won't get here soon enough to make plans."

"Simone D'Espere's in the Altar Guild?" JoAnne raised her eyebrows.

"I know." Marya laughed. "Go figure. She's the last person I would've expected to see at the church. Last I heard of her . . ."

"Excuse me just a minute, okay?" Linda stood and pushed her chair back. "I'm going to the ladies'."

"I'll come with you," Regina offered, standing, too. Maybe being off balance, right much wine under her belt, Linda Lee might loosen up a little, say something about her and Jack and Simone D'Espere.

JoAnne interrupted. "It's a single. Only one stall." She'd suggested this restaurant, so Regina figured she knew the lay of the land. Damn.

"You go ahead, then, Linda Lee. I'll wait." Regina sat down again and leaned forward while Linda walked toward the back of the room.

". . . she had married some hundred-year-old man who was at death's door, for his money," Marya continued.

"Sounds about right," JoAnne added. JoAnne was the only one who still lived in Morgantown, but she was the least likely to tell girl stories, or gossip. "I always wondered why she and her twin both stayed here, what kept them coming back."

"Her twin, too?" Regina asked.

"Yeah. She married some one-armed man from California, I think somebody said he was a psychiatrist, and as soon as that ended, she was back here in Morgantown, too."

Jo shook her head, her disapproval easy to read. "Those two gals were their own Morgantown soap opera."

"I'm surprised she even remembered me, for God's sake," Marya went on. "I mean, Paulo hung out with Jack a lot, but I rarely saw Simone D'Espere after that baby was born."

JoAnne smirked. "I saw plenty of her. Or should I say plenty of the baby and Jack, not her. Jack would bring him over around supper time, and I'd end up feeding them both." Her voice dripped disapproval. "According to Jack, she never cooked a single meal the whole time they were married."

"That wasn't that long." Marya added. "Shhh . . . maybe we should hold out on the details." She nodded her head toward Linda, moving back toward the table.

Linda rejoined them, lipstick fresh, smile pasted on. "What did I miss?"

"Manny and I spent a lot of time with Jack and Simone." Regina had their full attention now. Perhaps she'd overserved herself a bit. She made sure to sit up straight and speak clearly.

"You did?" Linda took a sip of wine as soon as she sat down.

"By then I'd decided Manny was the one for me . . . after that summer . . . so when we got back to school in September, I accepted his pin, remember?" She looked at JoAnne for approval. Linda twisted her wine glass while Gina continued. "Seemed like I was the only one of us who didn't have to study that much, once I got out of science and into Phys Ed. Let's just say all you guys were more studious, so seems like I only saw you at the House my last two years. And Manny and Jack hung out a lot while she was pregnant, before the baby came. Jack almost never spent time at their apartment."

Linda was watching Regina, like she'd opened some dark magic kit and was making things disappear and reappear.

"I kinda liked her, to tell you the truth. She never put on any airs. And there she was pregnant—and a townie—around all of us college girls." Regina kept on.

Linda looked startled.

"Well I did. I mean, it's not like you were giving us the time of day." Sometimes, when she'd had a bit more to drink than usual, she could get a teensy little edge. Especially if Manny wasn't around. She maintained control around Manny. Gina could tell this was getting to Linda—hadn't she clammed up like a nun at an orgy when Marya brought up Simone D'Espere?—but she couldn't stop herself. Linda Lee cut them all off without so much as a word. She could take a little heat. She'd keep her tone normal, light, though. Avoid unpleasantness.

"I thought she could barely speak English." Marya said.

"Don't be silly. She could speak English—she just had that accent that the guys drooled over. We'd drive out to Cooper's Rock or go to the Greek's . . . This one time, she came in after we'd all ordered, and she reached over for one of Jack's French fries, and he said, 'Get your own damn fries,' real angry-like. I'll never forget that cause I'd never seen Jack act so . . . impolite."

"Simone D'Espere brought out the worst in him," Marya added, pouring herself more wine. She offered the bottle around, but Linda and JoAnne shook their heads no.

Regina nodded yes. "A splash more, please."

"Paulo's told that story about Jack and the French fries at least a hundred times, I think, to let me know how lucky I am. He'd never snap at me like that. He knows better."

Regina smiled. "Our guys are certainly the sweeties, Marya, no doubt about it."

"Jack's a gentleman, too," Linda said, her voice quiet.

The others laughed. "Of course he is," Regina added. "He always was. That's why that one time was so hilarious."

"He did drag that baby around a lot, you have to admit," Marya said.

JoAnne nodded agreement. "He hardly ever came to the house for parties that year, and when he did he came by himself."

"Well most guys wouldn't bring their pregnant wife to a fraternity party. That would be . . . awkward." Gina knew she should drop it, but this was the most alive she'd felt all day. "Did I tell y'all that she flirted with Manny? I didn't care. He was kind of freaked—you know Manny—that this pregnant gal, who was actually Jack's wife, would be flirting—like it was gross, some mortal sin."

"You've never had to worry about Manny," Linda said.

"Not for a second."

Linda drank a large sip of wine, held her glass toward Marya. "I guess that means Simone D'Espere will be at the funeral." Her voice was normal now, but Regina could tell that she was off guard about the possibility of running into Simone D'Espere.

Marya poured the wine. "Seems like."

"I've never met her, never even seen her except in pictures," Linda added, looking at each of them. "But it sounds like after Jack and I broke up, things changed for all of us. I mean, not just me."

Regina pushed her chair back. "You said it, not me. Now will y'all 'scuse me, please." She would not let her wicked side take over; she would walk slowly, carefully, to the ladies' room. And she would not rush her afternoon cigarette. She'd wait until she was back at the hotel. But she had to have a breath to herself, or she'd explode. Thank heaven for gin and white wine. All this talking and remembering and talking. And Linda getting so . . . what? Sad-like? . . . 'cause she told that story about Jack and Simone D'Espere? Linda Lee was the one who snubbed them. Hadn't they been writing her and calling her and trying hard as hell to let her know they cared about her, not Simone D'Espere? She wasn't some prodigal daughter. She had no business acting all hurt about this thing. She left. If talking about all that made her uncomfortable, so what? She'd made her choice about their friendship crystal clear. Regina pushed the door into the ladies' room. So what if seeing Simone upset her? Hadn't they all worried about seeing *her* again, after all these years, after she'd snubbed every single one of them? So much for female bonding.

She wouldn't smoke. She wet a paper towel, put it up to her temples. That was cool. She would not have a headache here. Manny knew about the headaches, but the gals didn't. Sometimes she got so sick with a headache that she had to go to the hospital so they could knock her out and give her IV fluids. She could not, would not have a headache here. The damp towel helped. A cigarette would help, too, a lot, but she would wait. It was too early. She'd eat a bite of roll, that's what she'd do. And order hot tea. Earl Gray. That always helped.

This Linda Lee thing had her a tiny bit off balance. She was trying. Let bygones be bygones. They were all strangers, polite strangers—but they weren't really strangers. They had history; the guys had history. What did they have? Memories. A few memories. Okay. Feelings? Connections? Linda Lee had been her friend. She'd thought she was her friend. Now, all these years later, what was she trying to prove? That they could pick up where they left off and be all close? Regina found her lipstick in her bag, added a fresh layer. Pinched her cheeks.

There. No headache. Still her cigarette to look forward to in a bit. She touched the hard pack of Virginia Slims in her purse.

When Regina got back, the waiter was putting the bill folders by their plates. She wouldn't order tea. But the rolls were there, untouched. Poor guy. Leave him a sizable tip. Make his day.

She served herself a roll while the other three women continued to jabber about . . . what? No butter, just a few bites of dry bread. She'd be good to go. She smiled and let them talk around her while she chewed, slowly, tiny bite by tiny bite.

Back at her house, JoAnne was bustling about starting a fire. "Who wants more wine? Coffee? Something else?"

"I won't say no," Marya responded.

"I'm afraid I don't have a Sancerre, but I do have a pretty good Helfrich Pinot Gris in the wine cooler. A 2008."

"I'm crazy about that! Perfect!"

"And Gina, I know you don't do red."

"Thanks, Jo. Pinot Gris's great." Regina petted the dog while Linda and Marya bustled around trying to help. "I love your sweet Golden. Makes me miss my Nugget," she called to the kitchen. *When were the guys going to get back?* she wondered She walked over to the sofa, reached for the magazines on the coffee table. *Monticolas*—JoAnne must've gotten the yearbook?—were stacked there. Three of them. How odd. Gina had never gotten a yearbook—but, then, she hadn't been in any of the clubs, either. JoAnne had been the doer. Hadn't she actually pledged a sorority for a while?

"*Monticolas?* You have *Monticolas?* Did you pull them out for the reunion? Have y'all looked everybody up?" Regina asked, riffling through the pages of the top book. "Were we ever this young and goofy looking? That hair! My God—these people look about twelve years old."

JoAnne set a tray of cheese and crackers and fruit on the other end of the table. "To tell you the truth, I don't remember buying yearbooks—I guess my parents ordered them. They'd come in the mail every summer. I hardly looked at them. Marc dug them out of boxes in the attic after everybody came over the other night. He thought we'd get a kick out of them, the women. Don't ask me why."

"Are any of us in there?" Gina asked.

"The guys are, on the intramural sports pages. And of course the Phi Kap composite. They look like such dorks."

"And there's one of you with the composite, Gina, cause you were Sweetheart. In the junior year there." JoAnne pointed. "And that *awful* one of me and Marc at the Fall Formal." She wrinkled her nose.

"It's like it's not even the same world—they look like little boys. They thought they were so cool. Look at those tacky sports jackets!" Regina held up the fraternity page. "I was pretty cute, though, wasn't I?" She couldn't even remember that fluffy formal.

"And yet so much is the same. Marc called while I was in the kitchen. You'll never guess where the guys have ended up on their memory lane tour."

"I'll bite," said Linda.

"The Olympia!"

"You have got to be kidding!" Regina shrieked. "How many times did we go to the Olympia?"

Marya laughed. "Only every Friday happy hour."

"I didn't start coming till I was going out with Jack," Linda said, turning toward Marya. "But I went once with you, before then. The first time I tasted beer."

"Really? We drank *so* much beer—remember, they sold quarts?" Regina poured herself a glass of wine.

"We'd rally there before the fraternity parties even started, make our plans for the night. Where to start. We'd always plan to end up at Phi Kap, though, remember? They had the best bands."

"I can't believe how much beer I drank back then. How did we do it?"

"We danced for hours—I guess we'd sweat it out!"

"It was so loud we didn't even try to talk."

"Hell no—if anybody talked, it would be one of the guys, telling some outrageous story about how they'd done something stupid like streak across the quad or show up for practice tanked or drive all the way to Pittsburgh for a Primanti sub and right back just to win some stupid bet."

"We gals never did talk, unless we went to the bathroom—and somebody was always in there throwing up."

"I am *not* ready for Emma to go away to college!"

JoAnne shook her head. "It was terrible when Charlie left. It wasn't so bad when young Marc left." She reached for a slice of cheese. "I feel like, with Marky, I was a kind of a 'lick and a promise' mother. I did better with Charlie."

"I'll bet you were super." Linda with the pats. "Jack and I were married a year before I'd even talk about having a baby. Even though I loved him like crazy I had to be sure . . ."

JoAnne interrupted. "When he'd stop by, after y'all started dating again, you were all he could talk about. Marc and I would beg him to bring you to visit . . ."

Linda shook her head.

"I'll bet it was hard for you to believe him . . ." Regina prodded. "Once burned and all that." Enough of the goodie-sweetsie girl stuff. Let's have some dirt!

"I swore to myself I'd never be dependent on a man again, after what he did to me at the end of sophomore year."

Everyone looked at Linda, a bit daunted by the edgy tone in her voice. Oooh-la.

"And I haven't."

"Really?" Marya asked.

"Nope. I've made my own money ever since I started working, and that didn't change when we got married."

"Me too, come to think of it, though I never thought about it in those terms," JoAnne said. "I've always put my salary in savings and bonds, so I guess if I had to, I could be independent." She took a sip of wine. "Of course if Marc ever said he was going to leave me he'd be a dead man."

"Amen to that," Regina laughed. "I could hock my jewelry and live well for the rest of my life!" She flashed her diamond rings, on both hands. "Thank God and all his holy angels. Hey, do you still play guitar, Jo?"

"You'll never believe it, but I do. And Marc's taken up banjo, just this past year. It's kind of a thing we all do together now, with Charlie. Neither of us is a bit good, like Charlie."

"Come on," Linda said, "you were terrific in college. You remember any of the songs we'd sing?"

"Are you kidding—it's like riding a bike. I play right much in the evenings, when Marc's not here. I'm not much of a TV person."

"Me either," Regina agreed. "So why don't you play something for us?"

"Okay. But only if y'all promise to sing, too," she called over her shoulder as she left the room.

Regina was glad that she'd diverted the conversation away from all that independent woman crap, but no way was she going to join some days of yore singalong. Hell, if something happened to Manny, she'd be the richest woman in the room, and she'd never worked for pay for ten minutes since she'd gotten married. Why did they think that making their own money was such a big deal? Hadn't she earned her keep her own way? Hadn't she always been the A+ perfect business wife and homemaker and volunteer?

JoAnne walked back into the room tuning her guitar. "Linda, there was a message on the machine for you. Emma. She said she couldn't get you on your phone; she wanted you to know that she and Charlie would probably stay out until about twelve—they're jamming with some of his music friends. She left a number if you need her."

"Thanks. You know these people, Jo? Are they all right?"

"Will she *never* stop worrying for ten seconds?" Gina asked herself.

"They're great. Mostly old-timers who think Charlie set the moon. Good people."

"Anybody know when the guys are going to join us?" Marya asked.

"Marc said he was going to talk them into going to the Greeks for supper. I don't think we'll see them for a while."

"Y'all want to go out, then? So JoAnne doesn't have to mess with anything?" Regina suggested.

"How about we order in pizza?" Marya asked. "My treat. Does Vito's still deliver, JoAnne?"

"Is the Pope Catholic?" she answered, positioning herself on an ottoman with her guitar. "It'll be like old times."

Gina excused herself. "Y'all mind if I get a breath of fresh air before you start?"

"Go ahead," said Marya. "I'll call for the pizza."

Linda leaned forward, slicing cheese, "I'm going to look a little more at these two *Monticolas*."

"Okay. I'll be right back."

Regina walked down to the lake, to be certain the gals couldn't see her from the glass doors or if one of them came out on the patio looking for her. She used the silver lighter Manny gave her, initialed in fancy script, dated on their silver anniversary—it wasn't the only thing he gave her, by a long shot!—to light her Virginia Slim. All the better because she'd had to wait so long.

Ah—that first puff was heaven, a total relief from all the clatter and chatter and craziness of being back here with these women, waiting to bury ol' Ekim tomorrow. Or was it the next day? She was a little blurry. God she missed Nugget. Drawing on the cigarette, she felt that buzzy boost she loved. She did not want to sing old Pete Seeger protest songs—what a joke. She did not want to eat pizza. She didn't like pizza one bit. Messy, usually greasy, loaded with fat. But she had to eat something, that was a fact. As she smoked she decided: cheese, crackers, grapes. Were there celery sticks on that tray? That would work. And if she had to she'd put a piece of pizza on her plate and poke at it with her fork, that's what she'd do. She stubbed out her cigarette in the moist grass, buried it under some pine needles, and felt around in her purse for her Mentos and lip gloss.

The gals were struggling through "Cruel War" when Regina swooshed back in the glass door. She clapped her hands at them—"I loved that song!"— hurried over to the cheeseboard to put some food in her mouth to hide nicotine breath and also so she wouldn't have to join in the singing. JoAnne could still play and sing, but the other two were kinda gravelly, clearly way out of practice. But sincere. She'd grant them sincere. She'd never been much of a joiner-inner, even when she was in college, but strange enough she'd always felt easy talking to these three gals. They'd struck a nerve back when she was young and stupid and way too trusting. Her first time away from home, her daddy, all that. Talking, talking, talking. She'd told family stories she'd never told before or since. These three had been—what did the kids call it today on the talk shows?—her posse. That's it. We were a posse. She couldn't help but grin at that thought, imagining them all in Dale Evans' outfits.

As they finished the last "Yes, my love, yesssss," holding it out in a victorious long syllable, JoAnne turned toward Regina.

"Come join us. Your turn to pick an oldie."

Gina waved one hand in their direction. "You know I was never much more than a croaker. No, y'all go ahead. I need to snack a bit, and then I'll get the plates and all. Let me just enjoy listening."

Linda said, "You sure?" and then turned to Jo to suggest another song. "How about 'Blowin' in the Wind'? Can you play that?"

As the threesome started harmonizing, Gina scurried to the kitchen, relieved to have something to do. She was thrilled—thrilled!—to have these post-ciggie minutes to herself to enjoy the buzz. They moved on to "Where Have All the Flowers Gone?" Hell, next they'll be howling "We Shall Overcome"; couldn't they sing anything peppier than that? She yelled into the den, "Hey, how's about 'The Night They Drove Old Dixie Down' next?" They probably didn't know all the words. She certainly didn't.

She checked the cabinets and drawers for plates, forks, and napkins. JoAnne was clearly as organized a housekeeper as she was. That didn't surprise Gina. And everything was spic and span, despite the fact that she'd had people in and out for days. The kitchen and bathroom were always the giveaways, and these were spanking clean. Yessiree. Hmmmm; she hadn't seen any house help show up since Friday. Maybe Jo was a tad obsessive. As she was folding the napkins, Gina noticed the small desk nook—probably where JoAnne does her meal planning, she thought. Wonder if she does crosswords? Probably not.

A small silver Golden Retriever figurine was angled at the back by the small stained-glass lamp, behind some of the family pictures. Gina picked up the dog. It was cool in her hands, the face almost smiling—she could tell it was sterling just by the feel, but she checked the silver mark by force of habit. One of the boys probably gave her this for her birthday, or Mother's Day. Maybe Marc ordered it from the back of the New Yorker for their silver anniversary—nah, he wasn't that kind of sentimental guy. JoAnne probably only touched it once a week, when she dusted the desk, but Gina was certain she treasured it. IF she dusted the desk herself. She was bound to have a cleaning service in this big old barn. She set the curio back in its place. Bet some silversmith made that just for JoAnne, when her dog was a pup. From a photograph. Special.

She took the dinner things into the den just as the doorbell was ringing.

"I'll get it," JoAnne called.

"Let me. My treat," Marya yelled over her. Both hurried toward the front hall.

"Need any help?" Linda Lee asked, smiling.

"Nothing to do, really. You could move those books off the table there."

As she picked things up, Linda said in an uncertain voice, "I never drink this much wine. Not even on vacation. I don't know what got into me today . . ."

Regina was glad to hear a bit of hesitation in her voice. Maybe she hadn't grown up to be a feelingless robot after all. "Yeah, must be pretty weird, being back here for the first time in so long, and then Ekim dying."

"Yeah." Linda got up and walked over to stand by Gina. "I'm a nursing administrator, you know, so I'm always on call. Not really, like formally. But still. I want to be ready to go in if they need me. I never was much of a drinker, anyway. I mean, when we go on vacation I'll have a cocktail and a couple of glasses of wine . . ."

Finished with the dishes, Regina crossed her arms, smiled her cocktail party smile at Linda Lee. "We drink wine with dinner every night. Candles. The whole nine yards. We sort of got in the habit, doing so much entertaining for Manny's work."

Rolling her eyes, Linda reached out and tapped Regina on the arm. "Thank heaven Jack does most of his entertaining on the road. Nobody would call me the hostess with the mostess."

Surprised at the shred of self-revelation, Gina looked around the comfy yet stylish room. "JoAnne's clearly got that knocked. I guess with Marc a judge and all . . ."

"And you're right, this has been strange." Linda's voice caught. "At lunch, when you were talking about Jack breaking up with me, about that having an impact on all of you, too . . ."

"Well yeah." Now Regina was the one to poke Linda on the arm, her teensy bit of snideness hard to cover. "What in the world did you think, Linda Lee? I mean, we'd been so close, and then just . . . nothing. Nada."

Shaking her head back and forth, still with a doubtful expression, Linda continued, "I never thought about anybody else hurting."

"I can believe that!" Regina couldn't help but blurt.

Linda reached for her arm, her face almost tender, held onto it. "Really. That's the truth, I swear. You all had each other. And the guys at the House."

"Hell with the guys. We were *friends*!"

Marya and JoAnne walked in jabbering, holding two huge pizza boxes—why in the hell did they order two pizzas?—just as Gina shook off Linda's hand.

"Food's here," Marya called—why not just state the obvious, she thought.

JoAnne said, right behind her, "Everything okay in here?"

"Fine. I've got everything we need, I think," Gina, chipper to reassure JoAnne, hurried to make a place for the pizza boxes. "Why don't we put one of those in the oven?"

Linda stood quietly for a moment, then smiled up at JoAnne. "What can I do? Let me help." She wrapped her arms around one another, held onto her elbows.

"I got four halves of different things, so everybody could have something they'd like," Marya pointed to the boxes. "These smell soooo good. So help yourself. I didn't realize I was about to starve."

JoAnne patted Linda on the shoulder, all maternal. "You can have cleanup, Linda. Thanks." Again the pat. Linda sat on the sofa while JoAnne and Gina got the food and dishes organized.

As Marya and Linda started to serve themselves, Regina asked, "Hey, anybody want water? Let me get us all some water."

"Thanks, Gina. That would be great. I didn't realize I was this hungry, either. Is there a half with sausage?"

Gina headed for the kitchen, grabbing up her pocketbook. She found the fizzy water in the fridge, poured two glasses, made a point of singing "Michael Row the Boat Ashore" loud while she did it.

"Here you go," she said, as she carried those out to Linda and Marya. "I'll be right back with yours, Jo." She was satisfied that all three were sitting down eating.

She prepared the third and fourth glasses, then edged over to JoAnne's desk, with a glance at the open doorway. Quick as a hummingbird, she grabbed the silver dog and stuck it in her purse. *Ahhhhh*—she snapped the clasp. Oh *myyyyyyy*. Her breath got fast, deep.

"Wait a sec, JoAnne. I need to go to the little girls' room," she called, hurrying down the hall to the powder room off the foyer. As soon as she shut the door, she opened her purse, took out the puppy, held it in both hands up near her face. She would take it. Done. JoAnne wouldn't miss it for days—she'd never in a blue moon think one of them had taken it. It would be a mystery. Forever. Maybe she'd fire her cleaning service. She'd never know, but she'd always wonder. Emma had been here a lot. Maybe she'd blame it on Emma. Gina had to force herself to put the dog deep down in her pocketbook, then turn on the water. She had to control her breathing. God damn—she was really doing this. It had been a long time—since she'd taken that necklace at Manny's sister's, last year when they had the big reunion. She'd left it at a rest stop, when they were driving home. No one, not even Manny, knew this secret. This was all hers. It would be so easy—she'd just leave the dog in the bathroom in the Raleigh airport once they got home. There, on the sink in the bathroom, for someone to find. Maybe they'd turn it in to Lost and Found. Maybe they'd keep it. She'd never know. But doing this—this would be all hers. Her face was flushed; she felt *sooooo* good.

"Coming," she opened the door and called back to the den, putting her purse in the front hall, picking up the two water glasses on the way to the other room, smiling her extra perky smile. That's what Linda had called her at lunch, perky. "I swear that ol' Men-Oh-Paws will never behave," she said to the others, dripping fake sarcasm. "I think I finally know what's going on and swoosh—I'm caught by surprise. Y'all have that happen too?" She felt psyched. Absolutely exhilarated. Better than New Year's. She'd just pour herself a glass of that delicious wine and eat a slice of Vito's pizza after all. They'd always ordered Vito's, back in the day.

She was sitting cross-legged on the floor, a partially eaten slice of pizza on a plate in front of her. The others were rambling on about Ekim again—God, what more was there to say? Gina was feeling like she was about to pop. The wine helped take the edge off a little.

"I've got an idea," she interrupted, kinda loud.

The other three looked at her.

"How's about, for old time's sake, instead of talking about Ekim, we talk about us?"

"Sure," JoAnne said, the other two nodding.

"So how's about this: Each one of us tell something that happened at WVU that none of the rest of us know?" She looked at each of them, smiling her cheerleader smile.

"I don't know if I'd have anything to say," Linda said. "I mean, I was only there two years, and y'all pretty much knew everything there was to know . . ."

Regina made little click-click-clicking no's with her tongue and teeth. "Uh-uh, Linda Lee. *THINK*. I know you can think. I'll start, okay?"

"Let me open another bottle of wine, quick, before you start," JoAnne interrupted, jumping up and grabbing the empty pizza box.

"I've got something," said Marya. "This'll be fun."

"Gina, you put on some music, okay?" JoAnne said, using a JackRabbit to start on the fresh bottle. "I guess we do sometimes talk too much about the guys—they do, that's for sure."

Gina found a Doo-Wop boxset, put all three discs on shuffle, turned the volume down. "Okay: Here goes." She's standing while the others stay seated, feeling sort of like she's a stand-up comic. Pretty great. All the attention. "You all know about Dennis and all, you were talking about him today."

Puppetlike they all three nod.

"Right," said Marya.

"Well, you know I dated a LOT Freshman year, but I was still a virgin and all . . . I'd never even dated . . ."

"Weren't we all? That's no secret," JoAnne said.

"So, I went out with a lot of guys, close to whoever asked, but it was really Denny I was nuts about."

"Tell us something we don't know," Linda Lee said, finally smiling, looking around at the others.

"I'd dated him, off and on, a couple of months, and we'd petted pretty hot and heavy." Gina could see Marya's face flushing, but she was still smiling. Probably from the wine. They had all had a lot of wine, no doubt about it, but big so what? "Anyway, it was at one of the fraternity parties at his house, Sigma Nu, between Thanksgiving break and Christmas, and we'd been drinking Purple Passion . . ."

"You are NOT going to tell this!" JoAnne put her hand up to her mouth, laughing. "You have GOT to be kidding." Marya looked stunned.

Gina reached for JoAnne's knee, "Listen, really, I have NEVER told anybody this." This was fun; they all looked so off-balance. How long had it been since any of them had told girl secrets to other women? "So when the band took a break, Denny asked me if I wanted to come upstairs with him, just as normal as you please, like he was asking me if I wanted another drink. So I said, 'Sure,' all casual too, and he grabbed my hand and we headed upstairs. His room was grubby—I mean deep down guy grubby—but he slammed the door and started kissing me like there was no tomorrow."

"Gina!" Now Marya had her hand up to her mouth, too, but she didn't laugh. Her face had gone from blushed to white. *She's such a Catholic schoolgirl*, Gina thought. Linda just shook her head and grinned a too-much-wine grin.

"So he sorta dance/shoves me over to the bed and we sit down on it, and he starts pulling my sweater over my head. We'd done that before, in the car, but that was it—no bare tops, no nekkid bottoms." Gina couldn't help it, she started laughing. The others were laughing hard, too, even Marya—probably nervous—so she held up her hand, traffic cop style. "Listen, really, this is the God's truth. So he unhooked my bra, right—he did it fast, I'm sure he'd done it a million times—ol' Manny had to try and try his first time—anyway, there I was, bare, half naked," she caught her breath, "and it was SO EXCITING! I mean, it was SO GREAT! I thought, if it gets better than this, I'm *ready*."

"Gong!" Marya screeched. "Okay, that's enough, you've told us enough, Regina! No more details, please."

Regina put her hands on her hips. "Oh shut up, Marya. I know you and Paulo did everything but."

"Gina!" Marya yelled. "You know no such thing!"

"Of course I do. We were all technical virgins until we weren't. So you kept the bride prize? So what?" She stuck out her tongue at Marya, then reached over and patted her arm, to assure her she was only teasing. "Anyway, that's all. I was so scared someone was gonna come to the door, but crazy excited, too. That was quite a night! First time. I mean, I know y'all know I did it with Denny, but that was the first time."

Marya hugged her. "I didn't mean to ruin your story, Gina. Honest."

"No. You can't help it if you're a nun," she teased. "That's plenty anyway. You get the drift. Who's next?"

"I'll go," JoAnne said. "But mine's not funny. Or sexy. Is that okay?"

Figures, Gina thought. All logical and *right*. So right. "Absolutely. The only rule is none of us can know." Regina shoved JoAnne in front of the fire and took her place.

"Okay. Believe it or not, mine has to do with a paper I wrote, junior year, for my abnormal psychology class."

"Well I certainly won't know anything about this," Linda said, but she was not all mad or pouty sounding.

"It was toward the end of second semester, and I'd taken right many psych courses. This was the second class I'd had with Dr. Allen. Do y'all remember him? Very formal? All business?"

"I do, vaguely," said Marya while the others shook their heads no.

"Anyway, at the end of the lecture, when he was giving our papers back, he asked me to see him for a minute after class, just like that. I was scared to death to even look at my grade—remember how we'd fold our papers in half? So I just stuck it in my notebook and stood up and walked to the front of the room, waited for him."

"He did *not* make a play for you!" Gina yelled.

"Don't be silly. No. Never. He was super stand-offish. Which is why this is such a big deal. So," big intake of breath, "after everyone left he looked at me, and he said 'That was a fine paper, Miss Miller. Exceptional.' 'Why thank you, sir,' I answered, and turned to leave. 'One moment,' he said, so I turned back. 'I wanted to tell you that I hope you respect how smart you are.' 'Sir?' I said. I was flabbergasted. 'I see a lot of young women come through here, majoring in psychology, and many of them are just passing through. Pairing up. I hope you'll do something with your brains, young lady. That's all.' I must have stared at him, because he looked down and started gathering his papers. I said, 'Thank you, Professor Allen,' and left."

"Oh, JoAnne—that must have meant so much," Linda leaned toward her, touched her shoulder. "You always have been so smart."

Clapping, Gina asked, "You next, Marya. Ready?" Hot damn, JoAnne—so you *always* have to be the smartest one in the room?

"Well it's certainly not going to be about sex!" Marya laughed.

"Don't we all know that," JoAnne said.

"Does summer count? As long as we were students?" Marya asked.

"I don't see why not," Linda said, looking at the others.

"I tend to be pretty much an open book," Marya looked from face to face, "so I don't have many secrets." They all nodded agreement, even Linda. "You all were closer to me than my own sister, Debbie, and I'm not particularly exciting." She laughed a kind of nervous laugh.

Gina noticed that it looked like one corner of her mouth might actually be trembling. "Oh come on, just tell us," she insisted. Jo-Anne's story had taken some of the air out of her balloon. Now if Marya went all serious-stuffy on her, she wouldn't even want to hear what Linda Lee had to say.

"Okay. Here goes." Marya stood up. "This is harder than I thought." She sipped some water. "I've never told anybody this . . ."

"Marya, puh-leeze," Gina screamed.

"So, I went home after sophomore year. It was strange. Linda Lee took off, right when the guys found out Jack had broken up with her. You guys pretty much had your own things going on." Marya looked at each of them for verification. "So there I was, my daddy working most of the time, my mama and Debbie and her kids cooking or looking at soaps or shopping—I swear, I'd go to my room and write a note to Linda Lee begging her to write back, telling her we were ready to string up Jack Vanderbilt," the others nod.

Linda looked down, then mouthed "I'm so sorry."

"But the point is: I feel like I'm in prison. Or on that deserted island. Or in the Twilight Zone!"

Gina noticed that Marya's voice was trembly, and her mouth was shaking. Was she going to cry? Good grief—so she felt all lonesome? Haven't we all?

"I just couldn't figure out Linda Lee, couldn't understand. We'd been friends from the very first. Both of us are, I think, a little bit serious . . . maybe more than you, Gina."

"You think?" Gina howled. JoAnne shushed her.

"But this thing with my mother and my sister . . . it felt wrong, like an amputation. Like *I* had amputated myself from *them*, and I didn't even know I was doing it . . ."

Linda Lee reached for Marya's hand. Marya shook her away. *Rock on,* Gina thought. Linda leaned back, her face troubled.

"That was such a big deal to me. I mean, I was closer to you three than to my mother and my sister. You all knew me. When I got home that summer, I was like an alien to them. I didn't want to talk about anything they talked about. All I could tell them about was Paulo—that's all they wanted to hear about. That and were we going to get engaged."

"My family didn't get me either, if that's any comfort," Linda Lee whispered.

Looking almost embarrassed, but still somewhat pleased, Marya turned to Linda. "Your turn."

"Oh!" Linda Lee blurted, like it wasn't obvious it was her go.

Just then, "Book of Love" came on the CD, and JoAnne jumped up. "Let's dance, y'all. Come on. I'm going to open some Prosecco and let's dance!"

Regina stood up with the others. "Linda Lee's got to tell her secret!" she shouted. But Marya and JoAnne were already singing "Oh I wonder, wonder who, tell me who . . ." at the top of their lungs. Jo was pulling Linda Lee up off the sofa. *Damn, she gets a permission slip again,* Gina thought as she finished off her glass of water and headed toward the wine fridge to grab the Prosecco.

*****

Manny had left the bathroom light on, and the door cracked in the bedroom of their suite. He was making snuffling sounds when she came in.

"That you, Baby?" he mumbled when she crossed over to her side.

"Shhh, Manny."

They had been dancing and screeching out lyrics to "Rama Lama Ding Dong" when Emma and Charlie came through the patio doors. Gina noticed them right away.

"Hey, Cuties. Come on, dance with us!" she'd called, but they were less than excited. In the end, Charlie, sober as a judge, drove them all back to where they were staying. *What cute kids those two are,* Gina had thought. How were they so . . . what would the word be . . . together?

After she'd finished her bathroom routine and climbed under the warm covers, Manny readjusted a bit.

"You have fun, Babe?" he asked, his voice a little slurred but still lovey.

In the dark, she patted his shoulder; his back was to her, but she could tell he'd had quite a bit to drink by his voice, even though she couldn't smell his breath. Brown booze, no doubt. Cigars too. Gina knew him well.

"Lotsa girl-stuff, hon. How 'bout you?"

"Old times," he muttered. "Those guys are great."

"Yeah. Gals too." She rubbed the middle of his back, where it was always sore from too much driving and flying. She knew his back better than her own. She knew every shift in his voice, every signal in his movement.

"Damn that feels good. Over a little, to the left."

She moved her fingers to the side, his skin still taut and firm, though in the last few years, he'd gotten a lot more hair on his shoulders.

"You okay about tomorrow?"

"We told a million Ekim stories. He'd have loved it."

"I bet." She kept running her fingers from his shoulders down to that sweet curve at the base of his spine. "You need anything, hon?"

Gina was thinking: *When we're on vacation, she's on vacation. Still, something about tonight, about the way JoAnne was protective of Linda Lee, and Marya was almost what? Vulnerable there for a minute? Damn. That was some serious shit. But Linda Lee, she didn't tell her secret, did she? Hell no.*

Regina leaned gently toward the back of Manny's head. "I mean, do you *need* anything, sweetie?" she whispered as she reached for his crotch. She could make him happy. Taking care of his Big Boy would make Manny sooooo happy, and Her Highness wouldn't have to do a thing. Regina was still riled, agitated. While she rubbed Manny back and forth, back and forth, she could close her eyes and picture it, buried deep down in the dark inside her purse, her very own secret.

Linda,
Embassy Suites, Late

Buds on two of the yellow roses had collapsed onto the stems without the slightest bit of opening. Linda walked over, plucked them from the vase, and threw them in the trash. Why was that? The others were still fresh and upright. Jack never got greens or those white fillers, only the yellow roses. They both liked it that way, just the roses. Those that were left would bloom, she was certain.

"Jack?"

He appeared in the doorway between the suite's living room and bedroom, brushing his teeth, looking boyish in his pajama bottoms and white undershirt.

"Simone's probably going to be at the funeral."

"What?" He disappeared into the bathroom, was back beside her on the sofa in a minute. "Did you say Simone's going to be at the funeral?"

"According to Marya."

He shook his head.

"This gets stranger and stranger, doesn't it? Marya says she's one of the church ladies who prepares for the service."

"She was about as Catholic as I am."

Jack was raised Lutheran. "Should we tell Emma, since she'll probably run into her, or just let it play out?"

"Let me think about it." He patted my knee. "You okay?"

"Okay. Today with the gals was okay, I think."

"Good. You coming to bed?" He stood. "I'm about to fall over. Cigars. Drambuie."

Definitely not his style. "I'll be there in a sec."

He kissed the top of her head. "I've still gotta make a couple of calls, try to find some champagne for this Ekim thing in the morning."

"Beer might be more like it." She reached up to touch his hand as he left the room.

She leaned back against the sofa, curved into the cushions. *Was it my imagination, or was Regina a little hostile today?* Sometimes Regina acted concerned, curious—but at lunch, when Marya told them about running into Simone D'Espere, Regina had looked almost, what, gleeful there for a minute? And tonight: What was that Truth or Dare thing she came up with? Like she was trying to maybe shock Marya and JoAnne. They were so earnest with their so-called secrets. Thank goodness they'd skipped her turn. She didn't have a secret, not one she'd tell them anyway.

JoAnne made her feel at home, that was for real.

Linda closed her eyes, felt too heavy to stand. Dragging out to Coopers Rock in the morning. In the car Jack had begged: If the guys were gonna do this private Ekim send-off, he had to go. And he claimed he couldn't stand the thought of going back there, to begin with, but he'd especially hate going if she wouldn't come with him. Marya, Regina, and JoAnne had agreed, so she was captive.

She'd imagined this weekend being awkward, even sad, but no way could she have envisioned all this conflict and confusion. Jack needed her, he'd lost a friend, she was a grown person, she could deal with Cooper's Rock if she had to. Whatever Regina had going on, that was her stuff.

Marya,
At the GoMart on Cheat Road
September 18, Morning

"I still don't see why we had to stop here," Marya said, leaning toward Paulo's ear. The brightly-lit store smelled nasty—like some cheap cleaning product and fried sausage.

He hugged her shoulder. "Easy, hon. I'll get the Iron City and jerky and we'll be out of here in three minutes. Five minutes tops."

Marya's "you guys" was more teasing than annoyed, though she had not wanted to stop at this scruffy looking convenience store on the way to Coopers Rock, and she'd made that clear to Paulo when he pulled into the parking lot. She didn't want to go to Cooper's Rock this morning, period. It was hard to be tough on Paulo, though. He was always so easy-going and accommodating—except with Tony. Tony would try the patience of Matthew, Mark, Luke, and John, true. And Paulo thought he *had* to be firm with his boy. But still . . .

"I promised the guys. And it's for Ekim, really—you know that, babe."

"I still think it's crazy to go out there before the funeral. It's chilly and the weather says possible rain. And it's going to push us getting to church early enough to be sure everything's all right." Marya pulled her wool jacket around her, knotted the yellow and blue striped scarf up close to her neck. Thank heaven she'd brought these warm grubbies for the game. She hadn't planned on wearing jeans to any of the gatherings, but here she was. Her make-up was a lick and a promise. She'd have to take a shower and start over for church.

He grabbed two six-packs of beer and tucked one under his arm, reached for another. She shook her head no and headed toward the counter.

"Would you get some of that beef jerky?" he called after her—she veered off toward the snack aisle—"And maybe some deer, too, if they have it?"

"Jerky? Really?" Marya avoided looking at the daily values on the plastic tubes of nuclear meat. Did people really put this stuff into their mouths? No doubt Ekim hadn't paid much attention to nutrition. She sighed.

Paulo was already at the counter pulling out his wallet while two or three customers in denim work shirts rubbed lottery tickets.

She started to tell them you might as well throw your money in the street, but she resisted the urge. Paulo signaled for her to hurry.

"Here you go. I'm in the car." She handed him the food, flashed him her barely tolerant smile, pushed the closest glass door open. Marya did not want to know what that foolishness cost.

"Ekim loved this junk. You want anything?" he laughed and called after her as she shook her head.

She settled in the front seat of their Buick sedan and leaned back on the headrest, adjusted her back support, closed her eyes. Just for a minute of quiet. To ease the tension. She was going to have to tell Paulo about Tony's latest screw-up sooner rather than later. It had already been later, when they had to extend this reunion visit for the funeral. Now it was sooner, but not until after the service. On the drive home. He would get too upset, and he was already so sad about Ekim. She hated to see Paulo sad. She especially hated to tell him that Tony had messed up again, big time. This time involved pot.

"See, just a quick stop and we're on our way. It's not even 9:30. We're almost there." Paulo leaned over and kissed her cheek while he started the car. "You get enough sleep, babe?" Chipper as always.

"You know I didn't." He could sleep through an alien attack; she was lucky if she got five, six hours. Marya didn't open her eyes as he drove toward Pisgah and the Coopers Rock State Forest. They'd come out here together so many times when they were dating, by themselves, when she'd gotten tired of the loud music and crazy drunks at the House. Had talked and talked about getting married and having children and going into the medical field—her as a physical therapist, him as a pharmacist.

He'd even said, on their first date, a blind date, "You're the woman I want to marry."

Yep, they'd been sympatico from the get-go. And both Catholic. Her daddy had worried that she'd fall from her faith off at college, but she and Paulo had their belief in God in common. This was one of their favorite spots, when they were so young and hopeful and sure of themselves. Today they'd add a memory, the guys' hillbilly beer-and-jerky tribute to Ekim. Why had they insisted on dragging the wives along? She would've liked a couple of hours by herself in the hotel. This reunion had become far too together-y for her liking.

"Go ahead. Get some shuteye, babe. We'll be there in fifteen minutes. You always say a power nap is all you need." He patted her thigh. Paulo was always touching her, always pulling her down on his lap to 'nuggle, as he called it.

"You mind cutting off the radio? Please." Paulo was a sports junky—he knew more statistics than that crazy loud guy—what was his name? Howard somebody—but he was quick to turn it off for her. "Thanks." He was thoughtful like that. Always had been. He was more like JoAnne, trying to make everyone get along, everything went smoothly. Why did she have to be so glass half full?

Marya rubbed her arms with her hands.

"You cold, Ry? You want my sweater?"

She shook her head no. He was the only person in the world who called her Ry. The only one she'd let use a nickname. And he only did it when they were alone together. Paulo knew her so well, better than anybody else, living or dead. Probably the only way she got away with hiding this Tony mess from him was the fact that Ekim had died. He probably thought she was nervous and upset about that. She was, of course. But she dreaded telling him Tony's latest bad decision. Thank heaven Paulo'd been on a conference when the university security called last Tuesday night. Passed out on campus, when he wasn't even a student anymore. *And* he was on probation for pot. His guardian angel was with him that night, for sure. The Duquesne security guard worked off hours and weekends at the brewery. He'd called the house first, instead of the cops. Otherwise Antony would be behind bars right this minute. Paulo would *not* be sympathetic. He'd be furious. He probably wouldn't have allowed Antony to watch the house this weekend. But he'd been so excited about this reunion, and Jack and Linda Lee coming back, so she didn't have the heart to tell him before they left. And now Ekim . . .

He drove along, his fingers tapping the steering wheel. He could never sit still for five minutes. That's where Tony got it. But Paulo used that energy to earn his masters while they were married, open first one, then three drugstores in the Philly area, and now he'd started this microbrewery on the city's outskirts. As a hobby. And he wouldn't let Tony work there. Well, she couldn't blame him. Not after he took that check from Paulo's mama. That was the final straw. She'd tried to convince Paulo to give him another chance every way she knew—he was always such a soft touch, but not where Tony was concerned. Never.

Under his breath, Paulo was singing "Earth Angel." He loved to slow dance, still, and he loved to sing. One of their favorite things the past ten years had been going to Doo-Wop concerts. That was the most fun at JoAnne's last night, dancing. The "tell your secret" stuff she could've done without. The wine was good. And Gina was a hoot—though if she had to guess she'd say she was even skinnier than the last time she saw her. When was that? A game a few years ago, right after they got back?

But Linda Lee—JoAnne wanted them all to act like nothing had ever happened, let bygones be bygones—water under the porch she called it. JoAnne the peacemaker, the getter-together-er. The secret keeper. She was the one who'd gotten their two families together when Charlie and her two were little—first for ball games, then for mini vacations, then vacations. Jo knew all about Tony and Paulo—well, not quite all, not this latest fiasco, but most of it. Now the four of them were planning a trip to Italy next May, on a wine tasting/buying trip. Good Lord—would she want to invite Linda Lee and Jack? Marya's neck tensed just thinking about it.

"You think Linda Lee will be there?"

"Jack promised he'd come." Paulo hit the heel of his hand on the steering wheel. "Damn. What was I thinking? What are you girls going to drink?" He looked over at her like he'd sworn in front of his mama.

"Girls? Really? Girls?"

"Sorry." Sheepish grin. Old habits.

She waved her hand. "Not a big deal."

"You sure? We got this damn beer cause it was Ekim's favorite. I didn't even think about you girls—y'all. Should I head back to the GoMart? You think they have wine?"

"We're not going to be out here that long. It won't kill us to go without. Believe me, we had more than enough last night." She looked into the back. "We've got a water bottle somewhere in the car." She re-settled against the warm seat and headrest, closed her eyes again. "We drank gallons of wine. I wouldn't be surprised if Regina's still tipsy, if she even comes."

"There's a case of water in the trunk. Remind me to get some out when we stop, okay? For you girls."

She gave up on him calling them "girls." Why bother—he meant no harm. All the men were acting like boys anyway.

Paulo needn't have worried. Linda Lee and Jack brought a small cooler with three bottles of Zonin Prosecco.

"Where in heaven's name did you get that?" Marya asked.

Linda Lee's face looked tense, her smile was pasted on, but she managed a pleasant-enough reply. Maybe she had a headache from last night. "Jack's quite the talker, remember? He called someone who knew somebody who opened their wine store early for him, and voila." She signaled the cooler with her hand, her other hand up beside her mouth.

Marya thought, *Wonder what burr she's got up her butt this morning? She was all chummy last night after a few glasses of wine. Maybe I was a little too heavy-handed with the Simone D'Espere news yesterday. But she's a grown woman. It's not like she'd given them the time of day for years. A lifetime, really.*

"Well thank heavens for small favors."

Regina and JoAnne were sitting at a picnic table under the shelter, wiping glasses with paper napkins. Where in hell did Linda Lee get glasses? Marc and Manny were starting a fire in the huge CCC stone fireplace. The smell of pine and smoke in the air was welcoming, reminiscent of happier times. Anything to cut the dampness in the air.

"Bring me one of those Iron Cities, buddy," Marc yelled. Gina jumped up to get it for him.

"I ducked into Wal-Mart and got some glass flutes. They didn't have crystal, but I figured glass was better than plastic or paper, right?" Linda looked around, no doubt for approval, while JoAnne popped open the first bottle and the women had to say "Cheers" like this was some weirdo celebration.

"None for me," Marya said, showing them the green water bottle in her hand. "Anybody else?" She held it up. "We've got plenty."

"Hair of the dog," Regina said, holding out her glass while Jo poured her some of the bubbly.

"Why not? Come on—just a tad, for Ekim," JoAnne prodded, standing and leaning forward with the bottle. "Give me your glass, Linda."

Marya sipped her water, thinking maybe her tight neck and shoulders were a product of four days of too much wine, besides the other worry. All she could think was, *I wish I was back in the hotel room. With the curtains pulled, the Do Not Disturb sign on the door. I wish I'd thought of bringing something for the women myself. Damnit.*

"This is kind of the perfect day for a funeral, if there's any such thing," Regina said, raising her eyes toward the grey sky. "Eighty percent chance of rain by noon."

"Yeah. We need to get these guys out of here fast," JoAnne agreed. "But it's kind of sweet that they wanted to do something all their own for Ekim, don't you think?" she asked, raising her glass in a toast. They clinked with Marya's water bottle. "To Ekim."

"I wanted to get to the church early, to meet his sister and brother, talk to the priest, not run in at the last minute," Marya insisted. "Plus I'll have to do my hair again," looking skyward too. She'd pulled it back into a low ponytail, which looked fine for jeans and a jacket, but she thought she needed to do a bit more for the funeral. Somebody was bound to want pictures.

"Marc told me Annette and Johnny are going to greet the relatives. Johnny was his Big Brother, remember?" JoAnne: always smoothing the edges. "We can move the guys along. Let's give them an hour."

"I only let Paulo buy two six packs—he wanted to get a case, of course—so three each ought to be plenty to soften them up for the service."

Linda agreed: "More than enough. Jack had way too much to drink last night. He doesn't drink like that anymore."

"Really, Paulo did that on your say so?" JoAnne looked at Marya, surprised. "I'd like to see me tell Marc how much beer to buy."

"You know Paulo. So where's Jack?"

"We know you!" JoAnne said. The other two smiled while they sipped their Prosecco.

"What's that supposed to mean?" Marya bristled, spoke to JoAnne.

Linda indicated the nearby trees, "Gone for more wood. Before it rains."

She knew their drift. Paulo was a sweetie, but they all thought she was too bossy. Teased her about it. Deciding where they'd go eat, what wine they'd order, when it was bedtime for the children. But she liked to think of herself as . . . what? . . . direct, no-nonsense, assertive. Which are the things that make her such a good physical therapist—she could push those guys to work hard to rehabilitate their broken bodies like nobody's business. But she was never bossy with the children. If anything, she'd been too much of a softie, a "candy ass" as Samantha liked to say (lovingly). But then Samantha had been no trouble.

When neither of the women answered, she said, "Okay, give me a glass. My neck's killing me." She reached for the wine bottle while Regina passed her a glass. "Emma didn't come today?"

"She'll be at the funeral." Linda Lee reached over to clink glasses with Marya. "So tell me about your two." She acted curious, even though she still had that hangdog look on her face. A strained smile. Marya was dying to know what was going on with her. Did she and Jack have a fight? She'd never admit it. She had that protective shield thing going. Wait: Did she say back at the Fishbowl that Jack brought her out here that night he ditched her? Now that would be something—returning to the scene of the crime—no wonder Linda was so long-faced, and Jack was staying out of the way.

Regina walked over to the fire. Marya guessed the talk about their children could get old for her. Or she just preferred male company. Gina threw an arm around Marc's waist, gave him a squeeze. She was a flirt, but still, it could become annoying. *She'll be sitting on Jack's lap as soon as he gets back with the wood,* Marya thought.

She never messes with Paulo, though; she knows me too well. Manny always looks the other way when she flirts like a streetwalker. That had always been a bit of a mystery.

JoAnne filled in the blanks while Marya sipped her wine. "Marya has two beautiful young adults. Samantha's a few years older than Charlie, Tony's a few years younger."

"Yeah. Samantha's married with twins. Boys. They're Paulo's eyeballs," Marya added. "Samantha's his eyeballs too, for that matter."

"You and Samantha have always been close," JoAnne said.

"True. But she's a daddy's girl, no doubt about it."

"Sorta like her mama," JoAnne teased. "And let's not forget that Tony's his mama's boy."

"Let's go sit closer to the fire. It's too damp in here." No way was she going to blab on about Tony with Linda Lee and Regina around. Huh uh. No chance. Besides, the chilly air made the place downright clammy—and the gray sky made everything closed in, almost creepy.

"Tell me about him, about your son," Linda pressed as they wandered over to sit at a table nearer the fireplace, leaving the guys to talk. JoAnne grabbed another bottle of wine.

"Tony. His name's Antony, after Paulo's father." She found her throat tightening. What to say about her boy? "People say he looks like me, but I don't see it. He's taller than Paulo, slim like me. Gorgeous eyes."

"Almost green." JoAnne described, her own eyes wide in admiration. "He could always get you with those eyes."

"Everybody but Paulo." Why did she say that? Linda Lee raised her eyebrows, probably expecting more, some explanation. She wasn't about to say another word. "So where did you say Emma is?"

"She's sleeping in. Can you believe it? They stayed up playing music after they dropped us off. I was done in."

"Yeah, me too. They're night owls, all right." JoAnne, looking at Marya, said, "She stayed at the house again so Charlie could help her some more with the guitar. It's surprising how fast she's picked it up. If it was anybody but Charlie I'd say there's more than guitar going on," JoAnne wiggled her eyebrows. "But he's a music nut. Hasn't found time for a girlfriend yet."

"Emma's psyched about this old time." Linda Lee smiled. "She's played strings all her life, mostly classical. Started in Suzuki, with violin. Moved to cello when she was twelve. She's got some kind of musical wiring, like a songbird." Linda shook her head. "I wouldn't call her a music nut, though. She's more nuts about the computer."

Marya noticed Linda Lee relaxed when she talked about her daughter, her mouth less rigid. That girl did seem to have her act together, sorta like Samantha. Was it true that girls were easier than boys? How would she know? She hadn't had brothers, and her dad was a sweetheart. And nobody could have been harder to raise than Tony. When he'd been little, that's what everyone said while she tried to keep him off the ceiling: "Tony's all boy, that's for sure." Now, mostly, her friends didn't even bring up his name. "She seems pretty easygoing."

"She certainly didn't get that from me. Maybe Jack."

"Not Charlie." JoAnne shook her head. "Marc is *awful* on the banjo, but neither of us has the heart to tell him. Hey, remember back at school, when we pulled all-nighters?"

"I never did," Marya snapped. She would absolutely lose it if the gals started that old times crap again. Reaching across the table, she poured the last of the bottle. She needed quiet time, alone time, for a fact. The drive back to Pittsburgh with Paulo would be a nightmare, an absolute nightmare. And they still had Ekim's service and celebration. She could spit. Why had she let Paulo talk her into coming this morning? Normally she had no problem telling him no, but she knew what would be coming, wanted to please him as much as possible before the Tony bomb went off.

"That's true, you didn't." JoAnne said. "I'd forgotten."

"Marya always stuck to her schedule, remember?" Linda agreed.

Nodding, JoAnne added, "But we made time for one another, no matter what. That's what I mostly remember." She held up her glass in a toast.

"You were pretty organized, too, Linda Lee. We all were. Except Regina." Marya nodded at the guys. Sure enough, Regina was sitting on Jack's lap, one arm draped over his shoulder, whispering in his ear. Linda stared for a moment, a tiny furrow between her brows.

Marya opened a new bottle, held it up toward the fire: "Hey, Gina, I need you over here to stand up for me." Regina waved her off. How in the world did she get her kicks that way, knowing that Linda Lee was uneasy? And Manny was right there. Nobody could say she hadn't tried.

The guys' laughing sounded like they were back at the house telling their usual exaggerations and lies, and Regina smiling that coy smile of hers, laughing along at their stupid stories. Right now she was just plain worried about Tony: He'd promised not to have anybody over while they were gone. He was still on probation. Surely these extra days wouldn't be too much for him. Now would NOT be the time to test Paulo's patience. God she hoped Paulo didn't cry at the funeral. She'd lose it if he did. She was jangled already. Bringing up Tony only amped her worry. She'd call him when she got back to the room, be sure the house was okay. He was okay.

Just then the guys all stood up. "Come on. Time for Ekim's Phi Kap farewell," Paulo called, all cheerful and full of zippety-do-dah. The others grabbed more beer and headed toward Coopers' Rock. Like some initiation instead of a farewell. Paulo waited for the gals, gave them his encouraging smile. That man could smile.

"Y'all go ahead," JoAnne said. "We'll hang back here by the fire."

Linda shook her head, didn't say anything to Jack or even look at him. Marya had no intention of joining them for some juvenile send-off, so she just waved Paulo away.

"Come on, y'all," Regina said, signaling for them to join her. "For Ekim. He loved us. We were his lady loves."

Marya called, "Not a chance," so Gina hurried to catch up to the men. As she poured herself more wine and sat on the bench by the fire, she waved the others over. "It's nice over here." Linda and JoAnne joined her, warming their hands before they sat. Marya reached over and added another couple of logs. "Gina has always been a super flirt, hasn't she? I guess I'd put that out of my mind. She was all lovey with all the guys at the banquet—except Paulo. Even Frankie, although Baby Barbie gave her the serious stink eye."

JoAnne and Linda Lee mumbled agreement, and the three of them leaned toward the warmth.

Much as Marya wanted some peace and quiet, sitting with the two women without talking only made her more anxious. She floundered around in her brain for something to talk about that wasn't recipes or shopping or old times' sake. Or Tony.

"Hey, did either of you happen to see that movie that was so popular last year, *American Beauty?*" she added.

Both women looked up at her, JoAnne speaking first. "Marc went ga-ga over that sex scene, like the old lech he is." She was laughing, though, so Marya figured that was partly a joke. True things are said in jest, according to Willy Shakespeare.

"What about you, Linda? Did y'all see it?"

She nodded her head up and down. "We belong to a couples movie group—dinner out and a movie once a month, with after-dinner drinks at one of our houses. I tell you what: Jack was so upset by that dad going after that teenage girl, I thought he might leave in the middle of the movie. He barely said two words when we talked about it afterwards. And you know how he loves to talk."

"Come on, Kevin Spacey was pathetic . . ." Jo smiled.

"I know. I got the point. And supposedly we were supposed to be relieved that they didn't do IT, but watching him take her blouse off," now Linda shook her head no way. "You have to remember that Emma is about her age." If anything, she was looking more solemn, Marya thought, *like she might cry.* Probably Regina flirting with Jack was one straw too many.

"Or at least the age she was supposed to be in the movie. A minor couldn't do that scene."

"Oh I know that . . . still, Jack hated that movie."

"I'll tell you what I didn't like; I didn't like that wacky teenage boy next door one bit. He gave me the creeps." JoAnne fake shivered. "All that staring through windows and photographing people when they didn't know it."

"More than the dad?" Linda followed.

Marya thought she would throw up. She swallowed saliva. She had hated that boy in the movie. He was perverted in some serious, unfixable way. And the way his dad beat him . . . Tony had never done anything nearly that bad—certainly not sicko, like that. Okay, bad. But Paulo would never raise a hand to him. He never had. Not even when he caught him . . . gross. She couldn't think about it. Neither of them could. That dad in the movie was a pervert for sure; both the dads were. What was that about?

"So here in Morgantown the big deal was with the homosexuality," JoAnne offered. "Some of the fundamentalist churches picketed. And wrote letters to the editor."

"I guess in some ways Morgantown is pretty stuck in the sixties, huh?" Linda added, without much enthusiasm.

JoAnne said, "You okay?" to Linda, patting her shoulder—apparently without noticing that Marya was equally rattled. Why was Jo so daggone solicitous of Linda Lee? It's not like Linda Lee was her good buddy or cared about her feelings, back there when she turned her back on all of them.

"Not really. I probably shouldn't have come. But after last night . . . with you all . . ."

Marya smacked her thighs and stood, turned to Linda Lee. "So, you want to ride back with me?" JoAnne could let Paulo know she'd left. He'd be just as happy to ride with one of the guys anyway, to let the brotherhood linger. She was in no mood.

Linda Lee, all apologetic: "I don't want to rush you, Marya. I can stick it out. I'm just not going to the rock."

"Well, I'm going back, whether you want to come with me or not. Coming out here today was never my idea." She shrugged, picturing all the hearts and Susie Loves Jakes Forever written and carved out there on the ledge.

"I know what you mean. But it seems to mean a lot to the guys." JoAnne trying to smooth things over.

"The guys, the guys, the guys. Am I the only one who gets sick of what the guys want?" Marya searched her pockets for keys. "Damnit, Paulo must have the keys."

JoAnne reached into her fleece. "Here. Take mine. I'll get Charlie to pick it up later. Just leave it in the hotel parking lot."

"You sure?"

"Of course. We weren't going to take the four-runner to the funeral. Marc's ordered a limo."

Marya looked over at Linda perched on the edge of one of the benches looking like she wanted to rocket propel herself into another universe. "Might as well ride with me."

Linda stood. "Thanks. Jo, will you let Jack know?"

"Sure thing." Again with the patting Linda Lee on the shoulder. "I'll enjoy the fire for a few minutes. I never turn down a chance for a little peace and quiet."

Linda hadn't said a thing since they'd gotten in JoAnne's car, other than "Thanks again for the ride."

Marya drove with the classic rock station on low. Her neck, if anything, was even tenser than before. Even Elvis singing "Love Me Tender" couldn't relax her. They'd be back in Morgantown in twenty minutes or so. Then it would be three Excedrin and a hot shower, as hot as she could take it. Then the funeral. Would she be able to talk Paulo into leaving before the Celebration of Life? Probably not.

"Hey, Marya—thanks for trying to help out back there. With Regina and all."

Marya glanced at Linda sitting there on edge, like a puppy tucking its tail when its master is scolding it. "Oh, don't worry about that. We all know Gina's gotta flirt."

"Oh, I know. I'm not mad at her—but I appreciate what you did." She sat back, put her head on the headrest. "But I *am* dreading the Simone D'Espere thing. Do you think she'll try to talk to Jack?"

"That'd be my bet." Marya thought, *I can almost feel some sympathy for Linda Lee Barbour right about now.*

"I don't want to be that woman who flinches at the sight of first wife. I swear I don't. But I don't want to meet her, either. Even if she is Jay's mama."

"'Fraid you're not going to have too much sayso in that . . ."

Her phone ringer jangled, stopped her mid-sentence. Linda jumped a bit, too, looked around. It was in her purse, on the floor. She'd grabbed it from their car on her way to Jo's—the back was open after all.

"Want me to get that for you?"

"Nope. I never answer the phone when I'm driving. Paulo's got some setup on his steering wheel, but . . . damn, this is JoAnne's car. What am I thinking? You might see who it is? In case it's one of the kids. Just reach down in my bag."

Linda picked up the smartphone and glanced at the screen. "It says Tony Baloney." The ringer stopped.

"Damn. I need to pull over and call him back." She started looking for a pull-off. A driveway would have to do out there in the boonies.

As the car slowed to a stop, Linda tried to hand her the phone, but she shook her off as she opened the car door and stepped out onto the gravel drive. Marya paced back and forth for a minute or two before she turned back and retrieved the phone and shut the car door. She punched in the automatic number for Tony, and it only rang once before he answered.

"Mom!"

"What's going on? Everything okay?"

"You with Dad?"

"Nope. What's going on, Tony?"

"I'm okay."

"Tell me right this minute. Were you in an accident?"

"I swear it was Jeremy's, not mine . . ."

"What? Pot?" Tony, already on probation, from the last time, not another stupid, stupid decision. Please, God, not pot.

"No. Not pot."

Thank all the holy angels. "Antony, I'm going to scream here if you don't tell me . . ."

"Crank. We got caught with some crank. I swear it wasn't mine."

"Crank? What the hell? Where? Where are you now?"

"They let me call . . ."

"Who? Where?"

"I'm at the police station near the house. They know you and Dad, so they let me stay out here in the waiting area until I could get one of you. That guy from before."

Marya had to catch her breath. He was at the police station. Again. They were at least five hours away. Samantha wouldn't help Tony, even if she were closer, even if she begged. She had to think.

"Mom? You there, Mom?"

His voice sounded next door to panicky. "We were out on the football field last night, goofing around. See, I didn't have him come to the house. Like I promised. I swear I'd gotten a six pack, but Jeremy pulls out this pipe . . . anyway, I didn't know what to do . . ."

"Be quiet. Let me think." Marya walked back and forth with the phone at her ear. Was Crank worse than Crack? Or not as bad? Had he been sitting in the police station for what? Hours? Afraid to call. Why would a detective be involved? Thank God it was Simmons. She would have to tell Paulo—but she'd wait until they were on the way home. He didn't need to hear this now, with Ekim and all . . . she'd call Mac. "Tony? Who's on duty? Is it Detective Simmons?"

"Yeah. Him and some other guy who glares at me like he'd like to punch me."

"Shut up with the yeah. It's yes sir and no sir, you hear me? Can you put Simmons on the phone?" She waited for some shuffling around until she heard Ed Simmons' voice.

He sounded tense. "Marya? That you?"

"Yeah, Ed. How bad is it?" The rain started misting. She was cold, but she wasn't about to get in the car.

"This Jeremy kid is trouble. Do you know him?"

"No. Tony's been talking about him these last few weeks . . ."

"He's known down here. We were onto him . . ."

"Well Tony kinda is, too."

"Yeah, but like I said, this guy is bad news. The distributor kind of bad news."

Marya felt like her knees might buckle. "Oh God, Ed—please tell me Tony's not doing that, what, crack?"

"Crank." She'd heard Antony right the first time. "He was cranked out of his mind when we got to the field. This Jeremy kid may have been working him, you know . . ."

"No. I don't know. What can we do? We're at a funeral in Morgantown."

"I can't release him unless somebody comes in. And he's gonna be charged, at least for public nuisance. It's Jeremy we want."

"Okay, let me call Bobby MacNamara. He can get him out, right?"

"Yeah. He'll still have to go before a magistrate . . . And there'll be a hearing . . ."

"You're not going to put him in a cell, are you? I'll get Mac right now."

"I'll wait, Marya. Tell Paulo to give me a call?"

"Mac will be there as fast as I can get him there. I'll talk to Paulo. We'll be back tomorrow—or late tonight."

"You want me to let him go with Bobby MacNamara?"

"Yeah. And thanks. Bobby'll know what to do. Just don't call Paulo, cause of this funeral."

As she was about to shut off, she heard Tony in the background yelling, "Don't hang up."

He came on the line, out of breath. "Mom. I love you. I'm sorry. Really sorry for messing up again. Please . . ."

"Love you like crazy, Antony. But right this minute I could kill you." And she hit the red button.

She started scrolling through her contacts for Mac's number. He'd done their legal work since they'd closed on their first house years ago. He knew all about Tony's involvement with the law. He'd helped him before—how many times now? Three? This would be four. He'd know about this crack/crank whatever. He'd let them know if they needed to hire somebody else. What the hell was crank? The first time she'd heard it, she'd thought Tony was misspeaking. She startled as Linda walked up behind her. Marya hadn't heard the car door slam.

"You shocked me."

"I wasn't listening. I swear. But I can see you're upset. And it's raining. Let's get in the car. Anything I can do to help?"

"I'm not going to be able to drive. Can you drive?"

"Of course." Marya, hand trembling, gave Linda the keys and walked around to the passenger side. "Give me a minute. I've got to make another call."

Thank God Linda Lee didn't talk on the way back to Morgantown. Marya would have probably jumped out of the car if she'd asked her a lot of questions. As it was, she tried to calm her breathing. Deep breath in. Hold it. Slow breath out. When Paulo got back, he'd know something was wrong if she didn't get herself under control. She could blame her jumpiness on Ekim and the funeral and not getting back when they'd planned; he knew she couldn't stand it when plans were changed, but he was bound to know she was keeping something from him. They could finish one another's sentences. Right now she hated that he could do that.

When Linda pulled up in front of the Hilton, Marya grabbed her purse and said, "Thanks. Really. I'll see you at the service." She didn't wait to hear what Linda was saying.

Paulo still wasn't back when she finished her shower, so she lay on the bed in the dark trying to ward off a headache. Even warm from the shower, she couldn't stop shivering. How many years now had Tony managed to cut them off at the knees? First in high school, when he'd gotten caught passed out in the school bus after a football game. Then the pot started. They'd put him in a treatment center for a month before his senior year. Big waste of money. Then he'd gotten kicked out of college his freshman year—more pot, more antics. Worse trouble. But this. Crank. Simmons was saying it wasn't Tony's, wasn't he? Tony could probably testify against this Jeremy guy . . . Was she really thinking this, like some *Law and Order* episode? God this was a mess. She closed her eyes.

She'd loved the clean baby smell after Antony's bath, the way he arched his chubby tummy when she tickled him. They'd started calling him their wiggle worm as soon as Paulo held him that first time in the hospital. Tony was only still when he was nursing, and then he snuffled and nuzzled and sighed before he dropped off to sleep. She'd loved those 'nuggling' noises. He'd nursed every two hours for how long? Wore out his Johnny Jump Up. Slept no more than thirty minutes at a time forever. But he'd been a sweet baby, jolly as long as one of them paid attention to him. Mostly her, as long as she nursed.

Paulo had been patient taking turns with the bottle when she'd weaned Tony. He'd sung all his Doo-Wop songs in lullaby voice, rocking and singing and content to help with his baby boy. God she'd been exhausted. Samantha had slept through the night when she was two months old. Marya had congratulated herself on getting this nursing/schedule thing right. Who needed some new age nursing coach? Then Tony. Oh but he had the dearest baby laugh. She drifted off.

When Paulo crawled in bed beside her, she could smell his beery breath before he nuzzled her neck. "Hey, Babe. You mad at me?"

"Don't be silly." She turned toward him, wrapped one arm around his head.

"You should've stayed, I swear. It was good. Ekim would've liked it." He kissed her neck. "You smell damn good. Good enough to eat."

"What time is it?"

"Time to get a move on. You talked to Tony? Everything okay at the house?"

"If you're going to shower you better hurry. I want to meet Ekim's family." He could always read her mind. She'd have to talk about it soon enough, but not yet. "And brush your teeth."

Catholic funerals aren't personal at all—just a religious send-off of the Catholic soul to its heavenly reward. Some consecrated priest blessing him on his way, some consecrated angel, no doubt, welcoming him to his eternal home. Incense, prayers, litany, hymns that are more like dirges. Formal, impersonal, like God running the show, not Jesus. Marya lost herself in the sadness, her own sin of omission weighing on her shoulders like cement bags.

They'd been in such a hurry to get to the church that Paolo didn't seem to sniff out Marya's deeper layer of anxiety like he normally would. Now she sat crying steadily, quietly—that could be Tony there in that coffin. She couldn't bear the thought, couldn't stand keeping this closed up inside herself in that dark scary place where all the Tony anxiety lived. He was safe now, for the moment, with Bob MacNamara. She kept her handkerchief up to her mouth, trying to force the whimpers down, trying not to bawl out loud at the thought that each time her boy did something, it got worse and worse, and nothing she did or could imagine doing made a bit of difference. What was going to happen to Tony? Look at what happened to Ekim. Paulo put his arm around her just as a big intake of breath almost knocked her off the pew.

Deep breath in; hold it, slow breath out. Repeat. The priest droned on from the communion liturgy. Usually a priest's voice would comfort her. Not today. How much longer? At some point, he'd signal the guys to step forward. All of them were pallbearers. For now Paulo held her like he was trying to keep her skin from splitting, or his. Hardly anybody else here. No surprise. A few of the younger Phi Kaps from the House—probably the officers. Deep breath in; hold it, slow breath out.

She recited the "Christ have mercy on us" like a robot. When they'd been here, at WVU, when they'd all talked about their future like they could solve it like some geometry proof, they'd imagined being successful, making a difference, not being work slaves like their parents, having enough money to be able to *do* things, like actual vacations. All these plans as the keys to the kingdom, happily ever after, if they only did things right. And she had. Every step. Why had they thought they would be in control, could make life what they wanted? Is that what Regina and Manny had done by not having children? She didn't want what they had. She wanted Paulo and Samantha and Tony, even Tony, especially Tony. Deep breath in; hold it, slow breath out. Right this second they were all safe. Even Ekim, gone to spirit, pure spirit, free of his tormented body and soul.

Ekim's brother and sister were sending his body to be buried with his parents, thank God, so they didn't have to go to the cemetery on this grey, drizzly, sad enough already day. That would've been too much. They'd drive over to the gathering right after the service. This would be the last event, thank heaven, before they could go home. Maybe she'd tell Paulo about Tony tonight, back at the hotel, while they were in bed. In the dark. That might be better. He would be able to yell or cry or whatever he needed to do, so they could figure out, together, how to deal with their son, his non-stop problems. Or maybe she'd tell him in the car tomorrow, like she'd planned all along, so he couldn't cry or scream. Or wait until they were home, safe and secure. She had to admit to herself that there would be no best time, best place. She carried the dread, shoulders drooped, an ox weighted down with heavy buckets of water.

Marya,
The Celebration of Life

The Celebration of Life was in the same ballroom as the Phi Kap Frankie Gallucci tribute dinner. Marya noted the irony as they walked around to look at all the giant black and white photos of Ekim. He'd been such a walking disaster the last time he was here, right here in this room. Surely the official photographer hadn't included him in any shots from that night, except that group shot. In his football uniform in high school, he'd been such a cutie, with a mischievous glint in his eyes. His first communion, in a little grey suit and white shirt and a striped bowtie, hair slick with Bryllcreem. His sister must have brought these shots. Who'd had them blown up? Maybe that had been Frankie's contribution. She had to smile at that thought. He'd made it back for the funeral, without pregnant Barbie.

There Ekim was in his military uniform, beside his helicopter, his helmet under his arm. Had he been drinking then? He looked clear-eyed, self-assured. The guys said he had been a good pilot. And of course another blow up of the composite, all the brothers, forever young. Ekim in his tie and cheap sports coat looking like he was prouder than the president to be a Phi Kap. There, in color, surprisingly, the "formal" portrait of the Phi Kaps from a few nights ago—without the finger sticking out of the fly, thank God. They all looked handsome and happy—even Ekim, though he'd been drunk as a monkey. The times, they are a–changin'.

Paulo walked around with her, holding her hand snug, like he was holding onto a child crossing the street. He had little to say. Since he and his Phi Kap brothers had escorted the casket to the hearse, even Paulo was solemn. The place was surprisingly crowded and noisy—nothing like the funeral—probably all the current brothers from the house with their girlfriends or dates showing up for the party. Frankie probably arranged that, too. A Motown band was warming up. Kegs instead of liquor, thank God.

Paulo told her that the meal was going to be an Ekim send-off—meatballs and kibbie and Syrian bread with Mediterranean salads. Galaktoboureko and baklava for dessert. It smelled like a family reunion. Who had they found on short notice to cater such a spread? The guys could get it together when they needed to; they'd proven that time and again. All of them except Ekim.

They were looking for the others when Marya saw Simone D'Espere framed in the doorway, silver raincoat with collar up, black scarf wrapped around her head and neck like a forties movie star. Marya stood frozen while Simone turned over her coat and umbrella to one of the young guys doing coat-check duty—probably a pledge—and watched as she unwound the scarf and bounced up to them.

Simone smiled and pointed, breathless, "Aren't those pictures fabulous? Don't you just love that one—the one of Ekim as a little boy?" She was wearing a tiny black dress, cut just above her slender knees. The sleeveless V-neck was flattering—not a bit of flab on those arms. And of course, the demure gold cross. What was that scent? Belle Fleur? A young woman's perfume. Marya nodded to Simone, forced herself to smile with her lips.

"These photographs make me think of young Jack. He so wanted to be here. Did your children come, Marya?"

She shook her head no—Linda had said they all called Jack's son Jay, not Jack—as she continued searching the room for JoAnne and Marc while Paulo filled in the conversational gap. Simone, shaking her cap of dirty blond hair, tossing her crystal drop earrings around as she talked, was acting like they were continuing some lifelong dialogue, like they had some lasting connection or relationship. Paulo, of course, gave her a hug. He would hug G. Gordon Liddy.

"He was such a sweetie pie, wasn't he? It's just too very sad," Simone continued, that hint of a French accent making her voice chipper at the same time it was supposed to suggest dismay. She was still sexy.

Paulo patted her shoulder. God there was a lot of shoulder-patting this weekend. They weren't ready for the nursing home, for heaven's sake. She sighted JoAnne near the food line, was about to say to Paulo . . .

"So would you mind introducing me to her?"

"To who?" Marya blurted.

"Linda Lee. Jack's wife." She smiled like she was asking for sugar with her coffee.

"Of course," Paulo offered, taking her by the elbow. "Marya? Honey?"

"You go ahead. I was just about to . . ." She let her sentence trail off. He would probably think she meant go to the bathroom, which she almost never said out loud in public.

As they strolled across the floor, heads leaning in toward one another, Marya scanned the room looking for JoAnne's curly head. She saw her near the service door—of course, she'd offer to help. She turned toward her and waved. JoAnne connected, waved back, smiling, but Marya shook her head no and signaled for the exit door. Jo put her platter on the nearest table and walked toward her, meeting her about six feet from the entrance.

Marya said "Shhh, please," and pushed Jo through the door, across the foyer, toward the entranceway. "You are not going to believe what just happened," she whispered.

"What?" JoAnne looked worried. "Tony?" They stepped outside; only a few people were there, smoking. Young people. Nobody they knew.

"Simone D'Espere. She's getting Paulo to introduce her to Linda Lee. And she's acting all lovey/dovey. Like one of us."

"That's not going to be good. What do we do?"

Marya looked through the sidelight, could see Paulo and Simone still wandering the room. "Maybe you could go talk to her?"

Just then, near the memory book table, Paulo tapped Jack on the shoulder. Marya pulled Jo closer. "Look. We're too late." She grabbed Jo's hand and pointed across the room. They could see Paulo and Jack and Simone talking. Simone's back was to them—she could have been one of the college girls, she was that trim, if WVU girls dressed that stylishly. She was talking with her hands, Jack was back as far against the table as he could get, and Paulo had one hand on Jack's shoulder. Where was Linda Lee?

"See? She's over there with Jack. Have you talked to her?" Jo was whispering now, though there was nobody to hear them.

"No. Why don't you head over there? I'll look for Linda Lee, try to distract her, give her a head's up." As they walked back into the room and separated, Marya headed for the bar. Maybe besides water and soda they'd have some decent wine. Maybe Linda Lee would be getting a glass. She needed something for her nerves; this weekend she had been a bundle of nerves. As she got closer, she saw Regina and Linda Lee in the line. Thank goodness.

"Hey, y'all," she called. They looked up at her, smiled.

"Just like the guys to have kegs," Regina laughed. "I understand they ordered some wine for the ladies, though. If Manny hadn't . . ."

"Probably undrinkable," Marya cut her off while Linda Lee shrugged. Apparently she hadn't seen Simone talking to Jack. Good. She stood on that side of Linda, blocking her view of the food table, "if they had the young frat guys do the ordering."

"So the service was nice," Linda Lee said. "The guys appreciated it."

"At least it's over," Regina added.

Marya had to agree. There was nothing personal to recommend the funeral service, but that's the way Catholics did it—at least the Catholic church she and Paulo attended. They'd never go for one of those guitar and home-baked bread services. Church was somber, to give you hope AND make you worry. Besides, Ekim was Catholic.

"I am so ready to go home," Marya said, not certain what to do. She was no member of the Linda Lee fan club, but still, going out to Cooper's Rock was bad enough. It would be cruel and unusual punishment for Linda Lee to have to phony-talk with Simone D'Espere. Or, rather, Simone Vanderbilt. Or to watch her fawn all over Jack with her girly/sexy voice. That would burn. She and Linda Lee had been close friends once upon a time. And she had no love lost for women like Simone D'Espere.

The band started playing "Hold On," and a crowd of the college age-group got up to dance, or rather, to wiggle around close to one another. None of them actually knew how to dance-dance, not like they all did. Thank goodness the dancers blocked the view across the room. Marya relaxed a bit, trying to think.

"The band's good," Gina said. "Ekim would like this band."

"Yeah." Linda Lee turned toward the stage. "That was the idea, I guess. I still love this music. It's strange to me, how the young people love our music."

"Me too," Gina said. "Usually I'd make Manny wait in line for our wine—usually he'd offer, he's such a gentleman—but this is really their day."

"Linda Lee—do you mind if Regina gets our wine? Would you mind coming outside with me for a minute? I'm getting kinda nervous."

"Of course, Marya. Do you mind, Regina? Whatever dry white they have?"

"Sure. And you're always red, right Marya?"

"Unless it sparkles," she snapped. She'd never been good at hiding emotions. She tried to lighten, since Regina looked puzzled. "I can't imagine Jesus blessed Chardonnay at the wedding in Cana, can you?" she said, forcing a smile, grabbing Linda Lee by the elbow, and walking away.

As they worked their way through the dancing young people, Marya couldn't help wondering if she'd lost her scrambled mind. Why was she all of a sudden the Linda Lee Whisperer? Everything was off balance. She could scream or dig a hole and crawl in it.

In a flash, they shut the door on the pounding music and stood outside on the walkway, where she'd been with JoAnne only minutes before.

"What's wrong? How can I help?" Linda Lee's eyes were worried. "Is it that phone call earlier? I could tell you were upset . . ."

"Let me get my breath, okay?"

Linda Lee looked around, pointed to a bench under a maple tree off to the side. "Want to sit down?" She guided Marya over.

Marya wasn't any good at pretense; she knew that. Before, at lunch, she'd wanted to see how Linda Lee would react when she told her Simone D'Espere would be at the funeral. Be hardhearted, like

Linda Lee had been to them when she'd cut them off without a single word. Now she felt like one of those women she hated, the ones who are cruel to other women for the fun of it. She'd spoken out of her own old hurt feelings. That had been wrong. She had startled Linda Lee, caught her off guard, caused her discomfort, probably even pain. On purpose. What could she say now?

"I'm okay. Really. It's just, I'm really sorry for what I said at lunch yesterday."

"What do you mean?" Linda was clearly caught off guard.

"Dropping that Simone stuff on you like that."

She shook her head. "Listen, I'm glad you did. Really. I would've hated to have run into her at the funeral, not knowing she'd be there. You did me a favor. And I didn't see her anyway."

Marya didn't answer, her guilt settling uneasily on her already frazzled nerves.

"Marya, please," Linda Lee moved closer, "I appreciate you telling me. I mean it, no need to apologize."

"Okay. Thanks." She twisted her hands in her lap. "But she's here. And she's talking to Jack and Paulo."

"Oh." Linda Lee's face froze.

Marya reached over for her hand. "I thought you ought to know."

"You're right. Thanks for the heads up."

"And she's acting all friendly, like we're all old best buds."

Linda Lee patted Marya's hand so they made a hand mound, like that old game they'd played as children. "Please. This was inevitable, I guess. It had to happen sometime. And Jack is fine. He's better than fine. I'm okay with it. Honest."

"Still, let me warn you: She's already flirting with Paulo."

Shrugging, Linda Lee stood. "I'll just pretend she has on dirty underwear. That'll help." Marya was startled—Linda Lee wasn't usually the crude one. That was Regina's area.

Linda Lee tried to laugh, but the sound was not convincing.

"Listen," Marya held onto her hand, tugged. "I mean it. I'm sorry for springing that on you at lunch."

"You know what? Screw Simone D'Espere. Let's go back inside and get this over with."

Regina met them at the door with their wine. "Everything okay?"

"Yeah. I just had to get out of here for a minute, catch my breath."

"I know what you mean." Gina rolled her eyes toward the food table. Manny, Jack, and Paulo were standing there, talking to Simone D'Espere. "The black widow."

"Thanks for the wine, Regina. I could use it! Maybe intravenous." Linda Lee took her glass and took a sip, then another sip. "It's not bad, Marya."

"This merlot tastes like dog piss—or what I'd imagine dog piss tastes like." Marya frowned.

They stood there drinking for a moment. Marya heard a "Hey, Mom," and looked up automatically. Emma and Charlie were hurrying toward them. They were holding hands. Was she just pulling him along or were they actually holding hands?

"Emma." Linda Lee smiled, reached out to hug her daughter.

"Mrs. Vanderbilt," Charlie said.

"Come on—it's Linda to you and your family. Please."

He grinned and Emma let go of his hand, grinned at her mother. "Isn't this band terrific? We've been dancing."

"They definitely have that sixties sound down pat," Regina offered, upbeat.

"So are you and Dad going to dance? Come on," Emma reached for her mother's hand. "Let's grab Dad."

The women followed as Emma led them around the outer edge of the dancers to the food table. Marya thought it might be helpful to have the young ones as a buffer. Even Simone D'Espere wouldn't come on to Charlie.

"Dad!" Emma called, her voice full of music.

Jack looked up and smiled. "There they are, my two best girls." Was that relief on his face, Marya wondered?

Followed quickly by the French lilt, "Linda Lee Barbour? Can you believe, all these years, and it takes a funeral for us to finally meet?"

JoAnne and Marc walked up at that moment. "Hey, y'all. I've been looking for you," Jo said, looking right at Linda Lee.

"Hey, JoAnne," Simone D'Espere said. "It's been too long."

Simone leaned forward as if to cheek kiss Jo, but JoAnne pulled back just a hair, so Simone hugged Marc instead.

She stepped back from him, gave Marc her full-on gaze. "Hear you're a judge now, Marc. I'd better mind my p's and q's."

"So they tell me," Marc responded, moving toward Jack.

Simone acted as if she didn't notice the slight. "I thought maybe one day we'd all get together at young Jack's wedding, but so far he's managed to stay single."

Jack was holding Linda Lee's hand now. "Jay still hasn't brought a serious girl home," he said. Linda nodded her head in agreement.

"He hasn't rushed to the altar like all of us did," Simone added, laughing as if she'd told some clever joke.

"Our young folks are smarter than we were," JoAnne popped in. "Way."

"Thank God," said Marya. "Antony better not even think about getting married until he starts paying his own bills."

Linda Lee looked from one to the other, her face contained, grateful.

"We were all more grown-up, don't you think?" Regina interrupted. "I mean, the war and Civil Rights and all . . ." Gina wasn't usually the one to get all serious, or to save the day. But thank goodness for her right that second.

"Charlie's got it together for somebody his age," Emma piped in, clearly unaware of the discomfort.

"You must be Emma." Simone turned her intense, cheerful stare on her.

"Yep. The one and only," Emma smiled back. "And you're Jay's mother?"

"You look a lot like your daddy looked when he was young."

"Most people say she looks like me," Linda Lee said quietly.

"Hmmm. I don't really see it," Simone responded, looking closely at Linda Lee for the first time, one hand up toward her mouth, as though she were studying her. "Maybe around the mouth."

"Tell you what," Jack said. "I can't listen to this band one more minute without dancing. Come on, Linda. This is one of our songs." The singer was on the first verse of "Unchained Melody."

"You, too, babe," said Paulo, pulling Marya close, waltzing her out onto the floor. "Body rubbing music."

Marya followed, nestled her chin into his chest. Had he even noticed how awkward that had been?

"That Simone is a piece of work, isn't she?" he whispered in her ear.

"Oh, Paulo," was all she could get out. His familiar body was comforting up against hers, his voice soothing, his manner always loving, thoughtful. Just right.

"I thought that Jack might punch her if she said one more word."

Wrapping her arms around his neck, smiling up into his smiling face, Marya, safe herself for that one moment, whispered, "You have no idea how much I love you."

LINDA

Head tucked under Jack's chin, eyes closed, Linda felt safe, safe and breathless. Marya, Regina, JoAnne—they'd tried to protect her. And Jack had rescued her.

Dancing slow and easy with her husband, as she had to this very song back at the House many times all those years ago, for just this moment past and this present merged in a way that wasn't cause for despair.

Life's ironies: Simone D'Espere was on the sidelines, without a partner, no doubt watching as they slow danced. Imagining such a moment before today, Linda would have felt that gut-punch sensation, that kicked in the teeth feeling of that long ago, deep betrayal. All she felt now was relief. Relief and a tickle of pleasure that Emma had been such a natural buffer, totally unaware of her mother's discomfort.

If she'd imagined such a moment—and no way could she have ever imagined any of this—it would never have been Marya who dragged her out to warn her. Marya, who'd acted all approach-avoidance at lunch when she told her Simone would be at the funeral. And Regina speaking up about Civil Rights—that she would not have dreamed in a thousand and one nights.

These women were not cardboard cut-outs like those Disney princess figures in the lobby at the movies when she took Emma and her friends. She had to admit that she'd been guilty, despite her feminist leanings, of freezing them in the identities she'd known, of framing her thinking of them as a group, the group of women she'd abandoned. Her own guilt prevailing, not any notion of their world. Not flesh and blood individuals with their own knocks and losses and hurdles. Had they done the same thing, in their thinking of her? She had no way of knowing, but for now she could enjoy this dance with Jack, feel relief at the way the women had thrown up a protective fence around her, and enjoy the grace of a daughter who adapted and engaged in a natural, welcoming way with that stranger, Simone D'Espere

JoAnne,
At the Celebration of Life

Now that the band had stopped playing, JoAnne was anxious to leave. Boxing up the old yearbooks and photos and memorabilia they'd brought along to remind everyone of happier times—Marc had insisted on bringing his Phi Kap paddle—she paused and picked up a campaign poster of Frankie Galluci for Student Government President. She'd forgotten that. He looked like such an impressionable, earnest boy. Now he was Frank instead of Frankie, and they'd given him a black hat, but he wasn't that boy anymore, not even close. None of them were.

And look at all the photos from Cheat Lake—so many dances, such confident broad smiles. Band flyers—The Bonnevilles. Even the band looked young. They'd all been so happy in the moment. Other wives from nearby had brought pictures and scrapbooks, news articles about football and basketball games, composites from other years. The Phi Kaps had a history, no doubt about it.

She scanned the room, almost empty now, and tried to signal Marc with a come-on curl of her fingers. If she didn't get his attention, he'd stay till they turned the lights off, hanging out with his buds. He was talking, and the others looked at him as if he were revealing the secret to youth. He wouldn't look her way. She knew that was on purpose. She kept on packing the box of memories. Would she always associate that faint smell of baklava and roses and garlic with tonight, with Ekim?

A few of the college guys were intent on killing the keg. Wait-staff and busboys slumped against the wall, waiting to break down all the round eight-seaters skirting the empty dance floor. The band was packing up, having a few beers on the bandstand. Some of the pledges were clearly still having a blast, clumsy and no doubt wasted, laughing and talking and taking down the giant photos—creating their own tales to elaborate for years to come, she figured. What in the world would they do with those pictures? Store them at the House, in the attic or basement, pull them out for some oldies/sixties party some day? Is that ironic or what? They looked like children—some were Charlie's age! She'd felt so sophisticated when she was their age, so know-it-all and self-assured. *Do these guys feel that way now,* she wondered. Regina had acted confident; Marya had always been in charge. But Linda Lee, she was a tabula rasa. The times they are a 'changin.

She and Marc had had such a good time dancing tonight, moving together naturally—God they were good together, all their body moves, the touching and holding and loving, always had been. Those few moments of dancing let her forget the reason they were here for a bit. But now she was tired, and a tad let down, and he was ignoring her.

She could see Linda leaning against Jack, his arm easy around her hip. They fit right in today, like they'd never left. Regina batted her eyes at who? Not Frankie Galluci? JoAnne smiled. Second Wife would not approve. Gina was incorrigible. They loved her despite her naughtiness. Rich as Croesus, but she still had that Little Matchgirl aura. How Manny put up with her she would never understand, but he always had.

One of the fraternity guys, obviously blotto, staggered up. "Hey? I saw ya dancin. Ya wanna dance?"

JoAnne looked at him, caught off guard, like he had to be kidding. "The band's packing up."

He looked toward the bandstand, pulled his chin back in surprise. "Oh. Ya wanna drink then?"

Jo shook her head no, said, "Thanks, I've had plenty. You might think about calling it quits, yourself." He stumbled off to the keg, calling "Later, then" over his shoulder. She might've been flattered, but he was blind drunk.

As she gathered the last of her photos, she thought, *Overall this reunion has turned out as well as possible, given the iffy/anxious part about having Linda and Jack coming back as a couple, and then Ekim's shock.* Linda was easy with them now—well, easier, especially tonight. The Celebration of Life was a good idea, she had to admit, much as she'd objected. It would've been too fragmented and unfinished for everyone to leave right after the funeral. Wonder how Marc assessed these last few days. He certainly couldn't have dreamed of losing one of his fraternity brothers. Not yet. It was too soon. But it had been a kind of tonic to have Jack and Linda here for everything, even that.

Leaving the box on the table for Marc to carry, she headed across the room to drag him away. Out of the corner of her eye, she noticed Marya, shoulders slumped, seated alone at one of the messy tables that still needed to be cleared. She hated to see her so dejected. She'd always been gritty, practical, a friend she could count on. Not one to cave during tough times. True, Marya loved to know all the dirt about everybody, even if she acted like she had never made mud pies herself—so why wasn't she over there with the others? Jo was struck by the fact that Marya had been more buttoned up all weekend, when she and Marc had hoped everything would be upbeat, that everybody would have big fun. Like "old times" would be too much to ask—ridiculous, really—but revitalized friendship, more than a Christmas card acquaintance, lots of laughs and new experiences together, that's what they'd wanted to happen.

At first, JoAnne had figured Marya was only cranky around Linda—Marya held more of a grudge than she did, though her reasoning that Linda had dumped them, so why even bother, had never felt convincing to JoAnne. But she'd been subdued the whole weekend, whether Linda was in the room or not. Except at lunch, when she'd announced Simone D'Espere would be at the funeral. Now that was the feisty Marya she knew. Digging. Otherwise, she hadn't been herself. Paulo was his usual Mr. Positive, putting everybody at ease. Then Ekim died. That took the air out of them all.

Leaning against the table, she wondered, *Could it ever be close to the same again?* After the service, Marya and Linda had been talking, getting along—not all best friendy, but less tense. Marya had even been a bit of a Mama Bear when Simone showed up. Now she looked miserable at that table all by herself, done in. She had to be brooding over something. She'd never been one to tell all, like Gina—she liked to know everything about everybody, but she was private about her own business—but they'd talked more over the years since they'd gotten together as families, especially about the children. She'd been pretty open when it was only the two of them, even about Antony's bad judgment. Besides, Marya was never a pouter, never one to give in to the blues. She was always stretching for the sensible solution. This had to be about Antony. Nothing else that Jo knew of got to Marya like that boy of hers. He'd dragged her down right much these last few years. *Wonder what it could be now? God I'm lucky Charlie's such a sweetheart.*

She wandered over to the messy table and sat beside Marya, pulled her close for a hug. Her hair smelled like herbal tea, maybe ginger and chamomile.

"We're looking forward to Italy. Marc has been busy, keeping ahead of his legal calendar and planning this get together. I've seen him more the last few days than I have in months. It'll be great for us to get away with you guys."

"Us too. We're happy when we're in Italy." Marya sat up a little, pulled away, pushed her hair behind her ear. Same gold hoops—had she always worn those?

"I can see why. After we went to Paris last year, we wanted to keep travelling, especially to Spain and Italy. But it's hard to pry Marc away from the bench. He's gotten serious in his old age." She made an exaggerated stern Marc face, grinned.

"Yeah. We can't wait to show you around to our favorite cafes and vineyards. You're gonna love it." Marya actually smiled, relaxing against the back of the chair. "Paulo found 'his people' in this tiny village; it's like he's found a whole new fraternity."

JoAnne put her elbows on the table, rested her head in her hands.

Marya looked over her shoulder to where the guys were hanging out near the kegs. Jo followed her glance: Regina and Linda were still with them. Nobody was making a move toward the door, but Frankie wasn't there anymore. Must've left. She was feeling restless herself.

JoAnne reached for Marya's hand. "Hey, you okay?"

"I told you I'm fine."

"Is something wrong with Antony? You can tell me . . . I'm worried about you."

Marya pulled her hand away, flapped it in that "go away" fashion. "Leave it alone, okay?"

JoAnne nodded agreement, though nothing Marya had said had made her feel any better. She could hear Marc's laughter above the other noises. "You know, I've been thinking, with all the guys back this weekend, Marc is so happy. It struck me that he's never really made close friends except these guys. He's not even that close with his real brother, Matt."

"Paulo always says I'm his best friend. I'm pretty sure he means it." Marya rested her chin on her fist. "But he loves these guys, too. Really loves them."

"I don't know the last time Marc's let loose, laughed so much. This has been good for him . . . well, of course I don't mean . . ."

"Of course not. I know what you mean." Marya leaned toward her. "You know Paulo—he always looks on the bright side." Marya tried to smile, but it was a flop. JoAnne was afraid, for a moment, that she'd cry, but instead she looked around in her pocketbook and pulled out a lipstick. "I'm sure I look like Who Shot John."

"Look at me—this mess of hair has gone wild, I guess from all the rain. I think it stopped a little bit ago, thank goodness." She ran her fingers through her corkscrew curls. They blossomed and frizzed even more. "All of us are a little worn at the edges." She rubbed Marya's shoulder. "Can I get you anything? Another glass of wine?"

"God, no. I stopped drinking that rotgut a couple of hours ago. It'd gag a corpse."

JoAnne was feeling bone weary, actually—but the more tired she got, the more wound up she felt. "I wish the guys would call it quits, so the staff could finish cleaning up these tables and we could all go home."

"Plus my feet hurt like hell." Marya stuck out her stockinged feet, big toe pointing to the black pumps she'd shed. "I'm not used to wearing heels for what, eight hours? At work we wear those ugly orthotic shoes."

"Hey, I was wondering, Marya—you okay with Linda being here?"

"Did I have a choice?" She looked up with a jerk. "I'm sorry. I shouldn't take it out on you." She shrugged. "She's okay. Today I've actually been glad she came back."

JoAnne considered that progress. "God I could jump out of my skin. I wish Marc would come on." She twiddled her fingers on the table. "I wish I'd gone for a run this morning."

"I wish I'd slept in." She leaned her chin on one hand. "Going to Cooper's Rock was a big deal for the guys. At least it was for Paulo. But I should've stayed in the hotel."

"Marc too." Jo looked across the room at the men again. Marc still wouldn't meet her eye. "I miss the days when Marc and I used to get up and run together every morning."

"You always were more of a jock than the rest of us." Marya rubbed her feet, one after the other.

"Yep, I was a regular tomboy when I was little. Climbing trees, riding my bike till all hours, catching crawly things. Fishing with my dad."

"Not me. Huh-uh. I was your girly-girl from day one."

"Oh, my dear, I was a cheerleader, too," JoAnne laughed. "But being outside has always been my favorite. Doing something. Working in my yard. I'd rather be outside in the cold taking a walk than stuck inside playing bridge."

"Give me a book and my sofa or a new *People* magazine any day." Marya crossed her ankles, sat back.

"Hey," JoAnne reached for Marya's hands. "Let's hurry them along. They want us to get out of here." She nodded toward the bored staff. Most days she felt like one of those sheep dogs, herding everybody where they were supposed to be. Now that Marc was a judge, they had so many evenings out—too many. They'd always been busy, but everybody wanted a piece of him now. And there was the next election pressure. They'd missed a few of their weekly date nights recently, but they still had lots of laughs when it was just the two of them—hiking, skiing, sitting at a bar talking, going to concerts, music festivals.

Marya reached down to put her shoes back on. "I am SOOO ready to go."

They moseyed over to the group. The others didn't look up until they were right on top of them, they were talking with such animation.

"Hey, babe," Paulo said, looking pleased. "You ready?" Marya rested her head on his shoulder.

Marc gave JoAnne a quick smile, kept talking. Jack was leaning in listening. Linda turned her way. "Broken records, right?"

"You haven't had to put up with it for the last thirty years," Marya said, no humor whatsoever in her voice.

"Boys will be boys," JoAnne jumped in, though Linda's face had already lost its ease. Why did Marya have to say that? "What do you say, Marc, let's let these people finish cleaning up." She pulled on his elbow.

"Come on, guys. Come back to the house with us. The evening's young. I've got some Drambuie that will even out any rough edges."

Jo didn't dare give him a disapproving look, but inside she wanted to smack him senseless. Not that she'd ever do that, but she wanted to. "Of course, y'all come on. We'll build a fire. I'll make us some eggs a little later. Soak up all that alcohol."

"Huh-uh. No way. I'll fall down if I don't get to bed soon," Marya said, leaning against Paulo.

"We're on our way, babe." Paulo grabbed Marya around the shoulders. "Thanks, y'all. Jack, don't be a stranger." He shook hands all around with the guys and then steered his wife toward the door to the foyer. "See you in the funny papers!" he called over his shoulder.

Marc laughed and yelled, "Don't take any wooden nickels!"

"What about you, Linda? You ready to head back to the hotel?" Jack asked.

Linda looked at him, raised her eyebrows as if to say, "What do you want?"

"Hey, come on," Regina said. "Don't be party poopers. Who knows when we'll be together again?"

"Charlie and Emma are at the house. You've got to come by and get her, anyway, don't you, if you're leaving first thing tomorrow?" Marc reminded Jack in his old "I dare you" voice. "Come on, have a nightcap. I'm nowhere near sleepy."

"Don't forget that box over there on the table, hon," Jo added, trying to move them along.

"Well, Manny and I are in, aren't we Manny?" Regina batted her lashes up to her husband, grabbing his bicep, flirting like she was trying to get him to propose. Manny smiled down at her and agreed.

"Okay, then, it's settled. See you all back at the house." Marc smacked his hands together, smacked Manny and Jack on the shoulder.

Marc still hadn't met JoAnne's eyes. He was like that, determined when he made up his mind, when he wanted something. Jo sighed. "Don't forget that box, Marc!" At least they were finally leaving.

Outside on the brick patio, the air had that clean woodsy smell, that coolness off the lake that made everything fresh, crisp this time of year. Jo breathed in deeply, like she might be getting ready to meditate. Down by the lake, the firepit was blazing. Charlie could build a fire in a snowstorm. She could see the huddled shadows, like animals gathered for warmth or protection or both. At least five or six people. She listened to the instruments—mandolin, fiddle, guitar, was that a banjo?

"Emma has had a way better time than she expected, believe me." Linda handed Jo a glass of ice water. "That lamb was salty."

"But delicious." JoAnne drank a long draught of the cool water. "Thanks." She tipped the glass toward Linda.

"Regina's in there helping the guys get drinks. Some things never change," Linda smiled.

"But some things do," Jo answered quietly, giving Linda an approving look. "Thanks for coming. Really. I'm glad I had a chance to say that. This has meant so much to all of us. It's good Jack was here to see Ekim for this last time. Who knew?" she sighed.

"I know. Thank God." Linda took a sip of her water. "I couldn't have forgiven myself if he'd died and I'd been the reason Jack wasn't here. I'm so grateful Marc insisted." She smiled, gazing through the thirty-year film that lingered in the air between them. "But then he's always been a persuasive kinda guy."

"Ask somebody who knows." The haunting music drifted up, notes echoing through the dark as if they could've come from some log cabin built on the property two hundred years before.

"This is a beautiful spot. I know I've told you that already—I'm sure anybody who comes here says the same thing."

"The lake and these woods—three acres—that's what sealed it for us."

"I'll bet."

"When we bought this house, I think Marc finally felt like he'd accomplished something."

"No kidding? I mean, he graduated from law school—none of the guys would've predicted that, right?—and he'd been practicing a while before y'all moved in here, right?"

"Oh yeah. We lived down in Charleston for a time. But we both wanted to come back to Morgantown. And he was driven to be a success by his own standards, and being an attorney wasn't near good enough." She scanned the grounds. "Every time he gets there, to his invisible, nigh-upon-impossible standard, he ups the ante."

"Jack loves his work, but I wouldn't call him driven. He's more of a homebody than you'd guess. He's on the road so much that he doesn't much care if we just kick back at home when he's there, watch a movie, order in. In fact he prefers it."

"You know Marc—an extrovert's extrovert. He'd probably break the scale on that Myers-Briggs personality test if they could get him to sit still long enough to take it."

"Jack is still super outgoing—but he's mellowed, I think. Especially after Emma. He's been a terrific dad. Way more involved than my dad ever was with his kids. But times were different."

"Some people say a woman marries her father." JoAnne shook her head, her frizzy curls bobbing all over the place. "I miss mine all the time. Daddy took me and my sister everywhere. To car shows. minor league ball games. Mountie games. I thought my daddy set the moon."

"Charlie and Marc are good together. At least that's what it's looked like to me this weekend."

"Charlie's easygoing." She pressed her lips together, paused. "We were both better with Charlie than with Marky." With Marky, they could snow ski and water ski, and he and Marc could hunt—young Marc'd never be close to them, especially to his daddy. She kept her counsel about that because Marc didn't like her to bring it up. He'd bristle, "The boy had way more than we ever did."

"I'm sorry I didn't get to meet him this weekend."

"Me too." Jo took a deep breath, a sip of water. "He comes back for Thanksgiving. All that week. The three of them hunt for the turkey. Family tradition—one of the men brings home the turkey."

"That sounds like fun for them."

"Some years he's come home for Christmas, too, but mostly it's just once a year. Every now and then we go out to visit and ski, but we don't like to push it."

"Is he married?"

"Divorced. No children. Looks like it'll be a while before I'm a grandma, but that's okay. Marc and I are pretty satisfied empty nesters. We've always gotten along."

"I loved watching you two dance."

"Thanks. Remember, we used to say we'd never marry a man who couldn't dance?" She smiled, a pleased-we're-sharing-this-memory smile.

"Oh yeah. Jack'll dance with me at a wedding or company event now, but that's about it. He's still got it going on, though. He's more likely to go out on the dance floor than I am."

"Marc and I put on oldies sometimes and dance out here. It can be . . . magical."

"I'll bet. This place was made for romance."

JoAnne smiled agreement; she could look through the double doors, see the fire roaring in the den, look toward the lake and see her son's sister fire. Her men could keep the home fires burning, that was for sure.

"Gina and Manny can still dance, too, can't they?" Linda's voice had a faint question in it.

"Yeah." JoAnne looked through the shadow and caught Linda's eye. "They could win a dance contest, probably."

"But it's not the same, do you know what I mean? You and Marc have that spark—you always did."

Jo didn't answer for a moment, looked down toward the bonfire, listened to the old-time tune. "I do know what you mean."

"Gina could act in make-up commercials for mature women—don't you hate that word mature?—skin products or hair products, either one. Or maybe one of those workout tapes. She looks fantastic."

"Don't you think she's too skinny?"

"Skinny is fashionable, right? Gina is all about fashion."

"I guess. She's too bony for me." JoAnne shook her ice. "But she's never lost any of her Regina allure, the old come-hither for

Manny—and any guy she's talking to—I'll say that for her. She still craves men's attention."

"Marc is nuts about you, too."

"He is. They're just different guys—in some ways, different creatures."

"You and I picked individuals, didn't we?"

The tune now was upbeat, the fiddle—two fiddles?—sounding like whistles in the night, a train headed somewhere, away. The mandolin curling under them made the tune hopeful, happy.

"Those kids are good."

"Charlie's found his passion, as they say, that's for sure."

"I think Emma may've gotten into guitar this weekend. Charlie's been patient with her tagging along."

"I'm not sure it's just been patience."

"You think?" Linda sounded uncertain, a little uneasy.

"He's not a smooth operator, by any means, Linda—like his dad was back in the day—not to worry. But I think he's enjoyed having Emma around. They've kept one another company through all this Phi Kap Tilt-A-Whirl craziness."

"She's never been out with anybody older, a guy in college."

"Really, don't give it a thought."

"Okay. If you say so." She rattled her ice, looked at JoAnne. "Just goes to show you. I thought it was going to be kind of a bore and a snore for her, the obligatory tour of WVU. Hanging out with the oldsters."

The glass door slid open, and Regina bounced out.

"Look what the cat dragged in," JoAnne laughed. "Or out, I should say."

"You gals are missing a mighty fine fire."

"Out here we're serenaded." JoAnne laughed, pointing down to the gathering by the lake. "And I'm not coming in there if the guys are gonna smoke cigars. No way. Out here is too yummy. Why don't you stay out here with us?"

"It's gotten too chilly for me. I'm shivering standing here talking to you. Come on." She brushed her arm toward the den, bowed as if she were a doorman. "I've made the men promise to smoke in Marc's study."

"How do they stand those nasty cigars?"

"Don't you think it's probably just some penis thing?" Gina made a naughty, leery face.

Laughing, the three women walked inside, toward the welcoming fire. No men in sight, JoAnne noticed.

She brought afghans and a pot of lemon-ginger tea, and the women sat on the floor in front of the fire. Regina wrapped the throw around her and shook her head no to the tea—she was sipping Drambuie. Linda hugged her mug near her face, the slight steam making her features blurry, like through a shower curtain.

"I wish Marya had come," Gina said.

"Me too," Linda sighed. "I think we're getting along pretty well now."

"You are," JoAnne agreed, settling to her side. "You like this tea? It's my favorite."

"I'm just enjoying the smell right now," Linda smiled.

"Has Marya been grumpy or is it my imagination?" Regina asked.

Both sipped tea, made unclear responses—um huh? Uh uh? Huhhh?—noncommital.

"This Drambuie is so warm going down—y'all ought to have some."

"I've drunk more this weekend than I usually drink in a month. Two months." Linda shook her head no. "Tea is perfect."

"Maybe you were drinking so much cause you were nervous?" Gina leaned forward, looking directly into Linda's face.

Linda shrugged, met Gina's stare. "I'm not going to say I wasn't nervous."

"Come on, Regina. We've all put that behind us." JoAnne smacked Gina's knee.

"Ouch!" Gina glared at the other two. "Maybe Marya hasn't. Maybe that's why she's not here."

"She said she was exhausted," JoAnne started, but Regina gave her a come on, be real look. "I think she's probably got other things on her mind besides Linda," JoAnne insisted.

"She sure looked more nervous than I remember . . . but Gina's right, it's been a long time."

"Life happens," Gina said, leaning back, looking into the fire. "Even for Ms. Perfect Marya."

"Come on, Gina," JoAnne said, "Marya never held herself up as some paragon of perfection. She just made different choices than we did. She was always more focused on school. And virtue." All three smiled, now. "And she certainly never judged you—or any of us, for that matter."

"I'm not judging her now. I'm just saying. She was Polly Pure back in the day, and you know it."

"Marya has always had her own way of dealing with things."

"Come on, Gina. Lighten up." Linda cleared her throat. "Her family were pretty hardcore Catholics, remember?"

JoAnne agreed. "She and Paulo have stuck by the church, even with all this gross news about priests and little boys."

"Please don't mention that." Gina made a gag signal with her finger to her throat.

"I'm just saying . . ."

"I know what you're saying. You're saying Marya held onto religion while the rest of us turned away from it. So? It was the sixties. That whole God is Dead movement."

"You were never much of a Catholic anyway, were you, Gina?"

"You were never much of a Methodist anyway, were you, JoAnne?" Gina drained her glass. "I never noticed you getting down on your knees, except, of course, when Marc . . ."

"Easy there, Regina. You didn't exactly take some purity pledge yourself."

"I never said otherwise." Gina stood. "I'm going to get another jig of this. Check on the guys. Y'all want anything?"

"No. Not a thing."

"Your choice." Regina sashayed out of the room, like it was 8:00 and she was ordering her first drink.

"What was that all about?"

"Don't ask me. Regina's been known to drink a bit too much. And she's been kind of quiet all through this whole Ekim mess; quiet for Gina, anyway. But I've never known her to be all sensitive about the Catholic church—have you?"

"You're asking me? I don't exactly have a lot to go on." Linda sipped her tea. "But I do seem to remember that her daddy was against the church, for some reason we never really talked about. Or excommunicated. Something. Anyway, he hated the church."

"She doesn't say much about her daddy, ever, except that he was strict and kinda mean."

"More like a monster, if I remember."

"She didn't go to mass or confession when we were in school. She was probably a lapsed Catholic, like most of us were lapsed something."

"Marya went, didn't she?"

"She did. And after they got together, Paulo started going with her—if she'd go to Saturday night mass instead of Sunday morning."

"The doors are always open for the confessing sinner." Linda put her teacup on the hearth, leaned back. "Why do you think Marya was edgy? Do you think it was my fault? We had a pretty good long walk at the Fishbowl the other day."

"I wouldn't worry about it, Linda. Marya's complicated."

"Aren't we all?" Linda pulled the afghan tighter. "But Gina's right, in a way—things always went right for her, just the way she planned. And she and Paulo are still crazy about each other. Never a bump in their road, right?"

"Yeah." Jo shook her head. "But nobody's life is perfect. Believe me."

"Didn't I learn that the hard way?"

"You weren't all churchy either, were you?"

"Nope. My family went, but they didn't preach at home—we said the blessing, but that was about it. No prayer plaques in the kitchen."

"So when this whole Jack thing happened, I know you didn't go to the church for comfort. Who did you talk to, since you wouldn't talk to us?"

Linda shut her eyes for a moment, as if trying to get a picture in her mind. "I didn't talk to anybody."

JoAnne paused, quiet, then whispered, "That must've been horrible."

"It was a bad time." She shut her eyes again.

Was she trying to cut JoAnne off, or was she trying to say more? JoAnne waited.

"But I got through it. On my own."

"Didn't you miss us?"

"Hell yes, Jo—like crazy."

"Then why didn't you get in touch with one of us? Any one of us?"

"It would've been you."

"But it wasn't."

Gina hurried back into the room with a small glass of Drambuie. "The guys are playing 'A Big Fat Hen'—do you remember that stupid game?" She's laughing. "Why in the world do they find that so funny?"

"Tell me they're not drinking shots?" JoAnne sat up.

"Nope. They've moved to beer. You'd think they were eighteen—or maybe twelve."

"Jack hasn't done anything quite that silly since I don't know when—certainly not since we got married."

"I can assure you Marc hasn't been playing any drinking games in a while!" She laughed. "Can you picture that? Judge Bonheur, passed out from playing Whales Tales?"

Gina said, "Shhh—listen." Sure enough, the sound of male laughter made it from two rooms over.

"We didn't play games." JoAnne said. "But we laughed a lot, didn't we?"

"We played bridge sometimes. We all wanted Marya for our partner, remember? She could remember every card, every suit, every bid. But never drinking games. That was the guy's thing. After hours."

"Yeah. We tended to talk," JoAnne observed, while Gina hunkered down by Linda and wrapped herself up like a mummy. "And talk. Hey, how come you know so much about after hours? Marc has never told me anything about that."

"Manny is not a man of secrets. I can get him to tell me just about anything."

"I'm sure." JoAnne made a wrapped around the little finger gesture.

Gina took a sip of her drink. "That can go two ways, you know."

JoAnne laughed. "Oh come on, when has Manny kept you from having your way."

Gina didn't answer. She just pulled her afghan closer around her and leaned back against one of the leather banquettes.

Linda looked from JoAnne to Gina, her smile fading. "Gina. You okay?"

"Not really."

"Hey, Gina, sorry if I touched a nerve. Rattling on like that." JoAnne tried to put an arm around her shoulder, but Gina shook her off.

"You have no idea." Gina stared at them both, a strange, open look on her face Jo had never seen before—some combination of anger and pain that was not Gina-like at all.

The fire crackled, the women sat quietly, and Gina huddled in her wrap, her chin down, shoulders hunched.

"I had four miscarriages when we were in South America," Gina whispered. "Four."

Linda and JoAnne sat stunned for a moment. Jo inhaled, put a hand on Gina's knees. "Oh, honey—we didn't know."

"Of course you didn't know. I didn't tell anybody. I didn't even tell my mama."

Linda didn't speak. JoAnne continued. "I wish you'd told me."

"And what could you have done, Jo? How would you have fixed that? I'd like to know."

"I could've comforted you, at least."

"A couple of the times Manny was travelling when it happened. I'd find out I was expecting, we'd celebrate, I'd be about twelve weeks along, then . . . then that awful mess . . . then, nothing."

"Gina—I didn't know you and Manny wanted children."

"Of course I wanted children. Did you think I was some kind of selfish bitch?"

"No, we didn't, we don't," JoAnne said.

They were quiet again for a few minutes, staring into the fire. Linda looked down at her hands, didn't move a muscle. Gina leaned back, sighed, exhausted.

JoAnne stood. "Hey, y'all: I've got a bottle of Chartreuse we bought in France. I've been waiting for something special to open it."

"That'd be good, Jo. Thanks." Gina was subdued—again, a pretty non-Gina demeanor. "Marya will be mad she missed it."

"Sure. I've never tried it," Linda said, her voice little more than a whisper.

JoAnne left the room and Linda slid closer to Gina.

JoAnne couldn't hear them as she hurried about getting the tray and the cordial and the glasses. She opened the bottle, the floral scent strong, straining to figure out if they were saying anything, but the room was still. Walking toward the den, she stopped at the doorway.

"I know how you feel, Gina."

Gina looked up. "Did you have a miscarriage?"

"That's not what I mean," Linda swallowed. "I wanted children, too. I didn't think I'd have them, either. Even with Jack."

"Oh."

"It took us a few months. Then we had Emma. Jack wanted more."

"Manny didn't want children."

"What? I can't believe that."

"Believe it." Regina looked over her shoulder, toward the kitchen. "After I had my surgery . . . after the doc said no more miscarriages . . . Manny wouldn't even talk about adopting."

Jo thought, *Did Linda say she had a miscarriage? Or did she say she didn't?* She cleared her throat, walked back in the room holding the silver tray with the greenish bottle and three jeweled liqueur glasses—red, blue, green.

"We deserve something special, don't you think?" She held up the tray and then put it down on the coffee table. "This is made by monks, cloistered in the mountains. Tres chic. Let's drink to us."

"Why not?" Linda said and stood. "Let me help you up, Regina."

Regina stood, too, dropped the comforter. "Thanks, y'all."

"For what?" Jo passed around the three vintage glasses, the liquid smelling like a field of wildflowers.

"For letting me be real there, for a sec." Regina grinned her typical grin, the cheerful one she used with women. "A teensy, tinsy moment." Her laugh was brittle.

"To Regina and Linda and JoAnne—for being real." They toasted and each took a cautious sip.

"That is strong!" Linda said. "Licorice?"

"Yummy," Regina added. "Kinda sweet, like Galliano—but not too sweet."

JoAnne took a second sip. "Worth waiting for. Glad I kept it to have with you two." She raised her glass again. They did too. "And to Marya. Always real."

JoAnne lifted the tray and put it on the hearth. "So: We'd better sit down." They moved even closer to the fire, and each bundled up again. "Doesn't sound like the guys are ready to quit any time soon."

They drank and stared into the fire. Regina looked over at Linda. "Hey, Linda Lee, you never told us your college secret."

Linda tried to smile, but her face looked sheepish. "I didn't, did I?"

"You don't have to if you don't want to," JoAnne said, looking at Gina for agreement. Regina only shrugged her shoulders, like why not?

"No. I should. You all did. So I ought to." She held out her glass and JoAnne poured a bit more of the Chartreuse. "It's hard for me to tell secrets . . ."

"Oh, come on—really, you don't have to." JoAnne insisted again. "We'd all had too much to drink the other night."

"No, actually, I want to. Y'all have been great, the way you've welcomed me back."

"Like we said all along, Linda, you were our friend. Don't be such a dope!" Gina reached over and poured herself more of the liqueur.

That made Linda smile. "Who's the dope?" she said. "I saw you flirting with Frankie Galluci."

Gina made a yuk face.

"Am I right?"

She nodded a reluctant yes. "Guilty as charged."

"And by the way, Linda," JoAnne interrupted, "you were pretty damn cool with Simone D'Espere acting all buddy-buddy today."

"She is such a phony, isn't she? I'm amazed at how little I felt when I finally met her. But she's Jay's mother. Which is so sad. I tried to be civil."

"Plus she obviously had that boob job," Gina said, cupping her hands beneath her own tiny breasts.

"Anyway, a secret." Linda took another sip, looked from one to the other. "That night, that night that Jack told me he was going to marry Simone D'Espere because she was pregnant," she sipped again. JoAnne and Regina looked at her, not moving. "That night I . . . I . . ." her breath caught, that big gasp just before a person cries.

"Linda. Stop. You don't have to do this."

Linda put down her glass and rubbed her eyes, blinked. "Let me get my breath, okay?"

"Sure."

"I've never told anybody this, not even Jack—especially not Jack."

"We'd never tell," JoAnne said.

"I never tell Manny anything . . . well, anything that's a real secret."

"Okay." Linda picked up her glass again and finished the drink. JoAnne lifted the bottle, but she shook her head no. "I was pregnant, too."

"Oh!" Gina blurted. JoAnne didn't speak, her mouth in a stunned O.

"That's it: I was pregnant too. Of course I couldn't tell anybody." She's trembling, looks up at them. "I didn't know myself. Until a few weeks later. And then I was so scared. It's not an excuse, I know that, but it's the reason."

"Oh my God, Linda, I should've come to your house. I should have made you talk to me." JoAnne raised her voice.

"Shh." Linda shook her head no. "Who can say? It's behind me now." She looked at Gina. "So that's why I was worried I wouldn't have any children."

"You had a miscarriage? All by yourself?"

Linda didn't speak. She turned her head away, chin wobbling like she was trying to keep from crying. She just brushed her hand, like she couldn't speak.

Now Gina raised her voice. "That is *so* fucked up! No wonder you wouldn't talk to us. You couldn't. Jack Vanderbilt would be a dead man!"

"Shhhh! The guys'll hear," JoAnne whispered, finger to mouth.

Linda still didn't say a word. JoAnne hugged her, so she put her head on Jo's shoulder.

"Just as well Marya wasn't here," Linda whispered.

"You poor girl. All alone with that." Gina looked like she'd like to punch somebody. JoAnne had tears in her eyes. "And nobody to talk to."

"It was a bad time. An awful time. The worst." Linda swallowed. "Then, I was still somehow connected to Jack all those years, I guess, when I thought I was over him. But even when he came back, I never told him. Ever. Why make him sad over something he can never change? Sometimes you have to deal with things on your own. Alone."

Gina and JoAnne were quiet.

"What good would it have done to tell him? He was already marrying Simone."

Gina stared into the fire. "If that doesn't beat all. I had no idea."

"No. Me either. I thought we were going to get pinned that night, get married soon."

"I am so mad at myself that I didn't drive right to your house and make you talk to me." JoAnne hit a fist on her knee.

"Thanks, Jo. I know that."

Regina stood. "I would've shot the son of a bitch, no problem."

Now Linda shrugged. "It worked out. In the end. Here we are."

They stared into the fire, the three women, still, quiet, all thinking their own sad, secret thoughts. JoAnne reached over and held Linda's hand. "I'm so sorry." She wondered, *How in heaven's name could Linda Lee deal with that, all by herself? What happened? Did she have a miscarriage, like Gina? Or not?* She couldn't ask, wouldn't ask, but Linda wasn't telling them all of her secret. *She could've had the baby and given it up! What if that's what she did! No wonder she hadn't answered, had stayed away. Was that it?*

The glass door slid quietly, and Emma and Charlie tiptoed in, both with Mexican blankets wrapped around them. Old Christmas gifts from Marky, JoAnne noted.

"Hey you two. Jam over?"

Linda and Regina looked up and smiled, too. "Hey, Emma. Y'all have fun, sweetie?"

"We were trying to stay quiet, so we wouldn't wake you, but I guess that isn't an issue," Charlie said, putting his mandolin case inside the door. Emma stepped in, did the same. JoAnne noticed Charlie putting his hand in the middle of Emma's back, guiding her toward the kitchen. *That was not a pal-sy way for a guy to touch a girl,* Jo thought. It seemed kind of intimate to her.

They looked at one another and stopped. Emma laughed. "It got too cold out there for the instruments, and for us." She made shivery movements. JoAnne noticed that her face was flushed: the cold? the fire? necking?

"Don't worry—we put the fire out. Is that Dad?" Raucous male laughter from two rooms over.

JoAnne nodded. "Some male bonding ritual I guess—or just pure-tee foolishness."

"We're gonna get something hot, okay? Then head upstairs to listen to music?"

"Sure. Okay. There are some Ramen packets in the pantry." Charlie loved Ramen, took it with him all the time to festivals and jams. JoAnne looked over at Linda, who was still smiling.

"Okay with you, Mom?" Emma called as they headed again for the kitchen, more like a statement than a question.

"Sure. Okay." Linda mimicked Jo's answer. *Now why did she do that?* JoAnne wondered.

"Remember to turn off the tea kettle?"

"Sure thing. Thanks, Mom."

"Thanks, Miz Bonheur. Want anything?" Emma stuck her head back out the doorway. Face still rosy. Cheeks cold, or whisker-scratched? JoAnne didn't usually have to figure out what was going on with guys. She could pretty easily read Charlie and Marky. But Emma's expression was inscrutable.

"No, dear. Thanks. We're fine." JoAnne moved back toward the fire, added a few more logs.

"I forgot they were even out there," Linda said. "Emma's been so reliable, and her friends are all so nice—we've known them all for years—I've never had to worry about her."

"Charlie's a great guy, too." JoAnne settled back down beside Linda. "You don't have to worry about him for a second."

"Y'all mind if I stretch out on the couch?" Regina yawned.

"Go right ahead, make yourself comfy." JoAnne poured herself a tiny bit more of the Chartreuse. "The guys shouldn't be too much longer."

"Manny has to get his beauty sleep," Regina said, dragging her cover over to the sofa. "I'm gonna be listening, now. So don't you dare talk about me."

"Promise," Linda answered, smiling at JoAnne.

"Or say anything I wouldn't want to miss," she added as she cuddled down and closed her eyes.

"You got it, Miss Thing." JoAnne shook her head slightly and Linda smiled in return. "I guess we better whisper."

"Right. At least for the next thirty seconds." They both looked over at Regina, or the bundle that was Regina, with only half her head showing, the streaked hair somehow still shiny.

"She could be eighteen again, couldn't she?" Linda noted.

They leaned back toward the fire. JoAnne stabbed at the new logs with the poker until they settled into the coals. "You said Emma's what? Sixteen?"

"Almost seventeen. Next month. She's a Thanksgiving baby."

"Better than a Christmas baby, huh?" JoAnne leaned again the leather bench. "Charlie's twenty-one. We held him a second year in kindergarten—probably one reason he's always seemed more mature than the guys he used to hang with."

"You did a great job, JoAnne. You're a good mama."

Jo closed her eyes, sighed. "Thanks." She kept her eyes closed. "I think Charlie would agree. I'm not so sure about Marky."

"I kinda got a feeling earlier, when we were talking . . ." She paused. "Say, do you think Regina's really okay?"

"I do. What makes you ask?"

"Part of my nursing development was classes in identifying traumatized women."

"What? Why would you say that?" That word "traumatized" stunned her.

"To tell you the truth, I've been watching Gina—not in a bad way, just kind of paying attention, you know—and it seems like there's more beneath the surface, you know what I mean?"

"You mean all the flirting? That's harmless. She's always done that, remember?"

"I mean the needing attention all the time. And talking about sex. And acting all lovey dovey with Manny when the guys are around. And the not eating. Have you noticed that?"

JoAnne opened her eyes, sat up. "You are quite the observer, Linda." She covered her mouth with one hand for a moment. "But don't worry about Regina. She can take care of herself. She always has."

"If you say so."

"I say so." JoAnne smiled. "You were the best listener, Linda. I hadn't thought of that in a long time, until right this minute."

"Thanks, I think."

"It's a huge compliment. And I mean it." She grabbed one of Linda's hands. "That's one of the things I missed, after you were gone: Somebody I could talk to who would listen."

"Well then, thanks, really."

"Regina is still a chatterbox." She looked over her shoulder, but Gina wasn't moving. "Always was. But I've never thought of her as traumatized. And Marya—we started seeing less and less of her after she was pinned to Paulo, remember? And studying so hard for PT school. Except at the House."

"You and I had the best talks—remember driving out to tutor, and driving back, how we'd jabber away the whole time?"

"I did a lot of the jabbering . . ."

"Back home, with so many people, nobody even noticed if I didn't say much. Plus I was always reading or drawing—listening, mostly, I guess. I couldn't have gotten a word in anyway."

"I have missed that so much!" JoAnne said, as if she'd just come to that realization. "Marc is *not* a listener."

"Really? Y'all seem so close."

"We are—we really are. But we're definitely two different people. And he's always been so driven." She takes a big breath, blows out slowly, sighing. "But Marc's the leader of the pack. He asks for my advice on a lot—with these judge elections, especially, and sometimes with legal stuff—but he's been more 'traditional' than I would have imagined back when we were dating."

"You two were pretty much the free spirits, then," Linda agreed. She tilted her head. "But how traditional?"

"Like when Marky was born, he was my responsibility. Marc about missed that child's first five years; he was so busy being the biggest and best lawyer in Charleston." She crossed her legs, sat up straighter. "I had to finish law school, study for the bar, and then take care of a baby pretty much by myself. It was not a good time for us."

Linda rubbed her hands together in front of the fire. "I didn't know."

"Nobody knew. Except maybe Ekim. And he was too drunk to pay much attention. We were down in Charleston." Linda picked up her glass, poured some more of the thick, greenish Chartreuse, took a slow sip. "Marc drank way too much, there, for a couple of years."

"You're kidding."

"No. I'm not. He had the reputation, there for a while, of being a bit of a party guy."

"Really? After y'all were married?"

"I was, of course, home with a baby, a nervous wreck."

"You? You've always been so together."

"I was *not* together for those couple of years. Not at all."

"Now I feel like more of a terrible friend. A terrible, selfish friend."

"I finally confronted Marc. I got a babysitter one night, went to the bar where I knew he hung out after hours and there he sat, all smiling and flirty, with one of his paralegals leaning toward him with those disgusting ooey-gooey adoring eyes."

"No!"

"Yep." She put her glass down. "I never asked about that gal. But I told him, right there at the table, in front of her, I said, 'You either get your act together and act like a husband and father, or I'm out of here. For good.'"

Linda didn't speak.

"And he got his act together all right. And we've been a team ever since, a partnership, me Yin to his Yang, or however that works. We moved here pretty soon after."

"That must have been horrible."

"We love each other. Still. But Marky got the worst of it," she whispered. "He's pretty much a loner, now, prefers 'smelling the flowers'—which is actually smoking pot and doing as little as possible. Works for Game and Fisheries, some kind of computer sharpshooter. Hikes, camps, bow hunts. Drives Marc crazy." She shook her head. "Oh well: Sin loi minoi."

"Huh? What did you say?"

"Sin loi minoi." She looked at Linda. "It's something Ekim used to say, when he was at the House. Marc would go out drinking with him sometimes, but then he stopped doing that. And Ekim left. And that happened."

"What in the world does that mean, sin whatever?"

JoAnne laughed, a quiet laugh. "Whatever. Don't worry."

"Huh?"

JoAnne kept laughing, because she'd never known herself; when she'd asked Ekim that very question, whether that's what it meant—whatever, don't worry—or whether he was just telling her not to bother. "It's Vietnamese. I don't really know what it means."

*****

JoAnne sat at the edge of the bed, took her time rubbing Jergens into her hands. Her mother had used it, and she'd always loved the comforting smell. Around one in the morning, she'd called cabs— Regina was sound asleep, she and Linda could hardly keep their eyes

240

open—and finally everyone had left—Emma too. Lots of hugs and promises and thanks and plans to get together again soon.

Marc had his light out. He was turned toward the window, away from her, but she could tell he wasn't asleep yet. He smelled like clean cotton and Colgate toothpaste and faint cigar smoke, even though he'd washed his face and hands. She reached over and rubbed his shoulder; he turned toward her, smiling, a hazy boozy look on his face. She hadn't seen that look in a long time.

"You take care of the fire?"

"You know I did. Don't I always."

"You do." JoAnne snuggled down beneath the covers. His feet knit themselves between her legs.

"You are so warm, babe." His grin was like a boy's—he reminded her of Marky, with that silly grin on his face. They looked so much alike. He pulled her closer.

"Did you have fun with Manny and Jack? Sure sounded like it."

"It was great. Jack's great. And that Linda—I swear, she hasn't changed a bit."

JoAnne pulled away. "We've all changed, Marc. Every one of us."

"I guess." He begins to rub her hip in that place she loved. "You gals have fun?"

"We did. Do you think Charlie is interested in their daughter?"

"She's a cutie all right. Nah. I don't think so." He sat up on one elbow. "Hey, thanks for all your help this weekend." He kissed her, a sweet, lingering kiss. "You're my rock, you know that, don't you? You're my rock, babe." He turned back toward the window and sighed. "Poor Ekim, damn him."

JoAnne scooted down, turned off her bedside lamp. But she didn't close her eyes—couldn't. *Who wants to be a rock?* she thought. *Who wants to be a god damn rock?* She turned her back toward Marc. Maybe I'm a pillow, a soft reliable pillow—your favorite. Or maybe I'm a table, somewhere to gather and talk and figure things out. Or maybe, just maybe, I'm a volcano. That would be a rock, wouldn't it, with all that hot lava inside? Bubbling? What had happened in Pompeii? Hadn't they thought Vesuvius would never erupt again? But it did. Were they all volcanoes, her and Regina and Marya? Maybe. But not Linda. Linda had had her eruption, back when she was young, when she left WVU. She'd been pregnant. Pregnant. How could they have not known? She must've had a miscarriage—Regina telling about hers is what they were talking about. All alone, knowing Jack was marrying Simone D'Espere because she was pregnant. Talk about messed up. But she'd made her own way, somehow, despite all that. Gotten away from West Virginia. JoAnne stared at the ceiling. *I've always been part of an us, all this time. The peacemaker. The mama. The supportive wife. The rock.*

Marc made those ruffly noises he made instead of snores. She had to smile. That was it: He still made her smile. And he respected her. That was true. Her intelligence. Her capability. Her steadiness. They had fun together. And she respected him. Look what he'd accomplished. And he had settled down, like he'd promised. He'd been a great dad to Charlie. He loved her. She loved him. They still had great sex.

That made her think of Gina's travel ban. *When we're on vacation, she's on vacation; her 'gina, as we used to call it back in the day. Regina. So sad about those miscarriages.* She'd had no idea. Regina was a rock, she guessed. And they'd always taken her for the lightweight. They were wrong about Marya, too. Her life wasn't perfect, even if she tried to act that way. If she doesn't look out, Jo-Anne thought, she could become even tougher, harder. And Paulo so sweet to her. When was the last time she'd talked with friends about personal, secret things? She couldn't even remember.

All those things could be true, she realized, every single one of them—wife, mother, lawyer, competent woman—and she could still feel like she felt right this minute, like something had passed her by, something she could never have again.

She got up, quiet as a feather, eased her feet into her slippers, and walked through the dark room to the stairs. She knew what she needed. She needed to be outside, by herself. At the hall closet, she grabbed a jacket—the same one she'd worn to Cooper's Rock this morning. Was it only this morning? It seemed like forever ago. And a scarf. It was nippy out.

JoAnne opened the door to the patio and walked down the brick path toward Cheat Lake. The air had that damp chill that seeps into your bones, but she didn't mind. Out here it smelled like grass and charred wood and the lake water. It was noisy out here, too, she thought. Nature is always noisy. Animals scurrying away—probably squirrels—bats chirping overhead, hunting at night, some insect making a racket. Was it a cricket? A tree frog? And messy. Nature was messy. Vultures were the nastiest creatures on earth. But they were necessary. *It's clean out here, really clean,* JoAnne thought as she wrapped her arms around herself. After all that rain, it's clean. She walked down to the dock, where the water lapped against the retaining wall every now and then. She loved it out here. Tomorrow, after everyone was gone, she'd call the office and tell them she wasn't coming in for one more day. And she'd hike Cheat Mountain. That's what she'd do. She'd hike Cheat Mountain all by herself.

Linda,
Later, At the Motel

Linda, eyes closed, head nestled into the pillow she'd brought from home, turned toward Jack, couldn't drop off to sleep. They'd packed their bags, put them by the door, ready to walk out as soon as the alarm went off. Brush teeth, grab a cup of coffee in the lobby, hit the road for home. That was the plan. Emma begged them to let her sleep, promised she'd wrap in her quilt in her peejays and sleep in the backseat until they pulled into the driveway. When Linda asked her to set her travel clock for 6:15, she'd called "Uhhh" over her shoulder.

That look on Emma's face when she and Charlie came inside from their fire. *Had they been making out?* She'd never had that suspicion before, not once, when Emma was out with her friends. Was it even her business? Should she broach the subject of Charlie as maybe a boyfriend friend, or wait and see if Emma had anything to say? Emma was so young—but was she really? Almost seventeen any minute. What was she when she fell for Jack, nineteen? She didn't like this train of thought one bit.

That Chartreuse—is that what it was called, Chartreuse? Linda tried to envision monks on some hillside in France gathering wildflowers. Of course they were doing it by hand. Of course they were singing or chanting—something like that upbeat, happy song that singing nun made popular all those years back, when she was in high school. Dominique da da da da—she could hear it in her head. Funny how songs stuck in your head. They'd be singing that, picking the flowers by hand. The monks looked like Friar Tuck on the Disney Robinhood.

Dominique da da da da—it was like she and Jack had background music throughout their lives. Certainly when they were dating. Like dancing to "Unchained Melody" tonight. Those years she was by herself, she hadn't been as conscious of music accompanying her. She did buy that one album, *Who's to Bless and Who's to Blame,* by Kris Kristofferson. The first time she heard the title song she'd had to sit down. She'd never forget those lyrics that hit her like a brick: "If a cheated man's a loser/ And a cheater never wins/ And if beggars can't be choosers/ 'Til they're weak and wealthy men." She went to Plan 9 and bought the album that day and played it for weeks like some mantra. She could hear that song in her head right now. "And a cheater never wins." Everything was too complicated.

She couldn't believe she'd told JoAnne and Regina she was pregnant. Was that Chartreuse like truth serum, some hallucinogen? She'd never intended to tell them, to tell anybody. What did JoAnne say? She should have come to the house and knocked on the door? And Regina said she would've shot Jack Vanderbilt if she'd known. They'd reacted like it mattered to them, like they wanted to *do* something, to take care of her. She was still reeling from how they reacted. Her mind wouldn't rest. Still, she had that remnant of her secret, that piece she'd never tell anyone, no matter how much secret syrup she drank.

Jack jerked, that final falling off to sleep jerk. He didn't know any of it, not the part she told JoAnne and Regina, not the part she kept to herself. She was closer to Jack than any human who walked the earth, but now two of the women knew more than he would ever know about their breakup. It was so weird, the way the past and present wafted like smoke in the fireplace, weaving and crossing and rising together, fading up and away into the ether, waning but never vanishing.

Regina had four miscarriages. Four. And she'd been shot. And had a heart attack. But she kept on primping and flirting and taking care of NICU babies. Remarkable. And Jo: Making everybody she met feel important, feel like they mattered, feel welcome. Poor Marya, dealing with that son she adores, trying to be invulnerable when her heart hurts. Linda was glad to know these women, glad to reconnect, glad she'd come after all.

She leaned closer to Jack, tried to match her breathing with his breathing, tried to envision the smoke from the fireplace at JoAnne's filtering up through the chimney, out to the night sky, off into the foggy night, merging and blending and floating up, up, up.

III. The Home

September 19, 2000

The drive from Morgantown to Lynchburg takes over five hours. We left the motel by 6:30—Jack's request, his desire for home taking over—and I decided I'd drive. I was too wired to sleep or sit and chitchat about the weekend.

Emma wrapped up in her quilt in the backseat, told us "Don't wake me if you stop, okay?" in that groggy sleep-deprived voice teenagers have.

Jack started out with his hand on my right shoulder, offering pennies for my thoughts, wondering how I'd connected with "the girls." (He actually said "the girls"—jumpy as I was, he was lucky I didn't bite his head off. But he'd been such a trooper these four days.) How could he want to talk more, after talking constantly while we were in Morgantown? I asked him to put on NPR; he was asleep in five minutes.

I turned the radio down, grateful for the quiet in the morning hours before there was much traffic on the interstate. Home beckoned, the familiarity of our own sofas and chairs and beds, the food we keep in the refrigerator, the grass that needs to be cut.

But so much was cramming my brain. This drive was nothing like the Greyhound ride all those years ago, crowded in an unfamiliar space with strangers when I was a stumbling zombie, feeling unwanted and scared and dirty. Jack was beside me now; he loved me. Emma was our own child, a different child than the one I was harboring then, but ours all the same. I could think of that time now with sadness for that girl; yes, but without overpowering despair—a realization that made me take a deep breath. I'd been carrying that lump of shame and guilt around all this time, even if it was buried where I rarely paid attention to it. I could face it with a sense of loss, true, but also acceptance, now that the sadness would always be mine alone. There was no virtue in telling Jack or one of the women who offered me the fragile possibility of friendship again. Telling would enable Regina and Marya and JoAnne to understand better why I shut down and hid from them all those years ago, but their understanding of that deeper secret wasn't necessary. Telling Jack now would be selfish. I'd hand him grief he didn't need, loss he could do nothing about. We'd both made our choices way back when. Those choices were our burden and our reality, pieces of who we are, but not the only pieces.

That one piece of it would remain inside me, like some bullet fragment the surgeon can't remove. I could've told Marya; she was so much more vulnerable now. Or I was more aware of her vulnerability. Or JoAnne, no nonsense, ever-forgiving JoAnne. I'd had the chance to tell each of them. Why hadn't I? Did I expect they'd be too judgmental—especially Marya—or was I the one who was still judgmental? Regina and I had been close, once, but she was walled off now, no matter how "out there" and open she appeared. Still individuals, all three of them, no doubt about that, but hardly the "girls" Jack implied. We were different women now. Complex and individual, definitely no longer naive, but giving them my secret would add nothing to our relationship. It was mine alone.

Emma turned into a chatterbox as soon as we pulled into the driveway. She was hungry; why hadn't we stopped at Tudor Biscuit World one last time? How come we didn't wake her up to eat? Forget her insistence we let her sleep. As she helped take the suitcases into the house, she asked if we were going back any time soon, say for a football game? Were any of the families going to come visit? Could she take guitar lessons?

I let Jack field her energy while I rolled my suitcase into the laundry room. The clean sheet smell that permeated the space made me feel at home. I welcomed the quiet as I sorted my clothes into piles and shut out the jabber in the kitchen while they pulled out bread and sandwich fixings.

"Want a sandwich, Mom? Dad's making tuna fish. With pickle, like you like it," Emma called as I headed up the back stairs with my toiletry bag and my few remaining clean clothes. I shouted down a quick no thanks and kept going. I wasn't ready to give up my alone time while I was easing into the calm familiarity of our house. Plus I was about to drop from driving straight through.

Our bedroom, with some of my favorite paintings hanging as well as photos of me and Jack, Emma growing up, and shots of our parents and kin, welcomed me like a security blanket. I sat on the bed, let the clothes and toiletries drop beside me. I fell back against the decorative pillows, giving over to the comfort of being in my own space.

My sketchpad slipped out of my carry-all. I picked it up, realized I'd only drawn one pencil drawing the whole time we'd been away: Emma, sleeping, peaceful.

"Linda, you want anything from the store? I'm going to pick up Freida, and I need to get a few things—the cupboard's almost bare," Jack called from the bottom of the stairs. Jack and his clichés.

It was all I could do to call back "Huh-uh," let that settle in the quiet of the house after Jack shut the door.

My body settled into the firm comfort of our bed. When Jack and I had moved into this house, right before Emma was born, we'd decided on mid-century modern for our bedroom, for its clean lines, the mellow wood, and the difference from the heavy mahogany and oak and walnut of our growing up. When I'd suggested that, he'd said, "Why not? My parents' bedroom was like a cave." The bamboo floors—no dusty rugs or carpets—shone in the sunlight. I closed my eyes, floated in the safe sense of being home. Work tomorrow—thinking about that re-entry could wait.

The house was still.

Wait. I hadn't heard Emma come up. That was strange. I would've expected her to hurry to her room, her sanctuary, and begin calling her friends she'd undoubtedly missed to catch up. I sat and listened. I didn't hear any voices, or music, or anyone moving around downstairs. That was odd.

I headed down the back stairs calling, "Emma," but she didn't answer. I still heard the washer churning, but no Emma. The kitchen was empty, too—Jack and Emma had cleaned up after making their sandwiches. "Emma," I called again.

"In here, Mom," she answered from the den. I followed her flat voice—odd, she hadn't put on any of her music—and was surprised to see her wrapped up in her quilt on the sofa, no computer in her lap, no portable CD player in her hand, no earphones. Like all the air had been let out.

"Honey—you okay?" Emma was always practicing her cello or talking on the phone or working on an animation on the computer or running out the door to catch up with her pals. This still, quiet Emma caught me by surprise, especially since she'd slept all the way home and jabbered like a magpie when we got here.

When she pulled her feet aside and I sat down next to her I could see she looked puzzled, maybe a tad sad. "You glad to be home, Emma?"

"Kinda yes, kinda no."

"You want to tell me about it."

"Not really. I'm trying to figure it out."

"Did you let Witt or Zoe or any of the others know you're back?"

"Not yet."

"Oh." I stayed beside her, uncertain whether to leave her be and respect her privacy, like she was suggesting, or sit a while and hope she would want to talk. Emma wasn't a brooder, or at least she hadn't been.

When I heard the washer signal done I stood. "I'll put my clothes in the drier. You want me to put in anything of yours?"

"Huh-uh," she answered, meek.

She looked up when I came back, her expression an uncharacteristic grimace. "Could I ask you something?"

"Anything. Since when do you have to ask?" I patted her feet, propped them into my lap as I sat.

"There's something that's bugging me."

"So tell me."

"I just don't get it. How all this time you haven't wanted to be friends with those women who went to college with you."

Sucker punch. Big time. So now Emma wanted to know about that moment in my life when I blew it. Apparently the sampling I'd offered hadn't satisfied her. Just when I was ready to stuff it into the bag in my brain marked "rags."

She kept on, like she wasn't expecting an answer. "I liked them all, especially JoAnne. Marya is a kinda happy/sad person—she didn't talk to me much. And Regina was like some Peter Pan character—not Wendy, maybe even Peter—'I'll never grow up.' Has she always been such a big flirt?" She shook her head. "I just don't get it, why you didn't stay in touch with your friends."

"Who said I didn't want to?" That came out more defensive than I'd intended.

"You never called them or talked about them or asked to speak to one of them when Dad was talking to the guys."

"Oh." The critical tone of her voice put me on edge. I wasn't used to that. We talked about anything she brought up, the sex stuff and the confusion stuff and all the things I couldn't talk about when I was growing up, especially with my parents. She and her friends, at sixteen, seemed far more open and together than I was at her age. Or when I left Morgantown at twenty, for that matter.

"What can I tell you? Like I said before, I needed a change in my life. I couldn't get what I needed at WVU." That sounded thin, even to me.

"They have nursing. And a medical school." Digging. Like she was cross-examining me.

I didn't want to come off wary, but that's how I was feeling. I didn't want to shut her out, either, like I'd shut out JoAnne and Regina and Marya. She didn't need to know the gritty personal details, though. But this was Emma, and I'd tried to be the mom I'd wanted, one she could come to for straight answers.

"Charlie says his mom didn't understand either."

"Oh." I was staring, now, alarmed, all pretense of maternal control out the door.

Emma sat up, leaned toward me. "Mom? What in the world is this about?"

The concern in her voice grated my jagged feelings more than the probing. I came close to crying. Was this secret going to pull sneak attacks and throw grenades my whole life?

"People make choices, Emma. People need change."

She hugged me and I let myself put my head on her shoulder. "I like them. I like them all. Especially JoAnne and Regina."

"I know. They're impressive, aren't they? Strong individuals."

"And Charlie, Mom. Charlie got to me."

I pulled back and looked at her troubled face. "Got to you? Like . . . you don't mean in a bad way?" alarm for her taking over.

"Mom! Of course not! He's like, the nicest guy I've ever met. I'd say gentleman, only I hate that word."

"Oh. Okay." I leaned back.

"I wanted to hug him more than just friends, and kiss him more than pals, and being around him . . . I felt tingly . . ."

"I see." I struggled to keep my face calm, open.

"Every time I was around him I, . . ." she hesitated, her face intent, "I wanted his attention on *me,* just me."

All I could do was nod. I knew those sensations well.

"But he wasn't looking at me like that, Mom."

"Oh."

"And he'd hold my hand to take me somewhere, but it was a brother/sister hand holding, you know what I mean?"

"I do."

"And I liked his parents a lot, especially JoAnne, and the way they wanted everybody to feel at home but didn't put on a big show about it, you know? I liked the whole family."

I put my fingers to my mouth to keep my lips from trembling.

"So aren't you going to say anything? I just can't understand how you cut them out of your life like you did, never even mentioned them."

"I see." I stood, looked around the room. "Let me check my clothes in the drier, okay? I don't want them to get wrinkled."

I stood in the laundry room, my hands on the washer propping me up, as this insight and questioning from Emma bounced around in my head. Just when I was feeling some peace from this. I took deep breaths, let the tumbling of the drier grab my mind. I walked back to the den, sat in a chair kitty-korner from the sofa.

"Emma, I've promised myself I won't mislead you or lie to you, and I'm not going to start now."

She nodded, quiet, waiting. My wise Emma.

"I know exactly how you feel about Charlie. That's how I felt about your dad the first time I met him. First love—nothing more powerful."

She leaned toward me.

"But I was too young and too . . . I don't know, what's the right word? Insecure? JoAnne and the others, they knew themselves and what they wanted so much better than I did. Were more open. They were more like you. Or at least that's how I saw them at the time."

Emma reached for my hand.

"When I left, I made a choice. At the time I thought it was the right choice. You know your dad married Simone, right?"

She nods yes. "And they had Jay."

"When I found out he was going to marry her, it broke my heart, like to have killed me, so I ran away, without even thinking. I just did it. After I could think again, I decided to put him and those two years behind me, to start fresh. That was my decision, good, bad, or otherwise." I swallowed the part I can't tell. "JoAnne and Regina and Marya tried to stay friends, but I cut them off, too. Out of my own immaturity."

"You were twenty by then, weren't you? I would've thought that . . ."

I held up my hand. "The only thing right about my choice was that I *was* too young to get attached. I did need to grow up and stand on my own two feet. I wouldn't have done that if I'd stayed at WVU."

"But WHY? Look at how well they've all done. JoAnne and Marc are so good together, and they were first loves. Marya and Paulo too."

"I know." I shook my head. "I wish I hadn't let my heartbreak get in the way of my friendships. I can see that was stupid. Hindsight and all. I made mistakes."

Emma shrugged, like she thought I'd been stupid, too.

"It's your daddy's stubbornness that got the two of us back together, eventually. I would have never gone after him. I wouldn't have had the courage."

"Thank God. Imagine: You could've lost Dad, too." Now Emma shakes her head, no doubt realizing that I almost blew having her.

"Seeing JoAnne and the others . . . I see that we all had our own problems, we were all in different places trying to figure out how to grow up. No excuse. Just reality."

"Poor Dad. It's so strange, meeting Simone, knowing she's Jay's mother. I can't see her married to Dad. Not for five minutes."

That "poor Dad" stung. But it wouldn't be right for me to go deeper. That was my stuff. "Charlie was right. I was the one who ran away, who cut them out of my life. They're amazing women, aren't they? And to let me back in."

Emma shrugged, still not satisfied. "For thirty years? After you'd graduated and all . . ."

"I know, Emma. Sometimes the brain and the gut don't communicate, you know? I should've reached out. It was up to me." I slumped. "But I didn't."

She stood, her quilt wrapped around her like some mummy come to life. "Your loss, like you always tell me." That face was sad.

"Emma," but she hobbled away toward the stairs. I couldn't miss it. She wanted to be alone now.

Supper was a sorry affair around the kitchen table. Jack talked nonstop about the weekend, either ignoring the fact that Emma and I didn't have much to say other than "Uh huh" or "Uh-uh," or clueless that we weren't in the mood to replay the reunion and all its ups and downs.

"I'll get the dishes, Mom. I know you're wiped," Emma said as soon as Jack took the last bite of stir-fry. Was that a peace offering, or a way to get rid of us?

"There's so little. How about we skip the dishwasher. You wash, I'll dry. Okay?"

"Sure," she answered, her back to me, scraping plates.

"Guess I'll check out the news. Seems like we've been away a month, doesn't it?" Jack kissed us both on the forehead and headed for the den. "Come on Freida, girl," he called. I was betting clueless.

Emma and I worked together with ease, standing in front of this kitchen sink where I'd washed dishes and baby Emma had played on the floor beside me with her Speak 'n Spin.

"So how did you and Charlie leave it?"

She shrugged.

"Are you going to keep in touch?" Wisdom told me to back off, but maternal protectiveness made me forge ahead.

"Mom."

"Okay." I folded the dishcloth. "What do you want to know?"

"So you said you knew how I'm feeling, that you felt that way about dad when you all met."

"Yes." I sat at the table, and she joined me.

"You just let him go. Like you let your friends go. That doesn't make any sense to me."

"Maybe I didn't let him go. Maybe he let me go. And I had to deal with it."

"Oh." She shrugged again.

I reached for both Emma's hands, remembering when one tiny fist was smaller than the palm of mine. "I see you and your friends, and how you all trust one another, and I'm happy for you, Emma, I really am.

"When I was your age I hadn't had a real boyfriend. One of the guys in high school, he was fun to kiss, but I didn't think about him from one day till the next."

"Charlie didn't kiss me, except on the cheek."

"I liked him a lot, too, Emma. I like them all. Very much. But I can't rewrite my history to make it come out the way I might like it. Or the way you might like it, for that matter."

"So should I call Charlie? Or write an email and ask him to keep in touch? About that collaboration we talked about? What should I do?" Her sad eyes were hopeful.

What if I'd asked my mother, all those years ago, "What should I do?" Or JoAnne? But I didn't think I could.

"Emma, Emma . . . I wish I had an easy answer, but I don't. Charlie's a great guy. He'd be lucky to fall in love with you."

She pulled away. "Sounds like a 'but' is coming."

"Listen to yourself, Emma. What's your gut telling you?"

She slumped, tugged at a piece of her hair. "He wants to be friends."

I stood and hugged her. "You have such strong instincts. You always have."

"Big fat deal." Tears were trickling down her cheeks, but her voice was steady.

"All those years ago, I ran away out of fear. Plain old garden variety fear. And hurt. I didn't think I had anybody I could talk to. So I ran."

She turned around and hugged me back. "I'm so sorry, Mom. That must have been horrible."

"It was, Emma. It really was. But maybe if I'd known myself better, had more confidence or grit or whatever it is you have, I wouldn't have hurt so many people, including myself."

She hugged harder, her head nuzzled into my shoulder.

"Pain's going to be a piece of it, but I found out the hard way that you can't run away from the pain. You think you can . . . I was lucky, though. Your daddy found me. In the end, he didn't let me pretend I was independent and satisfied being alone, when I wasn't."

"You've always been so confident, Mama."

I raised my eyebrows. "Remember that silly song you loved when you were about ten, 'Listen to Your Heart'? You'd belt it out like a lounge singer."

Emma smiled, tears still on her face. But she smiled.

"When you finished, you'd laugh and say, 'That is SOOOOO ooey-gooey,' and your dad and I would laugh, too?"

"Of course. Didn't I lip sync it in the talent show that year?"

"You did. You were hilarious. But you were right. It *was* too gooey. Listening to a heart that's broken, that's not exactly smart, you know? You need to talk to your friends, and if you're lucky enough, some grown up you can trust. Your heart's gonna hurt too much to be much help."

"So I probably shouldn't email Charlie?"

"That's not what I'm saying. I don't have that answer for you. But take some time and make up your mind. Don't just 'listen to your heart' when it's a mess. Or rush your decisions. Talk to Zoe about this. Or Witt. Or Martin—you and Martin are always good for one another. Maybe you'll decide to go for it, maybe you won't, but it's up to you. Charlie could be a great friend. Or he could be more. Or less. I have no idea. But I trust you to think it through. And talk it through with your friends."

Emma hugged me then, and I hugged her back, kissed the top of her head.

"I lost all that when I ran away. I had my painting, thank goodness, and my nursing studies, which gave me a sense of purpose when I was so lonely. I needed that. But I *was* lonely, and afraid of relationships. Then your father found me, and I was ready for him."

"Thank GOD!" Emma laughed.

"You know, all this time I underestimated all of those guys, Dad's fraternity brothers. I thought they were superficial, cause they always talked on the surface about things I considered trivial, like football or old fraternity pranks or who's golf game is better than who else's. But look at them this weekend, how they dealt with Ekim. They really are close. And they care about one another. I'm envious of that. I don't have that. I gave it up."

"Maybe you and JoAnne will try again."

"Maybe. We'll see."

"Can I tell you something else?" She pulled away. "It's kinda embarrassing." She had that look on her face, that I'm going to tell you something you're not gonna like look. I nodded, grateful she could still trust me.

"I made myself available to Charlie, Mama, leaning against him after a song, sitting extra close when he was showing me something on the guitar. He was always sweet, and he'd touch the middle of my back to get me to go somewhere, but he never did anything like that to me. Like flirting. I kinda threw myself at him."

I smoothed her hair. This must be so hard for her.

"Do you think I turned him off? Like he ended up thinking I was some slutty kid? Should I message him, stay in touch? What should I do? I feel so different about him."

"Oh, Emma." I backed up so I could look her in the face. "JoAnne says he hasn't had any interest in girlfriends yet, that he loves hanging around with the old-time musicians. Maybe it's not you. Maybe Charlie's not ready for a girlfriend. Like I was too insecure to trust my friends. Wise in some things, not so wise in others."

"He sure wasn't picking up on my signals. Or maybe he was and . . . ugh!"

"He reminds me of an old soul. His mama says he's always been like that."

"Yeah. I can see that. His music is what matters to him, no doubt about that." She looked straight at me now, no longer self-conscious. "Can I start guitar lessons? I promise I won't slack on cello. I loved playing like that, without sheet music or stands or a conductor. It was different. And . . . real."

"Of course you can. If that's what you want. If you're not doing it to please Charlie in some way."

"We connected with the music, Mama. We really did."

"Great. I'm glad."

"So I'm gonna call Martin, see who's a great guitar teacher around here. Can he come over? I promise we won't be up late."

"School tomorrow. Definitely."

"Definitely." She gave me a real hug, a nothing-held-back-be-tween-us hug.

She hurried upstairs, lighter, I could tell.

I was lighter, too, lighter than I'd been in forever. All I wanted to do was curl up on the sofa with Jack and shut my eyes and be right here, right now. Right this minute, that's all.

About the Author

Charlotte Morgan grew up in Richmond, Virginia. This is Charlotte's second book with Legacy Book Press, which published her memoir, *Are You Gregg's Mother?*, in January 2021. Her first novel, *One August Day,* was nominated for the annual fiction award by the Library of Virginia. *Protecting Elvis* is described in Kirkus Review as "A subtle, affecting glimpse into the lives of a trio of singular women molded by the words and personal character of a rock icon." *The Family* chronicles a young woman's search for faith, family, and friendship. Finishing Line Press published Morgan's poetry chapbook *Time Travel* in the summer of 2020. One of Morgan's short stories is included in *The Pushcart Prize Collection XXIV.* She holds an MFA from Virginia Commonwealth University. Morgan is a writer-in-residence each summer at Nimrod Hall Summer Arts Program. Her four adult children are individual and varied and independent in their lives and careers. She lives in Lynchburg, Virginia, with her artist husband John Dure Morgan and one sassy Standard Poodle.